# GRIMM

## NATE TEMPLE SERIES BOOK 3

## SHAYNE SILVERS

ARGENTO
PUBLISHING

Shayne Silvers

Grimm

Nate Temple Series Book 3

ISBN: **978-0-9980854-0-1**

© 2016, Shayne Silvers / Argento Publishing, LLC

info@shaynesilvers.com

For updates on new releases, promotions, and updates, please sign up for my mailing list on **shaynesilvers.com**.

# CONTENTS

# THE NATE TEMPLE SERIES—A WARNING

$\mathcal{N}$ate Temple starts out with everything most people could ever wish for—money, magic, and notoriety. He's a local celebrity in St. Louis, Missouri—even if the fact that he's a wizard is still a secret to the world at large.

Nate is also a bit of a...well, let's call a spade a spade. He can be a mouthy, smart-assed jerk. Like the infamous Sherlock Holmes, I specifically chose to give Nate glaring character flaws to overcome rather than making him a chivalrous Good Samaritan. He's a black hat wizard, an antihero—and you are now his partner in crime. He is going to make a *ton* of mistakes. And like a buddy cop movie, you are more than welcome to yell, laugh and curse at your new partner as you ride along together through the deadly streets of St. Louis.

Despite Nate's flaws, there's also something *endearing* about him...You soon catch whispers of a firm moral code buried deep under all his snark and arrogance. A diamond waiting to be polished. And you, the esteemed reader, will soon find yourself laughing at things you really shouldn't be laughing at. It's part of Nate's charm. Call it his magic...

So don't take yourself, or any of the characters in my world, too seriously. Life is too short for that nonsense.

Get ready to cringe, cackle, cry, curse, and—ultimately—*cheer* on this snarky wizard as he battles or befriends angels, demons, myths, gods, shifters, vampires and many other flavors of dangerous supernatural beings.

Let's see what Nate's up to this time.

The Brothers Grimm have come to town, and they have Nate's name on their hit list...

~

DON'T FORGET! VIP's get early access to all sorts of Temple-Verse goodies, including signed copies, private giveaways, and advance notice of future projects. AND A FREE NOVELLA! Click the image or join here: www.shaynesilvers.com/l/38599

*F*OLLOW and LIKE:

*S*hayne's FACEBOOK PAGE:
I try to respond to all messages, so don't hesitate to drop me a line. Not interacting with readers is the biggest travesty that most authors can make. Let me fix that.

# CHAPTER 1

*A* lot can happen between *now* and *never*.

    I once read that the phrase *it's now or never* was first coined to describe that moment that if one doesn't act upon right *now*, that they will never again get a second chance to do so. They would miss their one opportunity. Usually through their own fault, but sometimes that vindictive bitch named Karma could ninja flip out of a closet to give you a solid monkey fist to the stones.

You know…

Perhaps you had been facing a once in a lifetime opportunity – saying hello to the cute girl at the bar before anyone else; or maybe you had stood in silence for twenty seconds too long during your oral presentation in front of the classroom and desperately needed to formulate words that closely resembled anything intelligent.

Basically, you needed to do the thing *right freaking now*.

Carpe Diem.

Like me.

Right *now*, I was standing in the chilly sewers beneath the fine city of St. Louis in order to check off something on my to-do list. Something that was likely going to get my fancy new coat all smelly and icky in the process. Still, getting my coat smelly and icky was better than getting it bloody and hole-y. That's why I had brought backup. But the night was young. And I never counted my chickens before they hatched.

Especially when hunting vampires.

But I'll get to that in a minute.

Right *Now*, I was getting ready to do something marginally dangerous, and even with accomplices to watch my back, I wasn't quite ready to strap on my big boy pants. I was stalling.

I was here – hopefully – to save some lives. The victims didn't have Batman coming down to save them, or even the fine police persons of St. Louis. None of those upstanding people knew anyone was in danger down here, or would have even believed the intel that had led me here: a Greek hero gossiping at the bar over a beer. And all those victims had was one scraggly wizard, a disgraced werewolf FBI Agent, and a vanilla mortal to come save them.

*Now* was a brief period of time that was full of choices that would later result in more choices – harder ones – that would lead to penultimate consequences. The *now* part was pretty cut and dried for me. It was the consequences I was thinking about.

This whole mess had all started because of a favor I thought I owed Achilles.

Yes. *The* Achilles. The legendary Greek hero with – what some may call – vengeance issues.

And when one smashes up his place of business – allegedly – he could be known to display said vengeance issues by inflicting gratuitous amounts of pain upon the accused.

No thanks.

So, I wanted to make it up to him before the thought even crossed his mind. It wasn't like I could blame the Angel for fluttering into Achilles' bar and picking a fight with Death – one of the Horsemen of the Apocalypse – and I a few months back. Angels were Holy, above the law, beyond reproach, *blah, blah, blah ad nauseam.*

So. Rather than tattling on the pigeon, I had nervously waited months for the chance to gain his gratitude by doing him a solid.

Over drinks at his bar earlier tonight, Achilles had idly mentioned rumors about a vampire kidnapping young girls to bring them down to the sewers, after which they were never heard from again. The most recent disappearance was one of Achilles' own bartenders, and he feared the worst for her.

That was how I found myself in the sewer with my girlfriend and my childhood best friend on a perfectly cold November night. To possibly prevent my sad rear end from being dragged across St. Louis behind Achilles' chariot.

I glanced at my dismal surroundings. Maybe the vampire was just looking to Netflix and chill in his spacious tunnel home. I studied the slick, slimy walls with a look of disgust. No, not a home… a lair. Definitely a lair.

But this was par for the course in my experience. Find bad guy. Exterminate bad guy. Keep young, pretty girls safe.

Or avenge them.

It's what we wizards did for a living. Well, most of us. The ones who didn't make millions of dollars per year on interest income from their daddy's technology company.

Ahem.

So maybe I was just doing it for the thrill. The challenge. Or maybe even to do the right thing. I grunted. *Who knows these things?* I asked myself with mild reproach. I shook my head before my inner Freud could psychoanalyze that too much further.

After the *Now* comes the *Never* part of the phrase. You know, the part where you won't be *here* anymore. The part where all of your family and loved ones have moved on and left you six feet under, while your soul is astral projected to the afterlife. Heaven. Hell. Atlantis. Nirvana. Or on a nice long boat ride with Charon – the chatty drunk Greek Boatman – who ferried souls on their trip to Hades in his Underworld funhouse.

Been there, done that. It didn't stick.

The point is, you're *dead*, so the consequences of your actions won't be your problem anymore. They will be felt by others, or by no one at all, leaving you with the peace of mind that you did all that you could, that it was worth it. That you made your move. Kissed the girl. Muttered something vaguely English in your speech class.

But you know what's in the middle of *now* and *never*?

Life.

Or in my case, annoying questions that interrupted my well thought out inner philosophical monologue.

"Remind me why we are standing in the literal filth of St. Louis in the middle of November, rather than back at *Chateau Falco* tipping one back before a roaring fire. Or why I'm here instead of curling up with my fiancé looking at wedding magazines and drinking a glass of wine," Gunnar complained. He lifted his boot with a disgusting squelch, emitting a whole new level of foulness to the brittle air. The dingy environment only seemed to amplify the stunningly royal bearing of my Viking friend. His golden hair was tucked up in a golden man bun, and his beard was impressively thicker than usual, as he had been growing it out for his upcoming wedding. Or so he had told me. I had recently had a nightmare where we were wrestling over a Monopoly argument involving my rapid construction of hotels, and I discovered that he was actually growing the beard out in order to hide a secret guardian inside – a leprechaun-sized werewolf willing and able to defend his master's honor in the event his master lost the wrestling match.

In my dream, I had lost to the violent little bastard.

So far, Gunnar's sniffer hadn't located any vampire scent at all, so I was appointed navigator based upon my eidetic memory of the scant information Achilles had provided.

"Well, if we're speaking of the latter, you should thank me," I muttered.

Indie punched me in the arm, scowling. I shook it off with an idle grin, glad that she had accepted my jibe at surface level. After all, I had been reading over every damn wedding magazine ever printed these past few weeks, which seemed to make my mother deliriously happy.

Yes, even a mother who recently died still went bonkers mad at the topic of gowns and weddings. You just had to find a way to talk to her spirit. Which I had. And she had commanded me to use her engagement ring when I asked Indie to share my life.

Which was the other reason I was down here, and the biggest reason I was stalling.

I was distracted. Conflicted. The vampire part of the trip was secondary in my mind.

Which wasn't good.

But I couldn't seem to shake it. I was going to ask Indie to marry me!

My stomach made a little flip-flop motion at the thought. I shot her a discreet glance, but she was too busy fidgeting with her gear to notice. She was so god damned beautiful that I found myself simply staring at her at times. Like now. Her long golden hair fell past her shoulders to frame her perfectly shaped curvaceous upper body, but tonight it was tied up in a pony-tail and sticking out the back of a Chicago Cubs baseball cap.

The St. Louis Cardinal in me growled territorially at that.

She was about my height, a hair under six-feet tall, with legs for days, and curves that most men would drool over. Her face was narrow with a thin nose and icy blue eyes like sun-kissed sapphires. I averted my eyes as she glanced up, seeming to notice my attention.

I pretended to scout our path as I mentally ran over my proposal plan. I had made reservations at *Vin de Set*, her favorite French restaurant. Two days from now. I had cleverly used the excuse that we were past due for our regular date night where we usually 'recalibrated' our relationship. We typically did this once or twice per month, but so far it had stretched into month two now without either of us bringing it up.

It might or might not have started as a result of Othello's visit to town a few months back when Indie had been out of town caring for her injured mother. Injured because of my enemies, we later found out. Either way, several events from that visit had created a bit of friction between us. Not because I had been unfaithful – not by *choice*, anyway – but because Othello had openly admitted her ongoing infatuation with me. One that she had secretly harbored since our brief romantic relationship in college several years back.

She had admitted this to Indie. In front of me. Without giving me any warning at all.

Which had required some deft maneuvering on my part, let me tell you.

The two were amicable now, but boy oh boy it had been interesting for a time.

My thoughts drifted back to my dinner plans as Gunnar began sniffing down one of the halls, hoping to catch a whiff of fanger, AKA *eau de corpse*. Vampire. Indie was still fidgeting with her gear.

Before the dinner proposal, I wanted to see how she handled tonight, because, well, this was my *life*.

Hunting.

At least a big *part* of my life. And even though she had told me before that she could handle it, I needed to *know* that she could. There's a difference, folks. The proposal details were all set. The venue picked. Dinner dishes and wine already ordered. Her favorite dessert, strawberry short-cake, ordered from a local bakery.

Everything was set.

Well, *almost* everything… Which led me back to my *third* reason for jumping on tonight's opportunity.

Indie readjusted the contraption dominating her cranium, tightening one of the straps so that the headlamp mounted on top didn't jiggle around so much with each movement. Despite me being chock full of power, able to cast a ball of light to float beside us and illuminate the darkness, and Gunnar's near night vision thanks to his werewolf genes, a girl needed to accessorize to feel complete in this world. Practicality and logic be damned. And no man would ever get in the way of accessorizing.

Ever.

Indie looked grim at the unexplained dangers of tonight's extermination – seeing as how I hadn't yet explained it to either of them in depth – but was also conflictingly excited to be included in the boy's club. Even if she was completely mundane – as without magic as a boiled egg – it really didn't seem to bother her. Where Gunnar and I were at the opposite end of the spectrum. Dare I say that Gunnar and I were legen–

*Wait for it…*

Dary.

Indie and I had been binge-watching *How I Met Your Mother* lately. So, sue me.

I smiled to myself, which only made Gunnar's eyes tighten, as if it confirmed his sneaking suspicion that I was as mad as a hatter.

"We're all mad here," I whispered softly.

"What?" Indie asked, having successfully completed readjusting her straps.

I mumbled nothing in particular, putting my head back in the game. "Alright, gang. We're hunting an Alucard named Dracula," I answered distractedly, focusing my ears towards the two tunnels that branched off ahead of us. One of them led to our target. The other led to more smelly things and my third reason for entering the sewers tonight.

"Are you drunk?" Gunnar asked, very seriously. Indie blinked, having not been around me for the past few hours and realizing that it could very possibly be a valid question.

"What? No. I'm not… I had one drink with Achilles, but…"

"You just keep staring off into the distance as if distracted. And you're not making any sense. It's… unsettling." He folded his arms.

"Yeah, sorry about that. Few other things on my mind."

He waited. And I realized what else was bothering him as I replayed our conversation in my head. "Oh. I see what you're getting at. I meant to say *a Dracula named Alucard.*" They stared at me, still not getting it. I rolled my eyes at Gunnar. "A vampire. The name *Alucard* is *Dracula* spelled backwards, you uneducated mutt," I turned to Indie, "and beautiful, intelligent lady."

Indie rolled her eyes. The silence grew before Gunnar finally let out a soft chuckle. "He seriously named himself *Alucard*? Does he have any idea how pretentious that is, or is it really his name?" He grinned hungrily. "I think I should ask him," he added, flexing his muscles. Or maybe he *hadn't* flexed. Regardless, his coat stretched along the seams of his arms and shoulders with a slight creaking sound.

"You're right. We should ask him. Word from Achilles is that he's kidnapped some girls. One of them was his. A bartender. I'm here to see if it's true. You two are here as witnesses. Especially you, Indie. No heroics. I'm serious. If he really is a vampire, stand back. Gunnar and I will handle it." She nodded her agreement, breath quickening slightly.

I consulted the mental map Achilles had shown me and took a left.

My posse followed me.

Which was good. Posses are supposed to do that sort of thing. It messed up the cool factor when they didn't.

We continued on for fifteen minutes or so until I began to hear faint whimpers coming from what sounded like only a dozen feet away. Still, with echoes it could be a mile. Gunnar took a big whiff of the air and nodded at me one time, looking suddenly relieved. Apparently, his sniffer was back on track. Or the vampire's apparent concealment spell didn't work this close up.

"Not far now. A few hundred feet at most," he whispered. "Won't they be able to sense us?"

I shook my head, mentally checking our map. "No. I masked our scent." There were two bends before any kind of opening that could house what might be used as living quarters.

I rolled my shoulders and patted my hip reassuringly.

Magic was suave and all, but I hadn't really mastered my new abilities yet. A few months back during *Mardi Gras* when my friends had been out of town, Othello and I had had a run in with Heaven. And Hell. And my previous governing institution, the Academy – which ruled and dictated the laws of the wizard nation. They had thought I was working for the demons. Heaven thought so too. I hadn't been, of course. But everyone and their mother wanted to get their grubby hands on the secret project my father had gifted to me prior to his death. An Armory of the deadliest supernatural weapons in recorded history.

During the struggle, my own people had taken away my magic, permanently, but my father had given me something else along with the Armory. A new, strange power that had historically been placed higher on the food chain than even a wizard's magic. To be honest, even months later, I was still struggling to wrap my head around it.

So, having not mastered my new abilities as a Maker, I liked to be reassured by the hundred-pound gun at my hip. Not really a hundred pounds, but the SIG Sauer X-Five Gunnar had given me a while back was definitely reassuring, and right now it really did feel like a hundred pounds of confidence.

"Alright, gang. It's now or never."

I lifted my foot to take a step, and a silver ball of light – I somehow had the presence of mind to notice that it resembled a stunningly attractive, anatomically correct, naked *Barbie* doll – struck me in the dome, knocking me clear on my ass and into a puddle of nastiness. I quickly scrambled to my feet, shivering, ready to obliterate the creature. She hovered where my head had been, staring directly at me. It *was* a naked Barbie.

And I recognized her.

"She looks familiar…" Gunnar murmured to Indie, who was staring wide-eyed at the silver sprite.

"What *is* she?" Indie asked bluntly, cocking her head sideways as she assessed the creature. "She's beautiful."

"A sprite. A fairy. A very dangerous fairy. Looks can be deceiving," I warned, shaking the cold sewage off my coat.

The sprite smiled in approval at the warning, flashing needle-like teeth at Indie, who flinched back a step. "He's back, and he's coming to murder you and all your friends." The glowing sprite hissed darkly to me, "it's time."

Like I said, a lot can happen between *now* and *never*.

# CHAPTER 2

*I* shook my coat off again with a growl, trying to detach, at least, the larger pieces of filth. Wet splashes marked my successes, adding to the fragrant stench filling my nose.

"Right before you sucker-punched me into that pile of defecation, we had been stealthily approaching the vermin in order to exterminate him. So, *shoo*, Barbie," I growled darkly. I didn't know what name she went by in casual circles, but I knew her True Name, the one able to compel her to obey if used three times in conjunction, which I was very tempted to use at the moment just to make a point. But I didn't. So, in my mind she was now *Barbie*, whereas before I had called her Nympho Sprite.

*Nympho* for nymphomaniac. Emphasis on *maniac*. I had met her before on an impromptu case that led to me opening my arcane bookstore, Plato's Cave – currently still under renovation from the gentle affections of a brawl involving a demon, an angel, and a Nephilim during *Mardi Gras* a few months back. This little light of mine had a thing for helping wizards in exchange for… well… *sexual favors*.

Look, I know, she looked all of twelve inches tall right *now*. But it's not as weird as it sounds. She could become *bigger* when she wanted to by shapeshifting to match her summoner's size. She had even hinted that she could shapeshift into other *creatures*, so being a werewolf for example wasn't an impediment to her, *erm*, bargaining price. I had also gotten the distinct impression that many didn't survive her affections, and that didn't seem to bother her in the least. If anything, it *pleased* her.

Creepy.

"Bah," she waved a hand at my comment. "Not the vampires, wiz–" She hesitated, eyes widening with sudden confusion. She stared at me more closely, assessing me on a deeper level than the mortal eye could, as if calculating a new equation in her mind. She must have realized I was no longer a wizard, but I didn't know how. She continued on a few seconds later, shelving the topic of my abilities, and returning to her initial purpose. "Interesting development." She murmured to herself before continuing. "The Grimm. Jacob is back. And he brought his brothers. To kill you and all your friends. I warned you of this when we first met."

An icy fist seemed to suddenly clench my vertebrae. Indie gasped.

The Brothers Grimm. They were back. For me. And my friends. Because I had taken their book from them a few years ago, and rather than destroying it like the sprite had advised, I had hoarded it away. And now I was going to pay for it.

As were my friends, apparently.

"I *knew* I recognized her. She used to work for Alistair. The book guy," Gunnar hissed. "Remember, Nate? Back in the old days." He looked at me.

She turned suddenly arctic eyes onto the wolf. "If you ever refer to him again as *the book guy* I will feast on your sclera." She licked her lips eagerly.

"No offense," he offered genuinely, taking a step back as he held up his hands to idly touch his eyes, which she had casually mentioned eating.

"Too late, wolf pup." She bared needle-like fangs in a hungry snarl.

Indie chimed in before the sprite could do anything. "Did you say vampires? As in, *plural?*" Gunnar and I froze, turning to the sprite.

She merely stared back, shaking her head in disbelief at our obviously limited mental capacity. "Good thing you brought the Regular along. She actually has a brain."

Gunnar and I began to sputter angry responses, but Indie beat us to it. "That's why they pay me the big bucks," she grinned.

Then I noticed the change in our surroundings. A faint rustling. And no more whimpering. Damn it. The sprite grinned in anticipation, looking eagerly delighted at the likely violence to come. "You seem to have stumbled upon a nest," she smiled.

Before I could respond with a sarcastic retort, a blinding flurry of tattered robes struck me like a Mizzou lineman. I purposely let him. A surprise counterattack.

No, really. It was on purpose.

So was the next part, when I let him slam my head into the brick wall behind us, eliciting an explosion of stars to swim across my vision. I dropped the pistol clutched in my hand and heard it splash deep into the muck at our feet. "Attack!" I managed to groan. Now I had him right where I wanted him. I heard Gunnar grunt in surprise and then the sound of him being tackled into the sewage. I briefly managed to wonder why I hadn't heard the explosion of fabric that resulted from him shifting into wolf form from human clothes. His giant snow-white mountain wolf form was much better suited to fighting vampires. In fact, it was designed to do *just that*. I don't know how I managed to notice any of this, seeing as how I had a frothing mad vampire chomping down towards my necksicle, but I did. I also saw Indie's flashlight go sailing off into the darkness before landing in a puddle of ick.

Barbie's ambient glow was the only thing protecting us from the natural darkness of the tunnels. For which I was grateful, but she apparently didn't have the patience to wait for a little thing like the result of a life or death fight to conclude our conversation.

"All because you took their book. I told you to destroy it. Admit it."

She folded her arms. I managed to get a forearm against the vampire's neck, barely keeping him from gobbling up my tender throat. Despite still coming to grips with using my new power, I somehow managed to cast out a weak spell of air and bowled over the pair of vampires that had attacked Indie. She looked unharmed, but to be honest I couldn't see very clearly, what with the animated Disney birds and stars dancing across my vision and the strain against keeping the vampire from tasting my esophagus. Since it was now pointless to continue masking our scent, I dropped the small spell I had held to get us here undetected. Twin shots shattered the air as Indie let loose with her pistol.

Hollow-point, oak-tipped bullets worked like garlic cupcakes on a vampire. They dropped in a puff of dust. I heard fists striking flesh, and wondered again why I heard no howling or growling from Gunnar. Had they gotten him? My vision began to turn red in anger, and the for the first time ever, the well of power that I presumed was available only to Makers called out to *me* rather than the other way around.

A river of molten lava flowing just beneath the surface of my mind invited me to play, and my vision pulsed from red to blue.

Before, as a wizard, I had essentially used the available elements around me to manipulate into magic. When the elements I needed were absent, I could draw from my own body for a limited time. But it was taxing.

The Maker power didn't quite work like that.

A constant pool of power resided just below the surface of the world around me, available to be manipulated into whatever the Maker saw fit to, well... *make*. To me, the well seemed bottomless in comparison to my old magic, but I was pretty sure it wasn't. It also wasn't as reliable, or I wasn't as gifted at using it as I had been with my magic. But then again, I had been a veritable force to be reckoned with as a wizard. Still, when the Maker power was harnessed, it could pack a punch that made a wizard look like a schoolyard bully. I began weaving the power together messily, still struggling against the vampire.

"Admit it, Temple," Barbie continued.

The vampire above me froze completely still. "Temple?" He hissed in alarm. I grunted an affirmative and he violently threw himself away before I could do anything. I fell into the muck at the sudden motion.

"The Maker!" One hissed from near Gunnar, who was holding a vampire's head under the filth, drowning him as he stared down the speaking vampire.

The one that had attacked me hissed again. "Retreat. None must harm the Maker."

I paused. *That* was never a good thing to hear. It usually implied worse, deadlier things were in store for you down the road. And they knew I was a Maker. Even though *I* didn't fully understand what that actually meant. Yet.

They disappeared back down the tunnel as fast as cockroaches when the lights were turned on. Vampires were *fast*. I took a deep breath, shook the stars from my eyes, and began to race after them, not wanting to give them a second longer than absolutely necessary with the victim I had heard whimpering earlier. I heard the clomping steps of my posse following me, and I felt Barbie latch onto my shoulder, getting a free ride.

Gunnar caught up to me easily so I shot him an angry glare. "You know, it would be really awesome if we had a werewolf to run them down right about now." Indie gamely let off a few pot shots as we ran.

He grunted in response. "Can't shift. Don't know why."

That dialed back my anger really quickly. What could prevent Gunnar from shifting? I hadn't even thought that was possible.

"Admit it, Temple. Admit you should have listened to me and I will take care of this… nuisance," Barbie spoke in my ear, interrupting our conversation.

I ignored her pointedly. We entered a cavernous space, and skidded to a stop. The vampires were scrabbling at a locked door, their fingers gouging at the wood to no effect.

"Rule number one, fangheads. Always have a back door ready."

They stopped, and then slowly turned to face me.

"We will leave you in peace," they offered, looking nervous.

"Not playing out that way," I muttered. The smell of blood and offal filled the space like a physical presence. My gaze swept the room quickly, searching for survivors.

But we were too late.

The girls were dead. I counted three bodies in direct sight. Two had been recently killed judging by the still-wet pools of blood around their crumpled bodies. Indie lifted her guns, pointing them at the vampires with a humorless grin on her beautiful face as Gunnar growled, taking a step forward. "Why can't I shift… fanghead?" He borrowed the nickname I had given them, somehow managing to tip an imaginary hat in my direction without averting his eyes from the vampires.

"Let us go and I will tell you. I'll even give it to you."

I laughed out loud. "Not too good at negotiating, are you? You just admitted that you have something that prevents my friend from letting his fur fly. That was your only bargaining chip. And you tossed it into the game without looking at your hand."

The vampires clammed up.

"We really do have more pressing matters, Temple," the sprite complained lazily. "Let's speed things up. They have a moonstone." She had drifted from my shoulders to float beside me. Most likely to avoid becoming collateral damage if they rushed me. I blinked at her. "Moonstone. A chunk of rock from the moon. It prevents a wolf from shifting," she elaborated. I exchanged a look with Gunnar. He shrugged with an arched brow. He hadn't heard of it either. I hated not knowing things.

"Why would you have something like that?" I asked them.

"Because he isn't the only wolf down here," the vampire snarled.

A piercing howl echoed throughout the tunnels. Followed by several answering calls.

The vampires tensed, arching up on the balls of their feet as if preparing to make a run for it. They weren't interested in tussling with us, let alone a pack of werewolves. The leader quickly reached into a pocket and pulled out a small stone. Before I could react, he slammed it into the wall, shattering it. Gunnar instantly sighed, his fists flexing into white furred claws.

"Admit it, Temple, and I will resolve this disagreement. You know you can't fight the vampires and the wolves at the same time. Time is wasting. They have your scent, and they will now be able to maintain their form when they get closer," the sprite whispered hungrily. I sighed.

"Okay, fine. I was right, you were wrong," I muttered. The howls grew closer, but silence still reigned supreme in our little alcove.

She shook her head, but didn't move. I saw the vampires tense up, ready to make their move.

"God damn it. *Fine. You* were right, and *I* was wrong." I shouted at her as the vamps took a step.

She beamed down at me for a few seconds, gloating, and the vampires were suddenly halfway out the room, escaping. But then Barbie snapped her dainty little toothpick fingers.

And a wave of pure silver light crashed down over the top of our heads like a heavy feather pillow. Not strong enough to knock me over, but enough to let me know it was definitely there. I heard an exclamation of surprise from my posse.

I stumbled a bit on wobbly legs, feeling oddly sensuous, as if all my senses were on high alert. I realized distantly that I was very definitely… in the *mood*. Like, instantly. I shook off the mental cloud and glared at the sprite. "If you hurt my friends, I'll roast you on a kabob." I took a threatening step towards her. "Or a toothpick, I guess."

"Tut, tut." She smiled, and I was knocked back on my ass, feeling dazed, and my pants just three sizes too small in the groin area. Indie let out a pleased whimper followed by a sharp exclamation of ecstasy. Then she folded to her feet with a dazed smile on her face. I blinked and turned my head to the sprite.

"That one was for free," she grinned.

"Did you just–"

"Granted, women are easier to please than men, if you know how we work. It just so happens that pleasure is my forte. Even *lethal* pleasure when the situation arises. But that's more for *my* enjoyment. This was just fore-play, a gift for your apology." She glanced at Indie, who was only now getting to her feet on shaky legs, looking excited and confused. She hadn't even commented on the filth covering her. "I think you may have an interesting night ahead of you, Temple," she smiled down at me. I shook the euphoria from my head, struggling to my feet. "You're welcome," she answered smugly.

Well, I didn't have anything to say to *that*. Thank you? A cigarette?

The vampires lay motionless on the cool stone floor. Their bodies slowly transformed into ash that was lighter than the air, before further disintegrating to nothing. Gunnar climbed to his feet, very obviously aroused, and even more obviously pleased at the situation. Great, everyone else seemed to get a happy ending, where I only got a case of metaphysical blue balls.

My life.

More howls punctuated my situation in a piercing lament.

# CHAPTER 3

"*A*lright. Time to scat."

"Where? If they don't have our scent yet they soon will," Gunnar answered, eyes darting back and forth anxiously.

"Follow me." I retraced our steps in a light jog back to the first intersection of tunnels, and veered down the other fork this time. The howls were coming from a different part of the sewer, which was a blessing, buying us a few minutes. The sprite whispered in my ear, having apparently hitched a ride on my shoulder again. Lazy freaking fairies.

"We have more pressing matters to discuss," she urged.

"I think survival is the most pressing issue," I argued. She grunted in disagreement. "Besides, I'm already working on the Grimms." She went silent, apparently satisfied at my answer and content to enjoy her free ride.

After several more turns we began to hear sounds above our heads.

"Is that a jackhammer?" Indie asked from my left shoulder, breathing heavily.

Gunnar tilted his head as we ran, remaining at my other shoulder. "It sounds like a construction site. Are we beneath roadwork?" He whispered softly, knowing how well werewolves could hear. "Is it safe for us to be down here?"

I grunted, spotting our next turn. They flowed with me. "Of course not. It's never safe down here. Remember all the signs I told you guys to ignore at the entrance?" Gunnar's eyes tightened, but he made no comment, focusing instead on our immediate survival.

We finally came to a gnarled iron door and I stopped. Water stains trailed down the brick-work surrounding the door, feeding a rather large patch of moss and algae of some kind. The construction sounds were louder now. I could imagine the familiar smells coming from the building above us. "It's louder now. It's definitely construction. Why did we stop?" A distant howl punctuated Gunnar's question.

"You're right. It does sound like construction. In fact, if I had to guess I would say we are directly underneath Plato's Cave." I reached into a pocket and nonchalantly withdrew an old-school iron key.

Gunnar muttered a curse. "This was your intention. You had this planned. No way we accidentally ended up underneath your bookstore." I smiled and shrugged innocently as I took a step forward and used the key to open the door to my hidey-hole.

Indie held up a hand, stalling Gunnar's impatience. "I got this. I speak Nate." She didn't try to hide her words. She turned to me, face deadpan. "Oh, Nate. You're so witty and clever. Why did you take us to your oh-so-secret underground lair? No, please, tell us. We can't take the suspense," she said, her voice monotone and dripping with sarcasm.

I scowled, and she winked, cracking a smile as she lifted her hands in a bow as if to tell Gunnar, *See?* She took all the fun out of it. I turned my back on them to address the door.

"No, really. Why are we here?" Indie asked seriously this time, peering over my shoulder with an affectionate squeeze as I struggled with the rusted lock on the door. I began to answer with the prearranged, carefully crafted lie on the tip of my tongue, but then I had a thought. Thanks to the sprite, I now had a justifiable excuse for wanting to stop by here. I didn't need to lie to cover the truth from her.

"I have a small vault down here as a precaution against the bookstore ever being robbed. I keep several things down here. The books the Grimms want are here. Lucky us, right?"

Gunnar studied me suspiciously, but didn't speak the question on his mind. If the sprite's visit was unplanned, why had I coincidentally known how to get to this place so quickly on a convenient vampire-hunting trip? I shrugged at him with a smile, silently urging him to drop it.

I finally wrestled the door open to loud screeching, which made me shiver.

The wolves had to have heard *that*.

I strode over to the hidden safe, the room comfortably illuminated by the sprite's presence on my shoulder. Several bookshelves lined two walls of the small storage room, filled with important-looking books, but they were just a front. I plucked a seemingly random loose brick free from the far wall to reveal a digital safe keypad. I heard grunts of surprise behind me but ignored them as I punched in the code. It beeped once, and a three-foot section of the brick wall swung silently towards me on well-oiled hinges, but the brick affixed to the small safe's door scratched the floor loudly. It had to be a tight fit to remain hidden, so there was nothing to do about it or else it would have been pretty obvious that it wasn't part of the wall.

I reached inside and plucked two books wrapped in silk from a jumble of random items. I also palmed a loose sapphire ring, glittering with a collection of tiny loose diamonds around its antique edges. The sprite – the only one close enough to see my hands and the contents of the vault – frowned at that, turning her gaze to the side of my face to regard me thoughtfully. I was too close to her physically to return the gesture so I merely pocketed the ring and lifted a finger to my lips, requesting her silence.

"Um, Nate? They're onto us. Did you get the books yet? If not, maybe we should come back later," Gunnar asked from out in the tunnel, speaking over his shoulder as he kept an eye out for us. Growling could be heard in the near distance, picking up on the sound of his voice and probably our scent too. They were close.

"Yes, I've got them." I tucked the books into my other coat pocket and shut the vault, carefully replacing the loose brick. The two books weren't particularly large, more journals than anything. Indie stepped closer to me, but hadn't seen the ring, thank god. It had belonged to my mother and I was going to use it when I proposed to her.

The growling suddenly ceased and I turned to find five figures facing Gunnar beyond the doorway.

"Wow, did I shake a bag of puppy chow or something?" I asked loud enough for everyone to hear as I stepped out of the room.

The leader stepped forward with a snarl. "Does he have it?" He asked one of his compatriots, staring past Gunnar and directly at me. He was a large specimen of a man, and sported a thick black beard that just touched his chest. They were dressed in casual clothes, grays and blacks, loose-fitting, and unremarkable. They all wore heavy hiking or combat boots, as if they had known they would be down here tonight. Which told me this wasn't a coincidence. The vampires had also been prepared for wolves. Blackbeard's eyes glittered expectantly in the darkness as he watched me.

One of the other wolves – a leaner, whip-thin scrapper, by the looks of it – took a deep whiff and nodded. "Yes. But he said nothing of the Maker being present. In fact, we are to avoid the Maker at all costs. Punishable by death," Scrappy warned Black Beard.

I was more startled to discover that yet another flavor of Freaks knew about my new powers, but I didn't have time to ask about it. Things escalated rather quickly.

"I know what our fucking orders were, pup!" Blackbeard bellowed as he backhanded the lean wolf without taking his gaze from me, sending the skinny werewolf into the wall with a hard thud. The other wolves shifted their shoulders reflexively but didn't avert their gaze from our party. They were all different flavors of Hard Ass. *Blackbeard, Shorty, Rhino, Arian, and Scrappy*, I silently nicknamed them in my head.

"Orders. Taking commands," I waved my hands to enunciate. "Wanting something of mine while tucking your tails between your legs in order to avoid a confrontation with me." I spoke softly but clearly. Gunnar grunted in agreement.

Indie piped up. "Gunnar, didn't you tell me werewolves were brave and honorable?"

He nodded. "I had thought so, but we're just people. Some good," he studied them each with a glare, "Some who shouldn't be let off their leashes." He yawned. Indie looked thoughtful, idly tapping a lip.

I nodded. "Not very impressive at all. In fact, you're boring me. Getting on my nerves, even. If you want to scrap, shed your human skin and let your fur fly, pups. We'll oblige. If not, Daddy's got important things to do. So, *shoo*," I flicked a dismissive hand.

Indie cocked her guns in the silence. Arian took a step forward. "Our orders were not to kill you. I can handle that." He took another step.

Gunnar growled, fists shifting into long black claws sheathed in thick white fur. "One more step and you're a sack of meat," he warned, looking resolved but distantly sickened at the potential for upcoming murder. The wolf snickered in doubtful reproach and took another step.

Before his foot touched the ground, Gunnar shifted entirely to wolf form in an explosion of tattered fabric. All I saw in the dull illumination was Arian, standing upright with his throat ripped out. Gunnar stood in his impressive wolf form, muscles bristling, on the other side of the pack, but still between the thieves and us. He growled a warning. The other wolves responded with menacing growls of their own.

Then the body thudded into the water.

Two of the others, Rhino and Shorty, instantly threw themselves forward and Indie's pistols *boomed*, sending Shorty back into the darkness with a cry. The other sailed right past Gunnar and Indie, straight for me. Of course, it was the bigger one, Rhino. I was fueled with plenty of rage at the moment, having anticipated a much calmer walk in the sewers than it had ended up being. The wolf's outstretched arms had been aimed at my feet, but since I had dropped to my knees, his fingertips managed to instead hit my side before time seemed to freeze. He was reaching for the books, but his hand got caught in the wrong pocket. The force of the burly were-wolf's attack would have folded most people or slammed them to the ground. But I'm a wizard, and I had let him get close enough to touch me on purpose.

You may not know this, but wizards are dirty cheats.

I had needed him to make physical contact with me in order for me to add his momentum to my magic. My fingertips broke the surface of the frigid water. As time seemed to stand still, I exploded upwards, a single drop of frozen shit water resting in the air before my face. My sudden motion caused his hand to tear open the pocket of my coat, but luckily the books were in my other pocket. I flicked my finger and the wolf was abruptly engulfed in a vortex of icy, stinky water. I used the rotating momentum to cast him straight back the way he had come. The explosion of frosty air hit the tunnels like a snow blower, coating the walls and ground in icy hoarfrost, a shining surface that was as slick as quicksilver. The wolf hit it.

And kept right on going at warp speed, right past Blackbeard and the others, fueled by the maelstrom of my magic.

He disappeared from sight and slid down the tunnel quite a ways before the chill began to wear off and the friction increased, hopefully giving him one serious rug burn. I heard a final yelp and then a crumple as he struck a wall that was no longer slick, well out of sight.

I brushed off my hands and turned to the remaining wolves. Only Black-beard and Scrappy remained in sight, looking startled. "Stomach shots. It won't kill him, but it will slow him down," Indie spoke clinically, thrusting her jaw at Shorty's groaning body.

Blackbeard growled menacingly and turned to Gunnar. "You will pay for that, rogue. Every wolf needs a pack. It's time you learned your place. The night is dangerous for a lone wolf."

Gunnar responded by shifting back to his human form. He stood from the ground, looking like a Viking from the Norse legends, blood dripping from his mouth. The sprite murmured appreciatively.

He only smiled. "I'll take my chances." His pecs glistened with the victo-rious sweat of a Roman Gladiator.

Either that or icy shit water.

But that kind of killed the sexy factor.

Blackbeard's eyes were murderous. "Gather the wounded. This wasn't as we were told it would be. No one else needs to die." He assessed Gunnar hungrily. "Tonight." He promised.

Then they were gone. Well, except for the dead werewolf. I looked at Barbie and then at the body. She rolled her eyes at me and he was suddenly gone. Disappeared or destroyed, I shivered to think about. Indie gasped too, and Barbie smiled darkly, licking her lips. I turned away from her. I had plenty of nightmare material already.

A few moments went by before Gunnar confirmed, "they're gone."

"Well," I sighed, "I don't know about you guys, but I'm exhausted from kicking ass all night. Let's head back. Gunnar, you're on point. Indie, in the middle. Barbie, watch our six."

"Oh, I'll definitely be watching *his* six." She pointed bluntly at Gunnar's prominent nakedness. He blushed. Indie burst out laughing.

"*Professionalism...*" I muttered, shaking my head as they began to follow me. I idly patted my pockets as we moved, my mind struggling to decipher why the sewers had been such a happening place tonight. And the coinci-dence that Achilles had sent us here, this night of all nights. Then I blinked, slowing my steps. I patted my pocket again more frantically as another second ticked by, feeling only the torn fabric hanging free. I halted, checking my other pocket now, turning it inside out.

I growled a curse as I came up empty handed. "Son of a bitch!"

The ring.

I searched the ground like a madman, scraping the puddles, ignoring everyone's incredulous faces and questions about what I was doing. I even cast out a bit of my new power, searching with magic for any traces of a small metal object under the filth, but I found nothing but a dented soda can. It was no use.

It was gone.

Rhino must have managed to swipe it when his hands got stuck in my pocket, tearing open the fabric.

I growled darkly as I climbed to my feet, glaring murder at the direction of the retreating werewolves.

Things can always get worse.

# CHAPTER 4

*W*e sat in my BMW X5, Gunnar behind the driver's wheel and Indie in the passenger seat as we headed back to *Chateau Falco*. Gunnar had thrown on some loose sweats and a tee that he always carried around with him in case of needing to re-clothe after a shift. I had also changed into an old gym outfit buried in my trunk, but still stunk to high heaven. Barbie had stuck by our side and was now hovering beside me in the backseat, looking pleasantly naked. I turned my head in embarrassment, which elicited a small smile from her silver lips.

Having survived the night, I was ready for a drink and a long massage, especially after Indie's very obvious innuendos on our way back to the vehicle. It seemed the sprite's magic had definitely lit a match in her that I wanted to explore. I cleared my head with a gentle slap to my cheeks.

Later. Business first. Beneath the more life-threatening situation, all I could think about was the lost ring. Had Rhino managed to nab it before I sent him on his icy waterslide? It seemed unlikely, but the bottom line was that I had assumed I was quicker than the lycanthrope gene, and now the ring was gone. I was confident it hadn't fallen into the muck. I had silently tested the tunnel with magic to no avail. I shook my head. I would just have to ask Rhino about it before my dinner date with Indie in a few days.

He and his pack weren't likely to want to see me.

I wasn't likely to be too concerned about that. I would just have to ask nicely.

Also known as walking loudly and swinging a big stick.

"So… the Grimms," I began, desperately needing to distract myself with something other than the ring. Barbie watched me hungrily as if waiting for me to finally tear off my clothes and submit to her allure. Dark sex may be appealing to some, but that was taking it to a whole different level. I shivered at the thought. "I take it that they aren't too happy with me?" In hindsight, it was a good reason I was down in the sewers tonight. It hadn't been my intention, but it seemed awfully coincidental that things had gone to hell the very night I had decided to make a trip to my previously secret vault for personal reasons.

But now that was dashed all to hell. No ring.

Barbie answered my rhetorical question. "To put it mildly. They want their book back. But besides that, they've also accepted a contract on your head. And all known associates, guilty or not." The temperature in the car grew frigid as the implication sunk in. She nodded before continuing, "I think it's time you destroy the book. You will die either way, but at least they won't be able to summon the rest of their brothers into our world. Or their pets. I believe you were lucky enough to have met one of *them* once." I nodded, grimacing at the memory of the demonic rooster horse Gunnar and I had fought and destroyed several years back.

"The rest? How many are there?" I asked, dumbfounded. I had assumed only a handful. Unless Jacob and Wilhelm's mom had been particularly amorous in her day.

She smiled icily. "Hundreds. Why do you think we locked them away?"

I blinked in astonishment. *Hundreds?*

"How many are here already?" I asked softly.

"A dozen."

"Oh. Well that doesn't sound like too many. I've got a few friends who can help–"

"A dozen of the most dangerous, bloodthirsty, savage, supernatural hit men that ever existed. A dozen creatures who spent hundreds of years destroying supernatural citizens, regardless of their powers and joint collaboration efforts. Even Makers." The silence was deafening. She drifted closer and lifted my chin. "You had a good round, Temple, but you played your last card. You lost. You just don't know it yet. At least you can make sure that the rest of us don't die too. Bring me the book. Sooner rather than later. I will help you destroy it. And say goodbye to you. I wish we could have gotten to know each other better..." With that, she was abruptly gone.

Indie and Gunnar merely stared at me with wide eyes before clamoring over each other with demands for an explanation. So, I told them. Everything. I had first run into Jacob Grimm years before. Our introduction had been the true reason behind my career as a used bookstore owner. I had opened Plato's Cave to hide the two books now resting in the satchel at my feet. I had been warned that I should destroy them. I hadn't listened, instead wanting to study them. In the years since, the fear had worn off and I had put it on my rainy-day list. As well as a zillion other things that always seemed to take precedence. So, they had sat buried in a vault beneath my third projector room in Plato's Cave for years. Unopened. Untouched. And now a liability.

The Hubris of youth...

Sharing the story with my friends helped clear my head a bit and come up with a game plan. If there was a contract out on my life, I knew a guy who might have heard about it. I told Gunnar where to turn. He did so without complaint, slowly beginning to unravel his clouded memory from the particular night we had met Jacob Grimm. After the events that transpired that fateful night, Barbie had wiped his mind clean to keep the information compartmentalized. But now I had told him the truth, and he didn't look pleased at my deceit. Even though, technically, it hadn't been me, I had been complicit in essentially helping him believe a lie. Which didn't sit well with the werewolf.

I would have to make it up to him somehow.

To be fair, the sprite had wiped everyone's memories from that night. Well, except mine. Even Kyle and Tammy, the two innocent college kids with unique healing abilities who had found themselves unwittingly entwined in the scheme to steal the books in the first place. Their accomplice had been working for the Grimms, but he was long gone now. I idly wondered what had happened to the two kids. If they even remembered why they had suddenly left town and dropped out of college.

I stared off into the distance, lost in memory, until Gunnar reached our destination and parked in a vacant spot on the side of the road. "I need to make a call." Gunnar nodded. I picked up my phone and dialed a familiar number, waiting for an answer. I had thought tonight was going to be a quick trip.

But it now seemed like my *never* was approaching earlier than I had anticipated. This was really going to mess up my five-year plan.

A familiar agitated voice answered the phone. I listened to him for a few more seconds before responding. "Are you sure you don't have time to talk right now?" I asked softly, eyeing a Kinko's just down the street, mind already formulating a sinister plan. Gunnar watched me warily, recognizing the familiar tone I had used, and knowing that the only safe response would have been to comply with my request. He had been on the receiving end of that tone one too many times.

But the person on the phone didn't know me well enough to realize that.

"I shouldn't even be talking to you at all! Fine. Give me a few hours. I need to clear up a few things first." The phone muffled and I heard a female complaining in the background.

"I guess that will have to work. Unless you... *clear a few things up* earlier than expected. If so, I'll be waiting." He grunted noncommittally and hung up.

I opened the door and stepped outside. "I'll be right back," I told them. Indie darted out of the car to join me with a curious frown. Rather than arguing, I figured the safest place for her was in my sight. I reached out and held her hand as we walked through the frigid streets. "Isn't that Tomas' apartment?" She asked, pointing a thumb over her shoulder. "The dragon hunter that you ran into a year ago?"

I nodded, smirking lightly.

"Why don't we just head up there and talk to him really quick? That was him on the phone, right?"

I smiled at her, nodding. "Because he wouldn't be focused. At this point I think he would tell us anything to get us out of his hair." She frowned. "He's got a girl up there. I think they are going out for dinner." She rolled her eyes in understanding.

"Men. One whiff of 'tang and they're off like a rocket. No loyalty."

I chuckled. "It's in our DNA, and written in our Man Bible. We all must abide by it," I answered solemnly.

"Right." She rolled her eyes. "Makes you very predictable." She squeezed my palm.

I turned my head and noticed her cheeks were rosy from the cold.

Snowflakes dotted her hair like ornaments, and her lips were a deep red shade like frozen raspberries. "We'll talk about predictable after you see my plan. I've been waiting a long time for something like this. The opportunity doesn't come up as often as you'd think."

I opened the door to the store and Indie studied me thoughtfully before entering first. I followed her and approached the register. "Good evening. I need you to do me a favor. I need some prints made," I addressed a matronly woman behind the counter with a dazzling array of badges and flair on her company vest. Her nametag read Nadine and she instantly noticed the smell suddenly permeating the room, but she didn't say anything about it. I handed her a flash drive I had swiped from my satchel, courtesy of Othello. I had held onto it for months, waiting for the perfect opportunity.

"Of course, how many would you two like?"

"Oh, quite a few. A hundred should suffice. You can pick your favorites." I told her. Indie managed to keep a straight face, even though she had no idea what I was doing.

"Well, that will take about an hour. Is that a problem?" She plugged in the flash drive as I answered, clicking buttons to get to the files. They were the only ones on the drive. It wouldn't take long for her to see them.

"No. But try to make it sooner. We can wait. We're parked just down the street. We'll also need a roll of packing tape and scissors."

She frowned. "Okay. Give me your number and I'll call you when it's all ready." Her frown was deepening at the items on the flash drive as the thumbnails pulled up on her screen. She glanced up at Indie thoughtfully, and then frowned. I barely managed to keep my face still.

"It's for a prank. Bachelor party. *Boys...*" Indie murmured, rolling her eyes in a *what can you do?* gesture. She deserved a Tony Award.

"O...Okay," Nadine finally responded.

"Perfect." I gave her three hundred-dollar bills, which she took gratefully as if it mitigated the questionable task I had just hired her to do, and then led Indie back outside. I spotted a coffee shop down the street and pointed at it. Indie squinted, and then grinned.

"Ooooh, hot chocolate!" She clapped her hands. We headed towards the coffee shop, Indie clutching my arm tightly while we crossed the street.

I could definitely get used to this.

She was forever material... as long as I could get my damn ring back from the fleabag werewolves.

~

"*Y*ou know, even though I'm no longer in law enforcement, breaking and entering still doesn't sit well with me," Gunnar complained. I opened my mouth to defend myself but he held up a finger. "Even if you did Shadow Walk in there. Probably wasn't a good idea to take Indie along with you. Who knows what that kind of magic does to a *Regular?*" He spat the last word like a particularly foul-tasting racial slur.

Indie swatted his arm. "Easy, dog," she grinned. "Nate's done it with me dozens of times."

"Heh… heh," I chuckled huskily in my creepiest tone.

Indie rolled her eyes. "Men. I'm surrounded by an adolescent boy who laughs at the word *boobs*, and a senior citizen who wants to keep me locked away in a bubble-wrapped house." We both piped up at that, arguing vehemently but she cut us off, face pressed against the glass eagerly. "Shhh… Pay attention. He's coming back!" She pointed up the street, but a row of cars blocked my vision. "This is going to be film-worthy…" I grinned at seeing her excitement, mildly surprised that for once she wasn't sitting beside Gunnar chastising me. In fact, she was defending my irresponsible use of magic.

I loved this woman.

Here she was, out of her league, and totally stoked at a supernatural B&E. It made me feel more comfortable about my upcoming proposal. Even if I *was* enabling her criminal skills.

Which brought me back to thoughts of the missing ring. At some point, tomorrow or the next day, I needed to pay the were-mutts a visit. But I had enough on my plate tonight.

Gunnar was arguing with Indie. "Film-worthy, as in you two caught on film breaking into his apartment? Why are we sitting here, and what exactly did you two do in there?"

Indie made a surprised grunt and lowered her body deeper in the seats. Gunnar and I instinctively mimicked her, finally noticing our target walking down the street with a girl on his arm. She was clinging to him as if he was the only source of heat on the planet.

That, and possibly the only way she could remain upright without breaking her heels.

Apparently, they had shared a few drinks while at dinner. She wasn't sloppy drunk, but she definitely needed his support. I smiled to myself, wishing I had a bird's eye view inside the apartment. Then I remembered my new magic.

As a Maker, I was supposedly able to create things that had never been accomplished before: new magic, more powerful artifacts, and spells – basically able to work outside the limitations of traditional magic. Where other wizards were limited by their innate ability – their body and the elements immediately around them – a Maker was supposedly limited only by his imagination, implying that if they put their mind to it, a Maker could quite literally do whatever crazy idea popped into their heads.

Of course, I had a long way to go before I would be doing anything like that.

I was having a hard-enough time trying to figure out how to reliably use it to recreate similar spells I had used when I was a regular old wizard. When it worked at all, my new magic worked *differently*.

Entirely differently.

Before the Event, I would see the world around me in Technicolor, able to grab and utilize gossamer threads of power that floated in the air, weaving them into balls of fire, attack spells, tracking spells, utilize my body's own energy for rituals to summon… things. Essentially, I used my immediate vicinity – all of it – and reshaped it to my will.

But I had been severely limited by the elements around me.

I had been a pretty big hitter compared to most wizards, but still.

I had limits.

But now…

The Maker power was incredibly different. Instead of pulling energy from the environment, it felt more like delving deep into the earth to reach through a secret portal to grasp power out of the very cosmos. A river of power flowed through the universe, and a small tributary of that river seemed to course beneath my feet at all times. The tough part was tapping into it. It was like knowing you were thirsty and seeing a fire hydrant jettisoning hundreds of gallons a minute into the air at fifty miles per hour. You had to find a way to use it, but you couldn't just slap your cheeks into the stream and hope for a refreshing sip. You had to think. Use your mind. Grab a cup to catch the falling water, decrease the pressure of the hydrant, slow time so that the force decreased, you know, hard things to think about when you were in the thick of things.

Seeing as how I generally didn't get much time to sit there and think during a brawl, I had spent my time trying to relearn the equivalent of my favorite attack and defense spells as a wizard, with marginal success. I could always *feel* the river of power.

It was *harnessing* it that was not very often successful.

I could spend an hour and my attempt would pass through the river every time. The next day I could get it seventy percent of the time. Other times I had been angry and it had instinctively been waiting for me, ready to be cast in any way I saw fit. Like when the power had first hit me and I found myself in a tussle involving Angels, Demons, Academy Justices, and the Horsemen of the Apocalypse. I had simply *thought* of what I wanted, and it happened without question or effort. Easy as pie.

Absolutely every time since then had been a grueling battle of wills. It was almost like a relationship. *His Needs, Her Needs.* I needed to establish the proper code of conduct in order to impress the river of power enough to give me what I wanted. Like foreplay before sex. It required a bit more work.

So essentially, I had a new imaginary girlfriend rather than my usual wizard's magic. And my imaginary friend was an invisible, unquenchable river of power coursing beneath my feet at all times. A river that I was confident actually came from the cosmos, or the *Big Bang.* It didn't feel terrestrial. It felt... alien. There had been times in my experimentation where the force had done things that completely went against every Law of Physics that I knew. And doing those things had been easier than trying to make a ball of fire, for example.

My hired thug, chauffeur, and cook – Mallory – had spent quite a bit of time with me in an attempt to help me learn. We had met with marginal success. I had discussed it with my parents – who now resided in an Ancient Armory hidden in *Chateau Falco* – my ancestral home. The librarian of the Armory, Pandora (yep, that one) had also been of little help as a teacher. No one knew what to tell me.

The last Maker had died many, many years ago, leaving me no one to learn from.

My mind snapped back to focus as Indie squeezed my arm excitedly. I stared out the window to see the apartment in question now had its light on. Indie's breath was fogging up the back window as she watched, eyes twinkling with mischief and anticipation.

"Any second now. What do you think they've been doing for the last ten minutes? I had figured he would have made his move by now." She spoke softly.

I blinked. *Ten minutes?* I needed to get my head back in the game. The Grimms were out there somewhere. I would be pretty easy meat if I zoned out like that again.

"You sure it wasn't too much?" She whispered.

Gunnar's face twitched. "Sure *what* wasn't too much? *Nate... what did you two—*"

The front door of the building suddenly slammed open and the drunken girl came stumbling out, yelling angrily over her shoulder as she struggled to toss her coat back on. Only one of the straps on her shirt was attached correctly, and it seemed to be tangled up with her arm because she was having a hell of a time putting the coat on. Her bra was also openly on display, and it, too, wasn't completely attached, flashing a pale expanse of skin to the peeping toms in our car. Indie slapped my arm with an anxious laugh, one of the guys, making sure I zeroed in on the almost escaped boob.

I grinned.

A half-naked man appeared in the doorway to the building, pleading with her to come back so he could explain. We could hear it through the windows, so he had to be shouting. But she shambled on down the street, storming off into the night and forcefully flipping the man the middle finger. His bare chest didn't seem to register the cold.

Then again, with what he had planned for the night so suddenly imploding on him, I could understand his mindset with the no doubt near superhuman spike of adrenaline and testosterone blocking his cold receptors.

I watched as his face slowly began to darken in anger, his eyes scanning the street like only an assassin could. His eyes landed on our car for a second, but then flicked past. I called him on my new phone – one that managed to encrypt calls, texts, and emails – from both ends of the line. Only retailed for $17,000. A steal. I had gotten one for all my friends earlier this year. With us occasionally taking on questionable jobs – legally, that is – I wanted as much security and deniability as possible. It was also designed and built by my own company, Temple Industries, so R&D took on the expense for it.

I spoke casually, bubbling with enthusiasm. "Hey, man. I was driving in your neighborhood and wanted to see if your plans had chang–"

"You miserable son of a bitch," he growled. "That was low. Even for you."

"If I don't ruin someone's day I don't sleep very well. It's one of my gifts."

He grunted, still scanning the street. Gunnar rolled his eyes and finally flashed his lights once. The man acknowledged us with a fiery glare. He flipped us off, and then motioned for us to come inside before doing so himself, deciding not to wait at the door.

"See you in a minute, bastard. Keep a low profile on your way in," he said cryptically before he hung up.

Gunnar merely shook his head at me. "You are a real piece of work. How did you manage to get the girl to leave so fast?"

"Oh, you'll see." Indie burst out laughing as we opened the car doors to follow my friend, the dragon hunter, inside his apartment.

# CHAPTER 5

*I* wasn't sure what I had expected, but as we stood in the dingy hallway outside the apartment door, I guessed I could have summed it up in one word. *More.* Tomas was a dragon hunter, a hit man. Surely, he made better money than the building led me to believe.

Tomas opened the door, scowled at me for good measure, and then while leaning out of the doorway to glance both ways behind us, he swiftly darted in to plant a quick wet smooch on Indie's cheek. I instinctively tensed up, my inner alpha male growling at the challenge, but Indie burst out laughing, calming my beast. She jabbed him playfully in the ribs as she forced her way past him and inside the apartment, darting immediately to the back room to inspect the masterpiece we had recently erected. Well, if that hadn't given us away I didn't know what would.

He quickly let Gunnar and I in the door, grimacing at our stench before locking and dead-bolting the door behind us. But he didn't question our smell, just accepted it. I wasn't sure what that said about me. Or him.

Tomas seemed nervous underneath his calm demeanor. Perhaps I thought so because he had asked us to be discreet upon entering the building, or because he had scanned the hallway before letting us in. Or maybe it was because he was now hurriedly dashing to the windows to close the thick curtains. Regardless, he wasn't a nervous guy. Hit men were notoriously calm, cool, and collected. I was pretty sure it was part of their job description. I raised an eyebrow at him, but he didn't explain. "Phones," he growled, holding out a beefy palm. Which pretty much confirmed my suspicions.

We complied and he carried them over to the microwave, carefully tucking them inside and shutting the door. Gunnar frowned at me as if attempting to telepathically ask me if Tomas had lost his marbles at some point.

"Faraday cage. Blocks the UHF frequencies." Gunnar continued staring at me.

"I hear words coming out of your mouth, but I don't know what they mean."

"No one can use them to hear us," Tomas clarified, striding towards us.

Indie returned from gloating over her masterpiece, instantly catching onto the tension as she watched the men folk stare each other down. Tomas pointed at the kitchen.

Her face clouded over in a heartbeat. "You think that because I'm a woman I'm going to go make you men sandwiches? Fat chance, dragon hunter. I have half a mind to–"

"Indie, can you put your phone in the microwave, please?" I interrupted her tirade.

"Oh. Yeah. Sure," she answered sheepishly, but Tomas was barely repressing his laughter as she made her way to the kitchen.

"While you're at it, I'll take a BLT." He finally burst out, roaring with laughter. An apple sailed out of the kitchen and clucked him on the back of the head, abruptly halting his laughter. My laughter began the millisecond his ended.

He sat down into a worn leather recliner with a grunt, picking up the projectile in his scarred hands. "I suppose I asked for that," he murmured, grinning. I nodded, and the room slowly began to fill with idle banter as they caught up with each other. I merely watched, mind combing the facts as I planned out my next moves.

Indie, dancing on her toes with anticipation finally convinced Tomas to let her show Gunnar the artwork in the bedroom. We spent a few minutes chuckling over it, even Gunnar. A hundred pictures of the same girl, all taken from different angles, formed a serial stalker collage that took up a good six-foot tall by four-foot wide section of the wall. They had been taken from some random woman's social media account. It had no doubt made

Tomas look, at best, like a crazy ex-boyfriend; and at worst, an obsessive stalker. Indie and I had efficiently *slaughtered* the mood. In my eyes, the elaborate joke made me feel that all was right with the world. Some good to balance the dire news I had learned today.

Pranks were soothing to the soul. They reminded you that if such an infinitesimal event like being cockblocked by an extremely well-thought-out master plan was the worst thing to happen to you that day, things were probably going to be more or less OK.

Also, my empathy factor was at an all time low at the moment. We had just survived a beating by two different supernatural groups in the sewers, but Tomas had been too busy planning on getting busy to spend five minutes of his time to talk with me. I had real world problems going on. I didn't have time for Tomas to get all twitter-pated for a few hours while I waited him out in a constant state of paranoia, anticipating a bullet to the head at any second.

Go Team Temple, crushing single guys' fantasies, one stalker collage at a time.

Tomas had taken a few minutes to truly calm down, but knowing who and what I was, he also likely knew there really wasn't anything he could do to me. *Hello, Maker.* Other than stealing a kiss from Indie's nonconsensual cheek. And accepting the fact that it really was quite an impressive prank, more than anything, seemed to cool him off. Also, seeing Gunnar, Indie and I burst out laughing at the impromptu mural had finally allowed him to admit the humor in it.

He signed in resignation. "Well, I definitely need a few drinks after that." He chuckled as he made his way into the kitchen. "Anyone else?" Everyone murmured agreement. He spoke over his shoulder as he began pouring drinks. "Bollocks! You should have seen her face. Hell, I'm sure mine looked just as shocked," he chuckled.

Gunnar pointed. "Where the hell did you get that many pictures of the same person? And who is she?" He asked me.

I shrugged. "Some girl. I have no idea who she is. I outsourced the job. Othello."

"Oh?" Indie said softly. Everyone knew about Othello and her *skills*... and our past relationship. The room grew brittle at Indie's tone. Then she let loose a dazzling smile. "Just kidding. She won't poach. We had a long... talk. Girl talk," she added as an afterthought. I shivered, wondering exactly what that meant. But I knew Indie had accepted my old college fling. Especially after *Mardi Gras* when Othello had literally died for me.

Othello loved me. But she also knew that it would never work out. And after a few 'talks' the girls seemed to get along splendidly, although I did always feel like I was walking on razor blades over a lava pit of fire-breathing ninja lemurs whenever I saw them spending time together. Especially when they grew quiet as soon as I entered the room, and then giggled loud enough for me to hear as I quickly walked away to do important man stuff like check the batteries in the remotes.

Freaking women.

"Anyway," I continued, "a few months ago, I told Othello to gather a slush pile of pictures of the same girl – any girl – so that I could do this to you or Raego the next time you got uppity." I smirked at Gunnar.

Tomas grunted, shaking his head in disbelief at my admitted depths of depravity. Gunnar merely scowled. "Well, I guess it's lucky for you it didn't work out like that…" he warned with a canine smile, letting his fangs lengthen as he partially shifted to his werewolf form. I rolled my eyes.

Tomas let out a belly laugh, watching Gunnar and I rib each other. "At least it's comforting to know that I'm not the only one on the receiving end of his stunts." He shook his head and took a deep drink of his wine. "I'm not going to lie. I played my cards right all night, told her suave stories, and made sure we both had plenty to drink. We got back to the apartment and I knew she was a sure thing." Indie shook her head and rolled her eyes in amusement. "We poured some drinks and took off to make some magic happen in the bedroom. I don't know who was more surprised to see my stalker collage. Linda certainly found zero humor in it," he muttered, shrugging his shoulders. "It was a good joke, even though it took me a few to realize it. I take it that this was your subtle way of telling me that your time was more important than my dating life?" He asked, risking a thoughtful look at me.

I smiled with my teeth. "Got it in one."

"Then I'm going to need another drink. We have some things we need to talk about. Quickly. In case anyone saw you come here," he spoke over his shoulder, heading back to the kitchen. We exchanged thoughtful looks as he left. He brought over the bottle and we all settled down around his rickety coffee table. My eyes idly roved the apartment and I was reminded again that being a hit man was apparently not a very lucrative career. Either that or Tomas was not a material girl. Or it was a front.

Bingo. That fit better. This was a disguise. A burner home in case he needed to flee.

"Out of respect, you go first, but then I have something important to tell you."

I didn't like the sound of that, but I rehashed our night's events. The vampires, the wolves, and their odd parting comments. As I took a second to wet my lips, he spoke.

"Promise you won't be upset..." he didn't make eye contact, looking ashamed.

"Don't tell me you know what's going on. Because that would mean I need to make a Tomas-sized smear on the wall," I growled, flexing my fists. Here he was, going on a date, all the while knowing I had been in danger.

"Possibly. This sounds similar to a strange contract I was offered a few weeks back. I didn't think it was related – and especially not that *you* were the mark – or I would have warned you sooner." Tomas was a mercenary, but he was loyal to me after the dragon ordeal a year back. I trusted him. "I didn't win the bid, and talk died down about it immediately. I had assumed it had been withdrawn. Then I got the update just tonight. I called you immediately, but your phone went straight to voicemail and I couldn't say anything sensitive on voicemail. I also couldn't say anything in front of Linda."

"Don't worry about that in the future. My phone is encrypted from both ends, so you can say whatever pleases you on my voicemail. Especially if it's important. Like a contract on my life." I stared daggers at him and watched him crumple a bit at the shoulders. Tomas was *good*. He and his crew were contacted for *all* the big hits. And when I say *hits*, I mean contracts involving an upcoming murder or kidnapping of a rogue Freak, or supernatural person. "So, spill," I demanded.

"No names were mentioned. Just a high-value target with strong defenses. A rogue wanted for punishment regarding unspecified crimes. No details on who the target was, who the employer was, or exactly what the mark had done. Just a lot of freaking money." I must have looked doubtful. "Enough money to make even *you* bat an eye." He amended, taking another drink. Which got my attention. "Then, a few hours ago, I was notified that the bidding for the contract was closed, and that the target must be avoided at all costs, except by the contracted team and their associates. Anyone interfering or getting involved in any way whatsoever with the target would be added to the hit list. They called it a Salted Earth Policy. All known acquaintances." He slowly lifted his gaze to meet mine. "And you are the primary target, Temple," he shivered.

I slowly relaxed. Then I began to laugh. Softly, but with great relief. I leaned back into the couch and took a long sip of my drink, crossing my feet on his coffee table. I had feared that Tomas would know more about the Grimms. Part of me was relieved to hear it wasn't so. Part of me wasn't. Gunnar and Indie looked just as confused, so I finally explained. "Well, if hiring a half-dozen werewolves to take me out is the extent of their genius, I'm not too worried. We already took care of them."

Tomas was shaking his head. "No. No. You don't understand. You didn't take care of anyone. Their first attack is always a probe to get to know their enemy. No one survives them. They are legion."

My shoulders went back to full anxiety mode.

I had heard of only one other group described as *legion*.

The Grimms.

Not only did they want to take me out for personal reasons, but also, they were now going to be paid a pile of money to do so. Oh, Capitalism. The thing that really got me was that no one should even know they were back in our world.

This smelled of the Academy. No one else was powerful enough, or ballsy enough, to risk contracting the Grimms. But I couldn't imagine even that being the case. That was blatantly illegal of the Academy. They literally couldn't touch me unless I openly attacked them. We had agreed that bygones were bygones. I had even attended a face-to-face meeting with the Grandmaster of the wizard nation after the events at *Mardi Gras*, accompanied by Death – a Horseman of the Apocalypse – and Eae, a freaking Angel of Heaven. If that wasn't a convincing team of people to have on your side, I didn't know what was.

The Academy had agreed, and written up a formal agreement that the past was behind us. I was a Maker, the sole member of my particular flavor of Freak, and thus outside their purview. Meaning they would leave me alone if I left them alone. We would be allies, with neither above the other.

So, what in the hell was going on?

"Just between us girls," Tomas continued, "chatter also says that this group is interested in acquiring a... *book* you may or may not have collected in your misspent youth." He glanced at me pointedly, eyes flicking to Gunnar and Indie with the silent question. I waved a hand, unconcerned.

"It's okay. They know what we're talking about. The Brothers Grimm, right?"

He frowned at me with his mouth open for a moment, and then regained his composure, letting out a single nod. "Aye. It was the book comment that made me think you might be the target. So, of course, I called you immediately."

Tomas polished off his drink and everyone sat in silence, pondering. A long minute later, he said a single word that sent a chill down my spine. "Run." He said it softly, but the emphasis made it a clarion call to my ears.

I was paranoid enough to actually jump to my feet, eyes darting to the windows, ready for an attack. But everything was safe and Tomas didn't look immediately concerned. I sat back down as Tomas chuckled.

"Not this *second*, Temple. But tonight. Or tomorrow. The earlier the better," he added, eyes darting to the windows instinctively. Which made sense now. He had said that anyone assisting or even interacting with me would be added to the list. I turned to see him watching me. He shrugged. "Yep. I'll be leaving town myself after your visit. Won't be returning here for quite some time. If that makes any difference or not. It was a burner house anyway. Temporary." He shrugged, not completely hiding the disappointment in his eyes at having to pack up and leave.

Because of me.

But he didn't say a word about me putting him in danger, which on a deeper level, meant a lot to me. I had shamed him in front of a lady friend, put his life in very real jeopardy, and instead of running to turn me in, he shrugged, laughed, gave me what information he could, and calmly told me that my visit had ruined his life in St. Louis and that he was leaving town – perhaps permanently. All without batting an eye.

Tomas was solid.

Indie chimed in, having been mostly silent up until now. "So, you said *Salted Earth Policy*. What exactly does that mean?"

"All known acquaintances, past and present," Tomas repeated softly, avoiding eye contact.

I spat on the ground in frustration, my mind racing. I doubted Tomas cared about getting his deposit back on the apartment. Gunnar's thoughts seemed to follow the same path, because his eyes suddenly widened and his hand went instinctively to his phone. But it was still in the microwave. Ashley was an acquaintance of mine. And she was his fiancé. Tomas clucked a warning, tapping his ears to signify the potential tapping of our phones.

"They're encrypted, remember?" I told him.

"Until you run into a hacker cleverer than your phone's engineer."

I folded my arms. "My company made them." Tomas merely stared back, unimpressed. "They cost $17,000. Each." His eyes widened a bit, but he shrugged anyway. "And Othello designed the encryption software." His face slowly morphed into a predatory smile.

"That one's a real piece of..." His eyes flashed to Indie, cheeks flushing, "Work," he clarified. Indie managed to grin and roll her eyes at the same time. "She's a real piece of *work*. Freaking cyber genius. I only got to speak with her for a few moments last time she was in town. Seems she helped me out on a few of my old contracts, not that I knew anything about it at the time, of course." Gunnar was already prowling to the microwave.

Tomas grew thoughtful. "Hey, when we first met you were able to dig up information on me that isn't available. To anyone." He watched me for a minute. "It was Othello, wasn't it?" I smiled and nodded. "Hot damn. You should arrange a more formal introduction sometime." He glanced back at his room. "Sans stalker collage..." His voice trailed off with a small smile. "Well, if there *is* a sometime in the future for any of us," he added. Gunnar was already shooting off a text, thumbs flying over the screen.

"The Brothers Grimm," Indie broke the tension slowly building in the room. "They wrote a collection of *fairy* tales. I still have a hard time believing they are the boogeymen of the supernatural community." She stated in disbelief.

Tomas shuddered. "You have no idea, little lady. No idea..." His eyes trailed off for a few moments before snapping back to me. "Wait a minute. How did you know guys already know about them? Remember, if anyone talks, they get added to the hit list. You should probably warn them. Whoever they are," he probed.

I smiled, detecting his ploy. "We've all got people, Tomas. Just remember that I've always got more people than anyone else and you'll be betting safe." Tomas blinked, no doubt wanting to hear the story, but I was done telling stories. As far as Tomas knew, someone I had pissed off at some point had been willing to pay a lot of money to get me and my friends dead. This someone was also well-connected enough to know that the Brothers Grimm were back in play. Which made no sense to me. "How do *you* know about the Grimms?" I asked instead, not wanting to admit my ignorance.

Tomas shrugged. "People talk on the tougher hits. Stakeouts get boring. We do what soldiers have done since time immemorial. We tell stories. I won't lie. Some of their stories are downright legendary. *Impossible* hits. No evidence. No calling card. No bragging rights. Just a job well done." His voice trailed off. "Of course, there are also the stories about totally innocent people disappearing under similar circumstances, but we all tell ourselves it's just a coincidence."

I nodded. I hadn't ever heard any stories, but I could imagine. "But how does anyone know they are back? Or that they are even real?" I wondered aloud.

"They weren't secretive about announcing it. Flyers went up every-where. Email notifications. Mailers. YouTube videos." He trailed off.

Indie and I turned to blink at him. "What?" We asked in disbelief.

He was nodding. "Yeah. Very odd. We all thought it was a prank. Looked like one of those *Anonymous* group's videos. Warning that they were back and they had some house cleaning to do. To stay out of their way until they came for you."

They had spent hundreds of years out of this world and their grand entrance includes a full social media blast? What the hell was going on? "How long ago was this?"

"Months," he answered. I blinked at him, my rage roaring to the surface. If I had only known sooner... But no, that wasn't Tomas' fault. No one had known that they had personal beef with me. Why would Tomas have even thought to tell me? He had no reason to do so. Other than as a professional courtesy. Hell, he probably assumed I saw the news like everyone else.

"Next time something like that happens, you get me on the phone imme-diately. I could have resolved this a long time ago without them having months to prepare." I warned. He swallowed guiltily, nodding.

My thoughts began to wander as I heard Gunnar speaking urgently into his phone. Indie was staring at me, but I didn't acknowledge her.

The Brothers Grimm were supernatural hit men – as in they killed *any* and *all* supernatural creatures, good or bad, naughty or not. Who ran in my circles that would be ballsy enough to hire a group of mad dogs to take me out? Mad dogs that would immediately turn around and kill them too? Who exactly had I pissed off?

Tomas spoke up. "The thing that gets me is why the wolves and fangers left you alone. Or why they were down there in the first place. If the wolves had orders not to kill you, why would they chance breaking into your vault when they could smell that you were down there?" I didn't tell him I had masked our scent from the vampires up until it had become obvious they were aware of our presence. Nor did I answer the unspoken question, *what are you hiding in a sewer vault that could attract a werewolf or vampire's attention?* Or the one he didn't know to ask. *How had they even known about the vault in the first place?*

I had enough problems on my mind, so I went along with the presumption that for now, it didn't matter how they learned about the vault. They simply knew.

So, next question.

I had no idea why they had been there, especially with conflicting orders. Rob from me, but don't kill me. They had to know that five wolves wouldn't have been enough for the job. Unless they hadn't planned on me being there. But then, how would they have broken into the vault in the first place? With me being a notorious wizard, my vault would undoubtedly be locked with *magic*. And why hadn't they tucked tail and run as soon as they discovered I was present? The wolves had scented us long before talking to us. Which meant they wanted something. Something they assumed I had hidden in a secret vault.

Questions piled on top of more questions. Maybe there was more than one thing going on here. I ran through the catalog of items in my vault, but couldn't think of anything particularly interesting to the supernatural community at large. Sure, there were nifty things in there, but all the super powerful and dangerous stuff was locked away in the Armory now. Maybe the wolves thought I had some kind of key to the Armory in my vault beneath Plato's Cave.

Still, these questions only led me back full circle to the most pressing issue.

No one knew about my vault.

I had *literally* told no one.

Not Gunnar. Not Indie. Not my parents. Not even my old traitorous friend, Peter.

*No one.*

And I couldn't remember the last time I had been down there, but it had been a long time. Which meant that someone must have followed me down there at some point, and then waited *years* until the perfect night to go get the goods. Tonight.

The same night I happened to be paying a visit.

Something smelled wrong about this whole thing, and I felt my face begin to scowl.

The only reason I had chosen tonight to visit could be summed up in one word.

Achilles.

# CHAPTER 6

*T*he room filled with soft chatter between Indie and Tomas as Gunnar continued to talk into his cell phone, no doubt warning Ashley of the situation. I was apparently setting off the vibe that I needed a few minutes to myself. This would typically be a time when I would have lit a cigarette to calm my racing mind.

But I had quit eight months ago, during the *Mardi Gras* fiasco. I didn't miss the habit much on a daily basis. Not at all, in fact. But times like this?

Yeah, a cigarette would have been nice. Or a stiffer drink. Thanks to Tomas' warning about possible surveillance, I couldn't open the windows to smoke anyway, so I settled in to attempt to think without the aid of stimulants.

Achilles had asked me to go down to the sewers tonight. If not for that, it could have been a long time until I went down there. The only other reason I had gone down there was to get the engagement ring, and I could have done that any time in the next few days. But I hadn't told a single person about either the ring *or* the vault. Ever. I began running through all my interactions for the past few days but came up with no smoking guns.

So, Achilles just happened to have a damsel in distress who needed saving in the sewers tonight. I had planned on going to the sewers to get the engagement ring in the next few days anyway, so I had decided to combine the two into one trip. Vampires first, to test Indie's mettle, *which she had passed with flying colors*, I thought to myself proudly. Then the engagement ring. Simple. Efficient.

*Right.*

I glanced at Indie discreetly, amazed by her natural beauty and genuine smile. Tomas was eating it up. A naturally beautiful woman with glittering pearly whites could make any man feel eight feet tall and bulletproof. And Indie had those traits in spades. I focused back on my dilemma.

So, the wolves had shown up at a vault that they shouldn't have even known existed, wanting to take some old books... that they also shouldn't have ever known existed. The only person who knew of the books was Gunnar, but even he didn't know what they truly were. Barbie had wiped everyone's memory of my first encounter with Jacob Grimm.

Everyone except me.

I shivered at that memory. Jacob had been a heavy hitter for sure, even all by himself. Now he had his brothers to help him take out the trash... *me*. And my loved ones. I shook that thought away. It wouldn't help me now.

The wolves had been commanded not to harm me. By their Alpha, if I guessed correctly. If that was true, why pick tonight? Why not yesterday or tomorrow?

Because someone had tipped them off.

My main question was whether it was the same person who sent me down there tonight or if there was a third-party lurking in the shadows somewhere. Regardless, the Brothers Grimm had taken a contract on us. I was on borrowed time, and the best defense I had were the books in my satchel. If I called anyone for help they would be placed on the kill list too, so reinforcements were out. I had only my motley crew of supernaturals who were by default on the list. Gunnar and who else? Indie, Ashley, Dean... the list grew on and on. How many people were on the list? Were Raego and Death included? How extensive was the assassination contract?

"Tomas." The room grew silent at my tone. He glanced up at me, looking nervous. "I need you to find out exactly who is on the list."

"Um, everyone."

"A little more specific. I'm a local celebrity. Is the gas station attendant I say good morning to every day on the list? His name is Juan. Is the news reporter I've sat down with a dozen times on the list? My employees? My dry cleaner? Indie? There could potentially be hundreds of victims here."

He thought about it for a moment. "I'll see what I can dig up. If they know about our meeting tonight, then I'm a dead man anyway. If not, I'll have to be discreet about it. Seem hungry. Like I'm willing to nab a few for myself if the Grimms will let me. Otherwise they will assume I'm fishing for intel and add me to the list, which will help no one. Least of all me."

"Good idea."

He was silent for a few moments. "Perhaps only the supernatural associates. From what I've read, the Grimms don't kill vanilla mortals. Only Freaks. So maybe your lady friends are safe. And the gas station attendant, employees, whoever else. That would make the most sense. They are, after all, against anyone able to use magic of any kind. Mortals should be safe."

"Well, I've taken on this particular chucklehead before and sent him packing. I'm sure I can do so again."

Tomas fidgeted. "Not just one."

I turned to him, remembering Barbie's warning. "How many are we talking?"

"Um… more than one?" I scowled back. He threw up his hands. "I just know there is a team of 'em. *Team* implies more than one. And if I were a betting man I would say both Jacob and Wilhelm Grimm, at least. The founding fathers, if you will."

"Well, if the vamps and wolves in the sewer were related to the Grimms – as unlikely as that is – at least I sent them packing. They won't be back in the picture anytime soon."

Tomas was shaking his head urgently. "No way. The stories always start the same. Their first attack is *always* a probe. They treat their kills like hunts. They lead their prey right where they want them. I think that's why the wolves were commanded not to kill."

Gunnar chimed in, having ended his phone call. "Either that or it's because they don't want to incur the wrath of the only Maker in centuries. They did mention that title specifically. And I'm pretty sure they said their orders came from their Alpha."

I was glad he had confirmed my thoughts. The Alpha. Not the Grimms. Maybe it wasn't related. I mean, what kind of idiots would the werewolves be to team up with a hit squad of assassins who killed *all* Freaks? I had met the local Alpha, and although he was powerful, I didn't remember him being particularly smart. Then I remembered that someone had hired the Grimms. Maybe even the wolves, but I doubted they had any significant means to pay the kind of sum Tomas had hinted at. And other than the scuffle during the *Mardi Gras* fiasco, I didn't think they had reason enough to take such drastic measures to kill me dead.

Or a regular could have hired the Grimms, which seemed just as unlikely. They wouldn't even *know* about the supernatural community. Well, probably not anyway.

I could think of only one freak with the brass balls to do something so stupid, and he was definitely in a position of power, maybe even enough to insulate him from the backlash of hiring the Grimms.

And I had pissed him off something fierce. In fact, he was the reason my new Maker powers were so much stronger than my parents' experiment had originally intended.

Jafar, the Captain of the Justices – the secret wizard police for the Academy. I was no longer a wizard, out of their jurisdiction, as was made abundantly clear with the signed agreement between us. But even if they wanted to flake on me, Death and Eae had also signed as witnesses, and the Academy wouldn't dare reneging on Heaven and Hell. That would cause fallout on a Biblical level.

I was a Maker, and that infuriated old Jafar, because it was essentially his fault I became such a nuisance. His fault that his boss had been forced to sign the agreement.

I stood and made a mental to-do list.

Step one, call Jafar. I needed to put a feeler out there. I couldn't let him know I was aware of the full picture. Just hint around the edges. Maybe something along the lines of bad magic was going on in my city and I wanted him to know about it ahead of time. A courtesy call. Like any good neighbor would do. But I was playing a dangerous game. They were either in on this Grimm business, or might know something about it. But to be completely honest, I was also just covering my ass. If they *weren't* involved, I *needed* to give them a heads-up as a token of good faith. It was part of our agreement. Even though I was no longer under their *jurisdiction*, that knife cut both ways. I was also out of their *protection*. I harbored no false belief that they would swoop in with a platoon to help me out, but figured they would instead likely find a political reason to declare my actions criminal when the dust settled – if I was still alive by then.

Step two, ask my parents for help. They were already dead, now residing in the Armory, so were in no danger by assisting me. I had to come clean with them about what Gunnar and I had really gotten into a few years ago, during our first encounter with Jacob Grimm. And the sole reason behind why I had opened Plato's Cave. To hide the deadly books now sitting a few feet away in my satchel.

After that, a chat with Achilles, who was legendary for his love of pointy things.

Gunnar and Indie followed me – saying their goodbyes on my behalf – as I wordlessly left the room. Tomas' advice echoed in my ears as I reached the door leading to the street.

*Run...*

As if that whispered word wasn't ominous enough, one sight of my parked car convinced me it was simply time to go home and hit the sheets.

I stopped on the steps, staring incredulously, first at the car – which had been beaten with a baseball bat, all the windows smashed out – and then at the street and rooftops for any hidden attackers.

The wind howled through the street, taunting my futile search.

They were gone, but they had left a poignant message.

Whoever they were.

# CHAPTER 7

"*I* don't like this," Gunnar growled, sniffing the remains of the car.

"It's not even your car. It's mine," I answered distractedly, eyeing the destruction clinically. The windows were shattered, the tires slashed, every section of metal dented, and a growing puddle of noxious liquids slowly grew from underneath the vehicle, inching towards our feet despite the cold weather. Which meant it was recent. The liquids hadn't had time to freeze. We probably should have heard something from Tomas' apartment. A car alarm at least.

But we hadn't heard a thing. Which was puzzling, and blatantly pointed towards a supernatural attack rather than a mundane crime of opportunity.

Now, *monetarily*, this was no big deal to me. But as a *message*, it was powerful indeed. Someone wanted me to know I was in their crosshairs, but I spotted no calling card or flashing neon sign stating his or her name. We were now stranded outside Tomas' apartment, so *someone* obviously knew we were here. The question was, did they already know Tomas lived here, or did they just happen to recognize my car and made a move? Regardless, if they didn't know yet, it was likely that they would soon connect the dots, realizing Tomas lived here, which explained what I was doing here. I had no other reason to be in this part of town. Which put him in danger. I shot him a text, warning him that he might already be compromised. Finished, I looked up to find Gunnar watching me.

51

"Call a cab. I need to make a quick call."

"Ashley's already on her way. She'll be here in ten minutes." He growled, still unsuccessfully trying to track the scent. Which was odd. A lot of sniffer problems for the werewolf lately. Maybe the thugs had another moonstone. Or maybe he was still feeling the effects from the vampire's moonstone in the sewer. It didn't matter now. I sensed no supernatural presence. At least I could reliably do *that* with my new powers.

"Good. I'm just going to step over here for a minute. We might want to walk a few blocks away. Let Ashley know to pick us up wherever you decide. As long as it's away from this." I waved a hand at the vehicle's remains.

Gunnar grunted, but began walking down the street, Indie hot on his heels, both of them giving me space. My phone vibrated, revealing a string of curse words from Tomas. I smiled at the screen as I followed a few steps behind Gunnar and Indie, scrolling through my contacts until I found the right name. *Arrogant prickface.* I clicked the name with a smile and readied myself for a cryptic, but not obviously so, conversation with a man who I hated and who hated me back even harder.

Jafar, Captain of the Justices.

"Who is this?" A scratchy, sleepy voice answered.

"It's your buddy. Your pal. Your BFF. Nate Temple. How you doing, sport?" I spoke, doing my best to sound overly positive and cheerful.

He growled back. "Do you know what time it is? What do you want?"

"To chat, of course. It's what friends... and *allies* do."

He waited a few seconds, gathering his sleepy thoughts together for an appropriate political response at the term *allies*. "I don't feel like chatting. What do you need?"

"Alright. No foreplay." I took a breath, forcing myself to sound confused and a little nervous. "Something is going on in town. I'm out of the loop, but everyone's acting... strange. Do you guys happen to know anything about it?" I waited a long second, replacing my fake anxiety with a harder tone. "If not, consider this a heads-up. When things get strange here, I usually end up taking out the trash, and I don't want you guys thinking I'm overstepping myself. You are more than welcome to come investigate, if you find it necessary."

I waited. The line was so quiet that I almost thought he had hung up. Then I heard faint rustling and some murmured words in the background. "Give me a minute," he muttered. He was apparently excusing himself to a more secure environment. "Okay. Strange how?" He finally asked.

I pondered how to answer that. If he was complicit, I didn't want to be sharing my movements with my hunters. If he wasn't, he needed a justifiable answer. He was a cop of sorts, after all, and even though I didn't personally like him, I was pretty sure he was good at his job.

*Wizard of the month* – or something like that – on the Academy's break room wall.

"I was jumped by a pack of wolves and then again by some fangs. In the same hour."

He grunted. "Sounds like a personal vendetta. You do have a reputation for making friends wherever you go." He sounded pleased at the snide comment.

I swallowed back a retort, taking a breath. This was to be a professional phone call. Even if it killed me. I needed to be able to claim deniability if things went downhill.

"They said they had orders not to harm me."

The line was quiet for a beat. "But you just said they jumped you."

"Exactly. Like I said, people are acting strange. It makes no sense. Vampires and wolves *hate* each other. So why would they have the same order not to harm me, but to jump me anyway?" I asked, not having to feign my confusion. "They were looking for something in my possession, but I'll be damned if I know what it was…" I teased, offering him something to bite. But he didn't take it.

"That *is* strange," he finally said. "What do you expect *me* to do about it? As you know, you aren't under our jurisdiction, much to my regret. So why should I send anyone to help you? It's obviously personal." He was quiet for a moment. *Then* he took my bait. "Unless… you wanted to make an exchange for our services. Say, unrestricted access to a certain Armory." I could practically hear him salivating.

"I'm not giving you the Armory."

"You don't have to give it to me. Or even the Academy. Just let us inventory it."

I laughed. "So you'll know exactly what you need to grab when you clowns finally make your move? Hard pass."

He growled. "Then I think we're finished here," he answered, sounding pompous. "Watch out for yourself, Temple. The night is dark and full of terrors." He roared in laughter at his own rapier wit.

"Fair warning. I'll put an end to whatever is going on, with, or without you. If I do it without you, I don't want to hear the Academy crying *foul* when the dust settles, declaring me some kind of vigilante. Consider this my 911 call. Next move is on your shoulders. If you don't do anything I'll do what I do best. Maybe test out my new powers. Who knows what could happen? I'd be lying if I said I wasn't curious..."

The line was silent again. Not much of a talker, old Jafar.

"I'll run it up the flagpole. That's all I can do," he finally grumbled, realizing that he had to do so, no matter how badly he wanted to see me dangling in the wind. I had made it official by calling him. If he didn't follow the proper channels it could backfire on him.

"That's all I'm asking. Call me back and let me know what you guys decide."

He had hung up at some point during my last comment. I cursed at my phone and tucked it into a pocket, lengthening my stride a bit to catch up with Gunnar and Indie. They were only a dozen feet ahead of me. I recognized Ashley's car double-parked outside an apartment building just ahead of us. Indie glanced over her shoulder, looking concerned at the expression on my face. Gunnar had eyes only for Ashley, but Indie slowed down and placed an arm around my shoulders, idly scratching her long fingernails through my scalp. "Bad?"

"On the contrary. It's kind of comforting to know that he's the same flavor of asshole he always was." Indie nodded, massaging my shoulder with one hand as we walked.

"Perhaps you just need an outlet to clear your head. Release some tension," she murmured.

I nodded. "Maybe I'll go hit the bag for an hour when we get home."

She stopped, her hand turning into a warning claw as she gripped my shoulder, forcing me to stop or fall over. I arched a confused brow at the hurt look on her face. "I don't know how much more obvious I can be, Nate. I would hope you consider *this*," she waved a hand at her body, "a better form of release than a dusty old punching bag," she warned.

I blinked, realizing my mistake too late. I couldn't believe I had missed such an obvious pass. Granted, I had a lot on my mind, but still. When a pretty girl flirts with you, you damn well better pay attention, Apocalypse or not. "Wow," I sighed. "I'm an idiot."

She nodded curtly. "Yes. You are." She folded her arms, tapping a foot as she arched a brow. "So, what does a girl have to do around here to get some claw marks on her back?"

I grinned, suddenly focused on only her. "Say no more." She smiled back and gripped my hand. "Still a little high-strung after Barbie's psychic attack, eh?" I teased.

Her eyes were dark and captivating. "Only one way to find out…" Then she smacked my ass as we stepped up to Gunnar and Ashley, who were unabashedly hugging and kissing each other outside of her idling car. The sound caused them to jump apart and stare at us. Indie burst out laughing. So did Ashley. I simply turned to glare at Indie in disbelief. She shrugged, folding her arms before her.

Then she did it again as I was climbing into the backseat.

"I'm not just some piece of meat, you know." I grumbled, only mildly upset that my ass-smacking authority had been stolen.

"Tonight, you are," she grinned, climbing in behind me. Gunnar rolled his eyes, but Ashley burst out laughing all over again.

"Looks like I missed a wild night." Ashley said, pulling out into traffic.

"Don't worry, we have a few more of them scheduled for the week." I grumbled.

"I'm guessing that's what the *car trouble* was really about?" She asked, glancing pointedly at Gunnar. His cheeks flushed slightly before he murmured an apology to her. I couldn't hear the words, but it looked like he was getting an earful.

He finally addressed me as we passed a row of commercial buildings. "*Chateau Falco?*" I nodded. "Might be a good idea for all of us to stick together for a few days. Until this, um, *car trouble* gets sorted out." He offered neutrally, giving me room to veto the idea if I wished. I glanced at Indie's hungry eyes and smiled. It was a big enough house. Plenty of rooms. I winked at her to let her know she still held priority of my attentions, guests be damned.

"Good idea. While you catch Ashley up I need to make another call."

They began talking softly together in the front seat while I made a call, feeling Indie's curious eyes on me the whole time. Even though I had warned Jafar on official channels, I wanted a more reliable insurance policy that was solely in my control rather than the shifting winds of political favor, and after events over the past year I had wisely planned for just such an event ahead of time. But it was risky. In fact, it was borderline *suicidal*.

"This can't be good," a familiar voice answered. I smiled.

"Consider this your answer. Commence *Operation White Knight*. Immediately. Then meet me at the ranch. Bring the family and anyone they care about." I hinted heavily, hoping he understood. "It's... bad." The line grew as cold as a grave.

"Are you *shitting* me? I thought that was just a doomsday plan. We only came up with it a few months ago, and you already need it?" I thought about it for a second, but I couldn't think of another option.

"Yes. Exercise extreme caution. Like we discussed. Don't harm them. Just hold them. If you *can*..." I added drily, knowing that his unique abilities made him the most capable of such a high-level operation.

The voice growled back defiantly. "Of course, I can hold them. Do you forget who you're talking to?" He challenged.

"Of course not. You're the Obsidian Son, *kid*." I teased.

"Damn right," Raego growled, the sound shifting to a deadlier timber, that of a giant black dragon partially shifting into a menacing creature of the night.

And he was my pal.

"I'll feel safer at my home, no offense. Plus, if things are about to go FUBAR, spreading out the risk might be a good idea."

I grunted agreement.

We hung up without further words. Indie's eyes were wide. "What did you just do?"

"Hopefully something that won't *immediately* get me killed." That didn't appease the fear on her face. "It should be fine. I'm sure of it."

Instead of poking holes in my plan she merely sighed, gripping my hand in support.

Damn fine woman. I squeezed back in silent thanks.

# CHAPTER 8

*I* woke up with a start. Indie had moaned in her sleep, sending an explosion of adrenaline through my veins. My eyes widened and my breathing came fast as I bolted up to a sitting position. It took me a few moments of frantic searching to calm down.

We were alone. Safe.

I stood and took a drink from a bottle of water on the bedside table. My body was practically quivering with energy. Great. I wasn't going back to sleep anytime soon. I quickly glanced at the satchel beside the bed, verifying its contents were safe. I decided that I might as well lock them away now. Perhaps the brief walk would put me back at ease so I could get some shut-eye. Check the wards, hide the books, and hit they hay. I had a long day tomorrow.

I climbed out from the covers and tossed the satchel over a shoulder before silently stealing from the room without waking Indie. I crept down the halls on the balls of my feet, pausing for a few seconds outside Gunnar and Ashley's room. Silence.

I continued on down the hallway, glancing idly over the balcony to the enormous sitting room below. A small fire burned lazily in the fireplace, casting a red soothing glow on the room. I watched it, trying to absorb the sense of tranquility.

A throat cleared behind me and I jumped out of my skin. I quickly spun, panting as I prepared to unleash hell. "Couldn't sleep either?" Gunnar whispered from the shadows.

"What the *hell*, man? Are you *trying* to give me a heart attack?"

He shrugged, smirking. His hands had shifted to his werewolf claws, long, obsidian talons against icy white fur. And they were idly scratching a steady line in the trim of a doorway. He'd been up for a while, judging by the curls of shavings at his feet. "Do you mind?" I growled, pointing at the damage to the woodwork.

He didn't meet my eyes, and continued scratching. "You're good for it."

"If you need to go outside to potty you don't need to scratch at the door." His eyes flashed an icy blue as his smirk widened.

"Figured it was easier to protect her from out here. In case anyone pays us a visit in the night," he answered softly. I nodded, stepping back up to lean on the banister. He approached on silent feet and copied me. We stood in silence, thinking dark protective thoughts. Our women were targets, and neither of us was powerful enough to defeat the Grimms. Hell, supernaturals didn't even have a good track record *surviving* them.

"I've got a pretty swanky security system. They're safer here than anywhere else."

He grunted. "Not good enough. You know who is after you. And me."

"Not just mundane security, wolf. I activated the *Guardians* tonight." He watched me curiously, having never heard me mention them before. I patted the beak of a stone griffin standing near my hip, using the motion to secretly tap my bracelet one time. The griffin was hidden in plain sight as a decoration. Stone creaked as it abruptly turned its head to assess the werewolf, sniffing. Then it cocked its neck, whipped its tail once to thump the floor in a warning thud, and then let out a soft caw. Gunnar's eyes widened.

After all, there were a few more gargoyles within throwing distance.

About three-dozen stone sentinels. Or gargoyles, as most knew them. Most depicted griffins, but there were a few other predatory creatures, including bears, wolves, lions, and even a few hybrid combinations as well.

They stretched the entire length of the impressive landing, a good hundred feet, give or take, and were spaced no more than ten feet apart. The bracelet on my wrist pulsed lightly to let me know everything was functional, but I avoided tapping into any of the live feeds, sensing no alarms. Doing so would have superimposed a visual sweep of each griffin's post over my own vision. A very disturbing sensation. Gunnar began to chuckle lightly. "Nice." I tapped my wrist in a quick double beat, reinitiating *sentinel* mode. The gargoyle cooed lightly and then shifted back to attention, appearing inanimate again.

"Puppy want to go for a walk?" I oozed in a high-pitched, animated voice. His face turned to stone. "I was planning on saying *hey* to my parents, see if they have any advice about the Grimms. Them or Pandora. I'd honestly take anything I can get right now."

Gunnar shrugged. "Why not?" He eyed the gargoyles again. "Sure they're enough?"

I smiled, nodding. "Yep. This is only one layer of protection. I'll know immediately if anyone shows up at the gate uninvited, giving us plenty of time to make it back here before anyone even gets near the front door of the house." He looked unconvinced.

"What if they can just Shadow Walk in here like you?"

"Warded. Only I can do that." It was one of the first things I figured out how to do with my new power. And the first thing I had tested against, much to Jafar's frustration.

"Okay. Let's be quick." He sighed, sounding resigned to leave his post to the *Guardians*. I rolled my eyes. Typical *Type A* personality trait.

Gunnar quickly matched my stride as I made my way towards the office. At times like this, it was still difficult for me to think of *Chateau Falco* as *mine*. I felt inadequate to the task of owning such an impressive and historic icon for a home. The grounds had been in the family since the 1700's. But now I was the last Temple. No other siblings or children to carry on the name. No one else to share the wandering halls with. A house deserved living bodies to fill it with laughter, cries, and life.

But it only had me. And my friends, I guess. Soon Indie would become a permanent staple of the rambling property, and I would get to show her all the Chateau's secrets. Gunnar knew quite a few of them, having practically grown up here with me, but he didn't know all of them. I wondered what it would be like to share my home with her, smiling distantly at the thought.

Gunnar spoke softly, "are you still planning on doing it this week?" He asked.

He was, of course, referring to my proposal. I nodded. "Yes."

He grunted. "Even with…" he waved a hand at, well, life in general, implying the Grimms. "All of this suddenly springing up on you?"

I thought about that for a few seconds and finally nodded. "Yeah. I guess

I am. I can't let them take something like that away from me. I've got to keep on living, man."

He smiled over at me, nodding. "Good." We walked on a bit longer in silence, enjoying each other's company. "I'm assuming that is why you originally planned the stop underneath Plato's Cave. At your secret vault. The one even I didn't know about." He sounded hurt. Slightly.

"Yes. The engagement ring was down there," I answered. Then I offered an olive branch. "No one knew about that vault. No. One. Not you. Not Indie. Not my parents. No one."

He glanced at me, waving a hand to signify burying the hatchet. "Except someone found out."

I muttered under my breath, which caused him to look at me again. "Yeah. They did. Kind of fortuitous that the vault also held the books."

"Fortuitous. Right." He growled, not sounding pleased. "Or it was a setup."

I nodded, my attitude growing darker. "Or that." I agreed. I felt his eyes rest on me, then he nodded, glad that I was on the same page.

I was on the same letter.

We finally reached the office and I pulled open the massive wooden doors. The fire was burning softly, casting the room in an orange glow.

And we weren't alone.

Mallory sat before the fire in my father's old armchair. He didn't even hear us enter at first, but jolted as the door clicked shut. He lurched to his feet, a crackling spear of electricity in one hand, and a tumbler of whisky in the other. He was breathing heavy until he recognized us. "Master Temple…" He said, sounding guilty at his aggressive reaction. The power coursing over the weapon zapped out and he tossed it on the ground at his feet. "Dean told me something rather troubling…" He hadn't been around when we got home. He was kind of an enigma, disappearing at odd times. But he had always been that way. In fact, I hadn't even seen him more than one time in the years he had worked for my father. I guessed he was supposed to be an added layer of security. And security worked best when none knew it was present.

I nodded at him. "It's true. The Grimms are back in town and they want to take me out. And any acquaintances." I let him chew on that, no holding back for my crew.

"Aye. What do ya' need me to do, Laddie?"

I lowered my head in gratitude. *Laddie* was an affectionate name from Mallory. And I cherished it in my current mentality of despair. "You just did it, Mallory. Thanks."

"Aye." He eyed us curiously. "Paying yer' respects?"

I nodded.

"I'll make the rounds then. I don't trust the security system, even with the *Guardians* online, as much as my own eyes." Gunnar grunted his agreement. Mallory left the fire after picking up his spear and downing the last of his drink. On the way past us he offered me his scarred, iron-hard forearm, his eyes twinkling with anticipation and support as he nodded a single time. I clasped it, squeezing once.

He did the same with Gunnar and then left. The resulting quiet felt like a heavy blanket over the office. Aged paintings of my parents hung above the fireplace, staring stoically down at us. Two smaller paintings of Gunnar and I as children in ridiculous superhero poses framed the fireplace, lending life and humor to the hooded stares of my parents. My father had taken the photos, had them painted, and had chosen to place them here of all places. Gunnar was shaking his head slowly with an amused grin at the memory of that day.

It had been the day my parents gave him his shifting rune. The rune that allowed him to master his werewolf skin rather than becoming a raving psychopath once a month.

I approached the bookshelf and reached for the lever that opened the secret passageway. The house was rife with them. If it wasn't for Death allowing me to speak with my parents after they had died, I may never have discovered that the primary entrance to the Armory was here at *Chateau Falco*. My house. I had thought the only entrance was at Temple Industries, but that had been destroyed by a rogue Academy Justice who had been trying to break in and take the Armory for himself in order to ignite a new world order during *Mardi Gras* not too long ago.

It had been under Jafar's watch.

Yet another reason he hated me. As if it had been my fault his employee went bonkers and tried to use my inheritance to lay waste to the Academy.

I shifted the pressure release valve and watched as the fire suddenly roared brighter. This wasn't the Armory yet, just a secret access point to the area that *housed* the entrance to the Armory. See, I told you my digs had all sorts of cool secret passageways and whatnot. Some more dangerous than others, and I was entirely confident that I knew only a fraction of what lay hidden beneath *Chateau Falco*'s skirts. I couldn't wait to explore my home with Indie.

Gunnar glanced thoughtfully behind us to the doorway leading back to the hallway and our women as if about to change his mind, but then back to me. "Nervous?" I asked.

"I've just never been in there before," he admitted. "And I worry for them…"

I nodded. "Don't worry. They're safe. Mallory is prowling the halls too. With his crazy ass lightning spear." I smiled.

Gunnar chuckled. "Someday you'll have to tell me where he got it."

I shrugged helplessly. "No clue." Like I said, Mallory was sort of an enigma to me. "You ready?" I asked. He nodded after a pause.

"Okay. We're not there yet. This is a secondary security measure my dad installed. The entrance to the Armory is only one of the things he hid down in the crypts. Follow me exactly." And then I stepped into the burning fire-place, which should have roasted me into bacon, but didn't.

Instead, I fell. At least it *felt* like falling. Pandora had told me it was really just a form of Shadow Walking to another dimension, or at least the shortcut that existed between two locations on the map. I had told her it felt similar to my Maker power. She had laughed, patting me on the back. *Who do you think made the magic in the first place? Wizards just found a way to copy it. Even if only primitively.*

I landed lightly on my feet and waited for Gunnar to appear beside me. He did so with wide eyes, glancing about nervously before spotting me. He brushed off his pants and stepped closer. "This Hogwarts stuff creeps me out," he grumbled.

"Just wait." I teased.

We walked for a few minutes, turning down several halls, until we approached a ten-foot tall door made of living stone.

When I say *living*, I'm being literal. The door depicted a woodland scene, complete with foliage, nocturnal creatures, a small pond, stars, and a full moon. But the carvings on the door darted about as if alive. Fish darted about between reeds in the pond, and an energetic pair of small owls flitted from one thick branch to another. A lone wolf sat on his haunches at the bank of the pond, hungrily eyeing the owls. The trees swayed in an unseen wind, and then one of the owls abruptly dove down into the pond, razor sharp claws extended. He scored a hit, flapping back to the tree to savor his fresh fish. Knowing what was about to happen, I pointed down at the bottom of the pond for Gunnar to see. The lone wolf also watched, no obvious reaction in his hungry eyes.

When the unlucky fish broke the surface of the water clutched in the owl's talons, another was instantaneously born at the base of the pond. A fishling? A fish baby? I shook my head. I wasn't a biologist.

Look, people, a tiny freaking fish.

It was magical. Obviously, of course, but I'm referring more to the *beauty* of someone, at some point in time, investing their power to create a living mural for no other reason than that they wanted to. That was what magic meant to me. It wasn't all about cool explosions and Hollywood-level special effects. Magic, at its core, was about life. And death. And the beauty of those two forces comingling. At least to me.

I smiled distantly as I pulled out a small penknife to slice the pad of my thumb enough to cause blood to spill. Then I reached out to caress the lone wolf's fur. He growled, but it wasn't the familiar friendly sound I was used to hearing after visiting the Armory so many times.

Usually he growled in contentment, appreciation for his master's touch.

This time it was a warning growl, and he abruptly snapped his jaws at me before padding over to the opposite end of the pond, as if that would keep me away from touching a two-dimensional carving.

I stood there in disbelief. That had never happened before.

The entrance to the Armory usually opened at the touch of my blood to the wolf's fur.

But this time it hadn't.

Gunnar was watching me expectantly, no doubt waiting for a great revelation of some kind. I hefted the satchel on my shoulder nervously, only too aware that for whatever reason, I could no longer plan on storing the books in the Armory.

It was locked to me.

I really didn't have time for this sort of thing.

"Hey, wolf."

"Yes?" Gunnar answered drily.

"No, not you. Him." The wolf in the carving watched me silently. "What gives?" I asked him.

His mane of fur lifted in warning as he growled again.

"I'm locked out." I clarified, in case it wasn't obvious. The wolf barked once.

"Was that a yes, Lassie?" I asked sarcastically. He barked again.

Huh.

"Why?" The wolf merely stared back at me this time.

"Is it permanent?" I asked. The wolf barked twice. "No?" I asked. He barked once for *yes*. Unless I was batshit crazy, I was now speaking wolf. I turned to Gunnar for help. "You getting any of this?" He shook his head, eyes studying the wolf carving with sudden interest at the possibility of understanding him. I turned back to the door.

"You aren't allowed to let anyone in?" I concluded. He confirmed with a single bark.

I turned to eye Gunnar over my shoulder and then shrugged. "Well, that's a first. Not sure what to make of it." I idly wondered if it was locked down due to me activating the *Guardians*. "Must be some kind of security measure." The wolf barked once, which made me shiver. I hadn't been addressing him, which meant that he could understand general conversations in his vicinity. I idly wondered if I had said anything to offend him in the past.

I didn't want to piss off the bouncer at the door.

Even if the bouncer was a living stone carving. "Look, when I referred to you as a fleabag mutt the other day, I was just kidding." The wolf merely turned his head away from me haughtily.

"How long is the door locked down?" The wolf glanced over a shoulder, but that was it, so I clarified my question. "Will it be locked down for long?" The wolf continued to stare back, which made me shiver. It meant that there wasn't a *yes* or *no* answer to the question. Which meant other variables were involved that could alter his answer, rendering him unable to respond. *What the hell?*

Maybe Pandora was just taking a bath and wanted some privacy. Or my parents were having a romantic stay-cation, and didn't want to be disturbed – the equivalent of a sock on the doorknob in a college dorm room. But that didn't sound right to me.

I turned back to Gunnar, a feeling of dread creeping over my shoulders. "We should probably get back to the girls. I don't like this."

His posture instantly grew rigid as the situation dawned on him. If the

Armory was on lockdown, something we probably wouldn't like was happening nearby.

Or, more likely, *had already happened.*

We began to run.

The wolf howled behind me, urging us on, the sound chilling as we raced back the way we had come, Gunnar hot on my heels.

# CHAPTER 9

*I*ndie had been justifiably alarmed at being woken up by her paranoid boyfriend in the middle of the night, who was freaking out about an impending attack, yelling gibberish about the Armory being on lockdown, gargoyles, and a talkative wolf carving refusing to open a door.

Especially after a growling werewolf forcibly shoved Ashley into our room. Indie had shrieked, tugging the sheets up above her nakedness. We hadn't immediately gone to sleep after all, thanks to Barbie's gift.

I owed Barbie for *that* memory reel.

And the best part?

After I proposed to Indie, she was mine forever.

Which was awesome, yet terrifying…

In my mad dash from the office, I had deemed it prudent to nab the feather that Pegasus' brother, Grimm – no relation to the psycho brothers currently hunting me – had once given me. I had wanted to make sure I had my bloodthirsty pony on call to get us out of Dodge if we needed to flee on the spot. I spotted the black feather with the red orb on the tip – like a demonic peacock's coloring – poking out from my satchel now on the far wall of the tunnels where I stood.

It had taken me quite a few deep breaths to calm down and share the full story with the girls, by which time Gunnar and I had mostly downgraded from a Defcon 1 threat assessment level and had returned to merely believing in general conspiracy theories.

My drifting thoughts earned me a solid *thwack* from Mallory's quarterstaff.

"Ow!" I spat, shaking my thumb in the air by my side to ease the pain.

Mallory only looked determined. Then he attacked me again.

I calmly embraced the raging river of power that seemed to constantly reside beneath my feet, or more accurately, beneath the surface of the earth, which just so happened to be beneath my feet. No matter where I stood at any given moment – from the top of a ten-story building, to a hot tub, to the secluded basement halls of *Chateau Falco* – I could now at least *feel* the power every time.

Progress!

But it was the harnessing of that power that constantly eluded me.

I reached for the overwhelming force, hoping to eke out a small defense against Mallory's rapidly approaching quarterstaff, and my hands sailed right through it. Which earned me a thump on the head this time, knocking me from my feet to land on my backside. Even with padded ends, Mallory's quarterstaff packed a punch. I growled a warning at him, but he merely shrugged.

"Your enemies enna' gonna' give you an inch, Laddie. You asked me to train you, so I'll be a doin' it right. Like you want me to. Even though right now you wonna' admit it." He held out a hand to help me to my feet.

"I just can't seem to get a consistent feel for it. At least I can always sense it now, but I can't always tap into it."

"That's better than when you started training." He offered with a shrug. "Baby steps, my son."

The words hung heavy in the air, and I could tell that Mallory wished them back. A slip of the tongue. Still.

Instead of climbing to my feet I stayed on the ground, patting the dirt floor beside me for him to sit down. He complied, looking uncomfortable. We were in the crypts before the door that led to the Armory. We watched the wolf chasing the owls, yapping excitedly as he eagerly hunted for a quick snack. I smiled. Which didn't last long. The door was no longer a door, but an obstacle in my mind. It was all that stood between me and possible answers to the Brothers Grimm. So close, but so far away.

"Any luck after you deactivated the *Guardians?*" He asked. I shook my head. He stared at the door thoughtfully, but didn't speak.

I turned to him, feigning nonchalance. "Who are you, anyway? I've never asked. Just took you on faith after my parents passed."

His face turned stony.

"I saw you only once before, you know. That day at the police station when you were driving my dad to bail me out. That was years ago. Before I opened the bookstore."

His features slowly melted to their usual sunny demeanor as he grunted with a distant smile. "Aye. I remember it well." He chewed on his lip, idly plucking unseen things from his pants. "A lot happened that day. Maybe not all of it seemed important, but me thinks it was. Especially now."

I nodded thoughtfully. No one knew what really happened that night. Well, now they did since I had spilled the beans last night. But before that, I had told no one. Not even my parents. So how was Mallory aware that something big had happened that night?

"Why do you say that?" I asked softly.

He was silent for a few moments. "Intuition. I remember the air feeling tense that night. The sea was wild. Air thick with unseen lightning. The Perfect Storm..." he trailed off.

"The *river.*" I said with a frown.

He chuckled. "Aye. The river," he corrected.

"Because claiming to know what the sea was like that night all the way from St. Louis would be crazy..."

"Well, I reckon I fit that bill, Laddie." He laughed lightly, squeezing his staff.

I let the silence calm me, focusing my mind. "You're not going to tell me."

"No." he finally answered with a sigh. But the word was apologetically firm.

"You know how that looks, right?"

He sighed. "Aye. I reckon I do."

"But that doesn't change anything."

"No. It doesna' change a thing." I let the tension in the air build, and was about to give him an ultimatum when he continued. "Your father swore that that was mine to keep. Even from you, his blood." He trailed off distantly. "I've done... things I'm enna' too proud of. I don't want to relive 'em. Or to

68

have someone judge me by me past." He looked at me. "I'm sure you understand." He winked. I was about to press the issue, but found myself calmly admitting that he had a point. I briefly pondered a suspicion that perhaps his accent was another form of disguise, because I had caught him slipping out of it several times over the past months. His next words caused me to look up. "Trust me by my actions, Laddie. Can't go wrong with that, can ye'?" His eyes twinkled in the dim torchlight.

I shrugged. "You've done right by me. I was just curious. I don't like puzzles."

"I know." He climbed to his feet, offering me his hand. "We have enough time for another few rounds if you want. After that ye' need to get going. Big meeting today."

I groaned, accepting his scarred hand to help me to my feet. I didn't want to think about that. "Are you trying to rile me up? You know how I feel about today's meeting, despite what the Board of Directors says."

He nodded. "Riling you up seemed to work a few times. You tapped into this... *well* of power almost seven of ten times. And you were as angry as a fisherman coming home after a voyage to find his wife porking the local baker!" He burst out laughing.

I hadn't been *that* angry. But he had a point. "I don't get it. I can sense it all the time now. It's everywhere. And yet it feels... alien." He watched me thoughtfully.

"I'm sure the first wizard said the same thing about magic."

"Yes, but a Maker *gave* the ability to use magic to wizards in the first place. Just makes me wonder if I'm playing with toys better left untouched. Well, if I can ever figure out how to consistently touch it," I complained.

He was silent for a few seconds, turning his back to me.

"That won't work out too well for your lady friend..." he muttered. "Makes me wonder how much you really care about her. Down here in your batcave whining about this and that when you should be focusing."

My vision went blue in a blink. I don't really know how else to describe it. I used to see red when angry, but after my transition in power, the world seemed to turn an arctic blue tint whenever I grew angry now.

"You don't get to talk about Indie like that," I warned, instinctively.

"Call 'em like I see 'em. Whining down here about billion dollar meetings, probing into my past like a gossipmonger. Like any of that really matters. You're running." He called over his shoulder, not even looking at me, apparently disgusted. I must have struck a nerve with my questions.

Still, that gave him no right to bring Indie into this. I pointed a finger at him and unbidden power abruptly launched from my fingertips, slamming him into the far wall. He bounced off and hit the ground with a groan. Crackling blue cuffs sailed from my fingertips and lifted him from the ground, pinning him at my eye level, facing me now. "Take it back, *whoever you are.*" I snarled.

I noticed that a single tear leaked down his cheek. Then he smiled sadly. "Told you it would work." He spat blood onto the floor.

I blinked.

He had riled me up.

And I had tapped into the power instinctively. I focused on it now, feeling it settling around my feet in a seeming unending well, hungry to be used. I mentally dipped my fingers into the torrent and felt galactic frost, scalding lava, razorblade air, moist earth full of life, and rock denser than anything on earth – all melded together into a single force.

And I was wielding it.

"Nate, you ready yet? We need to leave in ten minutes." A voice called from the distance.

Indie.

The power rushed out of me like water through a sieve, leaving me exhausted. Mallory slumped to the ground and took a deep breath. So did I.

"I'll be right up, mom," I muttered under my breath.

"I can hear you, Sir Echo. You're in a tunnel."

I muttered under my breath, softer this time. Mallory spat a bit more blood and saliva onto the dusty floor. "Sorry about that, Nate. Yer' easy to read. I needed ye' angry quick to see if ye' could do it on the fly."

I watched him, and his lone tear suddenly made much more sense. It had hurt him to hurt me. But he had done it anyway.

*Trust my actions*, he had said. Well, he had plum proven his character to me.

I thought about what he had done, and then began to laugh. "You taught me how to cheat." I finally said.

He grunted agreement, climbing to his feet. "If ye' can't consciously use your new power, at least ye' know how to cheat enough to keep yer' friends safe. One of yer' father's most valued lessons."

I lowered my head, nodding at the memory of my father. "Still, I'm sorry I reacted so strongly. You gave me a gift and I hurt you."

"The best gifts come at a cost. Now, it's time for you to get primped up. Big meeting today, whether ye' like it or not. Just don't get too angry with 'em." He winked, helping me to my feet again. "They're only doing their jobs, and they do work for you."

"Let's see what crazy scheme they have lined up for me this month," I muttered.

I made my way back to my room to rinse off and get ready to meet with Temple Industries' Board of Directors for an urgent meeting they had set up last minute.

Which was never a good thing.

I needed to be finished with this quickly. I had more important things to do than worry about my company right now.

The satchel with the books never left my sight.

Even from the shower.

# CHAPTER 10

*I* clicked the pen clutched in my fist, the sound surprisingly loud in the packed room.

Then I did it about a dozen more times in the space of a minute, while gazing lazily out the window of the twelve-story building. I shifted uncomfortably in the chair for a few seconds, and then finally lifted my feet up onto the table itself, letting out a soft contented sigh. That earned me a few thinly veiled looks of disapproval, but Mallory had beaten me up pretty good this morning, and my whole body seemed to throb with a dull, but constant pain, like a form of Chinese water torture.

I was waiting for the speaker to finish, ignoring the discreet glances of several more of my Board Members, who seemed more intent with my reaction to the speaker's words than the speech itself. Almost like they already knew the details... They seemed a tad concerned at my obvious display of disinterest, and I could feel their calculating eyes planning ahead for the next several days based on a million subtle clues they imagined they were cleverly deciphering from my body language.

It was enough to almost make me laugh aloud.

They thought they could read *me*? Every single move and reaction I made was deliberate, a disguise, purposely shown or hidden to lead them exactly where I wanted them to be. It was instinctual for me. These men and women thought they could out manipulate *me*? I was a *Temple*. I had attended dinner parties with more intrigue than they would experience in a lifetime.

But the thing about being known as a worthless, billionaire playboy was that people often forgot that I was eidetic, with a genius level IQ to boot. My cover persona was so blatant and obnoxious that many forgot this small fact. Which was purposeful, and I wielded this power like a razor in the night, quietly moving the chess pieces on the board to my desires, none the wiser.

I forced myself to take a soft, deep breath. But Mallory had been right. They didn't mean harm. Some of them were even ex-employees of the company while others had spent more than a decade serving on the Board for my parents. They thought they were doing the right thing. They just didn't know any better. We weren't enemies. They just needed… guidance. A firm hand. I glanced about the room. A *firmer* hand if they had thought this was going to fly with me.

They had worked very hard to broker this deal, without informing me ahead of time, which settled a threadbare cloak of barely constrained rage over my figurative shoulders.

Even if I hadn't been distracted with thoughts of the Brothers Grimm actively hunting me, I would have had the same response to the speaker's pitch.

Not *no*, but *hell no*.

Having already decided my response, I mentally began planning my day, idly tapping the satchel at my feet with my heavy winter boots. The satchel that held the two books that the Brothers Grimm wanted very badly. One was a book of summonings, and was how I had met Barbie the nympho-sprite in the first place. Some of the creatures in that book would be a fine catch indeed, for the Brothers Grimm. The book was essentially a free buffet menu to them. Open the cover, pick a page at random, perform the ritual depicted on the page, and a victim would be forced to answer the call – forced to appear against their will, trapped inside a nice summoning circle all neat and hogtied as you please for the Grimms to decapitate.

You see, with summoning rituals the creature called upon rarely had the power to stand up to the summoner – as long as they performed the ritual properly – and the pages in this book were very specific, leaving little room for error, and as a result, no way out for the victim. Well, Barbie's page had been smudged, causing a slight embarrassment for me when I first summoned her, but that is neither here nor there.

I shivered at that memory, and thought about the implications of the other creatures being called to their deaths. I had to keep the book out of the wrong hands or it would essentially be my fault when they were all killed.

The other book was the original edition of *Grimm's Fairy Tales*, or *Kinder- und Hausmärchen* in German. But it apparently was not only the first copy of the book, but actually held spells as well.

Of some kind or another.

I had flipped through the pages late last night, careful to make sure the protective ward remained intact so that the Grimms couldn't trace its location. Barbie had hinted at that being a likely possibility and I wasn't about to take any chances.

The first half of the book held the original stories: Snow White, the Princess and the Frog, and many, many more. Of course, these were the true, original tales, not the friendly *Disney* versions. For example, rather than kissing the frog, the Princess had dashed his body against a wall.

This was the *least* violent of the stories.

But then there was the second half of the book. It read more like a travel log, handwritten in big, loopy cursive German script. I wasn't fluent in German, but I caught enough recognizable words to get the main gist. It described creatures they had encountered while traveling the German countryside, and how they had murdered them.

Interspersed in the journal entries were sketches of supernatural creatures I had neither seen nor heard about before – likely long extinct thanks to the Grimms' hunting parties – and numerous depictions of diagrams, star positions, and plenty of vaguely alchemical or scientific calculations of some kind filling the margins. I shivered, glad that I couldn't read the language. The pictures had been gruesome enough.

I had scoured the text for one specific entry to no avail. I had been told that the book held the power to permanently lock away the Grimms or possibly kill them all. I didn't know if it was true or if it was in fact the opposite – a spell capable of drawing every Grimm in the universe to a single location in time and space. Cold fingers danced down my spine at the thought.

Whatever it was, the Grimms didn't want anyone else having access to the book. They had lost track of it at some point in recent history, and I had – completely by dumb luck – stumbled across it and decided to purchase it. Up until last night I hadn't really spent any time studying the tome, much to my embarrassment given the present circumstances. I had always told myself I would make time to study it… *tomorrow*. But, you know… *life* always seemed to get in the way.

After scarcely surviving my first encounter with a barely corporeal Jacob Grimm a few years ago, I had grown complacent, despite Barbie's persistent warning. I had thought he and his brothers safely locked away in a prison of sorts, and had been told that the book in my satchel was all they needed to escape. Perhaps that had been why I hadn't been too keen on reading it. I hadn't wanted to accidentally rub the proverbial lamp and let the genie out. Not that any of that mattered now. They had found their own way back, just like Jacob had told me he would. Perhaps if I could find out how he had accomplished this I could send him and his brothers back to the void. I grunted to myself, earning a few pointed looks from a Board Member sitting to my right. I ignored him.

And now Jakey and his brothers were coming for me. Not just to kill me for a personal offense, but now they were even going to get paid to do so! Talk about Karma. My arrogant pride had come full circle. The Minotaur would be hooting his nose ring off at the irony.

I was pretty sure I would need Barbie's help to either send them back or defeat them in battle.

Barbie had led me to believe that she had been involved in some capacity – a few hundred years ago – in imprisoning them in the first place. Or that she had at least witnessed it. I mean, she was powerful with a capital P, but I didn't really get an overwhelming combat vibe from her. Sure, she was sadistic, hyper violent, and savored murder by sex, but I hadn't ever really seen her Hulk out or anything, so wasn't sure what she could do in a battle. Which was sounding more and more likely.

I really could think of only one choice. I couldn't watch over and protect all my friends at once. I could only be in one place at a time. Which meant that I needed to bring the Grimms to me. I just needed to figure out how.

Someone cleared his throat, bringing me out of my reverie. I looked up to find everyone watching me expectantly. I put my worthless, billionaire playboy face in place, full of entitlement and general boredom at adult life. "Oh, thank God. Is he finished?" The gentleman beside me nodded, lips tight. "Good." I swept my gaze over each face for a few seconds, watching my Board squirm uncomfortably. "No." I took a casual sip of my bottled water, pretending not to notice the brittle tension in the room. "Now, is there anything else?" I asked, setting down my drink.

Ashley held a fist to her mouth and coughed lightly. She hadn't needed to mask it. The room suddenly roared with arguments, muffling her expulsion.

I let the sound build like a tidal wave for a handful of seconds. Then I held up a finger, breaking the sound wave like a cliff face suddenly rising out of the ocean, stopping it cold. I pointed at the man standing by the screen who was also taking a drink of water. "You've heard my answer. If you have anything to refute or add, I will give you thirty seconds to sell me. Give me the high points. I'm just a worthless heir after all, and you used a lot of big words."

He blinked, sputtered a bit, and then composed himself.

"We will pay ten times earnings for the last fiscal year. Your company's profits have plummeted since your father's... departure. We are offering you a golden parachute. An easy way out." That was an unheard-of offer. Easily double the industry standard.

"Now you're speaking my language." I finally answered, forcing myself to sound slightly interested. Several Board members seemed to relax in restrained triumph as the speaker babbled on a bit longer, biting onto my response hook, line, and sinker. I tuned him out, but still let on that I was completely focused on his words, nodding here and there convincingly.

But I was really assessing my Board with borderline murderous thoughts. They had set up this meeting behind my back. I could sense Ashley studying me, knowing I wasn't truly listening and that the other shoe was about to drop. I ignored her.

There would be repercussions for their actions.

Starting today.

No doubt the golden parachute would also be quite lucrative for each of the Board Members, seeing as how we collectively owned the majority of the publicly held company's shares. But I was the largest shareholder by far, and the heir to the company's founder, so my word was law. The speaker finally finished his spiel. I tapped my lip with a finger. "Thank you for your time... but my answer stands. Temple Industries won't be sold." A slip of rage escaped my carefully controlled façade as a sudden thought hit me. "Especially not to a German company."

The Grimms were German.

"We started here on US soil. I wouldn't be able to look myself in the mirror if I took those jobs away from American workers. *St. Louis* workers," I amended. "Some of them have been here for over twenty years."

"We would be inclined to leave your plant operational if that is a condition for your acceptance." He sounded eager.

I thought about that for a minute. But that wasn't truly my biggest problem with the pitch. Relocating the company would kill hundreds of jobs, which I of course wasn't okay with, but even if they kept the St. Louis plant operational, I didn't want to sell.

Temple Industries was *mine*. The last remnant of my parents' dynasty.

It wasn't for sale.

I shook my head. "No." The room imploded. I crossed my ankles and watched it play out. Sudden declarations of inattention on my part, no goal for the company's future growth or specific product lines to focus on, no plan for increasing or decreasing R&D, et cetera. I listened, nodding at the appropriate moments, remembering each comment, accusation, and face that dared speak.

"With this sale, you could focus on rebuilding your true passion, Plato's Cave. Especially after that explosion demolished your building earlier this year. That project requires a lot of focus on your part. Focus that you haven't given Temple Industries. Think about it, Nate. The company hasn't been a true focus for you, and it's suffered as a result." Of all the people who I had thought might challenge my authority, I hadn't anticipated Ashley.

My thirty pieces of silver. My Judas Iscariot with a kiss.

Her words were spoken softly, politely, but the voice swiftly cut through the outbursts of men ten years her senior like a hot knife through butter. The room grew silent, tension suddenly as thick as smoke.

I blinked, slowly swiveling to face her with barely masked shock. It was well known that she and I were more than just employer and employee. Everyone knew about her and Gunnar, and that he was my best friend, and that my parents had considered her a surrogate daughter.

And she had just sided against me. You could have heard a pin drop. My vision exploded blue and I couldn't contain myself.

"No." I growled savagely, slamming my fist onto the table enough to significantly crack it and send my water bottle splashing to the ground. Several Board members flinched at the impossible power of the strike, suddenly very, very nervous. After all, everyone had heard the news clips and general rumors about my exploits, even if they hadn't quite let themselves believe.

But that belief seemed to have changed in a microsecond.

I had fought a 'dragon' on the Eads Bridge, I had flown through a window to land on a Judge's lap – even though there was no possible explanation for how I had managed to jump through a third-story window with no balcony or stairway leading to it. I had started riots at *Mardi Gras* that ended with explosions at both my bookstore and Temple Industries. Brutally murdered bodies had been found at several of my properties throughout town. The police and FBI had held me in custody... several times. Regarding both my parents' murder and other crimes that had gone unsolved. I had allegedly burned down a strip club where a cop's mutilated body had later been discovered. I had been announced as a firm supporter of magical creatures coming out of the closet at a nationally-televised solar eclipse convention, standing arm in arm with senators and politicians. I had even been referred to – several times, and all by respected persons in the community – as a *wizard*, of all things.

All of these wild accusations and unbelievable stories strolled across the newsfeed of their memory as they stared at the cracked table.

And a longtime friend of mine who had supported me through all of that had just stood against me. Openly. My response was to crack a solid oak table with my bare fist. Which shouldn't have been possible. Seeing as how the room was filled with ex-scientists and engineers, they knew better than anyone the limitations of the human body.

But there the broken table sat, loudly defying every Law of Physics known to man.

The room was completely still.

"Now that you are finished airing our dirty laundry in front of our guest," I pointed a finger at the potential buyer of my father's company, causing him to flinch in fear as his eyes tore away from the damaged table, "I think we are finished here. You may leave," I whispered darkly to the German. He nodded quickly, eagerly gathering up his possessions under an arm – not wanting to waste any time putting them away properly, and bolted from the room. I swiveled in my chair, facing the windows and the winter wonderland outside. I let the silence build for a solid minute. I didn't turn around as I spoke. "You bring up valid points." I admitted, resulting in a soft, relieved collective breath. "I task you with forming plans to resolve our current deficiencies. We will discuss this at our next... *scheduled* meeting." I emphasized the word, spinning the chair slowly to face them again, letting them know with my glare and tone that this cloak and dagger shit would not happen again.

Ever.

"That is all." And I rose from the table. Everyone else did the same, bowing their heads deferentially. Concerned Board Members instantly swarmed Ashley as I strode out of the room and made my way to the elevator.

I had a few murders to plan. A trap to set up.

I would leave the bureaucrats to... well, *bureaucrat-ing*.

Because if I'm being honest with myself, I didn't think I was very good at it.

# CHAPTER 11

*I* strode towards the elevator, grinning to myself as I spotted the man waiting outside the polished doors. The German turned at the sound of my heels on marble, and his face paled, looking panicked that he would have to share an elevator with me. I smiled wider at him and his face blanched further.

I jabbed the button several times to increase the speed, and let my smile slowly fade.

Then I waited. "You know that doesn't help..." he nervously teased, aiming for small talk. I didn't respond. "I... I wanted to thank you for your time. I understand your position, but ask that you respectfully consider the offer when your emotions have cooled." I slowly turned my eyes to him, face unyielding. His already weak resolve shattered. "I... I think I need to use the necessities before I leave." He stammered, clutching the messy collection of PowerPoint handouts to his chest. "Good day." He practically whimpered.

I turned back to the elevator, waiting. After a minute, I jabbed the button again impatiently.

"You know that doesn't help, right?"

I briefly entertained murder.

I turned a fiery glare to find Ashley standing beside me. I spotted several heads quickly ducking back into the Board Room upon seeing her confront me.

Ashley held out her hand. "Peace offering?" I looked down and almost had a panic attack to see her holding out my satchel. I snatched it away eagerly. "You left this in the Board Room," she said softly.

"What the hell is wrong with me today?" I checked inside for the books and sighed in relief.

"Just today?" She teased.

"Touché." I muttered as the doors finally slid open. We stepped inside and I pressed the lobby button, preparing myself to brave the horde of reporters and TV anchors no doubt waiting outside the lobby doors. I glanced pointedly at her and pressed the button again, making sure she noticed. Then two more times. She rolled her eyes with a tired smile. "So… mind telling me what the hell that was about?" I growled.

She sighed, shoulders relaxing into a neutral position. "Just doing my job, Nate. I took off the *friend* hat and put on the *Temple Industries* hat. It's what you pay me for. It's nothing personal. My job is to be honest with you at all times. Especially when you don't want to hear it… and that was about as honest as one could get," she replied, respectfully.

I grunted. "I'm not selling the company. It belonged to my parents." I said stubbornly.

"I get that. I cared for your parents too," she responded softly, eyes glistening. I didn't give her an inch, remaining silent. Crocodile tears wouldn't fool me. She had challenged me in front of my Board, and I had considered her in my corner. "If you want to keep the company, you need to become more active in our future. No offense. Just my very expensive business degree at work." She smiled softly.

"They should know how to run a company. They've done it for years. It's a cash cow."

She was already shaking her head. "Wrong. Your father was directly involved in almost every aspect of the company. He lived and breathed it. True, he spent a lot of time on side projects, but never at the detriment of the company at large." She didn't add that I had done exactly that. "Just take the offer into consideration. No emotion. It's true you don't have to sell. With a little guidance, the company could become a Tech Titan again, but we need a captain to steer the ship."

"That's what your very expensive business degree is for. Not blindsiding me in front of the masses." I muttered frostily.

She nodded. "That's true. I could turn things around. But if you want me to do that, I'll need a raise."

I blinked at her. And then I began to laugh. I wasn't against the idea – I just found her segue so unexpected that it made me laugh. She was pining for a raise while I was pining to stay alive over the next few days. She smiled. "Not like that. Of course, I wouldn't object if it came with a compensation bonus. What I mean is that I need more authority to act. There are a couple of bottlenecks in the decision-making process. We should talk about it if you are serious about keeping the company. We have a great team, but a lot of potential projects went dark after your parents passed. We need to breathe some life back into them, and kill a few others."

I shrugged. "Done."

She shook her head. "I know you have more important things on your mind right now, but you can't let this be an emotional decision. We will talk about it at length before I agree to help. If not, consider this my resignation..." I blinked at her, dumbfounded. She went on as if not noticing, emotionless. "Which will of course mean several other key members would likely leave. Possibly moving to Germany to work for Mr. PowerPoint back there." She finally looked up at me, adjusting her librarian glasses with a manicured finger.

"You wouldn't."

"That's kind of where we are right now, Nate. This is your company now, and it's time you treated it like more than a hobby. Or sell it. Our key people feel like they have no voice, and that feeling breeds discontent, which inflates turnover. They. Will. Leave. Especially after *this*." She softened the blow with a sad smile. "You didn't really show much respect in there. This is their *life*. When employees feel that they are more dedicated than the owner, bad things tend to follow. You can't be mad at them for it. You come in once a month and dash their plans to pieces. How do you think they should feel? You're a bull in a china shop in their eyes. Some of them have been here for decades. You haven't. Yet you have the power to destroy their passion with a single growl, phone call, or click of a pen." She arched a brow and my shoulders sank a bit. She had a point. Even though it infuriated me to admit it. She touched my shoulder lightly as we continued our descent. "You need to stop straddling the fence. You want to keep the company, fine, let go of the reins completely or jump in headfirst. One or the other. Not both. A company this size is like a plant. It needs room to breathe. It's a living being wrapped in a concrete building." she poked my chest hard. "You're smothering it."

The doors opened but I didn't move. My vision was slowly turning blue. Which wasn't good. It meant my anger was rising, and with it, the leviathan of power I now wielded. I assessed her words. She was right, of course. I held out my hand. She took it tentatively.

"You're right. When this is all over, we'll talk." She nodded her head once.

"That's all I ask."

"You're not allowed to quit. But a raise is definitely on the table. We should talk about that, too. As well as a list of other key personnel who you believe deserve a raise."

She nodded and then followed me into the posh lobby. The ceiling rested thirty feet above our heads, supported by thick marble columns. Several seating areas were present in case anyone needed to wait. I saw a small coffee shop in the corner, no customers present at the moment, leaving the two Rastafarian employees to thumb away on their cell phones.

Our heels clicked across the marble floor, two security guards tipping their hats our way as we approached the front doors. Ashley and I tugged on our coats, me wrapping the pea coat around my body tightly before buttoning it up and popping the collar to protect my neck from the wind and snow outside. Ashley wore a scarf, tucking it inside her coat.

Seeing as how the entire front of the building was glass, I could already see the frenzied horde waiting outside. News vans, and clusters of reporters filled the entryway, checking their recorders and microphones in eager anticipation to be the first to break the news – whatever it may be. They hadn't planned on the meeting ending early, and as soon as they saw me they began to scramble like a kicked anthill.

I wasn't quite sure how they even knew about the meeting in the first place. No doubt one of the Board Members had assumed a different ending to the meeting and had prepared accordingly, ready to steal the spotlight as soon as I agreed to sell. I wondered just how much money was riding on this deal for each Board Member and what it may have meant to their retirement plans. I would have to look into it. Because despite Ashley's advice, I was still pissed about how it had come to my attention. It would be a topic to discuss with Ashley in depth.

I was the freaking owner and I had found out via company email, which I checked only once a week. That would have to change if I was truly committed to following Ashley's advice.

Maybe I could negotiate up to twice a week. Max.

I took a deep breath, placing my hands on the door. Several people outside began eagerly pointing at me and raising their recording equipment. Ashley touched my shoulder in reassurance and support. "Your car ready?" I asked.

"I texted the driver from the Board Room." She pointed towards the street beyond the reporters.

"Good. Let's get you safely through the horde of vultures then. We'll talk later at the Chateau." She nodded and then followed me as I strode through the doors into the frenzy.

Camera flashes exploded across a sea of cold bodies, the tide of humanity practically frothing at the mouth to see that Nate Temple himself was the first to exit. I was a celebrity after all. For both good and bad reasons.

It began immediately, the crowd swarming us. *"Is it true that Temple Industries is selling to a German Industrial Company?"* One reporter shouted. What the hell was wrong with my Board? It seemed the media knew more than I myself, which meant someone had talked. Someone who had likely purchased *puts* – the right to sell at a fixed current price in case the stock crashed – or *calls* – the rights to buy my stock at a certain price in case the stock soared. Which, being insiders, would be illegal. Ashley's face went rigid, the same concern no doubt entering her mind. I forcibly continued to push us on through the crowd, tugging Ashley's hand firmly, forcing the crowd to part at a glacial pace. I may or may not have used subtle elbow strikes to speed things up.

*"How much are they buying the company for?"*

*"Will the factory remain on American soil?"* another shouted.

*"What do you have to say about this decision effectively killing hundreds of jobs in St. Louis, in an already precarious economy?"*

The cameras continued flashing and microphones dangled in front of me as I contemplated my response. My face remained expressionless out of experience, even though my mind was racing a million miles per hour. A gentle throb of warm energy seemed to abruptly fall over my shoulders, but I didn't have time to think about it.

Because that's when the *hit* went down.

Bullets began to fly.

# CHAPTER 12

*T*he glass walls of the lobby shuddered under a barrage of machine gun fire, shattering into millions of glittering crystals that spilled across the icy concrete. Ashley and I dove behind the back of a parked van, trying to determine who was shooting at us and from what direction. My eyes scanned the scene in a blur, searching for the shooter, but the fender suddenly lit up with sparks as bullets hammered just to the right of my skull. I ducked back, but not before a tracer of fire nicked my ear. Which pissed me off. The world morphed into an azure glow as magic beckoned to me. Ashley yanked me back further, whipping a pair of pistols out of her purse with the skilled precision of a practiced student. I recognized them as the pair Gunnar had given her for Christmas.

I still hadn't discovered exactly where the shooter was, but something persistently nagged at me until I finally gave it a second of attention.

Something was off about this situation.

You see, shootings are *loud*.

Rifle bullets fire at thousands of feet per second from tiny explosions of a hammer striking a casing of gunpowder. These thunderous concussions cause your brain to dampen your eardrums in an effort to preserve your hearing. Cordite fills the air in puffs of pungent smoke that makes it difficult to breathe fresh air, which you are desperately gulping, as adrenaline kicks in to fuel your muscles in order to help you run away faster.

Hot chunks of lead either strike people, causing screams of agony or death and sending gouts of blood into the air, or they strike stationary objects, splintering wood, shattering glass, or ricocheting off concrete and metal until they strike yet *another* target.

Hopefully not *you*.

A tangible fear swamps the air as screams of panic fill the night, accompanied by the whine of bullets flying past your ears like a persistent cloud of mosquitoes, and each one of them could end your life. Right here, right now.

It's chaos.

Having said that, this time was different.

For example, there was no screaming.

At all.

No cries, shouts, or yelling. Now, all of the other sounds were still there – bullets hammering into walls, snow embankments, cars, and the other equipment from the news crew, but the crew themselves were as silent as ghosts. Ashley seemed to realize the same phenomenon and glanced back at the crowd of news reporters at the same time I did.

Every single one of them stood completely still. Not even blinking.

"Shit…" I muttered, still scanning the crowd for any signs of movement.

But it was a sea of statues.

That explained the sensation of power I had briefly experienced prior to the first gunshot. Someone was altering time, or at least everyone's perception of it, which never ended well for the people affected.

I had only seen two creatures with that kind of power.

One was an Angel of Heaven, and the other was Jacob Grimm.

My anger evaporated to be replaced by true fear. Panic. My magic withered and died like a guttering candle as the anger disappeared. The Grimms had come for me and I had been caught with my pants down around my ankles, and with a crowd of helpless mortal targets as leverage, and I had no one to help me. No one to back me up as Ashley – a mortal – and I took on the world's most feared assassins.

"Nate?" Ashley asked in alarm. I shook my head, trying desperately to kill my fear. I needed to be angry. Not scared. Otherwise I was just dead weight. I was a spellslinger, god damn it. Ashley needed me to start throwing around balls of fire and death if we were going to survive this. The pep talk helped slowly wear away my fear, but it didn't entirely fade, and my anger remained stubbornly out of reach. And with it, the link to my power.

I needed a few minutes to get my head back in the game, so I assessed the situation.

Apparently, we were the only ones unaffected by the spell. I heard a muffled barking cough, followed by the sound of more cascading glass striking the pavement at the entrance to the building. I quickly peered around the edge of the van and discovered that the attack was coming from *inside* the building.

The security guards. One of them grinned at me from behind a pillar, drawing down.

Noticing my attention, Ashley leaned out over my shoulder and opened fire at the lobby. "Get down!" I yelled, pushing her back to safety.

Bullets pounded the front and side of the van in retaliation. One of the tires blew out with a hiss, and the van lurched downwards with a sharp groan. After a few seconds of constant shooting, I sensed a pause in the exchange, which usually signified reloading. I glanced around the corner, careful to keep my torso behind the fender. But the other shooter had apparently been waiting for me to make that mistake. Shots immediately rang out, hammering into the van all over again, one striking the passenger side mirror.

Which immediately tore free and struck me in the temple.

I hit the ground in a sprawl, ears ringing, and vision swirling lazily. I struggled to get my bearings and find the van but I couldn't make up from down. I was supposed to be doing something. *Get angry*, a voice whispered at the edge of my subconscious, but I couldn't understand how that would help. A wizard's magic had nothing to do with emotion. Sure, being emotional could increase your output, but you didn't have to be emotional to use a wizard's power. You had to be in control of your mind.

Then a thought slowly limped into the forefront of my brain.

*But you're not a wizard anymore...*

Then it hit me, my mind suddenly lurching back into gear. I struggled to get pissed, but the blow to the head had rattled me good. I felt fingers grip my ankle and begin pulling me back to cover, but they weren't fast enough.

Something tugged at the flap of my jacket with a significant amount of force, and I was jerked out of Ashley's reach as a single gunshot coughed. A silencer. Then another blow hammered into my belly and I temporarily lost control of my limbs as my breath shot out of me in a whoosh. The sound of a gunshot came a millisecond after the blow. I glanced down to find a sizeable amount of blood oozing from my stomach. Then the pain struck me. A searing hot stomach cramp from hell.

Then the pain doubled. Then trebled.

I could hear Ashley screaming something before more shots from her twin pistols cracked the air in a steady rhythm. Her barrage apparently gave the gunmen pause because I didn't hear return fire. She grasped my leg and successfully pulled me to safety this time, which felt truly horrible, my stomach knotting up into a tight ball of pain that forced me to curl up into a defensive ball.

I slowly uncurled, leaning my weight against the fender of the van as Ashley quickly checked my wound, hissing as her eyes fell on my stomach. I had been shot. And not by an amateur. Two direct hits with two measured pulls of the trigger.

A marksman. If they could hit that accurately through a glass wall and a hundred feet, they very easily could have killed me dead. Ashley let off another volley of shots around the side of the van, aiming at the interior of the building.

I peered around the corner, unable to stand yet, and saw the gunmen using lobby furniture for cover as they methodically approached, one covering the other's advance before they switched. My anger slowly began to wake, grumbling in response at their skilled approach. Ashley was no soldier. Neither was I. We didn't stand a chance playing the game by their rules. These guys were professional hunters. And I wasn't about to sit here and die behind a news van like some lamed deer. Rage rose like a leviathan out of the deeps, illuminating the world in a dim blue glow as my power roared to life with single-minded purpose.

Self-preservation.

So, it was time for me to do magic and stuff.

I leaned out with a hungry smile, feeling useful again as I cast a shield of air to protect me from oncoming lead. Ashley's bullets struck an invisible dome in front of the advancing gunman but they disintegrated to dusty motes rather than piercing flesh. That was both cool and practical. If I survived, I would have to learn it.

So, like I suspected. Grimms.

We needed a plan. I glanced down only to realize that the satchel was gone. My eyes quested for it in a panic. *There!* I instantly spotted it only a few feet away where I had been shot. Even with access to my power back online, I knew we needed to call in backup, but first I needed to protect the satchel. I began scrambling towards it as I maintained my shield, slipping and sliding in the light smear of blood pooling beneath me, but then a thought hit me and I froze. If I grabbed the satchel, they would know of its importance if they caught me. I quickly managed to scramble back behind the van.

Taking a deep breath filled with pain at my brief foray into the kill zone, I had time to see a bullet enter the crowd, striking one man in the hip, which caused him to drop the microphone pole clutched in his gloved hands before he flew backwards. The pole struck a woman in the temple and she collapsed in frosty silence, but I had seen the explosion of blood from the camera guy and was sure the woman would also have a noticeable lump on her dome, if not a concussion. I couldn't let the Grimms cause any more collateral damage. The reporters were defenseless. And they would die. I took a deep breath and tapped into the well of power, seizing it forcefully rather than wasting time trying to coerce it.

The pool of viscous power rippled in response as if pleased. I didn't have time to analyze that, so I simply latched onto it and sent it coursing deep down into my body, numbing all sensory receptors so that I could move.

"Ashley, cover me!" She didn't hesitate. She unleashed a barrage of lead with both pistols as fast as she could. They disintegrated on impact with the Grimms' shield, but had the desired effect. They paused. I quickly cast a concealment spell on the satchel and used a gust of air to send it deep into the crowd where I hoped it would remain hidden. I then delved deep into the reservoir of power at my feet and imagined a duplicate copy of the satchel and fastened it to my hip. It was weightless, but I hoped it would do the trick. I didn't know if they knew about the satchel of books, but if they did and they saw me fleeing without it – when I had been toting it while exiting the elevator – they might turn back to search for it. But step one, I needed them to *follow* us.

I didn't have a step two for my plan.

I took a deep breath, turning to Ashley with a macabre grin. She was staring at me nervously, no doubt wondering how I was still upright. "Get ready to run."

Her responding nod was less than encouraging.

"Memento Mori," I muttered. Her eyes widened, and she made the sign of the cross over her chest.

Which did absolutely nothing for my morale. She had zero faith in the wounded wizard. Maker. Whatever I was now.

I sighed, hoping she wasn't right.

# CHAPTER 13

*I* lurched to my feet, the pain of my wounds now a dull, distant ache. It would have to be enough. I made sure the shield spell stood between us and prepared to hoof it.

I snatched the back of Ashley's coat and tugged her off to the right, away from the crowd. We ran for several paces with her firing over her shoulder before her guns clicked empty. She muttered a curse, but immediately focused all of her attention on running away, racing beside me with panicked eyes. We were beyond the crowd in a blink, tearing off into the snow-covered grass surrounding the hotel.

Pounding boots tore after us in hot pursuit, somehow sounding like they were gaining on us. Several rounds hammered into my shield but we kept moving, Ashley's eyes were wild, as she no doubt anticipated being gunned down any second. I heard the attackers' guns run dry and I really laid on the speed, hoping they would slow as they reloaded.

Instead I heard one of them laugh hungrily, and the clatter of his gun hit the pavement. He was eager to confront us without guns. Which usually meant the person was experienced with inflicting pain via fists or magic. He let out a howl that turned into a leonine roar, dripping with the anticipation of a proper hunt. I glanced over my shoulder at the terrifying sound, fearing the worst. But I was wrong.

It was worse-er than I could have imagined in my darkest nightmares, and I had spent some time on the receiving end of a true master of the art personally sending me night and day terrors.

For months.

Needless to say, what I saw earned an *A-plus* in the nightmare department.

I stumbled a step in utter disbelief, and immediately decided that the only chance of survival required me to run backwards, even if I did lose speed. Ashley soon began to outpace me, not having turned around to look.

Which was probably better for her sanity.

Because a freaking lion was chasing us. With eyes and mane of living fire.

And the top of the lion's back was about the height of a small horse, making him more akin to a freaking *liger* – yes, they're real – the hybrid offspring of a lion and a tiger. But this one looked to have fed on annoying wizards and an unhealthy dose of steroids for breakfast every morning for the past twenty years.

The other Grimm somehow managed to maintain the same speed as the liger, which just wasn't fair. We didn't stand a chance outrunning them.

Then the freaking scenery changed and I suddenly found myself racing through the equivalent of the African Savannah rather than snow covered grass. I spotted a herd of motionless gazelles where the reporters had been, and felt a faint whisper of an icy wind ruffle my shaggy hair. I didn't even slow down, well past my disbelief quota for the day. So, I rolled with it, but I heard Ashley let out a sharp exhale of surprise. Still, she didn't slow down either, apparently accepting our teleportation without breaking stride. Either that or the Grimms had simply made it *look* like we had been teleported to a new location.

Yeah, that jived. *Fear.* They were trying to scare us. Now, being chased by a liger was terrifying. But being chased by a liger while suddenly being teleported to the African Savannah was a whole new level. Well, for most sane people anyway.

But Ashley and I were well beyond sane.

Without completely understanding how, I cast a cord of supercharged electricity behind us in a makeshift trip line. The spell crackled with purple energy across the ground, arcs of power sporadically zapping to ash anything it deemed alive. Then it disappeared from view. Invisible.

Huh.

I hadn't ever thought of doing anything like that before.

Without allowing myself to get caught up in the magic – *heh* – of my strange new powers, I copied the spell two more times, staggering their spacing in hopes that at least one would nab the liger, and switched the type of destructive power for each – one made of flowing lava and one of razor sharp crystals – both invisible. Remembering the size of the racing fire liger, I imagined that the height of the trip wires was a foot higher. Not being able to see it, I took it on faith that it was in fact higher than I had first seen it. I just hoped that the Grimms either hadn't seen it in their hunger for the chase, or at least didn't remember exactly where it had been.

Then the other Grimm decided he didn't want to be left out of the shapeshifting party, and shed his mortal skin midstride.

Again, it was really good that Ashley hadn't turned around. At least she wouldn't die with the shame of soiled pants. Even for me it was a close call as my eyes widened in further disbelief.

"Oh, come on!" I complained under my huffing breaths.

I managed to keep shuffling backwards in a clumsy run as I watched him shift into a freaking ape like Caesar from that new *Planet of the Apes* movie franchise, fully decked out in armor that covered his thickly muscled frame. He clutched a wicked looking bone-tipped spear in his stupid opposable thumbed fist. The twinkle in his eyes reminded me of how eerily intelligent Caesar had been in the movie.

But the Grimm looked smarter.

Proving this point, he launched himself onto the liger's back and they really began to pour on the speed, small craters of flame erupting with each strike of paw to sand.

The ape let out an ululating cry of glee from astride the liger as he pointed at my satchel with his spear.

The liger let out a roar of such ferocity I could practically feel it.

I opened my mouth to shout a defiant yell of my own, not wanting to feel left out, and immediately slammed into a warm body, my head cracking against another skull. My vision exploded in a supernova of stars. The sounds of pursuit rose in pitch. I managed to see Ashley lying beneath me, clutching her head with a groan. She had stopped for some reason, and since I had been running backwards I hadn't realized it until it was too late.

I managed to gain enough control over my body to look back and face our impending death. I realized my hand was resting on Ashley's rear end for support, which was firmer than I would have thought.

Gunnar and Indie would have killed me for that.

But I didn't have time to worry about Gunnar or Indie. It was over. Even as a Maker, I didn't have the juice to stand up to two of these things by myself, not while trying to keep an incapacitated Ashley safe. I murmured a goodbye to Indie under my breath, and pulled deep on the strange reservoir of power, clawing for something I could do to them as a final attack. I might die here, but at least I would go down fighting.

The liger jumped, fiery mane rippling in the wind as it sailed through the air in a parabolic arc that would end at my face. The ape reared back to launch his spear with a precision that had to have been rehearsed.

The motion drew my attention to a spot just below them a second before he loosed the spear.

A small purple flicker of hope among the desert brush.

I frantically imagined that the trip wire was higher. In fact, I imagined it was *exactly* where the Grimms were.

One second they were flying at my face, and the next thing I knew there was a purple implosion in the air. A wave of grit pelted us like a miniature sandstorm before I managed to shield my eyes with my sleeve.

I gagged, coughing up a mouthful of Grimm grit as I leaned to the side in case I retched. My head butted into a shaft of solid oak quivering in the earth beside me, directly between Ashley's legs. I looked up to see her staring at the spear that had almost killed her. Then her eyes rose to mine in wide-eyed disbelief. I'm sure my face was the same. The scenery abruptly snapped back to the chilly winter streets of St. Louis with a faint *pop*. She didn't even comment on *that*.

"A *liger?*" She whispered. "Why didn't you tell me there was a freaking liger chasing us?" She stammered in disbelief.

I shrugged, taking a shallow breath in case the air was still tainted with Grimm particles. I hadn't known she had seen any of it, assuming she had been down for the count. "That was nothing. Did you see the ape riding on his back?" She blinked at me. "That was his." I pointed at the spear. Her eyes darted to the spear, then back to me. "You can have it. I've already got one." I muttered woozily, clutching my stomach as a sharp burst of pain broke through my control. My fingers came back wet with blood, but I didn't let Ashley see.

And then she began to laugh, her brain unable to comprehend the situation in its entirety. After a few seconds, I joined her. I slowly climbed to my feet with a groan.

I glanced at the now snowy ground, idly wondering about the brief excursion into the Savannah and if it had merely been an illusion rather than a teleportation. Judging by its disappearance after the Grimms died I was betting so. Otherwise we would have been wandering around the desert right about now. "We probably need to get ba–"

"Your stomach!" Ashley jumped to her feet, gripping my shoulder as if I was about to fall down. "We need to get you to a hosp–"

"No," I gripped her arm to enunciate. She looked me in the eyes, frowning, ready to argue. "No way. No hospitals. I'm fine. For now, but we need to get back to the crowd and get my satchel. Now. Before it disappears or in case there were more of them."

I spotted a shiny item on the ground, and like all girls, squirrels, and toddlers, I made a move to grab it. I picked up a pair of ancient looking amulets right below where the Grimms had imploded in the air.

"What are they?" Ashley asked, peering over my shoulder curiously. I shoved them into my pocket for later.

"I have no idea. Let's go. Some of the reporters were injured."

We began to jog drunkenly back to the building, both our heads still a little woozy, but determined to retrieve the satchel and offer what help we could. We found the people milling about in a frenzied mass at the scene of the gunfight. Several Board Members stood apart, assessing the broken glass, and a small swarm surrounded the injured reporters, but the rest had turned on their cameras to document everything. Everyone froze at our approach.

And waited, unspeaking.

I cleared my throat, fighting my growing nausea. "The security guards tried to kill Ashley and me with machine guns." I mentally squirmed at the upcoming lie forming on my lips. "We chased them away, but they escaped in a waiting van and we lost them." I spotted the approximate location where the satchel should have been and sent out an invisible feeler to sweep the ground. I felt a slight resistance but when no one shrieked about someone grabbing their foot, I knew I had guessed right. I pulled it closer to hover beside me, still invisible. I could feel my power slowly fading, and the pain coming back.

"You chased them away…" One reporter murmured loud enough for all to hear. "Two men with machine guns." I nodded, trying to remain on my feet as the power began to leak out of me at a faster rate. The reporter met my eyes with a disbelieving look. "That none of us saw…"

I blinked sluggishly in response. Ashley swooped in to save me. "Yes. You'll find shell casings from my Glock 19's around here as well as those from the security guards."

"He's bleeding!" One of the reporters shouted, pointing at my stomach.

I glanced down and staggered at the sight. There was a lot of blood. Ashley suddenly gripped my arm, whispering in my ear. "We need to get you help, *now!*" She hissed. I nodded, feeling overwhelmingly dizzy as my magic went out with a weak puff, bringing back the pain like a surprise sledgehammer blow. My knees buckled at the agony, but Ashley held me, and immediately guided me towards a waiting taxi. I heard the sounds of her speaking to the driver, but couldn't understand the words. The world seemed muted by a fuzzy down blanket of lead, and a throbbing fire ate at my stomach.

I managed to mumble over my shoulder before Ashley was able to stop me. "I'm not selling Temple Industries." The crowd erupted with noise, before the car door slammed shut.

The car pulled out onto the icy streets and we fled, no doubt to avoid any authorities. I closed my eyes, and my breath began to increase in ragged pulls as I tried to remember the fight. Why hadn't the Grimms attacked in full force after the first salvo? Seeing a wounded wizard on the ground should have upped their bloodlust, but they hadn't come for me when they had held the best chance for success. Instead, their gaze had been fixated on my satchel. I had a leak somewhere. And only my inner circle knew what was inside the satchel. Unless it was just a lucky guess on their part.

I listened to the gentle lullaby of the tires on snow, trying to gather my thoughts. I glanced down and wished I hadn't. Apparently the Grimms had got me good and I had lost enough blood to convince my brain to do a hard reset. The darkness began to pull me under and I smiled, listening to Ashley yell something about a hospital to the driver.

"No, *Chateau Falco*." I murmured. Ashley shot me a nervous look, but I went *nighty-night* instead of waiting for her response.

# CHAPTER 14

*I* woke up a few subjective centuries later, instantly thrashing about wildly with my hands and breathing in short strangled gasps as I realized I didn't have-

"Easy, Nate. It's right here." Ashley offered the satchel to me. We were both in the back seat. I snatched it greedily from her hands, opening it to glance inside and verify the books were safe. I even risked lowering the wards for a moment to check that they weren't plants but the real books. We were driving, so I felt relatively safe that the Grimms would have a hard time tracking me while on the move. I hoped I wasn't underestimating them. I let out a sigh that sent a spasm of pain through my abdominal wall. I glanced down.

Oh yeah. Gut shot.

Curling my head to look at it caused the pain to flare again, but not as badly this time. My body had evidently grown used to the idea that the pain wasn't going anywhere anytime soon, so had welcomed the new wound to the numerous neighbors of older wounds I had accumulated over the years.

"So, how in the hell did we get back to St. Louis?" Ashley asked, noticing that I was fully awake.

"What?"

"I'm pretty sure we visited the desert for a while there."

I looked out the window, remembering the Grimm's transformation of their own bodies, and then the very reality around us. "What do you think of when you think of the African Savannah?"

She turned to look at me. "Danger. The hunt of predatory animals. Why?"

I nodded. "I don't think we actually changed locations. I think they just made the environment *look* like the Savannah. For the fear factor. To mess with us. Scared prey makes mistakes. I think it was a form of glamour." She blinked at me in disbelief. I could get that. I mean, on the fly they had managed to successfully alter every detail well enough to convince us we were on the Plains, running for our lives. "Did you see the gazelles?" She shook her head with furrowed eyebrows. "That was the reporters. Innocent, harmless, large group of creatures just standing there doing nothing." She blinked at me. Managing to make it look doubtful. "Look, a real herd of gazelles would have bolted at the first roar, right?" she looked thoughtful, nodding finally.

"Wow. That's... frightening. Is there a way to see through glamour? What if they do it again when we aren't expecting it? We think we're walking into *Chateau Falco* and really we're walking into their arms."

I shook my head. "It's not that easy. We were running for our lives. I'm pretty sure they would need us to be at least as keyed up as that in order to believe it. After all, they can't change every detail." At least these two Grimms hadn't been able to. "Did you feel the cool wind?"

She thought about it then shook her head.

"I did. It's what tipped me off. We just need to be hyper aware from now on. Look for inconsistencies in our environment."

She shivered. "Okay. I'll try. We need to warn the others. No wonder these guys have been so successful in killing off freaks. If they can trick their prey with glamour..."

I nodded morosely. She wasn't even bringing up the worst part. These two had shifted into uber-predator monsters. A fire-Liger and an intelligent cave-ape.

The driver made a left turn and I frowned. I hit the glass with a fist. "You're going the wrong way." The driver didn't acknowledge me and I felt a mild freak out coming on. Ashley noticed and began rattling the door handles and pushing the window buttons, but they were all locked up tight. She immediately pulled out one of her pistols and held it up to the window separating us from the driver. All I could see was a black, wiry beard and a

*Fidel Castro* looking cap – or whatever they were called. Then she tapped the window in warning, staring into the rearview mirror. "Stop. The. Car."

The man lifted his eyes to meet mine and I frowned. He looked familiar. Then he tore off his hat and his fake beard. He pulled out two molded hunks of silly putty from inside his mouth, deflating his cheeks, and peeled off both a wart and a particularly nasty liver spot stuck to his cheek with adhesive. I began to laugh and waved for Ashley to withdraw the gun.

"Laddie," the man spoke with his usual Scottish brogue after rolling the dividing window down. "Thought you might need an extra set of eyes. One of my boys was on sniper duty outside the hotel, but his shots didn't seem to bother 'em too much. We'll upgrade our arsenal. Apparently, we needed big game ammunition and an elephant rifle after they shifted." He grunted. I was still reeling from the fact that Mallory had *boys* on the payroll. "Ye' did good. But I reckon we stop and get ye' patched up. Here. Now." He pulled over into a deserted church parking lot in a quiet section of town.

"Why? Let's go to *Chateau Falco*. I need to talk to everyone."

"That can wait," he mumbled, and then climbed out of the car. I began to open my now unlocked door, but Ashley gripped my hand.

"He's probably right."

I frowned at her.

"I wasn't asking for a vote. The others could be in danger. I need to get to them before the Grimms do."

"Not with a leaky stomach." Mallory grunted, opening my door and letting out all the hot air. He was clutching a familiar leather valise that belonged to Dean. He knelt on the slushy asphalt, giving me no room to climb out. "Stay in the car. We don't want a crowd seeing what we're doing."

I grunted. "Well this sure won't attract a nosy old lady's attention." I motioned at the sight of a man kneeling over the lap of another man in a parked car in a church parking lot.

Mallory chuckled. "Your car door is facing the church, which is empty. No one to see what looks like your everyday... *man on man action.*" He laughed harder at Ashley's suddenly blushing cheeks. But instead of wimping out, Ashley held out her hands, inviting me to lean back so Mallory could get at my stomach. I sighed. Her chest did look rather comfortable – it came stocked with twin pillows that looked truly inviting – even if her werewolf fiancé would rip my eyes out for even teasing about it. Ashley shook her head and flicked my nose.

"I won't tell if you don't," she teased.

"Given your fiancé, that sounds almost as dire as you saying, *here, hold my beer for a second and watch this*! Usually never ends well." She laughed lightly and I turned my head before relaxing into her chest and lifting my shirt over my wound.

Yep.

Her pillows were great. In a strictly professional medical assessment. Better than any doctor's office bed I had sat in.

Mallory got to work instantly, cleaning the wound with iodine, which felt like slightly cooled lava and sulfuric acid had made a love child. I hissed a bit and Mallory rolled his eyes before continuing. I glanced down to see the wound and my guts did a nauseating little flip-flop. It wasn't pretty. The bullets had hit the side of my abdomen. I closed my eyes, not wanting to throw up on Ashley and ruin my very temporary pillows. Ashley sucked in a sharp breath as she saw the wound up close. Her hands instantly went to my scalp, fingers massaging idly.

"I'm so sorry, Nate. You should have had Gunnar or someone else here. Not me. I don't have a lick of power. This is my fault. If you hadn't been watching out for me, you could have laid waste to them without worrying about collateral damage."

I reached up and squeezed her hand, not immediately telling her the truth of the situation. I almost hadn't been able to tap into my power in time to do us any good. "You did great. Seriously. Great shooting skills. This had nothing to do with me being distracted. These guys are just that good. I'm lucky you were there." I hissed at a sharp pain from my stomach before admitting the truth aloud. "I'm not as formidable as I used to be. I'm still learning about my new powers. It will be a little while before I'm back to my old level. You saved us both, Annie Oakley."

She chuckled with a barely restrained sob, and then continued massaging my head.

"I'm going to take the bullet out now."

"If the bullet broke into my stomach wall, mind shoving a protein bar in there for me? I'm starving."

"Fresh out. But I think it missed the organ anyway."

"Okay. Ready, I guess."

Then the wound was spread open further, twisted up, squeezed, and generally abused for a few excruciating seconds. Ashley groaned at the sight, increasing her massage reflexively. It didn't help me ignore the pain.

Mallory finally grunted and pulled something out with a wet sucking sound. I looked down to see him holding up a small piece of metal. "Huh. Small caliber." He looked up at my eyes. "They weren't trying to kill you," he said ominously.

I shivered, kind of hoping it had been the opposite. I didn't want to imagine why they wanted me incapacitated but alive.

"Now if the bullet had been anything larger caliber, your coat wouldn't have prevented it from entering 'yer stomach, which would have guaranteed a hospital trip, and likely death," he added soberly. I grunted.

"Maybe I should go buy a lottery ticket."

Mallory wordlessly began closing up the wound. I suddenly felt a gentle warmth pulsing from his fingers and my eyes shot wide open as I watched him. He glanced up once, a look of mild embarrassment flashing to a warning frown, calmly, harshly, commanding me to seal my lips. I watched in awe as the power dribbled from his fingertips, a golden glow like magic dust forming the shape of a knot before settling inside my wounds. Ashley didn't seem to notice. With the sensation came the realization that my power was roaring back into me, leaving me feeling refreshed and no longer exhausted. In fact, I felt downright chipper. He wiped it down when finished, and wrapped me up with gauze before Ashley helped me to sit up fully. Mallory shot me a look, shook his head once, and then packed up his bag, closed the door, and got back behind the wheel. I stared at the back of his head thoughtfully as he started the car and we began to pull out of the parking lot, the talking heads on the radio idly chattering in the background.

Looks like Mallory and I needed to have a chat soon. But he was right. Not now.

I felt a weight in my coat pocket and stuck my fist in there to see what it was. My fingers closed around an unfamiliar shape and I blinked. I pulled out a long, heavy chain with an amulet attached to the end. Another rested within the pocket but I left it alone.

I held it up to the light and watched a pendant swing by a thick, linked chain of an unfamiliar metal. An obsidian gem hung in the shape of a double crescent, like that of an axe, encased in a ring of blood red stone to hold it in place. Power ebbed from the amulet, and I felt a minor resonance deep within my own reservoir of power.

But I also felt a darkness. A hunger to consume. I shivered and shoved it in my pocket. I hoped it wouldn't contaminate me or anything sinister like that.

*"In last night's news, a local land owner woke up in the middle of the night to find his fields burning with a wildfire the likes of which St. Louis has never seen. Police have been on site trying to discover the source of the blaze, but have found no help from the land owner, Mr. Kingston."*

My breath caught as the name rang a bell. "Stop the car."

Mallory did, looking around cautiously for an impending attack.

"We need to go to that farm."

"What farm, Laddie? We're in the middle of the city."

"The one on the radio. I know it. A friend lives there."

Ashley looked at me. "Do you really think you have time for that? They didn't say anything about any injuries. The landowner is fine. Just a fire."

"You're going to have to trust me on this. It's not the farmer I'm worried about."

Mallory eyed me in the rearview mirror. "If 'yer certain 'bout it..."

I nodded. "Drive."

I hoped Asterion, the Minotaur, was safe. His relationship with me had apparently made him a target too.

God damn the Grimms.

# CHAPTER 15

*W*e pulled up to the farmer's house, which looked much... wealthier than I remembered, although I really hadn't spent any time in any place but his fields. But I did remember seeing it from a distance, and I recalled it looking like any farm you might find in any section of the Midwest. Nothing special. But the home in front of me wasn't similar to any farm I had ever seen in my life.

At all. I briefly wondered if we were at the right place, but the heavy scent of smoke made it pretty obvious. There wasn't another home for miles.

Mr. Kingston's farming operation looked *mysteriously* successful. Something was odd about the structure, but I was too busy scanning for threats and masking my dull pain to spot what exactly had caught my attention. Mallory's unspoken power had helped, but not eliminated my discomfort. Still, my magic was back, which was a plus.

No police presence was in sight, but I was still nervous. I didn't want my name attached as a person of interest to whatever had gone down here, especially after the Board meeting. I'd had enough of affiliating with crime scenes in the past. In fact, I had once been arrested in the very field adjacent to Kingston's house, and declared high on 'shrooms. All because my car had been spotted outside the field and the police had wanted to question me about my parents' murder. Poor timing to say the least.

The detective in charge of that particular investigation had suffered quite the career change as a result of my not so subtle retaliation. Something to do with pictures of him in bondage gear or some kind of deviant outfit appearing in a file on a policeman's desk, as well as documentation of his secret interest in certain dark Craigslist ads, which had immediately been publicized via the local news channel. I actually wasn't sure if he was even in police work anymore. The world was a better place for it. He had been an incompetent hack, and a danger to citizens everywhere he had jurisdiction. He was more interested in the collar than the crime. The fame more than the justice.

I had... *fixed* that.

Allegedly.

Heh.

I studied the house, the shadows, the barn, the garage, and every single tree within jumping distance of a liger or an intelligent ape. But I saw nothing. If the Grimms had truly been behind the blaze, I didn't want to be caught with my pants around my ankles again. Especially after taking down two of their brothers. How many did that make now? Ten? More? Could they call in reinforcements quickly or did they need the book first?

Mallory clicked off the engine.

We sat there for a few minutes, listening to the engine cycle down.

Then the scene before us abruptly folded in on itself like a mirage, and a very normal quaint looking farm briefly stood in its place. Mallory grunted, and Ashley gasped. The familiar farm I had seen in the past, complete with a worn-out barn and broken fence stood before us. Then another ripple to the air and the wealthy farm was back. The scene remained solidly on the wealthy farm for a good ten seconds before I shook my head. My friends were staring at me, waiting for an explanation, but I had none. Well, *that* was a first. I was beginning to realize that perhaps it wasn't a coincidence that the Minotaur resided nearby.

There was magic hinkyness afoot.

Before anyone could speak I opened my door. The front door to the house opened at the exact same time. I stayed in place, not wanting to appear threatening to an elderly farmer. They tended to shoot trespassers. I imagined him growling, *Get off my lawn*, like that Clint Eastwood movie, before whipping out a twelve-gauge exclamation mark.

Listen, farmers don't mess around. Welcome to the Midwest, folks. It's dangerous.

I studied the man, face neutral and unthreatening, peaceful even.

Unless I was grimacing. I *was* in pain after all, despite Mallory's mysterious magic. The spell I used to mask pain worked to some extent, but only to hide it, not eliminate it. My face could have been set in a perpetual scowl without my realizing it. An instinctive muscle formation. I would have to look in the mirror to know for sure, but thought that would only encourage the farmer's *City Slicker* impression of me. I waved a hand and then shoved them in my coat pockets, looking relaxed.

The farmer stared at me.

Not Mallory or Ashley.

Me.

His glittering eyes didn't blink. We were close enough for me to see the hard lines on his face. He wore a casual fitting dress shirt, sported golden hair that just brushed his shoulders, and wore what looked like designer jeans and expensive as hell gator cowboy boots with a fat, glittering belt buckle.

In fact, despite the boots and belt buckle, he didn't look like a farmer at all.

My eyes roved to his face to see that he was still staring at me. He had a weathered face, with piercing hawk-like eyes that seemed to calculate me down to the individual hairs on my head, and his sudden grin looked like he was confident that his estimation was as accurate as only my accountant – or my mother – could ascertain.

It was chilling.

"Please. Come in." He called out in a clear, authoritative voice. Then he turned back into the house, not waiting for us.

Mallory and Ashley blinked and then looked at me to silently gauge my response. I shrugged with a smirk and said, "Let's go talk to Mr. Not Farmer."

Mallory grunted in agreement.

There were, after all, no plants anywhere. Only cows in the field beside the house. Now, I didn't know cows very well, but one thing stuck out as odd to me. These beasts were spotless. As in, they looked to have never experienced a fleck of dirt or shit on their coats for more than a day. And the fields were also pristine. No gaping mud pits, and it seemed the patties were more or less centralized to one corner of the field, because the section they were standing in was green as green could be, not a single defecation crater in sight. As if to point out this fact, one of the beasts slowly began meandering towards that section of the field, just like a regular person would head to the restroom. She did her business, turned around, and reentered the herd, tail still spotless.

Huh.

Trained to shit in one spot? Some trick.

I also noticed that the odorous part of the field was as far as possible from the house.

Then there was the house itself.

It was no farmhouse.

It more resembled a stone castle dressed in modern clothing, like it had harbored a brief real estate identity crisis. Pillars supported a second-floor balcony that wrapped around the entire front of the house, and I spotted a wide sliding glass door that no doubt led to a living area or the master bedroom on the upper floor. Expensive shutters hung outside the windows, looking to be painted gold, and immaculate garden work had turned the property to the American equivalent of an English Lord's estate, with plenty of large trees that hunched over soothing seating areas complete with benches or swings. The pile had to be several thousand square feet, but I only saw one car.

A Bentley.

New.

Gleaming farm equipment stood in an open barn that looked more like a luxury Quonset Hut that those modernists seemed to recently love as a primary home. Windows, log siding, and a spotless cement floor. The equipment all looked new. Unused.

Weird.

"Yeah," I muttered. "My Spidey sense is tingling. This guy seems like runner up to the most interesting man in the world."

Mallory and Ashley had followed my gaze, seeming to come to the same conclusion.

I reached the expensive oak door, complete with a distinct set of scales burned into the wood. I knocked. It was partly open, but still, even though he had invited us in I didn't want to just enter. What if he was a Grimm? Or the Grimms had him under duress? I readied my anger, feeling the pleasant thrum of power at my feet, even though less than an hour ago, I had been drained. I definitely needed to drill Mallory on his past. But not now. I checked the pistol Mallory had handed me, tucked it back in my coat, and entered after I heard a distant, *come in.*

I gently pushed the door open and it stopped after a foot, catching on a rich Persian Rug. Rich as in far superior to anything I had decorating *Chateau Falco.* My eyes traveled up to the walls to find true works of art casually adorning the plaster without embellishment – Renaissance pieces, portraits, battles, and then a smattering of specifically chosen more modern work that I also noticed were expensive – not worth the cost in my taste, but to each his own.

The floors were made of a single sheet of polished marble, not sections of tile, and tables lined each wall of the seven-foot wide entrance hall, each holding figurines, clay vases and bowls, and other decorations that were both tasteful and a profound display of wealth in their own right. Gold and jewels glittered like nightlights. And this was only the entrance to his home.

It was like standing in the waiting room outside Smaug's cave.

Was his wife a billionaire interior decorator? Or did he inherit a pile of money at some point? None of it made sense to me, which put me on edge.

Mallory and Ashley were no strangers to being around money, having spent a considerable amount of time around my parents, myself, and at *Chateau Falco,* but that only seemed to make their awe more impressive. They looked dumbstruck at the contradiction of a wealthy farmer. I snapped my fingers. "Pick up your jaws. We'll discuss it after. Act casual, friendly, and polite. Extremely polite. It's like cocaine to rich people. They want you to know how much better than you they are, and that you openly acknowledge it. Don't act like bumpkins or they will lose respect for you. Thank him for his hospitality. Compliment him on his beautiful home and things. Then politely sit there and let me do the talking."

They nodded and followed me down the hall. We entered a spacious living area that looked like it belonged on the cover of *Log Cabins for the Stupidly Rich.* A massive six-foot wide by four-foot tall two-way fireplace centered the room, also made of some flavor of marble, and a hundred thousand dollars' worth of aged leather Chesterfields (plural) formed an arc around each side of the soothing fire, essentially creating two living areas, or two sections of one giant living area, like an Aspen Ski Resort.

A bar stood off to the side, fully stocked with a selection that only a single man would need. No fruity drinks. Just scotch, whisky, and a twenty-foot tall glass-fronted wine rack, complete with amber lighting and title placards with a brief paragraph neatly written underneath each bottle. Notes on the taste, vintage, and grading of each bottle were scribbled in a precise hand. Was he a sommelier? I noticed that the wine closet extended several feet back, telling me that he didn't just have what was visible to the room, but at least six backups of *each visible bottle*. The guy obviously liked his wine. A quick scan of the selection let me know that he collected nothing costing less than two hundred bucks a bottle.

More exquisite artwork decorated the walls, entirely out of place in a farmhouse. In fact, it was more fitting for a wealthy European Baron of some kind. I didn't even bother to further assess the value of the rest of the shiny artifacts and *objets d'art* surrounding us. Safe to say, none of it would ever be sold at *Ikea*.

Farmer Kingston sat in one of the Chesterfield chairs facing away from us, watching the fire contentedly. His shoulders were entirely relaxed, and if I had to guess, he seemed genuinely pleased at the occasional sounds coming from our throats, as if he didn't often get the chance to share his collection and was enjoying our honest reaction, and giving us the solitude to enjoy it without him watching us.

My cynical side reared his ugly head. Pretty trusting guy to turn his back on us with all this money lying around. Three of us against a lone senior citizen. It wouldn't have been difficult to rob him blind.

Which usually was a sign that we really, *really* shouldn't think of robbing him blind.

He slowly turned to face me, sensing my gaze, and took a sip of the drink clutched in his scarred fist. His hard gaze told me that he knew what I had been thinking, and that I had been spot on. Ashley and Mallory had finished their circuit and now stood beside me.

His eyes crinkled at the corners as he slowly cracked a polite smile. He motioned for us to sit and join him. A serving tray with an unopened bottle of *Johnnie Walker Blue Label* and three fresh glasses with crisp white napkins artfully rolled inside each sat on the artful coffee table between us. A meat and cheese tray piled high with rolls of salami, hard cured sausage, and small wheels of assorted cheeses rested on a wooden platter beside a large bowl of fat, juicy grapes, complete with stems. None of it looked like it would be available at the local grocery store, but more like it had been harvested fresh on the property. Which obviously couldn't be true this time of year. But I didn't voice my thoughts. Instead, I smiled politely and took a seat in the chair opposite Kingston. Ashley and Mallory sat on the adjacent couch eagerly eyeing the platter.

"So, been farming lon–" I began.

Kingston cleared his throat pointedly with a sharp glance my way. "Please, be my guests. Help yourselves." He motioned to the food and drink. A bucket of ice sat on the opposite side of the tray as the bowl of grapes. Mallory began to reach for the ice but Kingston made a grunt. We all looked up at him. He pointed a finger at me. "Serve them." I blinked.

"I like this guy." Ashley murmured with a light laugh. I dipped my head in acknowledgment of Kingston's game. It seemed pretty obvious that he knew who I was and that he thought forcing me to perform an act of servitude would bother me. In all fairness, it definitely would have bothered most billionaire heirs.

But he didn't seem to know that I had basically been a bachelor for the past few years. Rather than freeloading at my parents' mansion, swimming in piles of money *Scrooge McDuck* style, I had instead chosen to open and operate a successful bookstore. By a combination of my bootstraps and a loan from my father to help purchase the real estate – which I had repaid in full and on time – I had opened the trendiest and most exclusive supernatural bookstore for hundreds of miles, only hiring help once the operation grew beyond my scope to efficiently handle. I hadn't outsourced it like most heirs did with new business ventures. I understood all too well that a true leader served from the front, rather than whipping his people from behind. And that no one could get behind a man's cause if he wasn't behind it himself.

But...

Hadn't I done exactly that with Temple Industries? The thought hit me like a slap to the cheek and I stood motionless for a subjective minute, but likely only an objective second.

Perhaps I had something to learn after all. I shelved the thought for later, avoiding Ashley's eyes out of guilt at my revelation.

But Kingston couldn't know any of that. So, a test.

I decided to have some fun with it.

I carefully plucked each napkin from the glass, and – mimicking my Butler, Dean – unfurled them with two sharp snaps of my wrist before expertly placing one on both Mallory and Ashley's laps. I selected one of their glasses, picked up the ice tongs from the bucket, and asked, "How many cubes, Miss?"

Ashley was gobbling it up. "Four, please, good sir." She answered haughtily.

I did as requested. "And how many fingers do you prefer, Miss?" I asked, keeping my face professionally servile, fighting to hide my smile at her instantly blushing face. She also looked confused. Served her right.

"Apologize." Kingston murmured, not looking amused.

I nodded, feigning confusion. "My apologies, Miss. I didn't mean to offend. Scotch is often measured in fingers, like so." I held up two fingers parallel to the bottom of the glass, "Two fingers," I added another digit, "And three fingers. How many would you prefer, Miss?"

She scowled up at me, no longer enjoying the game as much. "Two. I'm not much of a scotch drinker."

"I'm confident that your opinion is about to change. This is an exceptionally smooth scotch with sweet undertones. Our Host has excellent taste." I nodded deferentially at Kingston. "Let the drink rest for one minute or so to give time for the melting ice to break down the scotch a bit." She nodded, taking the glass from my outstretched hand.

I turned to Mallory, but he didn't let me speak. "Four fingers, one whisky ball." I managed to hide my scowl and turned to Kingston. He pointed at the bar with a faint grin.

"In the freezer. Don't dawdle now, son."

I stood, hiding my growing impatience. I had just wanted to see if my friend, the Minotaur, was safe from the fire, but here I was playing Jeeves to assure an old man I wasn't a worthless heir. This was going beyond the pale. But it was a test. And I always passed tests. I used the brief walk to cool my heels. A little humility was good for one's moral character. As long as this guy had something worthwhile to tell us and wasn't simply fishing for a fun story to share with his pals.

I withdrew a fresh glass from the bar and opened the freezer. I instantly spotted the row of spherical ice cubes the size of small racquetballs. I set one gently inside the glass, closed the freezer, and returned to the table. Mallory looked ready to critique, but I knew better. Dean had been the best Butler I had ever seen, he had served hundreds of guests thousands of drinks at Temple functions, and I had paid close attention to his process.

I poured four fingers into the empty glass before Mallory, whisked the glass up with a spare napkin I had nabbed from the bar, and finally poured it over the top of the ice ball in the fresh glass from the bar. He settled back in his seat, looking disappointed he hadn't been able to correct me. I offered him the drink, tucking the other glass behind my back. "I hope the Gentleman enjoys the drink. Is there anything else I may do for you?" I asked, risking a glance at Kingston after my minions shook their heads and took sips of their drinks. Ashley looked impressed, while Mallory looked as if he had found a second home. Kingston nodded in approval and motioned me to sit down. "Any more tests—"

"I find that on a regular basis, it is beneficial to realize where your enjoyments come from, and how much work is done to bring them to you. To put yourself in their shoes once in a while." He spoke in a deep baritone to no one in particular. I nodded.

"You obviously recognize me."

He nodded, unimpressed. "Pour yourself a drink, sit back, be quiet, and listen, Temple. You might learn something." Then he turned to Ashley and Mallory, leaving me to stare back in surprise. "My name is Kingston. Welcome to my humble estate. I'm sure you're interested in the fire last night, but I want to hear more about you before we talk business." He didn't look in my direction, and I could feel Ashley's tension grow as it became apparent that she was the center of attention, not me.

I poured a few fingers of scotch, and after a moment's hesitation added two more. I scowled at nothing in particular as I realized I also wanted one of those damn ice balls. I began to stand.

Kingston lifted a hooded glare my way. That was all. Just a look.

I found myself sitting back down by reflex. He nodded once, returning his attention to Ashley. I sighed, adding a few ice cubes to my drink. Then I leaned back as Kingston peppered Ashley and Mallory with polite questions. He was relentless, wanting to know everything about them.

But it was the darndest thing.

He wasn't interested in anything, well… *important.*

Instead, he seemed only interested in mundane things. *What they did for a living and if they enjoyed it? Their fondest childhood memory and what made it so important to them? Who would they most like to meet, both alive and dead? What did they do for enjoyment and why? If they had family, and if those loved ones lived nearby or out of town?* We had each managed to polish off a plate of the delicious food during our talk. Time stretched on, and I found myself feeling rather sleepy, the ache in my stomach a gentle lullaby of faint discomfort, manageable and almost possible to completely ignore thanks to the spell and the pain-calluses I had obviously formed.

The room grew silent, drawing me out of my daze to see Kingston nodding in genuine appreciation. "Thank you for sharing your life with me." He smiled at Ashley, eyes crinkling at the corners in worn, often used lines. "I find it beneficial to understand the true nature of a man – or woman – prior to discussing business. Now that you have satisfied a lonely old man's curiosity, how may I be of assistance?"

He turned to me, waiting expectantly. I guessed it was finally my turn, although I found it curious he hadn't also peppered me with a background check. Perhaps he already knew enough about me, or more likely, all he had had left to learn about me was my character, which I hoped had been learned by watching me play servant earlier.

I must have passed his test, so I leaned forward to play word games with the mysterious old man, wondering what I may have gotten us into by stopping in to check on Asterion, the Minotaur.

# CHAPTER 16

*I* chose my words carefully. We still knew nothing about the man. I couldn't confidently answer whether or not he was clued in on the supernatural community at large. He could just be a wealthy old guy living out his days at the back end of nowhere.

Or he could be something else entirely.

Mallory had eagerly filled a second plate at some point and was now wolfing it down as if it were his last meal. My own now empty plate sat before me. Ashley was leaning back into the couch, legs tucked beneath her hips, looking stuffed and sleepy.

"I was concerned when I heard about the fire. As I'm sure you are aware, I was once arrested on your property a few years ago, by an upstart police detective looking to make a name for himself by single-handedly solving a celebrity murder investigation."

"Your parents." He answered, eyes distant.

I didn't pounce on the answer like I would have in the past, demanding to hear if he had known my parents before their murder. One, because I had already found the killer, punished him personally, claiming my rightful vengeance and burying the hatchet, so to speak. It still hurt to think about, but not many people had the option to speak with the spirits of their deceased relatives from beyond the grave. I had it better than most, but it was still a sucky situation. I would have given anything to have them back in the land of the living. I could really use their help right about now, which briefly brought my thoughts back to the suspiciously locked-down Armory. Kingston watched my eyes thoughtfully but didn't speak.

"You didn't press charges, for which I thank you." He nodded, more in appreciation of my thanks than in acknowledgment of his choice to not press charges. I took a sip of my drink, thinking. "May I ask why you chose not to do so? I was obviously trespassing, and you must wonder what I was doing on your proper–"

"You were visiting a friend." He answered simply. I blinked, not sure how to respond. Kingston saved me from over thinking it. "He told me afterwards. Asked if I would grant you access to visit from time to time." I blinked again.

Well.

"You know the M... that Asterion resides on your property?" I changed what I had been about to say, still uneasy about speaking so openly with a stranger.

He nodded. "We have a lease and everything. Even among old friends, I don't do much without documentation. I learned long ago to keep my business separate from my pleasure." He smiled. "Our friend wanted a break from his past, a safe space to clear his head, and I had the ability to assist him. He's set up on auto draft somehow." He winked.

I leaned back, thinking. *A friend from his past. Payments. Documentation. Obvious wealth.* Who was this guy? He didn't grant me the time to ask.

"The Grimms or their functionaries burned down Asterion's field late last night. The cops came. Found nothing. Left. Then you three arrive," he pointed at my stomach casually, "When, *at the very least*, you should be in a hospital bed. It's... intriguing." He drummed fingertips on his glass, waiting for an explanation.

I smiled in acknowledgement of his fatherly concern. "There was a piece on the radio about it. Is... is my friend okay?" I asked, suddenly heartsick. This was all because of me. He was an associate of mine. Which was now synonymous with the word *target*.

*Salted Earth Policy.*

Kingston watched me with hooded eyes for a few moments, as if debating his answer. He spoke after an eternity, drumming his fingertips on his glass again as if to find the right words. "The attack... tried his faith. He is safe. Gone now, but safe. He left. Won't be able to come back for some time. Not sure if he wants to come back after that."

"Oh." I replied softly, looking down. My eyes were watering. Ashley reached out a hand and touched my arm, which was shaking slightly. I looked up and smiled gratefully at her, then set my glass down on the table, taking a deep breath as I faced Kingston. "The Grimms are after me. It's my fault your property suffered damage. I will repay you."

The farmer watched me, and then his face stretched into a tired smile. "Thank you for accepting responsibility. I was more concerned with the admission than the money. It was just a field, after all." He lifted a hand at the house in general and let out a soft chuckle. Then he abruptly stood, looking resigned to end the discussion as his eyes darted towards the front door curiously. "It seems you have an unscheduled appointment waiting outside. We've kept him waiting long enough. Don't damage the house, if you please." He added as an afterthought.

"Um... what do you mean unscheduled appointment?" I asked in bewilderment as he reached out to shake my hand. I took it, surprised at the force in his grip. He turned to kiss Ashley's hand and then traded grips with Mallory.

"Appointment?" I reminded him.

"It has been a pleasure meeting you in person. One hears so many things. It's nice when they end up being close to the truth, *Nathin Laurent Temple*." He winked.

I rocked back on my heels.

Wow.

He had gotten my name exactly right. And when I say *name*, I mean *True Name*. The dangerous kind. The one that could be used against you. For spells and dark intentions.

"Sure, Kingston..." I stammered, letting him politely lead us towards the front door. "Speaking of *names*," I enunciated the word, "What is your real name, if I may ask?"

He chuckled, reaching behind me to open the front door. "I suppose you've earned it." He turned to me with a faint grin, the opening door letting in a wash of frigid air that woke up the last vestige of my sleepiness. "My first name is Midas. I added the last bit to fit in with the age we now live in." Ashley and Mallory were studying the lawn warily. I blinked at the man before me. Midas Kingston... or was it *King Midas*?

He nodded in response to my unspoken question. "Now, you don't want to leave your guest waiting. Mind the rose bushes. They took forever to get right. Come back any time." He offered. I nodded numbly and stepped out the door, checking the pistol in my pocket as I scanned the front lawn.

I quested out with my power to locate the... *appointment* Midas had mentioned.

The door clicked softly behind us and I spotted a figure in black standing in the shade of a tree with an umbrella in one hand. He was tall, gaunt, and looked calmly menacing.

He didn't look familiar, but judging by his getup I was pretty sure I knew who he was. He waved lazily, motioning for me to approach him rather than the other way around. He couldn't come closer to the house uninvited. Either that, or it was the sunlight keeping him from attacking. An umbrella... yep, sunlight bothered this guy. Which meant... I scowled back at him, speaking over my shoulder to Ashley and Mallory. "Stay behind me. I think this is Alucard."

"Who?"

"The Vampire I thought I killed yesterday." And I trudged forward to stake a vampire.

One way or another, this would be over quickly.

For good this time.

# CHAPTER 17

*I* approached the stranger with caution. I was pretty sure he was a vampire, and not just any vampire, but the same conceited punk I thought we had killed yesterday in the sewers. The one who had led the kidnapping ring I had effectively shut down. The little shit that thought he was powerful enough to name himself *Dracula* spelled backwards – Alucard. But then again, he *was* in charge of the vampire coven, so it was a safe bet that he was at least marginally powerful, perhaps even a famed Master. With a name like his, he must have had something backing it up in order to prevent his metaphorical blood juice-box being taken away from him every day at vampire recess.

I needed to tread with caution.

My rage was steadily building as I realized I hadn't ended the problem last night, merely ending the operation – temporarily – by taking out his flunkies. Which tended to piss off the boss in most cases.

Which would make my upcoming conversation with Achilles – already a grim proposition since I was no doubt going to accuse him of setting me up – a tad bit harder. I hadn't taken out the leader, so the problem still existed. And his bartender was history.

I sighed, drawing in the power at my feet, glad that at least my anger was present. Thanks to Mallory, I felt strong enough for a scrap, but power like his usually had a cost. Typically spells like that laid the person out into a coma for a day or so, but so far, I was still going strong in the energy department. No time for half measures, I strode forward.

I reached the shade of the giant tree and stopped a few feet away from him. He didn't so much as shift his stance, remaining in a lazy lean against the trunk. Still, I kept my friends behind me with an outstretched arm as I nodded at him in greeting, my face set in a disgusted grimace. He tipped an imaginary hat back at me politely in greeting. His eyes were dark, distant, and lazily aware. Like a lion. Appearing bored and disinterested, but I would bet he didn't miss a thing going on around him.

Ever.

He wore trendy black slacks with the stereotypical loose-fitting white dress shirt of vampires from every movie ever made. A tailored coat hugged his torso before flaring out at the hips like a Steampunk piece, complete with oversized buttons and crisscrossing straps, reminding me of a 1700's era Colonial Pirate or Privateer. His hair was pulled back in a ponytail and a pair of heavy leather boots covered his feet, completing the look. His skin was naturally pale, but he had acquired a light tan somehow.

It seemed this vampire was willing to risk instant incineration along with sun cancer in order to obtain that perfect tan. Talk about priorities. He was also not one of the vampires from the sewer. Which was both good and bad.

"Aye aye, Captain." I sneered at his costume-like outfit.

He answered in a lazy New Orleans drawl. I noticed he was cleaning his teeth with some kind of toothpick. "Name's Alucard. You may have heard of me, Little Brother."

I didn't like vampires, but I *especially* didn't like one addressing me with an affectionate pet name. "Someone might have mentioned your name yesterday, but then they went and disappeared on me. Made quite the mess on their way out."

He nodded without taking immediate offense at me obliquely admitting to murdering his flunkies. "Yes. Glad you brought that up. Put me in a bit of a conundrum..."

He propped the umbrella against the tree beside him, but otherwise didn't shift his weight. He held up both hands, mimicking a scale as he left the toothpick in his mouth. "On one hand, you took care of some rogue associates of mine who had taken it upon themselves to open up a... snack bar without my express permission." He lowered one of his hands as if it were weighted down. "On the other hand, you killed my compatriots, Little Brother. Men – for better or worse – who were under my *Aegis*. My protection." His other hand shifted to more or less balance out the scales. I squinted, confused. Was he thanking me or threatening me?

"I came here for two reasons…" He waited patiently for me to speak. Instead I nodded, motioning with a wave of my hand for him to continue.

He tipped his imaginary hat again. I imagined it as a vintage Captain's hat for aesthetic reasons. "Obliged. First, to thank you for killing the vermin." He watched me, not speaking further.

I stared back in slight disbelief, waiting for a surprise attack of some kind, but nothing happened.

Apparently, I was quiet too long.

"Well, Little Brother. What do you say?"

"Um. You're welcome?"

He nodded, holding his hand to his stomach as he dipped his head politely. I found myself rather liking the guy, despite him being a blood-sucking parasite. I had dealt with many monsters over the years, and none of them had ever thanked me. Especially not for killing their men. "Next, I came here to kill you. For two offenses."

And my brief flicker of hope at gaining a new bestie died in a mental jet plane crash. He continued on, voice and tone even, despite the words that passed his lips. "One, because you slaughtered the several men that represented my entire St. Louis coven. Lowlife, greedy, treacherous bastards, but still. They were *mine*. And one must keep their… *street cred* intact. Now, I'm not particularly inclined to call in my other soldiers from down south to make your life a mess." He began ticking off fingers as he continued. "Logistics, required lodging, travel expenses, lot of additional death and collateral damage." He dropped his hand, meeting my eyes. He was very lucky that he hadn't glanced at Ashley and Mallory or I would have killed him on the spot. "My boys are a hungry sort, you see. I'd rather do it myself. One death. Clean. Neat. Professional. Respectful." He paused, plucking the toothpick out of his mouth with a wet *smacking* sound.

It was a finger bone.

He had been using a freaking metacarpal to clean his teeth. Yuck. And I had thought we could be friends. I really wasn't sure how to take this conversation. I mean, here he was threatening to kill me, yet he was being so freaking polite about it. It almost made me smile. It was a very old-school way of handling things. No shadowy revenge plots lurking over your shoulder for months or years, but an honorable, direct invitation to a duel. Brutal, yes. But also, honorable.

He continued speaking, satisfied his teeth were clean. "Second reason I came here to kill you is that I'm being coerced to do so. If I don't, a group that has some serious brass will raze my New Orleans coven to the ground. Reckon they been doing it for years. So. That about sums it up, Little Brother. Any last words?"

I stared back in masked disbelief. The Grimms? I turned my head to glance back at Mallory and Ashley. They looked just as surprised to hear that the Grimms had subcontracted my death, when the day before they had been adamant about leaving me unharmed.

A whir of fabric suddenly rustled past me and Ashley disappeared out from under my gaze. I spun with a snarl to find Alucard casually leaning against the tree in the same position as before except Ashley now knelt at his feet, and the tip of the umbrella – now a razor-sharp sword blade – was pressed gently into the back of her neck. "I asked you if you had anything to say and you turned your back on me. Can't really cry foul on that one, can ya', Little Brother? I stated my intent, no room for obfus... obfis..."

"Obfuscation," I offered in a snarl. He snapped his fingers together in agreement.

"That's the one, Little Brother. Obfuscation. So, you ready? Or does she die first? Either way we will fight. Here. Now. To the death."

I heard Mallory mutter a curse.

# CHAPTER 18

*A*lucard remained casually leaning against the tree, but I knew even a slight motion would kill Ashley. His glittering dark eyes watched me patiently, ready to react. I could sense that he didn't particularly want to kill Ashley, but that he would if I didn't give him the answer he sought.

"Leave her out of it and you have my word. We'll throw down within five minutes, Dracula."

He shivered at the name, shaking his head in amusement as he lowered the blade from her neck. I sighed in relief, but Ashley still knelt dangerously close to the blade for my comfort. She looked alert, ready to bolt at the first opening. But vampires were fast, so bad idea. I discreetly shook my head at her as Alucard continued. "Not my name. Parents thought it would keep the devil away to name me *Alucard*. Named my sister *Neveah*, of all things. *Heaven* spelled backwards. Now *she* was an evil little bint." He chuckled.

I didn't find anything funny. Threatening my friends did that to me for some reason. "Those are pretty elaborate names for little kids." I replied, thinking furiously.

He slapped his knees, shaking his head, which caused Ashley to flinch. "That's not even all of it! My middle name is Morningstar. *Morningstar!* It's almost like they *wanted* to set me up for failure. Not only was my first name associated with *Dracula*... my middle name was even *more* notorious! Bloody

Lucifer's last name! Two men who fell from Greatness." He shook his head, chuckling harder now. "Parents meant well, I suppose, but they obviously hadn't ever heard the phrase, *curiosity killed the cat*. It only made me want to learn more, so I did some... *research*. Imagine what my eight-year-old-self discovered about those names, and what that did to my impressionable, naïve self-image! I felt like a *god*. I was already an odd boy, interested in all sorts of mystical whatnots. Living in New Orleans with *voodoo* on every corner will do that to you. And being terrorized by larger kids for the formative years of your life put what some might call a *chip* on my shoulder. So, I hunted the vamps down, earned their respect, and joined up. Slowly but surely, I realized that the fangers were rather lazy. Regulars had heard all the stories, but thanks to Hollywood, no one believed them to be true. We could pretty much feast openly, which made the top fangs fat, rich, and apathetic. I built my powerbase, recruited new fangs, and used a little book to build a solid following behind me. The rest was inevitable."

"What book?" I asked, still formulating a plan to get Ashley to safety so we could conclude our duel without collateral damage.

"*The Prince*. Machiavelli," he grinned. "You like books, wizard?"

"A bit." I answered. This guy obviously didn't know much about me if he hadn't heard of *Plato's Cave*. It was mentioned in almost every news article about me. And that wasn't even considering the supernatural community to which I catered on a regular basis. "Alright, Alucard. Let her go and we'll settle this right now. I win – meaning you die – I get to put another set of fangs up on the fridge." His lips tightened a bit at that. After all, he had been exceedingly polite so far. But a thought was churning in my head as I realized where we stood. "You win, you owe me a favor, no questions asked." I folded my arms. He blinked in disbelief, opening his mouth to ask why I got something in return whether I won or lost, but I forestalled him. "I should correct you on one thing. Now that you told me your intention, I won't be letting you walk away without a fight. What kind of gentleman would I be to deny such an honest and polite duel? But I want you to know that I am no wizard." He frowned at both the threat and the statement, reading between the lines.

"Is that so, Little Brother?" He replied softly, like a dagger across velvet.

"Yep. I'm a Maker. Ever heard of that?"

His shoulders stiffened and his hand lifted up the umbrella faster than I could follow. It suddenly occupied the space between us, held in an upright defensive position. Ashley chose that moment to kick his ankle and roll away. Mallory snatched up her arm and yanked her to safety behind him, not letting her go even after she was safe. Alucard didn't even register the blow, other than a flicker of his eyes at her escape. He eyed me warily, thinking about my words.

"It's true?" He answered in a soft, curious voice.

I nodded.

He grunted. "Well, Little Brother. Can't claim as I believed that when I heard it. Thought it was a farce, a ruse, a legend spread by your own lips to keep your celebrity status going across the supernatural world. Heirs usually do such things."

I shook my head, sliced my mind with an imagined blade, tapping into the roaring torrent below, and spoke. "I swear on my power that I'm a Maker."

An invisible shockwave knocked everyone but me to a knee. Alucard was first to stand, assuming it had been an attack. But I stood neutrally with my arms hanging at my sides. He watched me for a few seconds. "Well, looks like you get something whether you win or lose, but I become a legend if I win. Agreed." He looked up at the sky and the bright ball of light that was the sun. Then at me. "Might have a bit of an advantage over me." He observed, not backing out, but simply stating a fact.

I looked up. Then back at him. Then off to the burnt-out field. Having him mention his disadvantage made what I had been about to propose even better. I smiled as I turned back to him, nodding. "I may have a solution. I'll give you at least a one-minute warning before I attack you. But until then I'm going to need you to trust me. Follow me step by step with no questions. I won't betray you or trap you anywhere. I know a place where the sun won't affect you. In fact, *you* will likely gain a slight advantage over *me*."

He frowned a bit at that. "Why would you do that? Why not take me here where I challenged you, Little Brother? Machiavelli would groan in his grave, he would."

I shrugged. "Usually I would do exactly that, but I'm not one for unfair fights when someone openly tells me exactly what they want to do. You've earned a fair... no, an *advantage* over me in a fair fight because of your honesty. Consider it a token of gratitude for not wasting my time with abductions and sneaky attacks over the next few days. I've got enough on my plate already."

He nodded in thoughtful thanks, and then motioned for me to lead on with a shrug.

Mallory quickly laid into me. "Just what the hell do ye' think 'yer doing? We have more important things to do! Now! You can't go throwing 'yer life around for every punk thug that wants a scrap, Laddie."

A veil of transparent blue silk seemed to settle over my vision as I tapped into my smoldering frustration and anger, using it to toss up a dome of power over my two friends, eliminating the possibility for sound to travel beyond us. Vampires had impeccable senses. I saw Alucard rub his arms idly as he watched me. I spoke to my friends. "Trust me. This is best. This way we aren't facing the Grimms while the vampire and his crew of blood-thirsty, hungry fangs sneaks up behind us. Remember, he also hinted that this was out of his hands, and that he was being extorted to kill me to save his coven from annihilation. Sounds like the Grimms. This way I can remove a player off the board. And I'm taking *no* risks to do so." They looked doubtful of that. "I want you two to leave. Now. Head to Chateau Falco. I'll be along shortly. Get Gunnar, Indie, and Raego to meet me there ready for war. I swear I will meet you there." It was hard not to gloat about my plan, but I didn't want to risk Alucard somehow overhearing. That was, if my crazy plan worked. "I'll explain later." I handed Ashley the satchel with the books, my eyes a silent warning to keep it safe. She nodded.

They blinked doubtfully despite the confident twinkle in my eyes. "You're up to something, boy." I nodded with a smile. Mallory shook his head and took Ashley by the arm. "Okay. Let's trust him and go. We're only dead weight here, at best. Collateral damage or leverage, at worst." I nodded my agreement. "You better be back, boy. I know where 'yer final resting place is. And I will make 'yer afterlife a living hell. Turn the family mausoleum into a museum. Maybe leave 'yer journal outside 'yer sarcoph-agus so everyone can read the true stories from 'yer youth." He winked darkly and I laughed aloud.

"You do that." I gripped forearms with him and hugged Ashley. Alucard watched us thoughtfully, but nodded his head in farewell to each of them as they swept past him. They didn't return the gesture, causing Alucard's lips to tighten in disapproval. Courtesy was a pretty big deal to this guy. I turned to look at him. "Alright. Just you and me. Come on. I've got an appointment in two hours, and I'd rather not be late."

Alucard blinked back incredulously. Almost as if bluntly stating that I couldn't possibly be that overconfident. That much ego simply couldn't fit into one person.

He didn't know me at all.

# CHAPTER 19

$\mathcal{A}$lucard clutched the umbrella over his head to protect himself from the sun, careful to keep every millimeter of flesh hidden. Lucky for him it was the size of one of those golf umbrellas. I thought myself very mature for not teasing him about how ridiculous he looked walking around in November under an umbrella. In a burned-down cow pasture.

We both looked utterly ridiculous.

I was very eager for the duel.

Listen, I'm not crazy or anything. Sure, it was a duel to the death, but I had a plan…

And I was finally getting the chance to field test my new powers in a battle setting. It would be a great opportunity for me to actually cut loose, to both try and replicate my old wizard's spells using my new power, but to also see exactly what strange new abilities I could dream up on the fly.

Sure, practicing with Mallory and Gunnar had been immeasurably helpful, but I couldn't go all out, and most of the magic I had been used to throwing around had definitely been focused on going all out. Overwhelming aggression. I wasn't really a half measure guy in *any* area of my life. I ate the whole pizza. If I wanted to order a plate of hot wings at a restaurant, and someone asked politely if they could have one, I was more likely to order them their own appetizer rather than sharing. I overfilled my dinner plates. Over-committed on estimated arrival times. What I mean to say is that you probably would never find me trying to learn swordplay by looking for me in a park, expecting to see me swinging foam swords with other errant knights in a cosplay outfit. You'd have better luck searching in a seedy warehouse district where I would be getting bloodied against experienced swordsmen using blunted wooden practice swords to teach me the hard way.

I looked at the world as all or nothing. An extremist, I had once heard it called. It might have stemmed from missing the *sharing lesson* day at Kindergarten. Then out of pure spite, refusing to learn it after I got back.

Alucard followed me along the once familiar – but now ashen – trail through the cow pasture. Neither of us spoke, although I could sense Alucard growing impatient, which just broke my little heart.

*Not too long now...*

As if on cue, the bright sun-filled sky suddenly winked out like someone had thrown a light switch, and was replaced by a dark, imposing sunset. A line of fire traced the edge of the earth in the distance. We stood in an impromptu ring of crepitating torches, and beyond that was only an impenetrable void of mist and blackness. Creatures of the night could be heard fighting, mating, and hunting in the void, but none entered the circle of fiery torchlight. And no sunlight actually touched the ground. Alucard's shoulders hitched in alarm at both the scene and the sounds of violence, but seemed to slightly relax at my lack of reaction.

I turned to him to see that he was watching our surroundings as if fearing a trap. I grinned. "Welcome to the *Dueling Grounds*. The farm has seen too much heat lately." He grunted at my pun. "I don't want the owner to pay the consequences if you and I make a bit of a ruckus." I leaned forward conspiratorially. "*Spoiler alert*. Causing a ruckus is kind of my thing." My grin stretched wider, darker. "Consider this my one minute warning. Here are the rules," I took a deep breath as if preparing to recite a laundry list, "Anything goes."

He watched me, calculating. "Anything goes." He repeated flatly.

I nodded. "No holds barred. To the death." I began to turn away but hesitated, holding a finger up over my shoulder. "Almost forgot," I said, glancing back at him. "If the chance arises, I will let you speak last words before I destroy you. I expect you to do the same... in the unlikely event that you win. No trickery, just out of respect. Agreed?"

He listened, eyes narrowing at the threat, but finally nodded. "I'll give you your minute to get your affairs in order." He muttered, rolling his eyes.

"And remember. You'll owe me a favor if you win."

He merely shook his head in disbelief. "Fine."

I tossed my coat off, rolled up my sleeves, and stood in the center of the clearing taking deep, relaxing breaths. Alucard watched me, reading me, waiting for a trick, and counting down. I closed my eyes.

I wasn't afraid in the slightest. For one, it was only one vampire. And for the most part, a single vampire was not evenly matched against a wizard as long as the wizard had fair warning. Even though I was no longer a wizard, but a *Maker*, I liked my odds. Secondly, there was no chance for cops to see me throwing magic around, which was an ever-present paranoia of mine. Thirdly, there was no chance for collateral damage – biological or architectural. We were alone, and in a cow pasture, or another dimension of some kind, for all I knew. The Minotaur had never elaborated.

I opened my eyes slightly, squinting at him. "Go time. In thirty seconds," I murmured softly, relaxing my shoulders as I closed my eyes again, opening my fingers to caress the warm air around us.

I cleared my mind of entirely all emotion, removing the crutch of anger that let me cheat to use my new powers. Once eliminated, I quested about in my peaceful, tranquil mind, trying to find a more reliable and natural way to tap into my new abilities. A stubborn, instant gratification fueled part of me began to mutter lazily. *Why? You already know how to use it. Stop wasting our time. Destroy him already!* I tuned the voice out.

But it had a point. Kind of.

I just didn't like having to rely on anything or anyone. It was a weakness in my eyes. A crutch. And anger could definitely be a weakness.

It was fairly safe to say that I was often angry in a fight, so that was good. But I had also managed to survive too many times to count where I had been too terrified to be angry. Therefore, it made sense to nip that reliance in the butt while I had the chance. Especially when tip off time with the Grimms was rapidly approaching.

I peeled away even more of myself, silencing the impatient voice still nagging at me. *Kill the fanger, nooowwww...* the voice trailed away as if falling down a deep dark hole.

I delved into my mind, emotionless, detached, analyzing my core belief system and pondering how I had used to tap into my powers as a wizard. I could still feel the familiar space in my soul where my power had once resided. Now it was empty, but...

*There.* Faint, fluid tendrils of... *something* weakly latched here and there like the appendages of a stubborn octopus, the other end leading off into the darkness. I smiled, mentally following the cords, watching them grow thicker as they flowed through each section of my body. They looped back and forth several times, wider, stronger, and more resilient the further I traveled, until finally darting off to end at two specific points in my body.

My head.

And my heart.

The two throbbed in opposing rhythm.

Their pulsing combined into a steady beat, like a steady drum roll that began to fill me with confidence, power, and...

Peace.

Like my own miniature soundtrack.

I sunk deeper into myself, allowing the pattern of sound to fill my body, mind, and soul. And then I submitted to the glorious power, anticipating an explosion of euphoric magical light that would cause Alucard to surrender in tears of awe at the dreaded power of the first Maker in centuries.

But nothing happened.

I waited some more.

Some more nothing happened.

"Time's up, Temple," Alucard hissed, and I felt the air shift as he threw himself at me, fangs aimed at my moneymaker.

# CHAPTER 20

*I* needed more time. I dove to the side to protect my face and throat, fingers latching onto the pistol in my pocket. I managed to squeeze off a few shots at a nearby blur of fabric, and heard a soft grunt before the pistol was knocked from my hand, instantly numbing my fingers. I kicked out with a boot, connecting solidly with Alucard's torso, sending him into a nearby bench where he folded.

My anger pulsed instinctively, fueling me with enough power to stay alive and add a little bit of oomph to my kick. Which was slightly alarming. I hadn't consciously chosen to use my power to kick him. Yet another reason I needed to get a grip on my new power.

Alucard groaned from across the clearing and I frantically dove back into my mind.

I knew the tendrils hadn't been there before my magic had been taken from me. I had to be on to something. I knew it.

As I drew closer to the nexuses of power over my heart and mind I realized that the pulses of sound were actually not sound at all. That was merely how I had translated it in my mind. The pulses were oddly akin to the reservoir of power I now constantly felt beneath my feet. I heard Alucard stumbling to his feet in the distance and knew I only had a few seconds.

When using my anger to tap into the power, I had apparently been forcing the power to obey my command by sheer strength, rage, and will.

Straight from the source. The never-ending river of power beneath the earth's crust. Which was a tad arrogant of me.

But apparently, I had a conduit right inside of me all along.

To use the river of power successfully, I had had to force it to my will, not submit.

Perhaps…

I opened my eyes in a squint, having lost track of time. Alucard was racing towards me, claws outstretched and a hungry gleam in his eyes. He launched himself at my throat again. "Gack!" I bellowed in challenge, diving away from his attack and rolling to safety. He didn't stop there. He landed in a skid, turned on a heel, and dove again. I reached out to the center of my heart and mind and instead of submitting to the power, I sent my essence out in a claw, clutching the cords of power in a metaphysical fist.

Then I squeezed.

Power exploded out of me in a torrent of wind and justice.

I felt like a god damned superhero.

A hot line of fire slashed across my throat, but the brief sensation of pain was instantly overwhelmed by magic so alien I could hardly comprehend it. My world suddenly exploded in a mushroom cloud of blue that resembled the color of the most ancient of arctic glaciers. Power ignited my veins like a lit fuse, flooding my body with raw, alien magic. A second shockwave shattered the night and I fell to my knees. I was sweating profusely around my neck and chest. I began to laugh in triumph, my voice sounding oddly raw.

I had done it.

I had learned how to use my power at will. All by myself. Which was important to me. It wouldn't have felt as good if I had accomplished it while training with Mallory. It had taken a real fight to break it out of me.

I began to feel very dizzy, but imagined a ball of fire, and it was suddenly there, although weak, sputtering. Then it died. I blinked. Tried it again, but all I saw was a spark before that too died.

I frowned and studied my surroundings, expecting to see a disheveled or disintegrated Alucard lying on the ground of a now dystopian world. The ground in a thirty-foot radius was completely clear of debris, and the torches all leaned away from me as if repelled. I looked up at a slight motion to see Alucard was hanging from a tree outside the clearing. He was staring at me in disbelief. He lifted up a bloody claw and I blinked. I touched my throat and it came away slick with blood, not sweat. I wasn't dizzy from the power. He had freaking cut my artery.

Sneaky bastard.

I fell to my back and heard Alucard land lightly on his feet. His footsteps approached closer as I struggled to breathe, my vision dwindling to a single point as a loud rushing sound began to fill my ears like ocean waves breaking over rocks.

I beckoned him closer. He watched me for a second, hesitating. "You made me promise to give you a chance to speak. No sucker punches, right?"

I nodded weakly. He shook his head, as if doubting his own sanity, but leaned over me, placing his ear near my lips. I whispered a few words. He leaned back with a frown, looking skeptical, but finally nodded. "Okay. I'll do it." He answered doubtfully. He watched me as I began to choke on my own blood. "Want me to make it clean?" I shook my head. I managed to speak louder than a whisper through another gurgle of blood.

"If I really die... bury me upside down," I gasped a short breath. "So the Grimms can kiss my ass." And I flashed him a peace sign before the world winked out to nothing.

# CHAPTER 21

*I* woke with a choked gasp, lurching into a coughing fit as my fingers instinctively flashed to my throat. I caressed the skin in a panic, practically hyperventilating as I tried to keep as much blood inside me as possible. I needed help. Immediately.

Then I paused as the pads of my fingers transmitted their observation to my brain.

My skin was perfectly smooth.

And not slick with blood.

Then I remembered. I had been at the *Dueling Grounds* with Alucard. And...

*That polite southern bastard had killed me!*

I managed to feel slightly betrayed and disappointed in him. He had displayed a level of genteel etiquette that was nonexistent these days. Just like my parents had tried to teach me. I had sensed potential camaraderie in him. A kindred spirit. A similar flavor of craziness.

But then I remembered seeing the beast in his eyes, the hunger for blood and vengeance. He was a *monster* first. *Human* last. I needed to remember that. People weren't always what they seemed. Or what we made them out to be. My breath had calmed down to the point where I merely felt like I had finished a brief jog, but my heart was still racing. I tried to let out a laugh, but it turned into a coughing rasp. I leaned back, contemplating my situation as I regained my breath.

The Minotaur had once told me that one couldn't truly die at the *Dueling Grounds*, but then again, he was also a monster. He could have been playing a long con on me.

I slowly stretched my neck, testing the motion, fearing that any second my head was going to just fall off. It felt like I had only just closed my eyes at the Dueling Grounds before abruptly waking here in my bed.

Wait, *my bed*. I was at Chateau Falco!

I lurched up to a sitting position, my eyes darting about wildly. I touched my throat again subconsciously, remembering the fiery slash of Alucard's claws and the sensation of drowning in my own blood. But now there wasn't even a tender scratch.

I jumped to my feet, testing my voice again.

"Tis' but a scratch!" I ran from the room, hooting and hollering as much as my throat would allow. "I'm invincib–" and I pummeled straight into Dean, tackling us both to the ground in an eruption of spilled cocktails, olives, and mint leaves. I sat up, coughing and wiping the booze from my face. "Where did *you* come from? Didn't you hear me yelling?"

He stood, brushing off his shoulders. "Yes, Master Temple. Of course. My apologies. I was just on my way to awaken the *Guardians* after I heard screaming and shouting erupting from a room that was empty when I passed by it less than three minutes ago, to gather refreshments for your guests. If you don't mind, I'll just be on my way now to activate them and exterminate the vermin."

"No one likes a wiseass, Dean. Unless it's me. I'm adorable. And apparently *invincible!*" He leaned to his right, peering at the side of my head as if checking for a head wound.

"Of course, Sir. Invincible. Quite right."

"I just *died!*"

"I'm sure it was most unpleasant. What would the Master Necromancer like to drink? Your undead servitors are waiting." He said, deadpan.

I scowled, not appreciating his lack of astonishment. "Water will suffice."

"Of course, Overlord. The Prince of Darkness may want to change. He's soiled himself." He plucked up the tray and turned on a heel, still brushing off his coat as he left. I didn't let his negative attitude kill my vibe.

But I did go change.

After a quick rinse, I headed to the office, anxious to share my plan with the team. I was sick of running. The Minotaur had been taken off the field, just for spending a bit of time with me over the past few years. Who would they go after next? I couldn't risk anyone else's life by waiting. It was time to bring the fight to the Grimms. It felt nice to finally have a plan. Once this was off my to-do list I could go visit the wolves to get my ring back. The way things were going my proposal would go off without a hitch after all.

My phone rang.

*Achilles.*

I groaned, sending it to voicemail with a nervous finger. One did not ignore a call from Achilles lightly. I waited for him to suddenly appear before me with a spear aimed at my throat, but nothing happened. I let out a sigh of relief. I would have to take care of him soon. He no doubt wanted an update on the vampire and bartender situation. Either that or he was checking to see if his ploy to have me killed had worked. I just didn't know whom to trust anymore, so I figured stalling was my best bet, short term.

Plus, the time on the screen told me we were running on a tight schedule.

Everyone turned to face me as I pocketed the phone and opened the office door. No one spoke, merely staring at me incredulously. Ah, they had heard about the vampire. Or the Grimms. Or both. I spotted my satchel on the ground near the door and picked it up, digging inside before letting out a sigh of relief. The amulet and books were safely tucked away inside. I nodded at Ashley as I approached. "What happened?" She asked carefully.

"I died. But it's okay. I was at the *Dueling Grounds.* You can't really die there. Vamp didn't know that though. Boy, is he going to be in for a surprise." Gunnar jumped to his feet, as did Indie. "What?!" They yelled in unison.

I waved them off. "No time. Drink up quickly. We're going on a field trip in ten minutes. I'll meet you outside by the stable." By now my friends knew *stable* meant *garage.* It was, after all, a converted stable. And it *had* temporarily housed a horse of the St. Louis Mounted Patrol Unit named Xavier in recent months. "I've got to round up a few things. Arm for bear." I thought about that for a second. "No. Liger. Arm for liger and intelligent apes." I nodded once to no one in particular, and then left the room without another word.

I made it a dozen feet before a hand latched onto me from behind, jerking me to a halt. Indie was breathing heavily. We didn't have time to stop and chat so I motioned for her to follow. She did, folding her arms and glaring at me.

"How have you been today?" I asked softly, wary of the apparent outburst forming behind her fiery glare. I knew I was treading on thin ice, but I needed to keep my head in the game if I was going to save everyone's lives. This was the biggest challenge I had ever encountered. I couldn't afford distractions.

"Oh, you know, I didn't die. You?" Her tone was arctic.

I gulped. "Yeah. It sounds worse saying it out loud. It really wasn't a big deal."

"What about the liger? Or the ape? Did they attend your meeting? Give a rousing presentation on the African Savannah?" Her words were clipped, precise, and full of venom. "You promised to call me after the meeting."

I groaned. It had completely slipped my mind after the attack, the gut shot, and then the race to Kingston's field. Then my duel with Alucard. "Listen, you're right. It's been kind of nonstop since the meeting. Some company from Germany wants to buy Temple Industrie–"

"I know. It's all over the news. I found out like that, rather than from my boyfriend, who attended the meeting, since, you know, it's *his company*." She sounded hurt.

"Right," I sighed in defeat, "Well, we were attacked on our way out the door by–"

"Shapeshifting Grimms. Yep. Heard that from Ashley. And Mallory, who I sent to look after you, by the way."

"Oh. Um. Thanks. I got scratched up a bit, but–"

"Nate…" She warned.

Crap. *Mallory, you loose-lipped bastard.* "Okay. I was shot. Mallory stitched me up." I patted my stomach by reflex and immediately froze. I tugged up my shirt…

And saw not a blemish. Nothing. "Huh…" I muttered lamely, thinking furiously.

Indie glanced down and frowned. "Are you saying Mallory lied? No, wait. You just said you were shot, too." Her face contorted in confusion and she rubbed her temples. "Nate, tell me what the hell is going on? My boyfriend is getting in fights anytime he leaves the house and I'm hearing about it from everyone but him. Then the dire wound I hear almost killed him suddenly disappears. Then you come in the office idly mentioning you died, but you're obviously not dead. *What. The. F?*" She folded her arms, scowling.

"I'm not really sure." I answered honestly.

And I wasn't.

Why was I healed? I mentally checked myself for all the scrapes and bruises from the last day, my astonishment continuing to grow. They were all gone. Did losing the fight at the *Dueling Grounds* ironically grant me a clean bill of health? I had bumped my shin two days ago, on our bedpost. I checked it. Still there. Huh. "I think dying at the Dueling Grounds carried an undisclosed perk. It healed me." I answered, amazed.

"Like twenty-four hours' worth, or one night to the next, or back up to a specific time?" She asked, thinking academically.

"I have no idea." I answered. I showed her my bruised shin. "Didn't cure this."

She pondered that. "We should probably find out." She grasped my hand. "Nate…"

I held up a hand to forestall her. "Indie, I'm going to be blunt. You mean the literal world to me, and I've kept you in the dark. I'm a big fat jerk." She nodded like a cat acknowledging their existence as the center of the universe, unimpressed. "Here's the thing. These guys are legendary. They never lose. And whoever hired them also ordered a hit on every one of my friends. That means I need you safe, but I have to be in the thick of battle on this one. Somewhere you can't be. I've been running around responding so far, trying to eliminate the problem before they come for *you*. That would…" I trailed off, my vision briefly flashing blue before I managed to calm my rage, "*End me. I would let them do anything to me if it kept you safe*." I paused. "Even let them kill me." I added softly.

She hissed. "Like hell you will." She growled, yanking me close into a hug. Her head tucked into my shoulder, the perfect height for a hug, just slightly shorter than me. I squeezed back with a sad smile. But I had been telling the truth.

I would do anything for this sweet, passionate, violent young woman.

I spoke into her hair. "That's why I've kept you back. I don't know what to do. Keep you locked away so you're safe until I can deal with them? But what if they take you while I'm away?" I shook my head in frustration, suddenly venting my impotent frustration with the only woman in the world I felt I could unconditionally trust. "I don't understand where they get their powers. Two could obviously shapeshift and use glamour, but that doesn't make any sense. They abhor freaks. So how can shifters also be Grimms?

"Or do I keep you close, stuck to my hip while bullets, fangs, blades, claws, and magic fills the night? You wouldn't survive." She began to argue, but I shook her gently. "Indiana Rippley. *Listen!*" I commanded, using her full name to get her attention. She blinked at me in surprise. "You *know* I'm right. That's not saying anything bad about you. Hell, I don't know how any of *us* can survive these guys. They never lose. Ever. It's why a whole nation of Freaks teamed up in secret to lock them away. Because they couldn't survive one by one. These groups *hated* each other," I paused for emphasis and she leaned back to stare at me through tear-filled eyes, frustrated at her helplessness. *"But they still teamed up to take the Grimms down."* I finally said.

She was quiet, sobbing softly. After a second, she nodded, and gently tugged my arm until we were walking again, headed towards the stable. Her voice was a venomous hiss, like the words of an ancient prophecy come to life. "You gather an army then. You've done it before." She said resolutely. "You've helped enough people. They owe you. Call in the banners, and *destroy them*. Let them know their place. With extreme prejudice."

I shook my head. "Anyone I call in on this gets added to the naughty list, earning an immediate death sentence. I can't do that to people I saved in the past. It's selfish and cruel. Save them from one death only to be available to die for me at a later, more convenient time? I couldn't live with myself."

"You do have a few allies who are already well-known acquaintances of yours. They will already be on the hit list. Gather *them*."

"Why do you think I raced to the Minotaur's field so quickly? They targeted him. Burned his field down. He's alive, but gone, whatever *that* means." I spoke softly, the rage patiently purring deep inside me. "They're going after my allies first."

Indie shivered, squeezing my arm compassionately. "What's the vampire's story?"

"It was Alucard. He was never down in the sewers. Those were several members of his coven that went rogue. They impersonated him to scare everyone away from their new abduction and murder business franchise. He thanked me for killing them, but since they *were* his coven, he was still forced to challenge me to save face. I get it." I shrugged.

She nodded. She had killed a few of them herself. It looked like she wanted to remind me of that superhero act, to prove her strength and usefulness in battle. I stopped her before she could voice it. "You did good down there. Seriously. But the Grimms... they're on a level above even me. Above *any* of us. Perhaps *all* of us." I sighed at the defiant look in her eyes. "Look, I don't know how to beat them. But I do know that waiting for them to attack us is off the table. I can't let them stack the deck anymore. I need to *act* rather than *react*. I need to lure them out. And for that, I'll keep you by my side. Hopefully, we can end it tonight."

She was opening her mouth to argue at the beginning of my speech, but wisely clicked her teeth shut as soon as I said I was taking her along with me. I still didn't know if it was a good idea, but I truly couldn't think of a safer alternative. At least I could keep an eye on her.

She kissed me on the lips. Then darted away. "I'm going to go arm myself for liger. You have some hunting rifles and pistols in the gun safe, right?" I smiled and nodded. "Okay, I'll meet you outside. Oh, and don't forget about the Armory. We need to check it again and see what the deal was last night. Maybe it's fixed now." I nodded, silently reaching inwards to clutch the nexus of wires powering my magic, allowing the current to course through me. Then I imagined pinching her butt. She yelped and shot a hungry glare over her shoulder. Then stopped. "You figured it out!" I nodded. "Go Team Rippley!" She squealed as she took off with renewed vigor, leaving me no time to correct her. I really needed to get t-shirts or something. Make it official. *Team Temple*.

I sighed, patted my satchel, and mentally prepped myself for battle as I headed outside. I entered the stable and spotted an old rusty knife on the workbench. I had stashed it here as a small project to work on after finding it inside my dad's desk. Dean made a habit of fixing things before I had a chance to do so, which he knew infuriated me. So, I had decided that someday I was going to fix this little old knife, because it may have been important to my dad for some small reason. Maybe I would even gift it to him when I saw him next. I sighed, admitting that I hadn't really needed to collect anything for the upcoming fight, only my thoughts.

But Indie had seen to that better than I could have on my own.

I promised myself that once this was over I was going to make her weep uncontrollably when I proposed tomorrow. Messy, snotty, mascara-thwarting tears of joy.

"*Team Rippley*," I muttered under my breath.

She had it coming to her.

# CHAPTER 22

*N*aturally, we didn't drive. We Shadow Walked to our destination. I had wanted to make sure I still had the strength to do so. And it was more efficient. It was the first time I had Shadow Walked such a large group. I had asked Mallory to stay behind and guard Chateau Falco with Dean. I didn't want to leave it unguarded. Especially with the Armory acting oddly. I also wanted Mallory to get a hold of Tomas, even though neither of us had had any luck with that over the past few hours.

But the rest of the gang was here. Gunnar, Ashley, and Indie.

If all worked out, I planned on having a few more in the next few minutes…

It was only an hour or so until sundown. We stood on the slushy streets just outside Alistair Specter Silverstein's old brownstone. Yes, his initials had been *ASS*. Poor guy.

But I didn't feel bad laughing at his initials. It was his fault I was even in this whole mess. He had listed an original 1812 edition of *Grimm's Fairy Tales* – known as *Kinder- und Hausmärchen* in German – at an auction house, which had ignited a murderous race to get the book first before ultimately leading me to the biggest bad I had ever faced, Jacob Grimm himself. And he hadn't liked me much afterwards.

It was a gift of mine. Annoying people to immeasurable levels of hatred.

It had been a while since I had been back to the old home. I had bought the place as a hidey-hole, and just in case ol' Alistair had secreted away any other potentially world-ending items in the walls or something. I didn't want a Regular couple to buy the place and accidentally uncover a weapon of mass destruction when renovating the bathroom.

*Team Temple* (not Rippley!) stood behind me, looking impressively foreboding. I was proud of them.

I glanced down at the prototype smart watch on my wrist. I had bullied the Board into funding the project, despite strong opposition, and was glad to have it today. After seeing the first test run they had quickly changed their tune and it was forecasted to sell extremely well upon release. I was ready to see a real-life field test. The weather wasn't optimal, which would make things difficult, but would also provide a plethora of information for the technicians to study later.

It also performed a truly magical action that many people took for granted these days.

It told the freaking time.

And we were on schedule. Now to see if a man was true to his word.

"Alucard," I called out in an inaudible whisper, knowing he could hear me. Vamps had supernatural hearing.

A man stepped out from behind a nearby tree, his predatory eyes quickly assessing each face in the group of thugs before him, searching for the man who had called his name. I stood behind my friends, biting back a laugh. He nodded at Ashley and Mallory in recognition, then his gaze continued to quickly rove over the rest of the group, searching. His gaze finally met mine and he froze.

Like, literally.

I waved at him cheerily. "I see you wore the sunblock, like I asked."

He lunged backwards, his coat suddenly flaring out in the shape of giant black bat wings that propelled him a safer distance away. A dozen feet now stood between us. I grunted, eyeing Alucard's coat thoughtfully. Perhaps this guy was the real thing. Alucard stared at me, dark eyes skeptical. "You're dead. I killed you. Not an hour ago."

I turned to my friends. "See? I'm invincible."

They contemplated that, then shrugged, still not convinced. I scowled back.

I lifted my collar to display my throat, where no injury remained from his claws. "Listen, Alucard. I wasn't completely honest with you. I didn't have time to really die. Had a few things to do first. But I let you have your revenge, and I will gladly tell everyone that you killed me in a duel to save face with your people." I shot him a winning smile. And waited.

He pondered that, frown growing. "Yes, that would... wait," a thought crossed his face, and then his eyes widened as my words dawned on him.

He was... *undeadly* silent for a solid minute.

Then he began a slow clap of approval, letting out an impressed laugh as he shook his head in disbelief. He began walking closer as he spoke. "Well *played*, Temple. That would most *certainly* improve your reputation quite a bit, wouldn't it, Little Brother? You dying and then coming back to life an hour later." I nodded, still smiling. My friends stepped back, giving me room to approach Alucard.

"Sure would." I said. He had no idea how much. This story would spread like wildfire, which just might keep the Academy off my back for a while. This would be the second tale of me defying death. Only one time had been authentic, but that was my little secret. I knew the guy on the other side.

But then for people to hear about me returning from certain death *again*? They would lose their minds. I managed to bury my grin as I addressed Alucard. "I understand your position. Your people need to know you handled the situation appropriately. *An eye for an eye.* I needed to keep on ticking. So, I found a win-win solution." I had taken a few steps towards him as I spoke. Gunnar's shoulders itched up protectively, but I had warned him ahead of time. Alucard noticed the werewolf's movement, but didn't react. "And now you owe me." I stated solemnly, extending a hand in a gentleman's agreement.

He flung up his hands, stammering. "But... people will think..."

I nodded. "You tell everyone you killed me. I back up your story with an oath on my power so people know I'm not lying. Your people respect you. My reputation *explodes*." I winked. "Or, you do nothing and people see you traipsing around with the guy who slaughtered your coven." I added softly. "I'll play it however you want, but you did make me a promise. And I think your word actually means something to you."

He just stared back, and I felt the concerned looks of my friends doing the same, as if suddenly wondering what level of sociopath they had attached themselves to. I let them think what they would. This was a high stakes game, and Alucard had no cards left.

He knew I was right, but he was right as well. He just couldn't force the dots into a more beneficial picture. He threw his hands up in defeat. "Fine. I've either failed or double-crossed the Grimms – which won't make them happy – and now we're all going to die." He squinted at me. "Unless you're not really going to die. I still don't quite get that part, but a promise is a promise." He met my hand in a tight grip.

"Nice meeting a man of his word. Even if you are a fanger." He peeled his lips back.

"Careful, wiz… Maker." He corrected. "I killed you once. We aren't friends." He studied me thoughtfully. "Yet. But I am mighty impressed. The thought of an alliance is… intriguing. It's a shame that our maiden voyage is a suicide mission. Great things could have been ours, I reckon."

"Nothing is written in stone."

"The Ten Commandments are. And I think we both know that neither of us would pull off an *A* on that grading scale." He winked. Then he turned away to formally introduce himself to the peanut gallery who was watching the exchange with masked emotion. They didn't know what the hell was going on either. I didn't have time for an explanation of the *Dueling Grounds*. I had listed the facts, told them to believe it, and that I would clarify any confusion – like my death and the lack of fatal wounds that Mallory had treated only hours ago – after the Grimms were dead.

I had a different story to share with the class today.

A *Fairy Tale*.

About how one little old wizard had managed to piss off the deadliest of supernatural exterminators in recorded history. And for that, I had brought a prop. Well, I had brought a prop that would *summon* someone who could share the story in *Dolby Digital Surround Sound*.

I scanned the skies. It would be dark soon, which was good for innocent bystanders. Harder to see what was going on. Snowflakes settled on my nose before melting to droplets of water. I closed my eyes for a moment, taking a deep breath. Now that I knew how to access it, it was time to begin pushing boundaries. I wanted to see if I could tap into it without imagining the pulsing tendrils of power, and me clutching them in my fist. I attempted it, faced a brief struggle of conflicting challenge, but then broke through and was instantly flooded with power. I grinned, eyes still closed as I assessed my mind for strain. It had felt more like using the reservoir that time, except I hadn't had to be angry.

Baby steps.

*Manly* baby steps.

Not wanting to tempt fate, I left my experimenting for later. When I opened my eyes, the world resembled a snow globe, tinted with blue sparkling snowflakes, visible as if under a microscope as I honed in on each one. Like a bird of prey. Was that a perk I hadn't noticed, or had I just imagined my vision sharper? I couldn't wait to play with my new toys.

If things played out as I hoped, that would happen all too soon.

Everyone was waiting for me, watching me grinning at nothing. I let out a sharp whistle. Then I turned to address the group. "The door's unlocked. I'll be right in. Gunnar knows the way." Gunnar grunted, eyeing Alucard warily, not letting him near the girls. I liked that.

Then I waited for a response to my whistle, shrugging my shoulders a few times for warmth, scanning the skies as I ran through my plan one last time.

# CHAPTER 23

*I* listened as the last of my gang finally gained entrance to the brownstone. The second the door closed, I heard a sharp crack of wings snapping in close to a body, a rush of wind, and then a pair of boots landed softly beside me. I thought I heard a second click of boots, but it was faint, almost inaudible. I turned and held out my hand, neutrally studying the air beside Raego, thankful he had already accomplished his mission.

My insurance policy. Delivered by my trusty weredragon pal.

Raego gripped my hand. "We're secure. No willpower. Only able to observe."

"You're sure?" He nodded. "You didn't harm them, right? That's not the intention. I just need an impartial witness." I thought about that. "Well, as impartial as possible. They obviously aren't going to be happy about this, but hopefully they will understand by the end," I added. Raego grunted doubtfully.

"No harm. Just control." He studied me thoughtfully. "Ballsy move."

"You did as commanded." I warned in a growl. "I'll take responsibility." Raego watched me intently, wisely not saying anything, his face a mask.

With that, he turned and began walking towards the brownstone. I followed him, trying to ignore the queasy flip-flopping motion in my stomach. Misha was no doubt watching the building from the rooftops. Raego rarely went anywhere these days without his red weredragon for a bodyguard. Being the leader of the dragon nation – the Obsidian Son – and the only black dragon in existence made a lot of dragon hunters grow dollar signs in their eyes when they saw Raego. And if Misha was here, I could safely assume that my friend Tory was roaming the streets in plain clothes, watching out for *her*.

I smiled at the unlikely union. Not the girl on girl part. The dragon on human part.

Well, technically Tory was more than just a human – being able to crush cars like beer cans kind of eliminated her from the human crowd. And she was an ex-cop, meaning she wasn't what you would call a *people person*, so perhaps meeting Misha was a better fit for her in the long run anyway.

We walked through the front door, following the voices heard coming from the back room. I idly thumbed the satchel at my side, slightly nervous. I was figuratively turning on a giant bat symbol to illuminate the skies and taunt the Grimms. Only it wouldn't be a bat symbol. To them, it would feel more like a cloud-sized depiction of a wizard humping a Grimm from behind.

But I needed to bait them, so it was necessary.

I think.

I shook off my doubts. Anything was better than being drawn into a fight on ground where I wasn't ready. I found everyone in the office, and silently went to work, not even needing magic for this next part. It was a ritual. Even Indie could have done it as long as she could follow directions. That was the scary part about rituals. They were predesigned to perform a supernatural function, and as long as the ritual was performed correctly, *anyone* could use it. It was only if the ritual was botched – which I had done the first time, in this very room – that things went downhill, and it was good to have a wizard nearby.

I had already performed this ritual before, and had been not-so-gently informed of what I had done wrong, so I was able to correctly prepare everything in only a few minutes. Then, rather than letting everyone hear what I was about to say, I decided to say it only in my mind. I called out a True Name.

Three times.

The air beside Raego shifted unnaturally, a bit. I frowned but didn't say anything. Useful to know.

A silver comet slammed down into the center of the ring before me, instantly zipping around in circles, agitated at the confinement, moving too fast to get a clear look at the creature's shape other than to determine that it was made of blinding silver light. Everyone stared at the circle after taking a few steps back and shielding their eyes from the pearlescent light.

I folded my arms. "Are you quite finished yet?" I asked.

The figure halted, revealing a twelve-inch tall action figure of a quick-silver playboy bunny. My Barbie doll.

Her hair, teeth, skin, and even the irises of her eyes, all glowed with mercurial light.

Because she was entirely naked. Which let me know all was right with the world.

She glared up at me. "Maker," she spat. "Release me or die."

"Hi, Barbie. I just want to pick you up and squeeze your tiny face!" I clapped. I felt the murderous gaze of every feminine pair of eyes hit me like bolts of lightning, but I stoically ignored them.

"I will let you touch mine if I can touch yours," she cooed, grinning murderously.

I shivered. "No, thanks." My gaze pointedly rose to acknowledge the group. "Group, meet Barbie. Barbie, meet Group." The sprite whirled with a hiss, craning her neck to see the large number of people here.

"You dare let them hear my name?" She shrieked.

"No. I spoke it in my mind. That's just our little secret. Listen, you helped me out by telling me about the Grimms. Now I need your help."

"I know. I reminded you of this yesterday. You have come to die."

"So… oh," I stammered, realizing I didn't have to persuade her and that she was already on board. But I wasn't really on board with the dying part. I had a different plan. I fast-forwarded my sales pitch. "I'm going to need you to-"

"This is tiring," she mumbled, interrupting me. I scowled back. *If she would just let me finish my sentence…* Suddenly a six-foot tall pinup version of the same sprite now occupied the ring, causing my friends to jump back a step in surprise. She rolled her shoulders, which did very nice things to her unclothed frame, earning pleased sounds from the men present in the room and arctic stares from the women. She shot Gunnar and Alucard a dark wink, and then turned to face me. "Let me out and I will aid you."

"Just to clarify, I do not consider killing me to be an aid." She frowned, but nodded.

I didn't even hesitate. There was no room around that agreement. Sure, she had helped me out before, a few times even, but there was this one time she had also threatened to sex me to death.

It's really not as weird as it sounds. Sex was her thing. She fed off of it. Some kind of succubus. But I trusted her. So, I scuffed the ring with my foot and let her out of her cage.

She instantly crouched, flung her fists up, and what looked like life-sized duplicates of Wolverine's Adamantium claws shot out the back of her wrist. She let out a deadly hiss, preparing to pounce and *snicker-snack* me to pieces with a *'Hey, Bub'* thrown in for good measure. Shouts filled the room as I tensed to defend myself.

But nothing happened.

She suddenly cackled with unabashed glee as she sheathed the claws. "Your face…"

Listen, creatures like her don't giggle. They cackle. Trust me.

I had been ready to clobber her with a giant-sized fly swatter of magic, and was reconsidering my decision to hold back. I was panting, and every woman in the room seemed suddenly pleased with the sprite they had recently scowled at. Women.

She walked past me, patting me on the shoulder with a demure wink.

My pants tightened a bit by default. I didn't know if she exuded some kind of pheromone or what, but it was impossible to ignore. I expected Indie to start shooting me with her hunting pistol, but instead she seemed to be having a similar reaction. She wasn't even looking my way, eyes locked on the sprite. I wrapped my power about me like a cloak, feeling a sudden drop in the euphoria. But still…

A naked chick stood a few feet away, walking around with such a blatant disregard that it really should have been a crime. She stopped before my friends, who stood at attention like kids in front of a teacher at the first day of school, waiting to be picked as the favorite student. "What a delightful platter you have brought me to nibble on, Nathaniel…" She hummed erotically.

"Not platter. Friends. Warriors all." She eyed Raego, who stared back with obvious interest, but his faint grin looked like a totally natural response to a beautiful naked woman standing before him, not influenced by her magic. He was, after all, well acquainted with mind magic. Dragons used a similar power. He stared deep into her eyes, and nodded back with a hungry smile. The sprite of death-by-sex, one who had literally carried hundreds if not thousands of men to their deaths aboard the eternal train of climax, *blushed*.

Well.

Okay.

I was a regular matchmaker. They *were* both shapeshifters... I stopped that train of thought quickly.

I cleared my throat. "I need you to show them what happened to start all this. Who we are up against, and why. The story of a few years ago when we first met should help out, too. You can leave out certain... details that are irrelevant to the Grimms," I added, silently and very obviously hinting at what I thought should be left out.

"You should have placed that limit on me before you freed me," she murmured, shooting one last look at Raego, who was still smiling at her.

She turned back to my friends. "Alright, children. Sit. Let me show you a story..." My friends complied, sitting in couches, on the ground, against a wall, wherever was comfortable. The sprite bowed her head, closed her eyes, and breathed deeply for a moment, murmuring softly under her breath. Then she began to whirl in a slow ballet, or a martial arts form, and the air suddenly thickened with fog. Then the fog began to shift and sway, coalescing into shapes, forms, landscapes, seasons, and instruments of death.

It was a war.

She showed us a story. One I hadn't known.

Her words filled the air like the voice of an angel over the swirling world of fog before us. I couldn't see her, or my friends, or even the room. It was as if she took us some place up in the clouds. As she spoke, those clouds pantomimed her story with crude figures, most forms of life unfinished, mere shapes representing a concept. A werewolf was obviously a werewolf, but if you looked closely there were no defining characteristics to distinguish it from another wolf, unless the character was essential to the story. Then it gained a few more details – just enough to catch our attention. I sat back and listened. A part of me was amazed at the magic, but the majority was amazed by the story itself, watching the dancing fog as I listened to her words.

# CHAPTER 24

"*D*uring the Crusades, there existed a tight-knit band of holy warriors who participated wherever the battle was thickest. It was said these men were filled with Holy Fire, and were unstoppable. They considered themselves judge, jury, and executioner, and didn't fit well among the other Crusaders, especially their commanding officers. In hushed tones, their fellow warriors nicknamed them the *Decapitares*, or 'ones who decapitate.' Then, the morning after a particularly vocal disagreement with their captain, they were simply gone, having drifted away like smoke in the night. Not a single sentry saw them leave, and none could find so much as a hoofprint marking their departure." She paused for emphasis. "This was the first time in recorded history that the so-called *Grimms* entered the world stage on an official level.

"But their origins go back further. Before that they were merely a group of supernaturals gifted with the ability to see through glamour. Any kind of glamour. They could look at you," she pointed at Gunnar, "and recognize you as a werewolf, or you," she pointed at Alucard, "and see you were a Master Vampire. They couldn't control it. Even worse, they were defenseless people, with no offensive power to balance out their vision. When they saw through someone's glamour the supernatural person in their gaze saw their eyes turn entirely black as a warning.

"One of them wisely realized that this ability made them targets, and in order to survive with such a dangerous power they needed to watch out for each other. His last name was Grimm, and at some point, the others inevitably adopted his name as a tribute to that man who saved them from eradication. They hid their powers as best they could, banding together for protection.

"After a time, these new Grimms convinced themselves – and then preached to the masses – that the reason their eyes turned black was proof that the accused were demons. That the change of eye color was a direct result of these seemingly normal people seeing a reflection of their dark, stained souls shining back at them. And that the *Grimms* were the only warning readily available to reveal these monsters for what they truly were. People believed them.

"So, as history would have it, the supernaturals of the age typically murdered them on the spot in order to maintain their anonymity among the other villagers. Because anyone outed as having powers back then was instantly killed. To protect the masses, of course," she added drily. The swirling fog shifted, showing us murder after murder, monsters of the night killing humans with black eyes. I shivered, trying not to imagine living in such a time where you were hated and killed for things you couldn't control. For something you were born with. Then I realized that for some, that time was now. That sobered me up.

Barbie continued on, interrupting my thoughts. "So, it was a time of *kill* or *be killed*. The Grimms suffered cataclysmic loss, but a familiar figure took heart on these poor creatures...

"Rumpelstiltskin." She paused as a figure loomed out of the fog, a twisted dwarf of a man with round lenses perched on his nose and a satchel over his shoulder. He handed the huddled Grimms something and the fog collapsed in on itself into a thick flat sheet.

"*What?*" I demanded.

"No questions until the end of the discussion, wizard." She admonished. "Now, Rumpelstiltskin, or someone very much like him, gave the Grimms an artifact that could absorb the power from a supernatural person, and allow the Grimm to wield it as their own. Then, if the Grimm was victorious the power permanently became theirs until they upgraded it to a new supernatural's power... by kidnapping or killing yet another supernatural. Rumpelstiltskin also showed them how to duplicate this artifact so that they could each have one someday."

"The Amulets." I exclaimed. Barbie nodded with a frown.

"So, they learned to defend themselves. Rather efficiently. Whatever flavor of supernatural they found themselves facing, they could match on even footing. A werewolf for a werewolf. Vampire for a vampire." That got my attention. It meant that whatever assistance I had on my side in the upcoming fight, the Grimms would be able to counter.

Well, *shit*.

"No longer in fear of being exterminated so easily, they sought training from experienced killers. And they each spent every moment learning these traits. Hunting, tracking, hiding, killing, escaping, and covering their tracks. Basically, espionage. They were the first super assassins. And being as how their eyes turned black upon seeing a supernatural, the opinion that this was a gift from god – the ability to see through the mists of hell to see the devils among us – took firmer root.

"Hard to blame them after a century of persecution, being on the run from any supernatural they happened to stumble across. Then they learned the study of law, seeing a perfect opportunity to sit in judgment of accused supernaturals. This was when they began to apply the definition of their adopted last name, Grimm, as a personal motto." She glanced around the room. "Grimm is German for *wrath*."

I shivered. Holy cow. Any time someone was accused of being a witch, wizard, or demon of some kind, with these guys on the panel as a judge they could *see* the truth and condemn as they saw fit. Which I assumed was usually an execution. The fog grew harder to watch at that point as I realized my own people were now being slaughtered at an alarming rate, and the Grimms seemed to grow taller, stronger, hungrier. Others seemed to have the same disgusted reaction to the story.

"Yes. Many died. Both good and bad people with supernatural abilities. The Grimms were ruthless. Then they decided to expand their business by becoming lawmen and hunting parties, actively pursuing the people who had murdered their ancestors for so many years. So, as you can see, our ancestors created their own worst enemy.

"I'm sure you can ascertain what happened to them after that. They entered government, the military, political offices, royal courts – any position that would give them the opportunity to expunge freaks from humanity. And they were good at it, assisting many of ancient history's most noted rulers. Every time a country went off in a ship to explore or take over new lands they typically had a secret Grimm or two in the party, willing to document, track, and kill any new creatures they might encounter.

"The American Colonies, Cortez' mission to South America, you name it. They took their family business global. Many of us in these undiscovered countries had no idea what hit us or where the Grimms' rage came from, but we soon found out. We were slaughtered for crimes we never committed. Until myself and hundreds of others collaborated to send them away." She grew quiet, remembering, and I suddenly realized that she was speaking first person. She had been there. Sure, I had heard her say that once already, but still, knowing the history now brought it into a whole new light.

"It was a big plan. Many died. We fed rumors into society that a meeting of freaks was organizing to take on the Grimms and also to coordinate the hiding of an artifact that could kill all supernatural persons if taken by the Grimms. Many died from the Grimms' torturous methods, many brave, brave souls. Men, women, and children. Totally harmless fairies, water spirits, woodland elves, and even a few of the more dangerous freaks, trolls, werewolves and vampires." She turned to me. "A *Master Temple* set up the plan. A distant ancestor of yours. It was his idea. A good one. A complicated one. And costly." I blinked in astonishment. My father had never told me *that*.

"How come I've never heard of it?" I asked.

She shook her head sadly. "Being a scribe of history, I'm almost confident that you have." She whispered. I waited, giving her a few seconds as silver tears filled her vision. "Roanoke."

I blinked. "The city in the American Colonies? Where everyone disappeared overnight?" I exclaimed in disbelief.

She nodded. "It was the location we led them to believe housed the artifact that could end us all for good."

I frowned. "But... that doesn't make any sense." Barbie smiled at me knowingly but didn't argue as she wiped away a lone tear. "Roanoke was abandoned around 1590, but *Grimm's Fairy Tales* was published in 1812..."

"You are correct, Temple. That's where the story gets *interesting*." I frowned again, but nodded, motioning for her to continue. "Now, it was around 1830 – my kind doesn't keep track of time like you mortals do – and Roanoke was now merely a shell of a town, having been abandoned long ago. The Grimms were full of bloodlust, hungry with the potential prize at their fingertips. Jacob and Wilhelm – who were actually related by blood to the real founding Grimm, not adopted to the name like others of the group – had managed to acquire the powers of a vampire so their life-span went considerably longer than history states, and they were much more than mere German professors and authors. They were brilliant, ruth-less, military leaders of a very literal army of assassins with one purpose. To end us all."

She paused, gathering her thoughts. "Master Temple, a *Maker*, in fact," she added, glancing at me, "Used his powers to create a doorway through time to Roanoke during the fateful disappearance hundreds of years in the past. The strain of such a mysterious historical event had left ripples, that he knew how to follow and pinpoint."

I blinked in astonishment, ready to pelt her with questions, but she continued on. "All of us leapt through the doorway to the past with the Grimms hot on our heels. We battled. Many died. Then he threw up a second portal leading into a void of darkness. He grabbed a bloodstained, weatherworn, fictitious map that supposedly held the directions to the arti-fact, and ran inside, leading the army away from our world. The Grimms followed. Most of them. Several more of us had to run into the gateway to convince all of them to follow. They sacrificed themselves for all of us.

"When they were all through, we carted the bodies into the dark void to eliminate any evidence and closed the gateway per Master Temple's instruc-tions. Then we returned to our time. In a way, he banished the Grimms twice. Once in the folds of time, then again in the folds of the universe itself. Quite an accomplishment. He timed it perfectly so that our wholesale slaughter could be hidden in the pages of history." The silence was deafen-ing. Ashley and Indie had tears in their eyes and were openly staring at me, seeming to empathize with the rollercoaster of emotions running through my mind. The Grimms had more than just one reason to kill me. My very ancestor had done this to them in the first place, sacrificing his life to save the world of magic. Gunnar slowly turned to me, but my vision was slightly blurry and I didn't acknowledge him.

"We carved the words *Roanoke* into every tree we could reach before fleeing. No one wanted to be found near the place when it was discovered by whatever authority happened to stumble upon the devastation and mystery that had housed a once thriving city on the fringes of the frontier. The event was hidden in history, a childhood mystery, the focus of many documentaries, but this is the true story. Perhaps the colony at Roanoke only disappeared *because* of what we did." Her eyes were distant, solemn, and almost regretful. "Without Master Temple back, we will never know the truth."

She turned to me. "Don't let them have died in vain. The Grimms must be ended, the bridge closed, and the rest of them prevented from coming over."

I had nothing to say to that.

It made me angry to realize that I didn't know if I could live up to the task of continuing or finishing what my ancestor had started. It was my fault they had found a way back. I just didn't know how to fix it.

This was well beyond me.

# CHAPTER 25

*I* sat in the corner, thinking furiously as I twirled the amulet in my fist, thinking of what needed to happen next. True, killing these asshats would give me immense satisfaction, but a small seed of empathy for their origin had also taken root. We had effectively *made* them. It didn't excuse their wholesale slaughter of Freaks, but I could understand a family feud that stretched over centuries. The supernatural community was rife with them. Even if they weren't all *technically* Grimms by *blood*. Even adopted family feuds could be violent, and as far as they saw it, they were true Grimms, blood or not.

I realized that the term *Grimm* was more accurately a sovereign nation of people with the unique ability to see through glamour. Not a last name, per se, but a *title*. And they took their jobs *very* seriously. But Jacob and Wilhelm were the real deal. Bloodline Grimms. Still, blood mattered little in this. Not at all, in fact.

And killing the ones already here would do nothing about the rest of them still waiting on the other side of the bridge. Somehow, some way, I needed to destroy this gateway or bridge or wormhole through time itself, and I didn't feel like visiting Roanoke to find it. To discover that my ancestor had been a Maker was astonishing. But to hear of the power he had wielded was even more inspiring. No wonder the world had crushed

Makers. With power like that... I had never before heard of such a thing. I would have loved to quiz my father about it, but the Armory was locked down. And I didn't have time anyway. It was history. Not relevant to our current situation.

Closing the gate would require abilities I didn't quite yet understand. Which wasn't good at all.

The sprite had just shown my friends a 'video' of how this had all come back into the light. From the auction, a few years ago, where I had tried to buy the original copy of *Grimm's Fairy Tales*. My resulting trip to Alistair's house where I met Gunnar responding to a report of gunshots, my first encounter of almost being raped by Barbie after a botched summoning, and my ultimate introduction with Jacob Grimm, visible only on a metaphysical level through a gateway of superblack darkness, the depth of which had never been replicated by man. I tapped the book cover in my hands, annoyed by the group's laughter at my failed summoning. She spent entirely too much time on that section of the story for my taste, so I had left to a quieter section of the room, refusing to be the butt of a joke when we had very real problems to deal with.

Out of professionalism, not embarrassment.

The discovery of their book had led me to opening Plato's Cave. With Alistair – St. Louis' primary arcane book dealer – murdered, someone had needed to fill his spot, and I had been fresh out of things to do.

And I loved books.

I had needed a place to hide the edition of *Grimm's Fairy Tales*, which although small, was much thicker and more ancient-looking than any copy you could find on a store's bookshelf. I had also needed to hide the book of summoning spells that Alistair had owned. The book that had introduced me to Barbie in the first place. The Grimm's had been very anxious to get their hands on it, as they could essentially summon defenseless supernaturals to their deaths. I had locked both books away underneath my store, underneath the third projector room that was used only for special occasions and was likely to be missed in the event of the store being attacked.

Like it had been earlier this year by a squad of vengeful Nephilim – the spawn of angels and humans – that had been sent to take me out. I had never told anyone about the vault beneath the store, but the very night I had gone down to pick up something entirely different from the books – the engagement ring I had been wanting to give Indie – no fewer than two groups of supernaturals had been waiting to nab the books from me. Someone knew my secret. Either I had an information leak or the spells I had used to conceal the books had faded and the Grimms could now sense it. Or my spells had never been strong enough. I had been a younger wizard back then. It was quite possible that my spells hadn't been strong enough to block it now that they were back in our world.

And I didn't even know *how* they were back in our world...

I looked down at the original edition of *Grimm's Fairy Tales* in my hands. It supposedly gave them the power to summon allies from the void of darkness where they had resided for a few centuries. I had met one of these lovely creatures already and barely survived. A demonic rooster horse I had turned into chicken nuggets. But it could also bring the rest of them back from the void. I had to keep it away from them. We needed more Grimms in St. Louis like we needed more Cubs fans in Ballpark Village.

At least I could try to even the scales a bit on the crew in my city.

This amulet thing made me nervous. Did it mean we were essentially evenly matched? I would have to change that.

Barbie had ended her story and everyone was now drifting my way. "You guys ready for a scrap?" I asked when they got closer. Their faces were grim, no pun intended, but they nodded as one, flexing fists and checking weapons. "Okay, it's now or never." I murmured, finally removing the warding spells from the books, hoping that would attract the Grimms like flies to shit. A greasy ball of acid wriggled its way into my stomach, but my magically enhanced gastrointestinal tract allowed me to hide the sensation.

I opened the book before me. It was filled with the traditional tales, all handwritten in German, but about halfway through the book morphed into a journal, complete with sketches, notes, and descriptions of various supernatural creatures no doubt encountered on their journey across the world. Power veritably throbbed from the pages, and I knew that my plan was a good one. This would attract them, all right.

I closed the book with a snap and tapped the screen of my watch a few times, setting the drone to watch the perimeter of the building. An added sentinel never hurt anyone. I wanted to know the second these punks showed up. I really hoped to see Jacob and Wilhelm. I also hoped that Misha and Tory would notice and respond quickly as a secret attack force.

"We should go outs–"

But I never got to finish that thought, because a freaking meteor hit the front door, sending it crashing inside the brownstone in an explosion of splinters and roaring sparks.

# CHAPTER 26

*E*veryone bolted to attack positions, racing for the door leading outside. No one wanted to be caught against a wall while fighting these guys. I led the gang, peering out the vacant hole in the wall where the door had been, staring into a winter wonderland. Snow was good. It would hide the battle. I turned to the sprite, "Mask the fight. I can't afford for the regulars to call the police when they see World War Three erupt on their front porches." She nodded, face tight, and cast a ball of condensed fog out the window that instantly expanded as it launched into the sky. I used the distraction to throw myself out the door, and also because I heard a monstrous roar of rage and an explosion of fire light up the sky.

I managed to glance at my watch's screen and my drone showed me a battle from the Apocalypse. A giant red dragon roared through the sky, casting jets of napalm flame down on a group of what appeared to be special-ops soldiers in all black outfits, complete with guns and night vision goggles. They scrambled, but didn't look afraid. They fled right into the waiting arms of Tory, who proceeded to Hulk Smash the first wave of Grimms with a city street trash can clutched in each manicured fist.

They didn't know what hit them.

Bodies went flying. Screams tore through the fog and snow.

The scent of blood struck me like a knife to the nose.

Then I was out the door entirely, using the diversion to cast familiar whips of molten fire and razor-sharp ice, using them like chains to harry a nearby group of ancient warriors as they opened fire on Misha and Tory. I tore them to shreds, watching their guns get slashed in half and their torsos explode in either flame or frost. I was cackling as my magic roared and hissed with unrestrained glee.

I heard a howl and Gunnar flew over my shoulder, tackling a black-eyed Grimm to the ground with his jaws snapping for a throat. Before he could kill him, the Grimm dropped his rifle and shifted to a wolf, rolling at the last second to land on his feet and twist out of Gunnar's jaws. He growled at Gunnar and then suddenly began packing on the pounds, doubling in size in a handful of seconds. Now, Gunnar was a huge freaking white werewolf. This one was now a twice-huge freaking white werewolf, and he gave Gunnar a lazy doggie grin before charging.

Gunnar barely paused, nothing but malice glittering in his eyes.

Twin shots retorted from out of a nearby window in Alistair's house and five-hundred-grain silver bullets hammered the Grimm Wolf to pulp. Gunnar looked over his shoulder and barked a complaint at Ashley who was leaning out the window with a defiant grin. But we didn't have time to revel in glory. There was the better part of a dozen more where these had come from.

Alucard was deep in the mix, tussling with two Grimms who had morphed into vampires and were trying to circle him as they lunged, swung, and bit empty air, razor sharp teeth clacking as loud as gunshots. Alucard whipped out his freaking umbrella again and withdrew a blade from the handle, spinning and whirling like a tornado as he threw himself at the nearest Grimm-pire.

*Heh.*

He was impressive. I wondered how old he was, because swordplay like that wasn't typically taught in school these days. But he sure knew how to party. His laughter filled the night as he moved in a blur, trails of blood painting the snow scarlet as he moved between the Grimms like a wraith.

I was kind of glad he had shown up.

As I picked out my next victim, preparing to face off with one who could duplicate my Maker abilities, I spotted a shady Grimm creeping among his own men, and silently slicing their throats with razor sharp claws. I watched in confusion, and then fascination, as I realized what I was seeing.

It took the Grimms only a minute to realize what was going on and discover the traitor in their midst.

Raego, using his shapeshifting abilities to look like whatever he wanted, had disguised himself as a Grimm. Two Grimms immediately exploded into half-formed black dragons, glanced down at their arms in apparent surprise at the color, and then looked up at him with pleased grins. Raego smiled back and black dragon arms replaced his own in a violent explosion of scales and claws, his face partially shifting into a dragon snout and his body doubling in size.

Let me tell you something. A dragon's roar is *loud*. I expected window-panes to shatter as the foreign vibration rattled the air, urging me to get further away from them.

The Grimms mimicked Raego and it was again two on one, but Raego was more familiar with his powers and used them to his advantage. Bodies struck bodies and razor-sharp claws slashed. One Grimm went down in a fountain of blood but no cry, and the other one redoubled his efforts. I could tell that the survivor was more talented.

I quickly glanced around, noticing another dragon racing through the sky chasing Misha, but overall it seemed like we were winning. I saw Tory swinging a car at another Grimm, who took the hit like a champ, and then swung a bigger car at her, striking her in the shoulder and sending her into a nearby tree where she crumpled. I watched anxiously, but she got back to her feet with a glare and a slight limp. I sighed in relief, scanning the streets. There weren't many Grimms left standing. Perhaps we could pull this off after all!

But I didn't have time to watch as another Grimm slowly turned to face me, a smile forming on his face. His eyes were as black as the depths of hell. Like the void my ancestor had trapped him in. I instantly recognized him from the pictures in the book. "Wilhelm," I growled hungrily. "Heard you guys swung by for the book sale I set up."

His black eyes sparkled as he nodded. "Aye."

"We already ran out of milk and cookies. Shame. But I made sure to schedule some entertainment for you while you waited. Hope you don't mind." I sneered.

"Oh, not at all. I've been aching for a good scrap for ages. Thanks to your ancestor." He grinned teasingly, flexing his fists and rolling his shoulders in preparation for a fight.

I nodded. "It runs in our blood. We're a sneaky bunch. My ancestor bested you guys what, almost half a millennium ago? Don't learn well, eh? Or are you just a sore loser? Speaking of losers, where's your big brother? Had to send the sniveling younger sibling to take me on? Was he too scared or were you just an easy sacrifice for him to make?" I smiled as his features grew still. "That must sting. Knowing he cast you into a situation you weren't equipped to handle." I teased. He glared, obviously upset that I already knew of my ancestor's involvement, and my mocking tone only fueled his anger further. He watched my whips of elemental power with a hungry gleam, but he didn't seem to tap into any kind of Maker power. Not yet anyway. "You probably should have learned. We Temples pretty much piss excellence. I guess I'm going to have to show–"

Something struck my skull from behind and the world exploded in pain. The whips of power went out as I crashed face-first into the snow. I managed to turn my head, spitting out slush, and all I could do was watch as Wilhelm slowly walked my way with lazy, plodding steps. My mind was scrambled. I struggled to gather my power, but then Wilhelm stomped on my wrist, which pretty much shut me down right there. Thankfully, no bones seemed to break, but I did feel an alarming creak of joints. Which wasn't pleasant.

"Listen up, boy. You really don't get it. You don't even stand a fraction of a chance against us. Literally." He let that sink in, the sounds of battle punctuating his words. I heard a lot of screams, and they didn't sound like Grimms. "I see you managed to swipe up the vampire. No matter. He wasn't key to our plans anyway. Just like the Minotaur wasn't key to our plans. Just a fun excursion." He chuckled. "Now, you've got something that belongs to my family. I'll be taking it back now. I'll pay you, of course. I'm not a robber." He patted his pockets and pantomimed a frown. "Well, that's embarrassing. I guess I didn't bring my wallet. Looks like I'll be accepting your generosity after all." Hands forcibly pinned me to the snow as he patted down my back, quickly finding the books I had hidden there. I hadn't wanted to risk leaving them out of my sight so had attached them to my torso with a belt, using a small spell to keep them from weighing me down. He cut the belt and plucked away the books, giving me a quick kick in the ribs.

Once.

Twice.

Three times.

Then someone flipped me onto my back. "Shame it had to end this way." Wilhelm looked around us, scanning the streets, no doubt realizing how many of them we had taken down. I followed his gaze with a satisfactory smirk.

And blinked.

There were *way* too many Grimms standing. And all my friends were down. Were they all dead? No, they were alive. I let out a relieved breath. Even if we were about to die, at least I would get the chance to look them in the eyes one last time.

I saw Ashley on the ground between two hulking Grimms who were glaring at Gunnar. He lay on the snow; face bloody, scratches on one cheek, glaring back with his lips peeled into a frozen snarl. But he didn't move. Everyone knelt in a line under direct observation of a row of Grimms. Each guard seemed to mimic the power of their captive, ready to respond in a blink if necessary, but they didn't seem very alert. In fact, they seemed rather unconcerned about the whole thing; conversing softly with each other while my crew knelt in the cold, wet snow. Nothing moved in the windows of nearby buildings, and I could hear nothing from the outside world.

Just us.

I saw another Grimm stand wearily from kneeling over a body on the ground. His neck had been slashed wide open by claws of some flavor.

Then the dead Grimm stood, shook his head, and wiped his hands on his pants. He bowed in thanks to the lean Grimm, and resumed his position beside his brothers. The Grimm who had apparently healed him or brought him back to life had an iron collar across his throat, etched with deep, mysterious looking runes. A *necromancer*? Able to bring those back from the *dead*? Come on! I idly remembered the two kids with extraordinary healing powers I had met several years ago. The brother and sister that the Grimms had hoped to recruit or kill. Looks like they had been taken, judging by this Grimm's incredible healing powers.

Wilhelm chuckled. "Thanks, Ichabod." The man grunted in acknowledgement, tired eyes passing over me in what looked like quiet rage and calloused disgust. His eyes twinkled with power, but I didn't know what kind, and they weren't black. Perhaps he was the one duplicating my Maker ability, because I sure as shit couldn't think of another power that could do what he just did – not counting the two kids with healing powers the Grimms had no doubt taken. Unless I myself could have someday learned necromancy with my Maker ability. Well, that pipeline thought ended here and now. We were through. Caught. Kidnapped. Bested. My trap turned on itself. Ichabod walked away to stand a bit apart from the rest of the men. I idly wondered if his power came from the banded collar around his neck rather than the amulets I had seen everyone wearing so far.

Wilhelm turned back to me. "I have no further use for your people, but I do have use for you. I'll let you off with a warning this time. I have what we need for now, so get your affairs in order. We're back and we're going to end your reign of terror. I need you... *cooperative*," he smiled darkly. "So, I'll let your people go as long as–"

A thunderous crack interrupted him and his shoulder exploded in blood, which liberally sprayed me. Wilhelm howled, pointing a finger at the house. "Get the bitch!"

Men darted for the house, and I realized something I had missed in my first glance. Indie was nowhere to be found.

Ichabod approached on tired feet and placed his hands on Wilhelm. I felt a gentle thrum of power similar to mine as the flesh began to knit itself back together. She had hit him in the joint, destroying his cartilage and tendons with a five-hundred-grain silver bullet, the kind used for hunting big game. My crew hadn't taken my caution lightly after hearing about the liger.

But it didn't matter. In seconds, Wilhelm was back to normal. He turned on me with a murderous scowl, rolling his shoulder. "You'll pay for that. Luckily, we don't typically kill humans or she would be dead. Instead, I think I'll keep her. For myself. After we conclude our business." I began to shake, trying to break free. My head was still scrambled from the unseen blow that had taken me down. And I couldn't touch my power.

"Stop struggling. I've got Ichabod blocking you anyway, even if you managed to get up." I stopped, spitting out blood, hitting his boots. He kicked me in the face. I came back to consciousness what felt like a few million years later.

The Grimms from the house were talking with Wilhelm, who was looking more furious by the minute. "What do you mean you can't find her? She's a god damn human. You're telling me you can battle monsters and demons but you can't find a young girl?" He backhanded the Grimm, knocking the man to his feet. A single tooth sailed into a pile of snow, but the Grimm merely spat, stood, and bowed apologetically.

He nodded to Wilhelm. "Aye, Sir. My apologies. I offer my life as payment."

"We don't have enough of us to go about tossing your lives about for these things, lucky for you. Just remember our goal. We need to get the rest of our brothers back." He scowled at the house, ignoring the nodding soldier. The man genuinely looked reprimanded. I shook my head in disbelief. These guys were true zealots. Wilhelm turned back to me, looking angry. "It seems I don't get my entertainment for tonight. Don't worry. You'll be hearing from us soon. She will be mine shortly thereafter. For now, we leave. I don't want to waste Ichabod's time bringing us back one by one if she decides to begin shooting again." He tipped an imaginary hat at me. "It's been a pleasure. Thanks for the... *book sale*. And also for masking the fight from the humans. We wouldn't want to show them your true colors, demon." He muttered, kicking me one more time for good measure.

Then, as one, they began trotting down the street, disappearing from view. Apparently, my people had been restrained, because none of them moved. They merely watched. None of it made sense to me. Why had Wilhelm let any of us live? The Grimms *hated* all freaks. I began to grow terrified as my mind stirred up all sorts of reasons for leaving any of us alive, and each was worse than the last.

As one, my friends suddenly jumped to their feet as if still in the thick of battle, glancing about frantically for enemies. I blinked at that. Then realized what had happened. The entire conversation had happened out of their time reference and I hadn't even realized it. As soon as Wilhelm began talking to me he must have frozen time, as I had seen his brothers do once before, so that our conversation remained private.

Raego exploded into his dragon form, snarling at the fog, droplets of fire splashing the snow in flashes of steam. After a few seconds, my friends saw me, no bad guys nearby, and bolted towards me to form a protective circle. They helped me to my feet, tossing questions back and forth and checking on each other. It seemed that more or less, everyone was okay. Flesh wounds all, but nothing requiring immediate attention. Other than rebuilding their dignity. I had brought a literal army to take on these clowns and it hadn't been enough. And Jacob hadn't even been here. He was apparently the bigger, badder brother. We had killed or injured plenty, but they had all been brought back by their spellslinger, Ichabod. He was the key to stopping them. I had to kill him next time we met. First. Fast. Without hesitation. Without his interference, we may have won.

"At least we still have the book. We lost the battle, but there is still the war." Gunnar was reminding Raego and Alucard, who looked as furious as it was likely to possibly get, having shifted back to their more or less human forms.

I cleared my throat, accepting Ashley's arm for support. "About that…" I said through pained breaths, sure my ribs had cracked or been broken from Wilhelm's well-placed kicks. My wrist throbbed. Everyone looked at me. "They took it." Faces turned white, lips setting in tight lines.

"Oh." Alucard mumbled. We absorbed that in silence as Ashley led me into the house. I had to find Indie. The rest of the world could burn for all I cared if Indie wasn't safe. The sprite appeared beside me, landing on my shoulder, now doll-sized again.

"She's okay. Don't worry. I led her to a safe place. She's in the office now. A nice shot." She murmured. I grunted, relief enveloping my shoulders. Indie was safe. I sighed as we entered the office. Indie stared at me, and her shoulders sank in relief. I gripped her in my arms, and then my legs gave out as the pain hit me. She fell along with me, cradling my head in her breasts. I began to cry.

I had been beaten, and I could think of no way to win. Soon they would bring over their brothers, and an already unbeatable crew of black ops mercenaries would get bigger. And badder.

I had thrown my best punch, setting the time, location, and we had been ready. We had been calmly swatted down like rueful puppies.

Mainly because of Ichabod. If we stood a chance of going back against them I needed to take him out first. Indie stroked my hair as the rest of my friends silently left, Gunnar and Alucard taking charge of two smaller groups, leading them deeper into the house to give us some privacy.

"I failed you. I failed all of us. Who did I think I was to lead us into that? Without Wilhelm's mercy, we would all be dead now."

Indie continued to silently stroke my hair, letting me vent. "We were winning. We were beating them. Then my mouth got in the way and someone sucker-punched me. I didn't see what happened next, but when I looked up, everyone was suddenly down."

I felt Indie mutter under her breath. "That man, Ichabod, happened. He did… something and everyone dropped. Then he calmly went from body to body bringing everyone back to life. Misha landed on a car, totaling it. No one could move. As he brought them back, they broke off into groups and gathered up everyone, leading them back to kneel before you in a line. Taunting and mocking them before Ichabod gave them a look and they stopped. I think even they are scared of him. Or wary of him. Was there a third brother in the stories?" I shook my head. "I wonder why he's so much more powerful than they are?" She asked to herself.

"He was using the power of a Maker. I think." I felt her look down at me, her body shifting. I shrugged. "Each Grimm duplicated our powers. I felt him use his power to heal Wilhelm. It felt familiar. I think he was the one blocking me. Except he knew how to use the power. I don't. At least not nearly as well. Maybe these amulets of theirs let them understand how to use their powers completely. Makes sense. Of course, they would have no idea how to use the abilities they steal beforehand, so it makes sense that they gain not only the power but knowledge of the power as well."

She grunted. "Scary." We were silent for a time, me trying to breathe deeper and stretch out the injured ribs as Indie continued stroking my cheeks and head. "He needs to die first," she finally said.

"My thoughts exactly," I growled.

"Consider this a test run. *Veni, Vidi… we got our asses kicked.*" I burst out laughing as she improvised the saying, *we came, we saw, we conquered.* "We should learn from it. This doesn't sound over. They haven't brought anyone else over yet. And they let us live. That means that they need something else."

I nodded, hissing at the resulting shooting pain in my skull caused by the motion. "Wilhelm said the same. That we would meet again soon." Another thought hit me. "You can't see him again. He has plans for you. Especially after shooting him. And he wants to hurt me. He gets you, and I'll do whatever he wants. I won't be able to help it." Indie began to growl an argument but I interrupted her. "I can sit here and tell you whatever you want to hear, that I'll take the right path and do the right thing, but let's be honest. When it comes to you, I'll choose you every time." I didn't mean it to sound romantic. I was just being honest, showing my flaw as a leader, but Indie squeezed me in a loving hug that hurt me so much I wanted to scream. But I didn't complain.

I could hear her crying, as well as sirens in the background. The damage in the street had been noticed and reported to the authorities. And it was outside another property I owned. This wasn't going to end well.

"Nate..." She didn't say *what are we going to do*, but she must have thought it very loudly.

I nodded. "I know..." I answered her unspoken question. "We need to vamoose." She helped me to my feet and we headed towards the others to Shadow Walk back to *Chateau Falco*, the only safe place I knew. As I began to cast the familiar spell of Shadow Walking, a thought whispered in my subconscious. I modified the spell a bit, and instead of ripping us to a new location, a vertical ring of blue fire erupted before us, revealing the snowy steps leading up to the front door of *Chateau Falco*. A gateway. That was new...

The sprite appeared before me, not giving me time to analyze the unique power I had instinctively used. I would worry about it later. Barbie shot me a silent look that said *call me when you are ready...* I nodded back and continued through the ring of fire, wondering if I would ever be ready to sentence my friends to die in order to save the supernatural community at large from the Grimms. It looked like sacrifice was our only option.

# CHAPTER 27

We had managed to get everyone into his or her own rooms, and when I say 'we' I really mean Dean, my Butler. But he worked for me, so I gain credit by extension.

The task seemed to have filled Dean with a level of pride and energy I hadn't seen in him in a long time. This was his job, and he took it very seriously. Each guest's request was met with an eager smile and then promptly satisfied. Mallory was ever present to help Dean out, but when I caught his eye he shook his head discreetly, letting me know that no one had tried to break in, but that he also hadn't located Tomas either.

With Jacob being absent from the fight earlier, I had feared that he had attempted to break into the Armory or something while his brothers kept us distracted. But it looked like all was clear.

Alucard was very pleased, studying my house with acute interest. He had shed blood for me, and even though we had met under less than ideal circumstances – him attempting to separate my head from my shoulders – I realized that I trusted him. I hoped that wasn't a mistake, but then again, I noticed Gunnar studying him several times, looking wary but also impressed. It was nice to see him also approving of the vampire, a natural enemy of a werewolf, but I knew he would keep an eye on things, leaving me to focus on our bigger problem.

Bros.

A powerful word.

Gunnar had been beaten, knocked down, but seeing that Ashley was more or less unharmed had given him renewed vigor, and a personal stake in the matter. In fact, everyone was now personally involved. It was no longer about helping me out of my own mess. They had all kicked ass, and had their asses kicked by the Grimms, and all looked anxious – and terrified – for round two. But none looked as downtrodden as I felt. They looked full of purpose, so I put on a mask, like my father had taught me long ago. A leader couldn't show weakness.

A leader was more than just the guy giving commands. He was the candle in the dark, the little light of fire that kept the team focused.

I must have done a decent job, because only the women seemed to see the truth. As was always the case. Ashley and Indie had several silent conversations with only their eyes. Tory and Misha jumped in on a few of these exchanges, learning the same information by estrogenic osmosis, and each of them silently proceeded to take care of the men, encouraging us, congratulating us, and generally building our self-esteem for round two, fueling our fires rather than putting them out with doubts and fears.

It was kind of magical.

I didn't let on that I knew their superpower, but Indie saw me watching and shrugged. "It's what we do."

"Hey, don't belittle yourself. You also bake cakes and clean the kitchen." Her eyes turned playfully aggressive. I grinned.

"If you weren't injured..." she growled, jokingly.

My injuries had slowly faded after eating what felt like a cereal bowl of painkillers, but I knew they would come back to haunt me soon. Indie grabbed my hand and we began to walk the halls of *Chateau Falco*, simply enjoying each other's company as we made our way to my office. I was anxious to get to the Armory and verify that all was safe and that hopefully the mysterious ward was down. Everyone else had gone to bed, leaving Indie and I to secretly check on the Armory and hopefully gain some insight into the Grimms from Pandora and my parents. As long as the door would open this time. I hadn't had time to really ponder that but it bothered me. It had never happened before and I didn't like surprises, especially when those surprises coincided with the Grimms' arrival.

We passed a small reading room to find Tory and Misha snuggling together, fast asleep. I smiled, nodding to Indie. She grinned back in silence.

As we took another step, Misha opened one eye to appraise us, no doubt making sure everything was safe for the woman in her arms. I wondered if she had even been asleep in the first place. Seeing it was just Indie and I, she winked and closed her eyes. Tory snuggled in closer to her chest with a sigh. Misha pulled a blanket over her shoulders and settled deeper into the couch, wrapping her arms around the ex-cop with a gentle kiss to the back of her head. I gently tugged Indie's hand, signaling for us to leave them in peace.

As we continued down the hall, I peppered Indie. "That's why I do this, Indie. To keep people like them safe from the Grimms." She nodded, eyes misty. We continued on for a few seconds in silence before I poked her playfully in the ribs. "You were saying something about me being injured...?" I teased, seeing the office just ahead.

She grinned mischievously. "I was saying that if you weren't injured, I'd have the sprite come over and remind me about the time you two met." My face turned red. "Then I would let her show me a few of her tricks for the next time you got out of hand." She winked darkly and I shook my head.

"I'd like to see you try that, woman. After you finish with the dishes, of course."

She lunged, chasing me, but I quickly darted into the office, pausing just past the threshold for her to catch me, so that I could possibly sneak in a kiss or two in private.

I had expected her to latch onto my shoulder, but nothing happened. I slowly turned and noticed that she was frozen in midair, arm outstretched to catch me. She was in the office, but completely immobile, still featuring a predator's grin as she reached out a playful hand, her eyes dancing with mischief. My good mood evaporated.

Indie was frozen, which could mean only one thing. Grimms.

I spun, fumbling to latch onto my power. We were under attack. And I hadn't activated the *Guardians*, fearing any misunderstandings with so many guests present.

I found the chair behind my desk slowly turning to face me. I didn't give him a chance to react. I launched a spear of ice directly at his cold, heartless chest, staring into his inky black eyes. I would finish what my ancestor started.

Here.

Now.

He waved a hand and the spear disappeared. He wiped off his hands with a smirk.

"Nate."

"Jacob." I acknowledged, forming another, more violent strike.

"I wouldn't."

"I would," I growled, tossing another lance of power, twice as strong.

The same thing happened. He wasn't even breathing hard. "We could do this all day. Or we could talk. I'm sure you've realized by now that I can duplicate all that you can do. Probably do it better, seeing as you don't yet know how to use your power, whereas I hold the knowledge of how to use it to its utmost potential." He held out a hand, palm up, waiting.

I grunted, flicking my head at Indie. "She's not a part of this." I warned.

"Why do you think I froze time?" He asked. His eyes slowly shifted from shiny black orbs to their normal blue shade as he stood. He shook his head. "Been a while since I had to deal with that." He approached me warily, not afraid, but as one would approach a skittish horse. It pissed me off. As if I needed to be calmed down. He was a murdering murderer. Of course, I was on edge. He carefully stepped to the side, studying Indie thoughtfully, not in a creepy way, but as if to see her for himself. "So, this is the one who shot my brother."

"Yep." I answered snidely. "And if Ichabod wouldn't have been there, boy, would his face have been red." I clapped a hand over my mouth and whispered pantomime. "Whoops. Too soon?"

He waved a hand, smirking. "Not at all. Wilhelm has always been... eager." He finally answered, face thoughtful. "It's why I lead. My younger brother can be very willful." He looked at me as if to give me inside information. "And he's very interested in taking your woman. As recompense." He watched me. "And that would be unpleasant for her."

"Yeah, well, that's not going to happen. I skipped class the day they taught *sharing*."

He blinked. "If he had his way, you wouldn't really have much say in the matter. Your body would be cold, providing sustenance for the worms." He added matter-of-fact.

"It wouldn't pan out like that," I said neutrally, letting him take what he would from my words. I was beginning to feel a little on edge. Why was he being so cordial? This was nothing like the monster I had first met several years ago.

175

He grunted. We studied each other. He was tall. Really tall. Well over six feet, and his hair was, *wait for it*, as white as snow, indicating his true age. Harnessing the powers of a vampire in his past had definitely agreed with his aging factor, because I spotted not a wrinkle. His features were long, harsh, and angular, as if he had recently vacated a sick bed, despite the healthy glow in his blue eyes. His long, bony fingers reached out from the sleeve of his black trench coat like a skeleton as he offered it to shake. I spat at it, hitting his palm with a satisfying *smack*. He frowned, shaking it off and then using a handkerchief to wipe it off. He tossed the soiled white kerchief on the ground.

"You surrendering?" I sneered.

He burst out laughing, patting his knees in amusement with those huge hands. They could very easily fit around my skull, which I wasn't interested in testing. "And why would I do such a thing? My... *B team* ate your lunch today, and you thought you were in *control* of the situation, setting a *trap* of all things. Cute. I see you've healed up a bit from my younger brother's... *ministrations.*" He smiled in amusement, acknowledging the injuries Wilhelm had given me. "That's nice, but we can heal better." He tapped his knee with a finger. "So, I must ask. What more could you *possibly* throw at me? The Minotaur? The turncoat vampire?" He smiled, not necessarily mocking me but instead asking with genuine interest.

I studied him thoughtfully. "You seem less... *psychotic* this time."

He nodded, eyes growing distant at the memory of our first meeting. "You must remember. The first time we met, I had been spending centuries in darkness." He watched me for a moment. "*426 years* to be precise. You should remember that number." He added cryptically with a twinkle in his eyes.

Oh, I remembered. Thanks to my ancestor their prison sentence had been extended through time itself. Poor guys. I was mildly curious how he had figured it out though. Because for all he knew, they had never traveled through time, so if he was looking at time by merely counting years then it had only been *186* years. But I didn't want to press too many of his buttons. If he didn't know, that was his problem. Maybe he had counted tally marks on a wall or something.

He continued. "And the first thing my eyes saw of my lost world was an abomination. Sorry, a *Freak*, as society rightfully calls you creatures these days." He waved his hand. "And not just any Freak, but a *Temple*. Ho' boy! An ancestor of the very man who put us in prison in the first place! I was a little… off my game." He smiled at the understatement. For all I knew, that first meeting was *on his game*, and this was merely a ruse. He waved his hand, motioning towards the fireplace, inviting me to sit. I complied, not knowing what else to do. I was essentially at his disposal; totally impotent to stop him from doing whatever it was he was trying to do. After all, if he had wanted to kill me he would have done so by now, and I didn't think I would have been able to stop him. He was right. He knew how to use the power of a Maker. I didn't.

Which blew.

So, I sat. With dignity. Realizing that with all my power and reputation, I was but a child to this legendary killer. My wrist ached. As did my ribs. Courtesy of his brother. I let none of it show. Let him think what he will.

He duplicated my motion, sitting across from me, steepling his fingers as he watched me like a bug in a box. "We have the book." He held up a finger. "We bested you in battle. Well, not *we*, but my brother." He held up another finger. "You and your motley crew of Freaks are injured, broken, and *you* don't even know how to properly use your power." He waited for me to argue, but I didn't. "There is a price on your head for me to take you out, which I had been planning on doing anyway." He held up a third finger, which was becoming damn annoying. "But you've done me a favor." He took a finger away. "And you have something else I want." He took away another finger. His gaze traveled to Indie, and he added as an afterthought, "And something my brother wants." He folded the last finger, and rested his palm in his lap. Then he waited.

"I don't understand."

He chuckled, nodding as he leaned forward. "I know."

I stared back, and decided to play my trump card. "You know I took out two of you single-handedly at the hotel." But he simply shrugged.

"A minor loss. They were hotheads, unworthy of life if they couldn't best you."

I hid a shiver at his callousness. "I have access to The Armory…" I stated, wondering if that name would mean anything to a man locked away for a few hundred years.

He clapped his hands. "Oh, you're not slow at *all*. That is *precisely* what I am speaking of!"

"And I could decimate you and your brothers with the weakest of toys from inside. Out of courtesy, I didn't bring them out to play today." I warned, smiling gently.

"Oh?" He asked, smiling.

I pressed on. "Yes. It really isn't even a question of the outcome. It's merely who you would like to sacrifice as cannon fodder." I said, tone neutral. "I'm willing to play. Are you willing to play, Jacob?"

He nodded eagerly, leaning further forward. "Oh, yes." Then he waited, watching me.

"Well, not this second." I finally said, growing frustrated.

"No, please. Go ahead. I will wait." He glanced at Indie thoughtfully, a frown growing on his face. "Oh, dear. I see now. You don't want to leave me with her. Wise choice." He tapped his lip thoughtfully before thrusting a finger in the air. "Ah! I could come with you and choose the weapon for you to slay me with." He offered.

I laughed. "Like I would show you where–"

He stood, leaned towards the mantle above the fireplace, and clicked a button I didn't even know existed. The fireplace roared like normal and he disappeared inside. I blinked, jumping to my feet a second later and rushing after him in a panic, torn between leaving Indie or leaving Jacob unattended. *How in the holy hell…*

And the bastard had moved so *fast*.

I landed in the familiar secret passageway ready to sprint and chase the fucker down, but found him casually leaning against the wall. "One hundred feet down, through the open room, second hallway on the right, last door on the first left hallway." He said laconically, smirking.

I blinked at him, not even attempting to hide my surprise. "How did you…"

"Yes, that is the proper sequence of words in the question, and ironically, my answer will start with the same three words." He maintained his smile as he continued. "How did you… *think we got here in the first place, Nathaniel Laurent Temple?*"

He strode past me with a whirl of his coat, rubbing his arms for warmth as he jumped back into the portal leading to the office. I blinked several times, then quickly followed, growing beyond agitated that he seemed to be one step ahead of me at every turn, but not wanting to leave him alone with Indie for one second.

When I appeared in the office he was already back in his chair, waiting.

I calmly sat down, checked on Indie, who remained frozen, and then stared into the fire. "What did you mean, Jacob?" I asked, voice dry as dust.

"The Armory. It was how we found our way back. Power calls power." He answered cryptically. Seeing my frown, he elaborated. "The fates would have it that you used it in recent months, and not just used it, but destroyed an existing gateway connected to it. Like all magic, power cannot be created nor destroyed, so the Armory sought out another gateway to connect to all on her own. Lucky for me, our calls coincided with her need and she let us link."

I blinked in astonishment. "She would never…"

He chuckled. "Oh, how delicious! I'm not speaking of your *librarian*." He emphasized quotes with his fingers, referring to Pandora. "I'm referring to the Arcanum itself, the Armory is a very literal being in its own right after so many years of housing the world's most deadly weapons. The items held in her clutches have tainted her – like magic does to everyone." He murmured with a bit of the zealot briefly peeking through his calm demeanor before he regained his composure. "The items have… awoken her. As any true guardian would know, if he had paid attention." His eyes looked me up and down with disappointment.

I shook my head in disbelief. "I'm kind of new to the position." I muttered defensively.

He reached out as if to touch my knee consolingly. I flinched away and he smiled. "I understand. Don't fret yourself, dear boy." That prickled up my spine, although I guessed he *was* several hundred years my senior. Technically. He watched me for a time before continuing. "Speaking of the Armory. Any luck trying to gain entrance lately?" His smile told me enough to know the awful truth.

Not only was he better than me in battle. He was also better than me at chess. I felt like I was in a philosophical debate with Gandhi, Aristotle, and Sun Tzu at the same time. "If you know enough to ask that you know the answer." I snarled in defeat.

"Yes. Well, you can blame me for that also. A few of us tried breaking in recently, but the Armory, or perhaps your *librarian*," he rolled his eyes. "Wouldn't let us in. Locked the door on us in fact." His eyes grew thoughtful as he studied me, no doubt pondering why he had failed. But I knew why. My blood was the key to the Armory. I kept my face blank as he watched me, but he finally sighed with an amused smile at my stubbornness. "No matter. It *is* quite the collection, I must say." My body tensed in alarm, wondering what devilish items he may have taken. He laughed at my bodily reaction. "Don't worry. I wasn't able to touch anything. Yet. Just a sight-seeing tour on our first time through." He watched me like a predator. "It was… enlightening. I saw…" his gaze trailed out the window, watching the snow fall for a few beats. "Vast potential for my brothers and I…" Silence stretched between us for a few moments longer before he resumed. "It will aid me immeasurably in the days to come. After I kill you, of course." He added as an afterthought, a slight crease in his forehead as if remembering he needed to take out the trash after dinner.

"Well, I'm not particularly fond of that plan." I was practically hyperventilating, but hiding it well. I hoped. He had taken a stroll through the Armory. Unaided. Had he hurt Pandora? Had she even known they were there? What about my parents? I buried those thoughts deep and faced him. "I'll take you on a tour myself if you wish. Why don't you and your brothers meet me here after I have a cup of coffee and I can show you my toys? And what they can do. Just me and your crew." I was almost whispering at the last, leaning forward with a hungry gleam in my eyes.

He watched me neutrally. "Tempting," he said, tapping his lips in thought, "But it will be mine soon enough. After you are expunged from this world."

"Well, I hate to ruin your plans, but killing me won't get you the Armory. It's keyed to my living blood." I answered honestly.

He nodded simply. "I know."

I felt smug with my small victory. I would win the war by losing the battle. Dying. Hoorah! Then he continued.

"But with my amulet, I'll absorb your very essence, able to do all that you can, be all that you are. Which means your powers will be mine, you will be dead, and the Armory will recognize me as her guardian." I began to shiver deep down in my soul. Would it really work out that way?

"Your amulet?" I asked, trying to stall for time.

He waved a hand at me, not even glancing my way. "Oh, come now. Don't act coy. I was waging wars before your Great ancestors were even a twinkle in another's eye. Judging by your reaction speed at the battle, you know all about our amulets and how they function. Else you would have shat yourself upon the first battle cry. I heard our old friend, Seraph, aided you in battle. I would so love to talk with her again. In private." His tone dripped venom, and I was pretty sure I knew whom he was talking about, even though I had never heard the name.

"Who?"

"The sprite that thwarted me when you and I first met." He amended. I managed to keep my face blank. I would have to warn her. At least she wasn't here. She was safe.

For now.

Jacob's forehead creased again as he continued to watch the snow fall outside. I was suddenly glad I had secreted away the amulets I had absconded from the liger and ape. I didn't know if he could have sensed them, but he likely would have taken them from me. And I wanted to study them. Jacob turned back to me. He looked supremely disappointed. "I grow weary of our talk. I had so hoped that you would be worth at least a little bit of banter."

He stood. "You know, I didn't even need to take the contract to want to kill you, but it was a large sum of money, and why do something for free when you can get paid? We have a lot to learn about this new world, and that costs money. We will kill you, my brother will play with your woman... for a time anyway, and then I will use my new Armory to bring back the rest of my brothers." He smiled in expectant euphoria. "Finally, to know that I avenged the fallen, taking down the very ancestor of our captor. To free my brothers, my family... I won't tell you how sweet that first breath of fresh air was..." His voice grew with excitement. "We will cleanse the world of the filth of magic once and for all." His eyes were glazed.

"You know, speaking of your brothers, I'm kind of offended you didn't bring all of them to our reunion. There won't be enough to kill for me to feel well and truly sated. It's kind of like when you take the last bite of a meal and you're still pretty hungry, but that's it. No more. It's a living hell, you know? Knowing you have to wait a few hours to get what you want..." I looked at him, eyes opening in embarrassment. "Oh, I didn't even... of *course* you know what I'm talking about. My ancestor gave you that gift already. *For four hundred years...* And here I am, talking about having to wait a few *hours*." I shook my head in faux embarrassment. "Must sting a bit, eh, Jakey?" I smiled good-naturedly at him, enjoying the slight reddening of his face. Finally, I had been able to get a rise out of him.

Then he calmed, watching me with a slight frown. "I truly wish I could spill the beans and tell you what you are missing. It's particularly sad that you genuinely have no idea what is about to happen. What *has* happened. And who the instrument of your destruction is. I guess you will die ignorant. Unless I decide to whisper the answer in your ear before I slice. Off. Your. Head." He shrugged his shoulders, truly not concerned about casually mentioning decapitation. *These freaking guys*, I shivered. And I wondered about his comment. Wilhelm had said something similar.

"You know... you're here, I'm here, your douche bag brother is torturing innocent kittens somewhere nearby. Why don't we just start the party already? Why don't–"

I blinked, feeling as if a bucket of ice water had just been dumped down my back.

A diversion.

Jacob began a slow clap. "My, my, *my*. The hamster finally learns how to use the wheel sitting in his cage. You're quite astute when you need to be, but boy does it take you a while to gain some traction. In my day, you would have been dashed against the rocks before two years old, supernatural or not." He shook his head in disgust. "Don't worry. We'll be seeing each other very soon, *Temple*." He shivered to himself, smiling in anticipation. "Damn it feels good to say that word with satisfaction rather than a soul deep rage." He winked. "I might as well tell you, you can believe me or not, but your Armory is on lockdown for another thirty-six hours. Thanks to our little stroll through her halls. In the meantime, don't worry about an impending attack. You'll receive plenty of warning when we desire to meet again. We don't need to surprise a group of mewling children. This diversion was about something else entirely." He smiled, almost laughing at my face as I waited to hear what he had done. "I recommend the... *television*, I think you call it." He shook his head. "Wonder of wonders what mortals have discovered without the use of magic. Anyway, you should find the local news particularly interesting." Then he disappeared in a puff of black smoke and a laugh, the perfect evil overlord exit.

Damn it.

"You'll pay for that, Nate!" Indie hissed, laughing as she suddenly lurched into the room, claws outstretched to latch onto my shirt where she had last seen me.

But I was no longer there.

Indie stumbled and blinked, finally spotting me by the fire. Then she grinned. "Did you really just Shadow Walk to the fire in order to escape me?

Wuss." She teased. Then she saw my face. "Nate?" she took an uncertain step closer. Rather than respond, I turned on the TV and sat in utter disbelief as the news report folded over me, numbing my brain.

"What in holy hell…" Indie began, collapsing into the other chair as a video played on the news.

# CHAPTER 28

*I* did what anyone would do when they find out their home has been frequented by a gang of monster killers.

I went exterminating.

Mallory and I had armed for bear, taking the West Wing of *Chateau Falco*, and I had kept my eyes open for any whisper of power emanating from the walls. Because, you know, Jacob seemed to know my house better than I did. Which made Mallory and Dean all sorts of offended. I hadn't told them that I hadn't known about the secret entrance, but simply that Jacob had *also* known about entrances he shouldn't have known about. It's called managing the chaos. I couldn't let them know how badly I had been outclassed.

Rage kept me warm as we traipsed through the halls, my power constantly beckoning to me. I almost *wanted* someone to jump out at me. We had left the girls with the other men, who had actively promised to guard them with their lives. Even Alucard. But I didn't think they needed any help. They were armed with a plethora of bullets, swords, and they had a Tory, a one-person wrecking crew. They needed no protection. Even if Alucard was handy in a scrap.

That small trusting part of me screamed at me not to be so foolish.

He was a vampire, and vampires couldn't be trusted.

Just like the Grimms thought that *none of us Freaks* could be trusted.

It sucks when your own arguments are thrown back at you. Unconditional bias towards a person or persons was a vicious poison.

As displayed by the Grimms.

It was time for me to open up my blinders a bit. A teeny bit. Vampires were after all murderers by default. That didn't mean that one couldn't rise above such little things.

Still, I would be on my guard. But I would also cut him a little slack. After all, he could have died several times today but he had been right there in the thick of battle.

But on the other hand, he had threatened, and actually killed me today.

I sighed, scanning the bookshelf before me, catching a newspaper clipping of my father and mother from several years before.

Standing in front of Temple Industries.

A part of me died with shame.

I had failed them. I had failed everyone. My friends. My company. Even the various Freaks of my city. They just didn't know it yet. I had given the Grimms access back to our world, and they were hungry to pick up where they had left off. The family business. Killing everything with even a drip of magic in their blood.

I realized I was growling when I saw the mirrored look on Mallory's face.

"We'll figure it out, son. Temple Industries will weather the storm." He trailed off, face distant, seeming as if even he didn't buy the words. "Somehow..."

I grunted.

We were back in the main living quarters. Raego and Misha were back from their section of the house, and they met us at the grand staircase, the obvious wealth of the marble balustrades and shining floors a blatant mockery of safety.

Chateau Falco had been invaded. Silently. Stealthily.

The Grimms had been in my home. And I hadn't known. I shivered. One night in the not too distant past I had been fast asleep beside Indie, and more than a dozen men had crept through my house.

And no one had noticed.

They could have even watched us for a time, unobserved, judging by Jacob's obvious knowledge of my floor plan. Just because he had entered through the Armory, that didn't explain how he knew of the secret entrance or how it had been activated. Unless his amulet did as he said, letting him know how to use his powers on a level so far above mine that I would snap my neck even trying to look up at him.

I knew the amulets could temporarily mirror whatever powers were thrown at it, but what was Jacob's *innate* power? The power permanently stored in the Amulet? Could the amulets store more than one type of power at a time? For how long? Centuries? And what had he meant by mentioning the *instrument of my destruction*? Was there a traitor in my midst? If so, I had no idea who it could be, although if I had to bet it would have been our newest member, Alucard. Or maybe that's what Jacob *wanted* me to think. To make me paranoid. I would just have to keep an eye on everyone. I shook my head as I silently began walking up the stairs. My friends followed me. No one spoke.

In one night, my whole world had collapsed. Every pillar that supported me shattered.

My own power was useless.

My friends were just as useless to defend themselves and had almost died trying.

I had unknowingly given a bus pass to history's baddest exterminators to come to St. Louis. And they were hungry to make up for lost time.

And my company...

I shook my head, glancing down at my phone. No missed calls. I angrily typed a text, demanding a response.

*Now*. Things needed to be done immediately if I stood a chance of surviving this.

Jacob had planned well. I just didn't know how he could have accomplished it. He had been locked away for centuries and had no idea how the world worked these days. I wouldn't have expected it of even the savviest of corporate lawyers – of which I had numerous on retainer, and not one had answered my calls – let alone a centuries-old assassin. It was almost worth an ovation, if I hadn't been on the receiving end.

I entered the office to find the television blaring, and my friends staring at the screen with ashen faces.

"In a late press release this evening, Nate Temple took to the camera to inform St. Louis of his resignation from Temple Industries." They played a clip of me standing there, in front of a gaggle of reporters, announcing my resignation, and then leaving with an insolent grin. Which was impossible.

186

The reporter continued. "The stock value crashed as a result. This all happened in the hours leading up to the closing bell, allowing time for the stock to drop lower than it ever has since its Initial Public Offering. Temple Industries is the largest employer of our city, and one of the larger technology companies in the world. Following the death of the founders, Nate Temple's parents, the company has struggled to find its way. Some say as a direct result of an absentee owner. A meeting was held this afternoon with the Board of Directors and Nate Temple to discuss the sale of the company to a German firm. Nate Temple later informed the media, who had been anxiously waiting outside the hotel, that the company was not for sale. Then he left without another word.

"Police were called to assist several injured reporters at the scene of what appears to have been a gunfight. Nate Temple could not be reached regarding the obvious violence, and speculation abounds as to who caused the injuries. Sources report that Nate Temple did leave with a gunshot wound. Details are being investigated at this time and we will inform you of any updates regarding the attack and the future of Temple Industries." Venom was thick in the reporter's voice. I had heard this already, but I wasn't sure if all of my friends had.

The television suddenly elicited an eruption of sparks and the screen cracked in half.

My friends turned to face me, eyes questioning. Alucard watched me, face blank. Ashley looked livid, but not at me. She had been in the meeting after all. She knew it to be a lie.

"Nate…" Gunnar began.

I held up a finger. "It's a lie. All of it."

Ashley watched me, brain practically buzzing with questions. "I've been with you all day. I am almost one hundred percent certain that this isn't possible. No offense." She answered my glare, speaking clinically. "Which means that this is corporate espionage, but who could have duplicated your every mannerism? I mean, that is *you*, Nate." She whispered. She began thumbing through her phone after a short vibration on the device.

I sighed, sitting down. "I have no idea. But to be honest, none of that matters. Stock values have plummeted. It almost doesn't matter now. Sure, we can fight it, saying it was fraudulent, and we will be in court for *years*. We will win, but will the company recover? Will anyone trust us long enough for the company to stay afloat?" I shook my head. "This almost *forces* us to sell in order to keep the doors open. I haven't been able to reach anyone, and you think my phone would be blowing up."

Ashley looked at me sharply. I nodded. "Which basically proves that this was set up by an insider. But who? And how are the Grimms involved? This is sophisticated stuff."

"We will be able to follow the money, sic a pack of angry lawyers at them. If it was an insider, someone had to profit off of it." I nodded, waving a hand to my previous point. "It looks like I'm going to have a busy day tomorrow."

"We all are. This was intentional. To keep me distracted. I just don't know why. We are obviously outclassed, why kick me while I'm down?"

Alucard piped up. "Because it's fun to dominate a victim."

We all turned to him, and Gunnar's hands rippled to claws. Alucard held out a placating hand. "I'm just telling the truth. I know a bit of how this works. I survived the vampire courts and excelled. You don't do that by collecting stamps. This is a calm, calculated full frontal attack from multiple directions. It was cleverly done. You can trace the money, sure, but Nate's point stands. Does that matter for tomorrow?" He shrugged. "I'm no CEO, but I think everyone is going to be very busy tomorrow. Lots of phone calls. Emails. Texts. Meetings. Then more meetings about *other* meetings. Bureaucracy. Busywork. Which will keep our hero occupied while something *else* happens."

I nodded, tipping an imaginary hat. "Regardless, we need to hit the hay. I had a run in with Jacob." The room erupted. Misha grasped Tory protectively, even though she didn't really need protection. She was tough cookies. I told them about my talk.

"He's going to let us know when we are going to die. That's... nice of him." Tory muttered, squeezing Misha's hand comfortingly. Misha looked as if she were in the middle of a war. Right here, right now. With enemies just around the corner. I was very glad Tory was trying to subtly calm her down.

I answered Tory. "He could have been lying, and a swarm of Grimms could already be outside my gates waiting to kill us all." My gaze settled on Misha, who nodded her approval. The room grew tense then. "But I don't think that's the case. He could have killed me tonight." I said softly.

Indie sobbed softly.

I regained my composure. "But he didn't. Which was a mistake. Now I'm ready for him. War Council time." I growled, motioning for them to gather round. I had some things to tell them, and we had some planning to do. I wasn't going down without a fight.

Hungry smiles met my words, and even if they didn't believe we stood a chance, at least they heard that it was going to be the most fun a failure ever had. Alucard laughed a few times, shaking his head in astonishment. Misha and Tory would return to Raego's compound to give him a heads-up. Because now more than ever, I needed to be sure that my insurance policy remained safe.

Also, Misha's daughters were with Raego, and the impending doom of battle had kicked on her Mom gene, flooding her with the need to protect her family at all costs.

I smiled, shooed them away with a last hug for each, and then the rest of us got ready to go back to bed. We needed our beauty sleep for tomorrow.

I did make sure to activate the *Guardians* before I followed Indie to our bedroom. I set them up to attack and destroy any living being attached to a Grimm's amulet. Which should be a nice surprise if Jacob thought to come back tonight.

I dreamt about Jacob's screams as a pack of *Guardians* tore him to shreds.

It was like a lullaby. A fairy tale.

## CHAPTER 29

"This is bad, Nate." I sipped my coffee, listening to my lawyer, Turner Locke, prepare to lay it out for me. I feared the worst, but knew it would be even worse than that.

"Proceed." I answered in a clipped voice, still unsatisfied with his response that he had been up all night putting out what fires he could, making phone calls, speaking with the mayor in my defense.

"As you surmised, several significant profits were made before closing bell." His voice trailed off. I waited. "Is there anything you want to tell me, Nate? You know I'm on your side, right? Anything we discuss is confidential."

I sighed. Sure, I could just tell him that a supernatural hit squad had physically attacked me outside the hotel after the meeting, and then again outside a brownstone near Cardinal Village. And then that this same group had hired my long-lost twin brother to do an official Press Release in order to announce my official resignation from Temple Industries. I could also just ask him to lock me up in a straightjacket now. Because he was a Regular. He *was* savvy to the world of magic, having worked for my father for years, but the story sounded far-fetched even to me. And I was the freaking *victim*.

"Nothing that would make a difference. Let's just say I was targeted."

The line was silent for a time. Then Turner began. "Documentation shows that you purchased one thousand married-put option contracts on Temple Industries stock, with the right to sell at five dollars below the previous day's closing value. Three months ago. The expiration date for these puts was tomorrow, but you exercised them yesterday, making you even richer than you already were. In an order of magnitude, thanks to the crash."

I dropped the coffee, causing Indie to gasp.

My vision flared blue, and the window exploded outwards. As did part of the wall.

"Nate?" Turner shouted into my ear. Indie had jumped to her feet with a shout and was now watching me as if having never seen me before. Her eyes darted from the explosion to me as if waiting for Grimms to appear out of the woodwork. Seeing me motionless seemed to calm her after a few seconds. Gunnar bounded into the room, already in his wolf form, Alucard hot on his heels. They swept outside into the frigid morning air, ready for war.

Still, I didn't move.

"*What?*" I whispered into the phone. Gunnar and Alucard reappeared, staring at me wild-eyed. I heard Indie speaking with them but didn't hear the words. A dull vibration filled my ears. I realized it was Turner talking.

"...what just happened? Is everything all right? Nate?" He sounded frantic.

"I... yes. Everything is... fine over here. Talk to me, Turner. I didn't have any put options on my stock. None. This was a setup."

"Well, I'm almost not sure it matters at this point." He responded after a beat. "Wait, you're on the news again. Let me catch this. I'll call you right back."

He hung up without waiting for an answer.

I pointed my remote at the TV and everyone turned to watch.

The reporter was animated.

"*This just in. Nate Temple has confirmed that his Press Release yesterday where he resigned from Temple Industries was some sort of prank. No further comment was given by Temple. New sources report that Master Temple sold options on his stocks, earning him a significant profit from the crash caused by his Press Release. The Board of Directors has stepped forth, issuing a unanimous statement voting Nate Temple out of the company for his reckless behavior. Ashley Belmont, CEO of Temple Industries, has not responded to numerous calls and it has come to the attention of our reporters that her stock portfolio also realized a substantial gain from the false press release, proving she was complicit in the fraud. Nate Temple has declined further comment on the matter, but effective immediately, he is no longer owner of Temple Industries. Having sold his majority share in the company, he is now only a minority owner, holding only 426 shares..."* I tuned out the rest of the report as the number struck a chord.

It was the exact number of years the Grimms had been imprisoned.

My phone vibrated. It was Turner.

"I couldn't have done this, Turner. Trust me. I haven't spoken to my broker in months."

"That was when the puts were ordered. The exact day you last spoke with him. It's all been recorded, and the broker has already met with the FBI." I blinked.

"Ashley has been with me. I know she isn't involved in this either." I tried to protect her a bit.

"Her puts were purchased at the same time as yours. Same day, in fact." Turner replied almost sadly. "And she's not answering her phone."

"That's... that's not possible. I saw her make over a dozen calls last night. She has been all *over* this."

"No one has heard from Ashley since the meeting with the German company. Tickets overseas were reported to the media. Even footage of her boarding the plane immediately after your Meeting."

That just wasn't... I growled to Gunnar. "Go. Get. Ashley. *Now.*" I snarled. Gunnar didn't even respond, his giant werewolf form disappearing in a blink. I had seen her only fifteen minutes ago. And she had practically been stuck to my hip since the meeting. What the hell was going on?

"Nate, as your lawyer, you need to be up front with me." He began.

I didn't let him continue. "Listen closely, Turner. You worked for my father for years. You know how important Temple Industries is to me. And was to him. I would *never*..." I calmed my tone, realizing I was shouting. I took a breath. "I would never do such a thing. It's a setup." I whispered.

"I'm going to be honest with you, Nate. Your actions to date haven't been particularly flattering when it comes to company loyalty. You've professed to me personally that you leave it all to your employees. The Press Release from the Board Meeting even has audio sound bites of you stating this very thing. Among other, more incriminating statements – not even counting the video footage of you – that are going to take me months to argue–"

"Turner. Listen. Shut this *down*. Now. It's what you are paid to do. I'm telling you right now, Ashley and I had *nothing* to do with this. Now, I've got bigger issues to deal with at the moment. Don't let me down."

"But–" I hung up the phone as Ashley came sprinting into the kitchen, Gunnar loping along behind her.

"What's wrong, Nate? I was getting ready to make a call when I–"

"You and I have been framed. You are apparently overseas after having sold your entire portfolio at full price, right before the crash. As did I, allegedly. No one can reach either of us by phone. They have footage of each of us doing things we never actually did. I have now *officially* been fired, having sold all my shares. I have no voice with the company anymore. This was prepared months ago, and enacted yesterday before closing bell. My broker is a witness."

She sat down. *"What?"* Her face was confused. "I've sent at *least* a dozen emails, and not one person has answered a call or text." She shouted.

An icy chill trickled down my neck. Our phones had been hacked. It was the only logical explanation.

We had been hacked by the Brothers Grimm, which was impossible. They couldn't have had the sophistication to... "They outsourced it. It's the only logical explanation. They must have a crew of hackers working on this. Setting up the dominos for yesterday. Then they flicked it while we were fighting in the streets. Which explains why Jacob was absent. He was flicking the domino." I growled.

Gunnar snarled.

Alucard hissed.

And the *women*. Well, let me just say that one should never hear the sounds that ripped out of their throats. It hit me like a primal chorus of mama bears roaring.

The women were pissed. And no one messed with angry women. It was almost enough to give me a smile. Instead, I motioned everyone closer. "Alright. Our timetable has accelerated. We act *now*."

I idly realized that my engagement plans might have to be delayed. Which would mean I was going to lose my deposit. Maybe I could squeeze in a dinner at home instead. I realized now more than ever that I needed to ask this woman to marry me.

Before it was too late.

The doorbell rang and we all looked at each other thoughtfully before racing towards the entrance. Dean stood before the door, scowling through the wood. "I'm not letting them in." He stated flatly. Then he turned on a heel and walked away.

My breathing slowed. The Grimms couldn't be here already.

I slowly leaned closer to the door and peered through. Three shady characters stood under the *Porte Cochère*, out of the sunlight, and I was suddenly shoved out of the way as Alucard let out a piercing hiss through his fangs. He flung open the door and his fingers abruptly elongated to lethal claws.

"What are you doing here?" He demanded of the people outside.

The closest figure leaned away from the door, almost looking as if he had been caught with his hand in the cookie jar. Then I realized how easy of a target I had made myself by peering through the keyhole. This son of a bitch had been ready to kill me through the wood. He smiled knowingly at me and then shrugged as if to say, *it's what I do.*

One of the others spoke. "We should ask the same of you… *Master.*" They wore long coats with hoods pulled up around their faces.

"It is not your place to question *me.*" Alucard warned.

The figures nodded as one, but the first figure continued. "The St. Louis Coven was murdered by this wizard," he pointed a claw at me, "and we hear you were to avenge them. Then we find you here. With him." His eyes flashed red. "So why is he breathing?"

The other two murmured their agreement.

Alucard swallowed as if eating something particularly vile before speaking. As he spoke, I understood why. He was being forced to comply with my demands from the *Dueling Grounds*, and to likely lose the support of his people. "I challenged Master Temple to a duel. I won. I killed him." One of the figures began to growl in protest, not pleased at the apparent mockery. Alucard held up his claw. "I swear it on my power. As does he." He pointed at me.

"Um. Yeah. What he said."

They stared at me.

Alucard turned a pained expression on me. "Perhaps you could elaborate that a bit. Prove your word." He offered, voice tight with frustration and embarrassment at my weak assistance.

"I swear it on my power that Alucard killed me." A slightly foreign – yet familiar – weight settled on my shoulders as I bound my new power to my words. I knew the vampires could feel it. "I used powers at my control to come back from the dead. I did this in order to prove to Alucard that we face a common enemy." They stared in disbelief. "And also, because I preferred not to die." I added drily. "Alucard avenged his people, as per your code, and now here we are."

The first vampire took a threatening step closer but Alucard was suddenly there.

"You expect me to believe this nonsense, *Master*?"

Alucard shook his head. "You felt his oath. I have nothing further to add. Other than to say that killing Master Temple, and seeing him come back from the grave altered my... perspective on the Grimm's contract."

The vampires turned to each other, staring at each other without speaking. Then I realized that they were likely conversing *mentally*. Creepy. The first figure broke away to address Alucard. "One does not break a contract with the Grimms lightly." He stated in warning. "You know the consequences of such an act."

Alucard nodded. "Not if we can beat them." He studied each face. "And after killing Nate here, only to see him come back, I have a good feeling about our chances."

The vampire stared at Alucard. "*Our...*" he repeated in disbelief. "Already you speak as his ally."

Alucard shrugged, and finally nodded.

"We cannot abide by this. I don't truly understand what happened here, but you can count on us holding our contract with the Grimms. The world must see that the vampires are no easy meat, and that attacks on them are met with extreme prejudice." Alucard's shoulders sagged ever so slightly. "Some would say that you are under his thrall."

"One does not enthrall a master vampire. A master vampire enthralls *others*."

The vampire merely shrugged. "We shall discuss this further. On the battlefield."

I cleared my throat. "By any chance, did you three trash my car last night?"

They stared at me as if witnessing a particularly slow-witted idiot declaring, "Chocolate ice cream! Trucks! Baseball!" I took their stares as a *no*.

And with a seemingly snide rustle of fabric, the vampires were simply gone.

Alucard turned to me, eyes pained. "Well, that could have gone better."

I patted him on the back. "You get used to it."

And I closed the door, mentally moving another chess piece to the Grimms side of the playing board.

# CHAPTER 30

*I* angrily shoved the new phone into my coat pocket. No answer. Which wasn't possible. Othello *always* answered. Thanks to the software we used to communicate – which was un-hackable according to her, and I believed it – she would have received the call and, unless she was dying, would have answered. This was my third phone call to her, which meant that I should have already received a response of some kind. Even a text saying, *on a date now, will call back in a minute.*

We had an agreement. I called. She answered or returned my call immediately.

Period.

But she hadn't.

Which made me all sorts of nervous. She had notifications set up on me, so anything on the Internet that involved *any* reference to my name would have instantly alerted her. And I would have received a call. Especially after the bombshell airing on the news right now. This had to be all over the Internet. Even with a new phone number, she would have been able to reach me.

But she hadn't.

As if in response to my thoughts, my phone suddenly vibrated and I jumped to answer, ready to unload in both anger and fear at my old fling, Othello, the internationally known – if only by an alias and an almost unflappable reputation – hacker. I needed her to fix this mess. Find out how it had happened and work with Turner to clear my – and Ashley's – name.

"Where are you?" A familiar voice spat.

But it wasn't Othello.

It was *Arrogant Prickface*, Jafar. I almost lost my bananas, succumbing to the full mental breakdown that had been growing in the back of my mind.

I managed to keep my tone dry, barely. "Oh, are you calling to offer your assistance to the situation I told you about? Because I never received the call that you promised."

"There will be no help," he snarled in pure rage. "Now, *where are you?*"

"Well, that's a shame. I'm at home, sipping a hot cocoa. Why?" I had expected this call, but the timing couldn't have been worse. I had known they wouldn't help, but I had expected a call telling me so. The car continued to move towards our destination, slush loudly smacking the undercarriage as Jafar replied, and his voice practically dripped with hatred. Gunnar's head leaned closer to me as he drove.

"Have you been here in the last twenty-four hours?" His voice was actually shaking he was so angry.

I laughed. "*What?* Did I happen to hop on a flight to *Egypt?* Are you kidding me? After you so bravely declined to help me by not calling me back? You guys aren't exactly on my Christmas card list. You know, for people who supposedly help others, you guys have a pretty strong track record of not showing up when the world is going to hell. Fucking pansies. If you recall, I'm also not one of you any longer, so get to your point." I didn't need to feign indignation. I also didn't have time to waste gabbing.

"I know your schemes, Temple. We refuse to help you out of a personal scuffle you no doubt brought upon yourself, and you retaliate by throwing a tantrum."

I kept my tone frosty, "I'm sure I don't know what you're talking about. If you need an alibi, I have a dozen. Things have gotten even *busier* for me since last we spoke." I paused significantly. "Know anything about that?"

"I already told you, *no.* Don't change the topic."

"Yeah, well. Funny thing about lying cowards is that I have trust issues with believing what they say when their lips move."

He grumbled in warning. "Your time is coming, Temple. I can only hope that I get to witness it."

"Get in line."

"Consider this fair warning," he snarled.

I hung up.

The car coasted to a stop. Gunnar and Indie remained silent. Ashley had decided to physically visit Temple Industries this morning, escorted by a very grim looking Mallory, who had received an earful and more from Gunnar about keeping her safe... or else. I had tried calling her a few times in the last hour but had heard no response, which also got under my skin. Mallory hadn't answered his phone either. Which made me angrier. I knew they were busy putting out fires, but now wasn't a good time to be ignoring their phones.

I kicked open the car door and approached the seedy bar, not waiting for my companions. I carefully pocketed the phone and stood in front of the entrance, staring at it angrily, a faint blue mist throbbing over my sight in tune with my heartbeat.

Then I blew the fucking door off its hinges.

I heard Gunnar grunt in surprise, jumping to shield Indie with his body. He hadn't needed to. I had made sure all the shrapnel went *inside* the building.

I strode into the dim bar to find two men sitting at a wooden table, calm as you please. The wooden door was leaning precariously against the bar, and then it crashed to the floor. The two men paid it no attention, staring at my silhouette in the doorway instead.

Achilles' skin was a burnished bronze, despite the season. The Greek Hero rippled with muscle, and was hauntingly handsome, golden hair tied back into a man bun, scalp buzzed on the sides. Like one of those CrossFit or UFC people. Death, one of the Four Horsemen of the Apocalypse, sat beside him, looking unimpressed. His skin was the exact opposite of Achilles, pale as fresh snow, or a skeleton, and he wore a heavy leather coat that hung to his knees. His gaze drifted to Indie, staring very intently, not speaking.

"Heard from Othello lately?" I asked him, pulling his attention from Indie. He frowned and shook his head, eyes distant at the question. He and Othello had shared a moment a few months back. I wasn't sure if they were an item or not, but figured it didn't hurt to ask. And he had been eyeing Indie too intently for my tastes. Jealousy?

*Nah...*

"Fine." I growled in frustration. I turned to Achilles. "Time to spill,

Myrmidon," I demanded, pulling up a chair. I held a hand over my shoulder, signaling my friends. "Sit over there." I pointed at an empty table off to the side. "Rip his throat out if I so much as frown," I told Gunnar, pointing at the men.

"You haven't stopped frowning for days though," he answered.

"If my frown grows... *frownier* then." I turned to address the two legends before me. Then called back out over my shoulder. "The tan one. *His* throat, if I wasn't clear. I haven't yet decided about the pasty one." I heard Gunnar grunt his acknowledgment.

Achilles laughed. And Death peeled his stare from Indie to me. Any other time I would have rocked back on my heels at the intensity of the glare. Not today.

"Balls. You've got them in spades," Achilles chuckled.

I nodded. "My balls have nothing to do with this. Or with spades, for that matter." Indie coughed, unsuccessfully hiding a laugh.

"You think I'm scared of your wolf?" He asked incredulously, leaning back in his chair.

"No. You should be scared of *me*. He's just the cannon fodder." I leaned forward, glad Gunnar or Indie hadn't made a surprised sound at my callous words. "I don't care how badass you are. Or how many Trojans you killed. That was a long time ago. This is now." I growled. "I can obliterate you with a thought," I snapped my fingers. I turned to Death. "Just ask pasty here."

Death leaned back contemplating, and then he gave Achilles a single nod.

"If I give you the time to have a thought, that would matter," Achilles answered softly, voice tight with a controlled fury at my blatant disrespect. I didn't care. I would go all out, right here, right now, even though I was severely outclassed. Achilles was allegedly a demigod, and a legendary fighter to boot. I wasn't even confident that my magic could harm the son of Zeus, if that's what he really was. But I was already on borrowed time anyway. I just didn't have the patience to be scared, what with the Grimms breathing down my back and all. I could die here toeing off with Achilles or die later at Jacob's hand. It was really just about timing at this point.

"Your ball. Talk. You sent me into a trap. Was there even a girl?"

Achilles watched me, and then finally shook his head. I took a deep, barely restrained breath, almost letting loose right then. "Why?" I asked, voice like an executioner's axe.

"Let me be clear. This isn't me submitting. I am not afraid of you, Maker or not." I shrugged, unconcerned with his precious ego. "You will pay for this offense, but to be fair, I understand your position." I wagged my fingers, not hiding my impatience for him to get to his point. His glare hardened. "I got a tip that your place was going to be robbed. The place no one should know about. Only reason I thought to tell you was that it was underneath that comic book shop you own, and wizards are notorious for hiding their stuff in obvious places. It only made sense that if there was a robbery going down beneath your store, it was likely to steal your stuff. I couldn't interfere openly, so..." he held out a palm as if that explained everything.

I grunted. "Bookstore. Not comic book store."

He rolled his eyes. "You also sell comics there, right?" He grinned darkly. I squinted back and nodded.

"Let's pretend I'm not going to kill you right now. We can talk hypothetically. What if I told you that the Brothers Grimm are back to add me to their trophy collection, and that the supernatural community has been acting... odd lately. Strangely. Out of character."

"I would say that it took you long enough to catch on."

"You knew about the Grimms?" I all but shouted.

He chuckled. "Who didn't?" He watched my eyes, face stretching into a smile. "No. Tell me you're not that blind," he finally said, my apparent ignorance too impossible to believe. Then he began to laugh, whipping out a scarred fist to slap Death on the shoulder in amusement. Despite Achilles being incredibly strong, and possibly a demigod, Death didn't budge.

Not even a little.

"I've had a lot on my plate lately," I grumbled. Achilles' laughter slowly died away.

"Let's put the pissing contest on hold," his eyes hardened as he spoke, and I saw his shoulders flex beneath his tee. "Until later." I nodded at the unspoken threat. "Talk."

I nodded agreement. And then I told him about the werewolves and vampires. About the books. About the attack after the Board meeting. Alucard. Kingston – to which his face grew instantly closed off. The attack at Alistair's old house, the Armory, my meeting with Jacob. And Temple Industries tanking. I took a breath, and noticed that a glass of water now sat before me. I blinked. I hadn't seen a bartender. I met Death's gaze, and he shrugged with a wry smile. I drank the water.

"I don't believe in coincidences," Achilles finally replied, words heavy with undertones.

I agreed. "Maybe you could bring a few of your pals to join me when I meet up with them again." A flickering candle of hope wavered inside my soul.

Achilles' return glare snuffed it out, and then proceeded to dump a bucket of water over the wick. "No. You broke my door." He folded his arms. I blinked back.

"Fine. I'll buy you a new one."

"I doubt your cash position will be the same in the near future. But that's not the point. You *disrespected* me." The air grew brittle and my shoulders tightened instinctively, remembering the memory Pandora had once showed me. Of Achilles battling Hector to the death outside the gates of Troy. The tension slowly faded and he sighed. "Also, I can play no part in this battle. Against the rules."

I opened my mouth to ask what he was talking about, but Death cleared his throat, and shook his head a single time, warning me.

"But I am interested to hear how you plan to defeat them," Achilles said, drinking from a glass of water that suddenly sat before him. *What the hell? Where were the drinks coming from?*

I withdrew one of the Grimm's amulets from my coat, and *boy oh boy* did the two legends before me suddenly look interested. "Is that..." I nodded. "But that means you *killed* one," Death stated in disbelief, glancing at Indie again. I was getting sick and tired of his wandering eyes. I snapped my fingers and he turned my way, looking surprised.

"Eyes over here. I'm territorial."

He smiled, holding up his hands in mock surrender. Achilles reached out for the amulet and I handed it to him after a second's hesitation. I had another. I didn't need two. I also didn't find a need to tell them I had killed two. I tapped the screen on my watch while they fidgeted with the amulet. The screen blinked to life, showing a live feed of the car parked just outside the door. My drone rested on the roof above the bar. I wasn't about to make things easier for the Grimms by being caught by surprise.

Achilles noticed the view and began to growl. "Relax. It's a drone. On your roof. I didn't secretly install permanent surveillance on your bar." I didn't add that I had *thought* about doing just that.

All was clear on my screen.

The two legends began murmuring to each other softly, holding the amulet up to the light and inspecting it from all angles. My phone rang.

My hands dove into my pocket to answer it.

"Hello?"

"Master Temple. This is Joe with Candy Cakes." A pause, waiting for me to acknowledge. I said nothing.

"Yes, well, I'm not sure how to say this, but... several of our bakers called in sick and... well, we won't be able to meet your deadline." He stammered, sounding terrified.

A calm, quiet rage replaced my smoldering fight or flight anger, and it felt deadlier to me. Less restrained and more eager to be used. I needed that cake. Tonight. No matter what it cost. I needed at least *one thing* to go my way. "You must be mistaken. Must have forgotten who I am. What I can do. Sure you want it to play out like this?" I spoke, voice dry as dust.

"Um, I don't think..."

"Exactly. *You. Don't. Think.*" I enunciated. The line grew silent. "You will have it ready on the contracted time, and I will come pick it up, as we agreed. Or... I foresee a rough year for you."

I carefully watched my words, all too aware that Indie sat only a few paces away.

"I'm sure that won't be possible. My boss was quite insistent." Then he threw in a doozy, and my vision practically wobbled. "Temple Industries is throwing a party of some kind, and have ordered a dozen specially designed cakes that we absolutely cannot refuse."

"You do realize who owns Temple Industries, you halfwit," I growled in disbelief.

"Yes, well... that would be the Board of Directors... not... not *you*," his voice was almost a whisper at the end.

"I will *destroy* you," I began to hyperventilate. "I'll burn-" Gunnar was suddenly beside me. He deftly reached over and grabbed the phone, terminating the call before I could say anything more. He handed it back to me, eyes wary of the manic look no doubt dancing in my eyes. *Burn it all*, a small voice teased in my ears. I squashed it quickly, taking a deep, calming breath.

"Might want to dial it back a bit. He's just doing his job." He placed a meaty hand on my shoulder, anchoring me back to reality.

I leaned forward, whispering so softly that I could barely even hear my own voice. "It was the baker. He can't make the cake! I need at least one freaking thing to go right, goddamnit!" Gunnar blinked back, looking amazed.

"You're still planning on..." He bit his tongue. I nodded.

"Now I'll have to get back to *Chateau Falco* and make my own." I sighed in resignation, realizing I had a better chance of sneaking up on a Grimm to pee on his leg than I did at making strawberry shortcake. I would have to make our go-to yellow cake with chocolate frosting. "There *will* be a cake, by seven hells!" I whispered violently.

"Do we really have time for that?" He asked softly.

I nodded. "That's really the only thing that matters to me. I want her to know that... in case... well..." He nodded sadly, understanding. "I'm probably going to need Dean's help. And yours. I need you to babysit her for me."

Gunnar's shoulders sagged. "I'm watching Ashley. I guess I can watch both. You doing it tonight?" I nodded. He sighed, gripped my shoulder as he stared deep into my eyes. "You're a good man, Nate. I'd say yes." His eyes twinkled in amusement.

I laughed. "Say yes to what?" Indie asked, sidling closer. "What's going on? Who did you just threaten?" She asked nervously, eyes assessing us, Gunnar's hand still gripping my shoulder. "Was it *them*?"

I opened my mouth, and then realized what it must have sounded like. "Kind of. An associate." I turned back to Achilles and Death. The Rider was watching Achilles fumble with the amulet. He set it down on the table and took a drink of his water, eyes peering over the rim of his glass, directly at me.

"I think it's time we leave." I snatched up the amulet, tucking it away inside my coat. I noted Death eyeing the amulet as I did so, looking thoughtful.

Achilles stood, so did Death. "We'll walk you out," he said under his breath.

I walked out the door, back into the cold. I began to turn around to say farewell and apologize when a fist latched onto my shoulder and I was suddenly sailing through the air, my ears whistling before my body slammed into the brick wall of the bar. I realized Achilles was holding me pinned against the stone, breathing heavily.

"Just so you understand. If you survive this mess, you and I are going to have a chat. A nice, long, *pointed* chat." His words were concise, clipped, and dripping with malice.

I used my power to sharply, but carefully pinch his Achilles tendon through his boots.

He yelped instinctively, dropping me as he darted back, fists up, ready to send an Olympian-sized fist at my delicate nose. I held up my hands. "I'm always up for a talk. But I don't take kindly to attacks when my back is turned." Achilles' face was red, heaving at the minor insult and obvious display of his only weakness. He was a hair away from Hulking out on me. "You want to talk? I love talks. To my face. Not as I'm walking out of a building. Your building. After we shared drinks with each other." My voice was low, dark, and imposing. Achilles eyes tightened, understanding, and looking slightly mollified at his action's lack of honor. One didn't attack a person they had just shared drinks with in their own place of business. Their *home*. "Just know. Next time you pull a stunt like that, Olympian or not, I will throw down without restraint. I'm awfully curious to see what a Maker can do when he really cuts loose." I was almost getting tired of using that threat. But the look in his eyes altered my opinion.

Perhaps I would use it a few more times.

Achilles took a step forward. I held up a hand. "Admit it. You sent me on a suicide mission. I survived, and came back pissed, as would anyone. I shouldn't have broken your door... but you shouldn't have tried to pull one over on me like that, good intentions or not." His shoulders sagged, and I happened to look over his shoulder for a millisecond. I stopped breathing for a second. A line of men stood on the opposite side of the street, watching us. They looked familiar. I began to growl, and Achilles whirled, knuckles cracking as he realized he had had his back to a gang of unsavory-looking individuals.

# CHAPTER 31

*T*hen I realized who and what they were as Gunnar began to growl.

Werewolves.

And my heart skipped a beat as I realized *another* thing.

They held Ashley, bound and gagged, in a rough grip. She had a burlap sack over her head, but I remembered her outfit. Gunnar took a step closer, sniffing the air with a growl of recognition.

My mind scrambled. If they had Ashley, what had happened to Mallory? He had been the one watching her back. My anger was there instantly like a comforting blanket.

Well, I had needed to talk with these clowns anyway. One of them likely had my ring.

A thought struck me.

"Hey, Hector." I said jovially. "How was your vacation to Greece?" The lead werewolf looked back at me, losing a bit of his composure.

"Who…" he began to respond, but Achilles interrupted him.

"*What*… what did you say his name was, Temple?" Achilles asked in a very soft, very deadly voice. I grinned.

Achilles *really* hated that name…

"Hector, meet Achilles. Achilles, this is Hector." I turned to Death with a slight frown. "I'm sensing Déjà vu. Anyone else?" Indie's eyes were wide.

"Huh. Damndest thing," I shrugged, turning back to the werewolves. Gunnar's claws were now out, and Achilles had effectively pinned the werewolves into place with only his eyes. A flicker of power danced over his frame, and I momentarily saw a much scarier Achilles. Dressed all in leather armor, clutching a shield in his left fist, a spear in his right, and a plumed, Greek helmet over his dome, like those ones in *300*. Then it winked out and street-clothes-clad Achilles again stood in his place.

I shivered a bit.

"My name is *not* Hector." The lead werewolf answered, staring warily at Achilles. The Olympian grunted, nodding as his shoulders relaxed, obviously recognizing him on closer inspection. He shot a disapproving frown my way before approaching Death. I recognized the lead werewolf, the Alpha of the local pack, from a few months back when I had met him at this very bar. It had ended in an epic bar fight where Tory had laid him out cold. Then later I had a little skirmish with him and his pack. A rogue Justice of the Academy had framed me as his mate's murderer. I had cleared it up, sending the Alpha the Justice's head, but we weren't friends.

Things were about to get hairy. They weren't here to chat. And I was pretty sure they weren't here to sell me a magazine subscription. Especially not with Ashley under guard.

Indie was holding Gunnar's sleeve, tugging with all her might as she tried to keep him on our side of the street. He was panting – arms rippling with tension under his coat, fighting the urge to shift and destroy the threat before us. The threat holding his fiancé captive. I noticed Death leaning against the brick wall, smoking a clove cigarette, and watching the scene unfold. His eyes darted to Indie twice, eyes contemplating. I didn't like his obvious interest in Indie. Not at all. I just didn't have time to discuss it with him.

I returned my gaze to the wolves. There had to be a dozen of them. I hid my gulp. I saw a sign dangling in the wind in the background behind them, and burst out laughing.

The lead wolf glared at me, pulling his eyes from Gunnar. "What exactly do you find humorous about this situation, Temple?"

I pointed at the sign, immediately folding over as I clutched my stomach. "It's... I can't..." The werewolf turned to look. *Johnson's Dog Park* was just legible under the snow that had accumulated on the sign. He turned back, eyes flashing, not finding anything funny about the sign. Indie stifled a laugh and Achilles chuckled before stepping up beside Death to lean against the brick wall. Death offered him a clove cigarette but Achilles waved him away. They murmured softly to each other for a second, and then turned to watch the result of the showdown.

I sighed. Obviously, we were on our own. I idly wondered about Death's allusion to Achilles not being allowed to interact in a battle with the Grimms, and thought maybe the same restraint held him back here.

I mimed rolling up my sleeves as I shot a pointed glance at Death, flicking my head to Indie. Death nodded, called out to Indie, and patted the wall beside him and Achilles. If that wasn't safe, I didn't know what was. Indie shot a look at me, pained and concerned, but complied.

I turned back to the werewolves, stepping up beside Gunnar. "Looks like we've got all the tools necessary for a brawl, gents. Any last words?" I smiled. No one spoke. "Okay. That works. Before I murder all of you, I think you should apologize for trashing my car last night after the sewer fiasco." The leader smiled, but didn't speak, the reaction basically admitting the crime. I continued. "Fine, I'll beat it out of you." They collectively growled at my threat, but I ignored them. "Also, one of your pups has something that belongs to me. Guy built like a rhino fancies himself a pickpocket." I didn't spot him in the crowd, but several of the wolves snickered. Death chuckled from behind me. "If you give it up now, I might not kill all of you," I shrugged out of my coat, folded it, and placed it on the hood of our car. "As slowly." I continued, turning back to them.

The lead werewolf scowled. "Before you get your panties in a twist, you should listen. The car was a warning. For him." He pointed at Gunnar. "We're not here for you. And your pack of spirit wolves is not permitted to participate." He added, shooting me a thoughtful scowl. I managed to hide my smile, remembering my second meeting with this guy. I had led him to believe I had a pack of spirit wolves at my beck and call. Apparently, he still believed it. He turned back to Gunnar. "You killed a member of my pack. I challenge you to a formal duel."

I blinked.

Well.

There was *that*.

I raised my hand. No one acknowledged me. "Hey, I might have killed one too, furface. Who do I get to fight?" I hopped up and down on my feet as if warming up. "I'm all dressed up with nowhere to go over here. And Rhino still has my property."

"*Rhino* survived. He's recovering. You're safe from repercussion." His eyes were cold, merciless. "For now. So. Please. Stop. Running. Your. Mouth." I stared back, incredulous. This was a first for me. I would have to let it play out and get my ring later. I turned to Death. He patted the wall beside him. Indie nodded furiously. My gaze tightened. But I couldn't leave Gunnar to fight the Alpha alone. What if he cheated and the pack swarmed him? But I thought about that. The leader had challenged him to a formal duel. Which meant...

If Gunnar won, he would become the de facto leader of the St. Louis werewolf pack. At least this guy's pack anyway. I wasn't sure how many packs were in St. Louis. It also meant that it would be a one-on-one fight. The pack wouldn't tolerate cheating. Even to help their Alpha. They valued strength and honor amongst themselves. Now, fighting another flavor of Freak was a different story. The victory was all that mattered there, but between wolves? Honor. Integrity. Duty. Responsibility.

So, Gunnar might actually have a chance here. I mean, Tory had taken this clown on. Then again, that had been a bar fight, not a no-holds-barred tooth and claw fight to the death. Still, Gunnar was downright scary when necessary.

And they had taken his girl, essentially forcing him to fight rather than submit. In their eyes, Gunnar had killed a packmate, and something needed to be done about it. Kind of like me having to fight Alucard yesterday.

Abruptly, a wolf stepped forward and spoke, eyes on the ground in submission. "Is this truly necessary, Ben? Surely you two can come to some sort of agreement. There are vampires in town, Grimms," he shivered slightly. "Other enemies. This will do nothing but divide us. I–"

The Alpha, Ben, turned on a heel and slammed a fist into the werewolf's stomach, causing him to fold to his knees. The Alpha stared down at him for a few silent seconds. "Anyone else?" No one moved. "I'm doing this to defend our pack's honor. It isn't a topic of conversation," he added. The injured werewolf took a shaky breath and climbed to his feet, keeping his eyes down, but I swear I saw murder in them. Perhaps this duel wouldn't be as professional as I hoped. The man nodded, and stepped back.

I kind of agreed with him. We were wasting time here, but I knew I would be outvoted. Even by Gunnar. Especially by Achilles, who was practically drooling at the chance to watch lethal violence outside the comfort of his own bar.

The Alpha turned back to Gunnar. "Your bitch hasn't been harmed. The one *protecting* her," he smiled wickedly, "was roughed up a bit, but should be fine." I almost used magic to kill him, duel be damned. They had beat up Mallory. That scarred old mystery man on my payroll with a murky past and a bit of secret magic. But *how?* I didn't have any time to think about it.

The Alpha waved a hand at Ashley. "She is merely... motivation. I've heard of your... distaste for battle when you didn't think it necessary." He glanced at Ashley. "She's here to convince you that this duel is indeed *necessary.*"

He stepped forward, claws suddenly appearing where his hands had been. Now, Gunnar had a rune on his wrist that allowed him to partially shift at will. The only other kind of werewolf that could partially shift at will was someone either very, *very* experienced with his or her power, or an Alpha. The primary purpose of Gunnar's rune was to prevent him from shifting into a raving psychopath on the full moon. All wolves were victim to this. Which was why they tended to live in packs, conveniently going on a long weekend trip or taking a few days off to go 'hunting,' far from civilization during these periods.

Alphas, on the other hand, were pretty similar to Gunnar. Not victim to the cycles of the moon, but *masters* of their beast.

Now that I thought about it, Gunnar's rune basically gave him the same abilities as an Alpha. He just didn't have a pack. But depending on the outcome of this fight, that story might change pretty damn quickly. And without a real job – having been fired from the FBI – maybe my friend *needed* a pack.

Then again, Ashley was a Regular, and would likely not be welcome in a pack. Possibly even seen as a sign of weakness or disrespect if their Alpha preferred a Regular to another wolf.

This political game was quite complicated now that I thought about it.

I turned to shoot Gunnar a questioning look. He shifted his eyes momentarily and gave me a single nod. I maintained eye contact, giving him a chance to change his mind. Instead, he shrugged out of his coat, set it on the hood, and tossed my coat back without actually looking at me. He stood in jeans and a white tee, muscles still rippling beneath as his beast struggled to break free.

I finally trotted over towards Indie. I glanced at Achilles. "Shouldn't we be worried about anyone seeing this?" I pointed at the windows.

Achilles shrugged. "No one looks. No one talks. Why do you think I chose this spot for my bar?" I didn't buy it, and my gaze must have relayed that. "It's mostly freaks in this part of town. They'll watch and leave it alone. The Regulars won't even notice. Not really a soft neighborhood, if you know what I mean. People usually duck and hide at the first sign of fighting in the streets." His gaze drifted to the wolves, conversation apparently over.

Indie smiled in relief that I wouldn't be fighting, and then shoved me lightly, noticing my distant gaze as my friend squared off with Ben.

"This really bothers you, doesn't it?"

I paused, thinking. "It's just... this is the first time the world hasn't revolved around me. It disproves years of scientific data. Did I not mock him enough?" She shook her head with a bemused sigh and we watched two werewolves get ready to claw the shit out of each other.

# CHAPTER 32

The pack formed a loose circle around the two wolves, blocking them from escape. I used the lull in action to shoot off a quick text to Mallory.

*Stay strong, buddy. We have Ashley.*

I pocketed my phone to watch the fight. This was to the death.

Speaking of which…

I shoved the Horseman out of my way to get between him and Indie. Or at least I tried to. Death didn't budge. Then he looked at me, gripped my coat with one idle hand, shook me a bit without any apparent effort, and then shoved me playfully, a gleam in his eyes as I stumbled a step, my coat caught in his fist. *Then* he let go. I glared back.

Freaking Horsemen.

He finally stepped aside, giving me enough room to take my space. I did so with a mutter, and turned to watch the fight. This was a new experience for me. Not being in the center of the chaos left me alone with my thoughts.

Standing next to the girl I wanted to propose to tonight. But I had no cake. And no ring. At least I still had the reservation at the French restaurant. As long as the Grimms didn't choose tonight to request my presence. If so, I would just have to propose in the car on the way to my death. Jacob had said something that had made me feel slightly better. They didn't typically harm mortals. Still, Indie had shot Wilhelm. I turned off those thoughts violently before they could escalate. Instead, I began running through scenarios, making sure I had enough time before our reservation to bake a freaking cake.

This was ridiculous.

I would have to get Indie out of my hair. I needed at least one part of my plan to go as scheduled. I had set everything up so meticulously and it had immediately begun to unravel with the arrival of the Grimms. I needed Gunnar to keep her busy while I *Cake Boss*'d my way through this proposal. Then I sobered a bit.

If, that is, Gunnar *won*.

My gaze swiveled to the impromptu fighting ring, and I settled back to watch. Two Alphas battling was rare. At least to non-werewolves.

Gunnar respectfully dipped his head, arms clad in fur with inch-long, razor sharp, inky black claws. They looked like they belonged on a freaking Polar Bear. Since he hadn't fully shifted they merely looked like an exceptionally muscular human's arm covered in fur, with wicked claws. It wasn't until he completed the shift that the joints popped into those more resembling a *steroid-infused* Arctic Wolf, the muscle mass shifting to the back, haunches, and jaws. But I idly began to wonder exactly *how* the transformation worked, on a magical or scientific level.

Then the leader snarled, and the fight was on.

Gunnar lurched back, barely dodging a fatal swipe of claws. It seemed this fight would take place in semi-shifted form, better able to take advantage of the mental cunning of humans rather than only the bloodlust of the wolf. A merging of the two forms. Perhaps that was normal. Not just showing brute strength but your humanity as well. I shrugged, wincing a bit as Gunnar dodged another swipe. He hadn't yet attacked. And it seemed he only moved enough to barely evade each attack. No more. No less.

I found myself fidgeting, impotent to help my friend.

As I watched, I noted that Gunnar was toying with him. After each failed attack, he took a step closer to his opponent, unapologetically, and unimpressed – face blank. Almost akin to how one allowed a toddler to throw his tantrum, and wear himself out, while the adult calmly watched, not feeding into the insanity. I grinned.

The Alpha lunged again, a flurry of claws. But Gunnar simply wasn't there. Then the leader fell over, grunting. Gunnar stood off to the side, holding a clawed hand in the air. It glistened crimson in the falling snow. He showed it to the pack, and then turned back to the Alpha, a questioning look on his face, "I'm finished if you are. Neither of us needs die today. I did what I had to do. I don't want to lead your pack. I was protecting a friend. That is all. Your wolves weren't following your orders. They stated you didn't want Temple harmed. But your soldiers didn't comply. They attacked anyway. After sufficient warning." He said softly, confidently, but voice still thick with menace. An olive branch. A chance to let both of them survive.

The Alpha roared in fury, pure carnage in his feral eyes. Gunnar sighed, and met him with a bodily impact I could practically feel. The wolves in the circle grew suddenly tense, fidgeting lightly from foot to foot. I heard a thickening crunch, and then watched as Gunnar lifted the Alpha over his head and tossed him into the nearby building. The werewolf slammed into the wall, brick crumbling slightly as his body crashed to the ground. He instantly climbed to his feet on shaky legs, eyes dancing with rage. Gunnar wasn't even breathing hard.

I told myself this was due to him sparring against a wizard on an almost daily basis for the past decade or so. But I was pretty sure I was witnessing Gunnar cut loose, and he was simply that *good*. It was pretty inspiring to see. After all, I had assumed he was just like every other wolf, that all of them were pretty much as skilled as he.

Apparently not.

I saw Ashley flinching with each sound, no doubt fearing that each was Gunnar receiving his last wound. With the bag over her head, she had no idea. "Go, Gunnar!" I cheered, clapping delightedly. More for Ashley's benefit than anything else. But it was like a shot of adrenaline for the Alpha. He launched himself at Gunnar in a blur and I heard a pained grunt from my friend, followed by a menacing growl. I darted forward without think-ing, shoving wolves aside with a growl, eager to see what had happened. The wall of fidgety wolves had blocked whatever just happened. I heard a few responding snarls.

"Not interfering, just can't see, mutt. Calm down." This comment did not make me any new friends, but they did move out of my way, giving me ample space to see. Some weren't even paying attention, eyes locked on the two figures standing in the circle.

I blinked as the tableau unfolded, my stomach tightening in revulsion.

The Alpha had his claws *inside* Gunnar's chest.

Gunnar merely stared back at the Alpha, gripping the offending wrist with one hand, and the other held safely out to the side. The Alpha's arms quivered with tension, but didn't move, unable to overpower my friend. "Last... Chance." Gunnar managed with a grunt. The Alpha went into a frenzy, redoubling his efforts. His claws sunk a bit deeper into Gunnar's chest before my friend sighed in both pain and resignation. "Sorry about this, brother."

And his arms began to flex, slowly forcing the claws from his chest like a sluggish glacier. The Alpha was drooling, spittle bursting from his lips as he fought to sink his claws to the hilt.

But he couldn't.

A millimeter at a time, Gunnar slowly forced the claws from his chest, and the wound instantly began to soak his gleaming white undershirt, the fabric straining, popping, and ripping along the seams as Gunnar continued to force the Alpha's claws away. And he never broke eye contact.

In fact, his face never changed at all. No strain. No pain. No mercy.

The Alpha's face was incredulous as he was slowly but surely forced from a killing strike. Gunnar held him there, arms to the side, leaned forward, and snarled, "No one touches my girl." Then, faster than I could register, he was inside the Alpha's claws, right up against his chest. His massive hands clutched both sides of the Alpha's face. Time seemed to slow as I saw the Alpha's eyes widen in alarm, arms beginning to swing down towards Gunnar in a last second attempt to kill his opponent. Gunnar twisted his mighty arms with a roar that set off car alarms, and a *snap, crackle, pop* ended the duel like a tiny drum solo. The once Alpha dropped like a sack of bricks to the snow.

Gunnar's chest heaved as he glared down at the body. Then he tore off his blood-soaked tee, rounded on the surrounding pack in a menacing snarl, and slammed the bloodied rag to the earth.

Then he began to move, purposefully, confidently, and menacingly, towards the werewolf holding Ashley. The werewolf flinched, his allies suddenly a few feet back, leaving him to face the new Alpha alone, and clutching the woman Gunnar loved as a hostage. His hands instantly released her, and then hastily tore off the hood, taking an urgent step backwards. "Just doing as commanded, Alpha," he offered weakly.

Gunnar's chest heaved, still leaking blood from five very distinct and impossibly deep wounds over his right pectoral muscle. The muscle just might have been thick enough to protect him.

He didn't take his murderous gaze from the wolf to look at Ashley, merely extended a thick, blood-smeared claw out to her. Her eyes blinked for a few seconds, assessing her surroundings in confusion. She latched onto the claw, not even caring that it wasn't a human hand. Her eyes tightened as they settled on his wounds. Her hand fell into the pads of his paw, his claws instantly sheathing upon contact, and her skin disappeared from view as white, bloody fur swamped her dainty fingers. Her red hair stood out like a flame against his white furred arms, emphasizing the blood on the ground. "I'm fine." She murmured softly to him.

Gunnar's lips pulled back, and still, he didn't remove his gaze from the now-terrified werewolf guard. He silently moved Ashley behind him, shoulders rippling like giant slabs of steak had been tucked beneath the skin. The fur stopped mid bicep, transitioning to his human form at the shoulder, to ultimately reveal a hairy blonde chest. His six-pack had a six-pack.

Listen, you get it. Gunnar was *ripped*, folks. Like, really jacked and stuff.

His voice was gravel. "Listen up. I don't care if you believe me or not. I killed your Alpha because he asked for it, and wouldn't back down despite numerous chances to do so. I don't tolerate anyone harming, or threatening to harm, my friends. At all." He waited for a response. They nodded as one. Gunnar seemed to accept this. "Same as down in the sewers. I gave them a chance to back down. They didn't. I did what I had to do. I don't like it any more than you do, but it had to be done. And I always do what has to be done. Understood?" Again, they nodded, staring at him in awe. I idly wondered where the wolf leading the others in the sewer was. Blackbeard. And how I could find this Rhino wolf to get my ring back.

No one even glanced at the Alpha on the ground. Well, the werewolf who had been punched in the stomach seemed to smile momentarily before nodding along with the rest of the pack.

Gunnar's pack.

Huh. This could come in handy.

"Hey, Gunnar. This might just help us out a bit. We could really use some backup when the Grimms come back. And now you have your own army."

Gunnar was already shaking his head to himself. He turned to face me, and then pointed a finger at the brick wall.

Achilles burst out laughing. Several of the wolves smiled proudly.

I blinked, and studying the ice-cold nature of his glacier blue eyes, I wisely turned back to do as requested. I wasn't obeying an order. I was complying with a friend's wish.

Seriously.

It wasn't like his Gladiator impersonation had rattled me a bit. I mean, I had known Gunnar his entire life and had never seen him like this. And I had put him in some pretty dire situations. But this time was different. I hadn't seen him resonate so much authority as he did now. It was almost as if his victory had granted him the ability to lead. And apparently, the pack seemed to agree. On the other hand, I realized him sending me away was a *very* wise move. His new pack would see him ordering a non-werewolf away rather than letting a friend jump into inner circle politics. This would earn their trust. Or solidify it. Just because he was my friend didn't mean I had any say whatsoever in future decisions regarding his pack.

I found myself smiling as I neared Indie. She was watching me incredulously. Achilles studied me, and nodded, realizing I had understood the underscored benefit of complying with Gunnar, even though I was used to ordering him around. Kind of.

In the *Nate and Gunnar* show, I was used to figuratively *wearing the pants*.

But in the *Gunnar and pack* show, I wasn't even a *consideration*.

I felt silently proud of my friend.

Then I saw a werewolf lunge at Gunnar's unsuspecting back, a wicked knife clutched in his fist as he closed in on Gunnar's neck. I didn't even have time to shout a warning.

# CHAPTER 33

*T*he werewolf's dagger was less than a foot away when he was suddenly tackled to the ground with enough force to give the attacker whiplash. Then his head cracked solidly into the fender of the jeep on the street and his body went limp. The defending werewolf snatched the dagger from his unconscious hands, and slammed it hilt deep into the attacker's eye socket with a grunt. The body flinched and went still. It was the werewolf from the sewers. Blackbeard.

Gunnar had whirled, claws out, eyes dancing from body to body, realizing he was surrounded. Then he noticed the two wolves on the ground. One stood with a bloody knife clutched in his fist. It was the werewolf who had attempted to stop the duel.

Blackbeard sat in a pool of blood.

You could have heard a pin drop.

The savior tossed the knife to the ground and dipped his head in respect. Gunnar grunted, nodding after a few seconds as he stared down at the familiar werewolf who had started the whole mess down in the sewer. "Thanks," he finally said to his hero.

The man shrugged. "You're our Alpha now. It's kind of my job. I'm your Geri."

Gunnar was silent for a moment. I grunted, recognizing the word. "The *Ravenous?*" I translated the Norse word. "One of Odin's two wolves." I elaborated. The wolves simply stared at me with surprise, except for Gunnar. He continued to stare at the werewolf. "We'll see about that," he replied softly.

The man cocked his head for a moment, but didn't say anything.

Gunnar elaborated. "I'm not fit to lead a pack. I guess you could say that I led a *pack* of FBI Agents once. And failed spectacularly. You deserve better."

The crowd lit up in an uproar, arguing over each other in variations of, "he has to lead us!"

Geri studied the crowd until they grew silent. Then he spoke to Gunnar as if no one else was present. "They are right. Our pack will devolve into civil war as we fight for a new leader. This saves bloodshed. That is the point of the Alpha Duel," he said gently.

Gunnar grunted again. I knew after being fired from the FBI he had a sore spot in the confidence department. Surely this would nip that in the bud. Geri seemed to notice this. "It is for the best."

Gunnar finally let out a snarl. "How can I trust you? *Any* of you?" He rounded on the pack, eyes glittering like shards of ice. "Despite what you were commanded to do, none should have obeyed. Kidnapping a Regular," he said in disgust. "If I ever hear of anyone doing that again," he pointed a thumb back at the dead body, "You will beg for such a clean end. Regulars, all of them, are off limits." His tone dripped menace.

The pack dropped their heads, looking ashamed.

I recalled the drone to me, where it calmly latched onto my wrist, folding neatly into my watch. Death and Achilles watched the tiny technology thoughtfully, saying nothing. My phone rang.

I answered it, confident that Gunnar could handle himself for a few minutes without me. "Yes," I answered apprehensively, recognizing the number.

"Get the fuck over here! We're being overwhelmed. Operation White Knight has been compromised!" An explosion roared in the background, and gunshots almost made the words illegible. Then the line went dead.

Shit. Raego was under attack.

# CHAPTER 34

*I* let out a sharp whistle and Gunnar spun, claws out, scanning the streets. His eyes latched onto me. "Time to roll," I yelled. "Raego's under attack!"

Gunnar stared back in shock. He was aware of my secret mission, *Operation White Knight*, and the implications of Raego being under attack were not lost on him. He practically picked up Ashley and raced towards the car. Indie never strayed from my side. I rested my hand on the door and paused, realizing there was no way we could take the girls with us. It had sounded like a war zone. And I didn't even know who the attackers were, or whom they had with them. I assumed the Grimms, but given the alliances they had made so far, I could be facing off against a gang of Trolls or vampires or wizards or possibly more wolves. My stomach roiled a little at that. What difference were Gunnar and I going to make? My gaze slowly followed Gunnar and Ashley as they raced towards us. The pack remained behind, looking agitated, but Geri was hot on Gunnar's heels, eyes hungry with anticipation of a scrap.

Gunnar had made new friends. Perhaps...

He met my eyes, and knowing me too well, he shook his head resolutely. "No," he said simply, under his breath.

I scowled. "But–"

"I can't bring them into that five minutes after I killed their leader."

"But—"

"The Maker is right. We want to be there by your side. Our old Alpha was boring. Fresh leadership and a fresh fight go hand in hand," Geri spoke respectfully. Gunnar grumbled under his breath, not pleased.

"What are you doing over here?" He demanded in a low voice.

"Where you go, I follow. It is my duty to be a voice of reason for you and to watch your back," he answered simply. "Despite the consequences, as you saw earlier." He added drily, reminding us of the previous Alpha decking him for speaking out.

I smiled smugly to myself, careful not to let Gunnar see. "We can't take the girls." They, of course objected to this with much yelling and shirt grabbing. Well, arm grabbing in Gunnar's case. "You didn't hear what it sounded like. A war zone." I added. "We can't help Raego and watch over you two at the same time."

Death approached on silent feet. "I can take Indie to safety," he offered softly, dangling his motorcycle keys. Gunnar whirled.

"Take both of them," he demanded.

Death studied him with a squint. "I ride a *motorcycle*, not a *minivan*."

Geri spoke up. "Let the pack watch over Ashley." Gunnar's fists flexed as he slowly rounded on his second in command.

"You honestly believe I can trust you five minutes after you *kidnapped* her?"

Geri lifted a hand in understanding. "But was she harmed?"

Gunnar's eyes danced dangerously. Geri held up his hands. "I'm not excusing our actions. But we *were* commanded to do a distasteful thing, which we could not disobey, and we did it professionally and gently. How many kidnappers act in such a way?" He added. I didn't like it, but he had a point. Then he drove that point home with a sledgehammer that made me angry for not remembering sooner. "Don't forget that we quite literally cannot disobey you. Only an Alpha potential could do such a thing, and I assure you none of us are up to the task." He glanced back at the two dead bodies. "I just killed the only other threat to your authority. If you missed it."

"What about you?" I asked.

He chuckled. "As a Geri, I have immense power over other wolves, but I forfeit any rights to Alpha-ship in exchange." He turned to Gunnar, eyes contemplating. "You do not know of this?" He asked.

Gunnar grunted. "I've never been much of a team player. Never really spent any length of time around other wolves," he admitted.

Geri nodded. "Understandable. Then our intelligence was sound, but it is still surprising to hear that you know nothing of our rules. I'll tell you true. None of the wolves are strong enough to challenge your order. None are strong enough to challenge your authority. All must obey. Even your Geri. *Especially* your Geri. You can trust us with your lives. And we are quite good as a pack," he promised darkly.

Gunnar sized up Geri for a few long moments. "But you were, by extension, working for the Grimms. My enemies," he added in a soft, iron-weighted voice that sent his words crashing to the ground like a crystal vase.

Geri winced, nodding. "True. By command of our Alpha." He waggled his fingers, as if having already explained that part. "We had no choice. By killing him, you severed our... agreement with the vile creatures. We are all a bit... perturbed about having to work for them, even though it was indirectly. It didn't sit well. To be honest, we were all quite glad our Alpha challenged you. Having heard the stories of you two, we thought we finally stood a chance of gaining new leadership. Perhaps the wolves you slew in the sewers were in fact martyrs, knowing that their deaths would cause a chain of events that would lead to the only other Alpha potential in town going claw-to-claw with our Alpha..." His words trailed off, and the sewer exchange grew a little more significant in my mind. Geri looked thoughtful, as if only just now thinking of the possibility himself.

And as I thought about it... It kind of made sense. After all, they had stated their orders not to *kill* me, but their orders hadn't said anything about *hurting* me. Fine distinction, but enough to skate by.

Ashley spoke up. "Gunnar." He turned to her, the same hard-eyed gaze fixating on her until she took an instinctive step back. "They were completely respectful about my kidnapping. Honestly. Not a hair on my head was harmed. If you must fight, I won't hold you back. It terrifies me, but I know you have no choice. Let them take me to safety. The Chateau or wherever you want." She paused. "Just murder some Grimms for me and get back home." She winked.

Gunnar smiled for the first time in a long time. Still looking concerned, but resolved to the situation. The clock was ticking. I could Shadow Walk us there in a blink, as long as I knew the girls were safe. He nodded, so I turned to Indie and Death.

"You will keep her safe. No matter what. Stick by her side until I call you. No deviations. Keep her away from Chateau Falco. The Grimms know the place like it's their own home. I would feel safer knowing she was at one of your safe-houses or whatever biker bar you call home." I remembered the one time I had tried summoning him, when I had been transported to some kind of seedy bar. It was a safe bet that not many knew of the place. Death nodded, looking oddly intense as his gaze shifted to Indie. I remembered his thoughtful looks at her over the past hour and felt a little anxiety creep up my neck. What had his interest been all about? Had he sensed something in my future? Or maybe things were simply serious enough for even him to be concerned.

I mean, to be honest, I didn't really have an idea what he could do. I had seen him get mildly perturbed before, and it had been downright terrifying, but I had never seen him really let loose. I would need to look into the Horsemen a bit further. If I survived this. But I trusted him enough to keep Indie safe. I couldn't imagine anyone attempting to pull one over on one of the Four Horsemen.

I kept my smile in check. If all went well at Raego's I could run home to bake my cake without fear of Indie catching me. I had effectively just hired a babysitter.

"You ready, Alpha?" I grinned.

He nodded back and extended his still bloody arm. I noticed that his chest wasn't bleeding so much anymore, thanks to his slow but steady healing factor. I blew a kiss at Indie. Then thought, *what the hell?*

I blew a kiss at Geri and Ashley.

But not Death.

One does not simply blow a kiss at Death.

Then instead of taking Gunnar's arm and Shadow Walking, I tried out the gateway spell I had recently learned. A ring of blue fire erupted before me, tall enough for Gunnar and I to walk through. Death flinched, but the sound on the other side of the gateway immediately drew everyone's attention. Raego's mansion rose up in the distance, but a war plagued the lawn. We dove through and I pulled it closed before Geri or anyone else decided they wanted to join the fight.

I immediately screamed as the world erupted in chaos; screams, dragon fire, machine guns, and the steady roar of *magic* shattered the air, causing my ears to instantly pop. Gunnar instantly shifted to full on giant werewolf. "Welcome to the jungle," I yelled for encouragement, whips of liquid fire and ice snapping to existence as extensions of my fists.

# CHAPTER 35

Two smaller than usual red dragons abruptly swooped down over our heads, missing me by inches, and snatching a stealthy Justice whom I hadn't noticed sneaking up behind me. Misha's daughters had come out to play. I smiled, but it didn't last long as the image finally struck my rational mind.

Justices.

That meant we weren't fighting Grimms. And I wasn't sure my allies knew the distinction. I had to stop this. We didn't stand a chance if any Justices were murdered. The entire Academy would come back and destroy everyone. These were supposedly the *good* guys.

I summoned up my new power, growing a large quivering orb of it to coalesce in front of me. I wasn't even sure what I was doing, merely trying to duplicate spells I had used as a wizard. Once complete, I shouted into the rippling orb at the top of my lungs.

My new powers might have beefed it up too much.

"PEACE! Everyone stop! Jafar! Show yourself!"

A nearby tree branch exploded as if struck by lightning, as the amplified sound of my voice struck it. Then the force hammered into the house, shattering the windows.

Absolutely everyone halted. The dragons in the skies pumped their powerful wings to land lightly atop the mansion before us. Everyone turned to me, looking startled.

Well, the Justices, of course, stared back at me with their stupid silver masks that replicated various forms of human emotion. *Sadness, laughter, rage, compassion,* and *hatred,* even an *expressionless* mask stared back at me. But I told myself that deep down they were scared.

Yeah.

One person touched his mask and it disintegrated, revealing Jafar. He approached me slowly, wary of a trap. I honestly had none. My only interest in this was everyone walking away more or less satisfied. Or dissatisfied on an equal level. Which I had heard was the sign of a good compromise.

"What is the meaning of this, Temple?" His voice dripped raw fury.

"What we have here is a grievous misunderstanding, obviously. You show up, for whatever reason, attacking the Dragon Lord's home. What did you expect?"

"We got a distress call." My inner psyche screamed in panic to kill him before he spoke any further, or discovered the truth. But I calmed it. Barely.

"What kind of distress call would warrant an entire battalion of Justices?" I asked carefully. "There must be some kind of mistake."

"Distress calls are not typically made by mistake."

"Well, *who* called you? I'd like to hire them. I call you guys all the time and you never answer. This person sounds handy if they can get you guys to actually show up and do your jobs," I muttered.

He flexed his fists. "I'm not at liberty to specify. A friend. That's all you need to know." He answered cryptically.

"Well, how am I supposed to help you with knowledge like that? You want me to prove that this imaginary person is not here?" I waited a breath. "See the problem?"

He merely stared back. "Someone important to... *me* called for my help." His eyes grew thoughtful. "I think."

"We're down to *I think,* now?" I asked in astonishment.

"The transmission was garbled."

I let him stew on that. "You rounded up an army to attack the Dragon Lord's home? For a *maybe*? Really subtle, Jafar. It's amazing we... *you* people haven't caused a war recently. But then again, that could change," I muttered, shaking my head, trying to intimidate him with consequences and get them out of here. I saw Raego approaching in human form. He nodded discreetly. I took a gamble.

"Scan the area. If your *friend* is here, you should be able to sense them. And before you get too pushy, I know you could break through any wards preventing it." I rolled my eyes. "So, you get to do it from here. Outside."

"What if she's been moved?"

*She*, I thought to myself, suddenly wary about exactly what Raego had done for *Operation White Knight*. "I'm the only other person with the ability to Shadow Walk, and I only just arrived." I muttered. "Had a disagreement with the local werewolf pack that made me fashionably late. Speaking of which, he's the new Alpha." I pointed at Gunnar, now back in his nude human form after having briefly shifted to wolf and back again.

He was also still liberally painted with blood from his fight.

He didn't smile or move in any way whatsoever other than to stare down the Justice.

Jafar blinked. I smiled. "All that blood almost lets you imagine the screams of the recently deceased Alpha. Cool." I let that sink in for a second or two. "So now you have managed to piss off the only Maker in existence, the Dragon Lord, and the local Alpha of the St. Louis werewolf pack. Because you *think* you got a distress call from a... *friend*. And our response was to defend Raego's home, and then offer you the opportunity to take a look around." I added softly. "We could have done much worse. Still could." I added as an afterthought.

Jafar growled, snapping a finger at a nearby Justice. He instantly shook his head. "No sign of her, Sir."

Jafar's face purpled. "This isn't over." He promised. "I *know* you're involved."

I shrugged. "You keep saying that. One of these days I'll actually believe you." He took a threatening step closer and I smiled, holding out my arms in invitation. "You're not the scariest thing I've run across today, Jafar. Not even close."

Jafar watched me, and without another word, every single Justice Shadow Walked out of existence, leaving us all alone.

"Well, that could have gone worse. Thanks, Nate. Gunnar." Raego muttered.

"I'm just glad no one died." Blank faces stared back at me. "No one *died*, right?"

Raego shook his head, but still didn't look pleased. "They attacked my house, Nate." He growled. "For something I did for you."

"I know." I admitted, not hiding my guilt. "How did it happen?" I asked carefully.

"She's clever." He muttered under his breath. I stared at him, not pleased to hear his defensive answer. "It's been resolved. Tory's on duty now." He promised, pointing at the house, where apparently Tory was now watching over *Operation White Knight*.

I nodded. "Good." We didn't have time to get in a tussle with the Justices. Not yet.

"Let's part ways. I'll get back with you soon. Right now, I have a few things to take care of. I need to go bake a cake."

"A cake." Raego answered flatly.

"Yes. After dinner, things are likely to get... *interesting*." He didn't even respond.

I turned away, Gunnar stepping up beside me. I spotted Misha speaking sternly with her two daughters, now in human form. They looked efficiently chastised. Then Misha let out a dazzling smile and wrapped them up in a group hug, murmuring to their heads. Her eyes shone with pride despite her previous scolding. I smiled, preparing to open a gateway out of there when a dragon let out a ferocious roar behind me. I whirled to see every single dragon staring at the tree line.

Which was suddenly filled with ten Grimms.

Without a word, they began to advance.

Then advance faster. I glanced at Gunnar with a groan, but he had already shifted back to wolf form and was growling territorially. Raego's face drained. "You were saying something about after dinner, Nate?"

"How god damn hard can it be to bake a cake?" I muttered. Raego frowned at me, no doubt wondering if I was still sane. I didn't elaborate. "Let's do this." And we were suddenly running to meet the Grimms as the dragons on the roof launched into the sky with peals of dinosaur-volume cries.

It really was too bad that the Justices had already fled. We really could have used some cannon fodder about now, and them being attacked might have even forced them to team up with me.

But, it just wasn't meant to be.

And just maybe, neither was my survival.
Or my cake.

# CHAPTER 36

*I* heard a piercing howl as Gunnar entered the fray.

I tipped an imaginary hat at Misha – now a giant red dragon – as she swooped down to incinerate a lone Grimm sneaking up to the side of the house. His scream was most satisfying.

Then a black blur slammed into her side, hammering her onto the roof of the mansion just over my shoulder. Tile and concrete exploded from the force of the impact, and a billow of fire erupted like someone had let loose the largest Molotov cocktail ever.

But I didn't have time to watch.

The air abruptly throbbed, sending me, and all my people to their knees. The air felt thick, soupy, and then it was abruptly gone and everyone climbed back to his or her feet, glancing back at me like it was my fault. I shrugged, and my whips of controlled fire and ice manifested as extensions of my hands – and my mind.

I wasn't sure how many dragons were currently in town, but I did know that Raego's operation was global, so it was likely he had only a skeleton force here. Which wouldn't be good for our odds. Then again, these punks could duplicate anything we could do, so it was almost counter-productive to have too many Freaks available.

Grimms exploded into new forms – dragons, a few werewolves, and a true berserker of a man. The last plucked up a tree with one hand, tore it out of the ground like a weed, and threw it at the house where it shattered the front door.

Body met body in heavy impacts, claws, and scales.

It was chaos.

Bolts of fire filled the sky. But not just fire. Lightning, Ice, Earth, and metal spears of gleaming silver. All weapons of the various Skittles bag of dragons fighting to defend their territory. Each color of dragon had a unique specialty and flavor of power.

Lightning shattered from one blue dragon's snout, lancing another green dragon from the sky. As if on cue, several more dazzling bolts of lightning shot from two other blue dragons, aimed at the first. The Grimms were learning quickly, I just didn't know friend from foe. Two quicksilver spears tagged the two dragons in the wings, sending them down to the earth with roars like thunder. I noticed that the two downed dragons seemed to have large chains around their throats, and then it hit me.

The amulets.

I yelled into the night, using my power to amplify my voice. "Look for the amulets! Means they are a Grimm, and not a friendly." Obviously, no one answered me. And it wouldn't have mattered if they had.

A pair of humans suddenly appeared out of thin air on either side of me, lunging to grapple me to the ground. But they stepped in direct striking range of my whips. I twirled the whips in a circle, managing to catch one of them by the ankle and send him flying towards the second floor of the house with major freezer burn. He screamed, and his foot dropped a few paces away as the body sailed away. A dragon with a chain around his neck swooped down at the last second to catch him, helping him land gently. One Grimm waited for him, suddenly kneeling over the body. Fucking Ichabod, bringing them back to life.

But I was too busy at the moment to do anything about him.

The remaining Grimm duplicated my whips of power, sending one at my face. I blocked it with my own. A coruscation of sparks exploded on impact, blinding both of us. I reacted first, even as I sensed his other fiery whip crackling towards my face. I imagined a pulsing body of water – vaguely humanoid and flipping off the Grimm where I had been standing as I simultaneously Shadow Walked thirty yards away. I reappeared facing the Grimm's side from a safe distance. His face was morphed into a triumphant smile, too caught up in the moment to realize it was just a doppelganger made of water. His napalm whip – a duplicate of my own raced towards the watery figure, pulsating with several thousand degrees of heat. See, it was more like lava than fire, and since he was copying me blindly, he hadn't thought of cause and effect.

I smiled.

The tip of his whip connected with the water, instantly superheating it.

The explosion of steam instantly melted the front of his body and sent him sailing off into the lawn, a smoking, screaming, wet mess to cool in a snow bank. I didn't gloat, but turned to see Ichabod no longer kneeling over the body of the first attacker, but rather helping him to his feet instead.

I snarled.

I had to take him out or it didn't matter how many we took down.

A werewolf launched out from behind a bush, hungrily snapping his jaws at my neck. Two hundred pounds of white fur – previously camouflaged by the snow – hit him like a truck, eliciting a yelp of pain. Gunnar bobbed his head at me, and the two wolves squared off. I began to run towards Ichabod, intent on murdering him quickly.

War raged around me, but I tuned it out, focusing on the man who stood silently watching me with sad, resolute eyes. Which gave me pause, slowing my steps. He looked over my shoulder, a mere flicker of his eyes.

So quickly that no one else would have even noticed it unless they were staring at him like I had been. I whirled, rolling to the side as a set of jaws clamped down on the earth where I had been standing. A werewolf I hadn't seen yelped as he struck his snout into the earth and flipped ass over teakettle. A dozen more stood behind him, growling and snapping at each other, forming a loose line.

And...

*Son of a bitch.*

They had Ashley.

Gunnar tore the throat out of his opponent, and was just standing to full height again, nose sniffing the air, suddenly interested in something familiar. His glacier-like eyes discovered the werewolves, and Ashley, and he stilled for a heartbeat. Then he was suddenly by my side, pacing back and forth, snapping, snarling, whining, and quivering with barely restrained impatience, hackles lifted until they made him look twice his normal size. His lips were pulled back in a permanent curl, but he obviously noticed the same thing I did.

There was nothing we could do. One move on our part and Ashley died.

Because werewolves gripped each of her arms in powerful jaws.

A shaggy, wood-colored wolf stepped forward, chain gleaming around his throat.

He watched us, intelligent eyes waiting for us to make a move. We didn't. My eyes instantly darted to a fierce battle just beyond the werewolves.

Two small red dragons were battling on the ground with another larger red silver dragon wearing the familiar Amulet.

Misha's daughters.

The two adolescent dragons fought like a pack, harrowing, and darting in for quick slashes and bites while the other distracted the silver monstrosity, dodging his silver spray of molten metal. But after a few seconds, the silver dragon suddenly spun and latched onto the leg of one of the smaller red dragons, and I heard a scream the likes of which I never wanted to hear again.

Their mother, Misha, diving to rescue her babies.

The giant red comet of motherly rage slammed into the silver dragon, pummeling it into the ground and knocking her offspring free from the attacker's jaws. The wounded dragonling limped to safety, her sister jumping in front of her to keep her safe as two more blue dragons dove to help the silver dragon battle Misha.

The two assailants roared, and let loose bolts of lightning directly into Misha's side. Her body arced up with a million volts of power and I managed to meet her eyes.

My.

Heart.

Stopped.

For an eternity, we stared at each other, neither able to move or look away. I saw a single tear, and then her eyes closed, and her body crashed to the ground, twitching. The Grimm dragons launched themselves up into the air, unconcerned with the dragonlings now racing to their mother's side.

Raego appeared like a shadowy nightmare, ripping off the head of one of the attacking dragons, and swallowing it in a single gulp. His wings snapped out and the air imploded in a shockwave of force that catapulted the other dragon into the side of the house. Purple motes rained down around him as he dove to Misha and her daughters.

But he was too late.

I turned to the werewolf before me. My body quivered with the power threatening to overwhelm me in order to destroy everything within a hundred paces. The werewolf seemed to smile, if that was possible, but he didn't turn to look at Raego. The Dragon Lord landed on the ground with the thud of a monstrous tree falling to the earth, and the sudden roar that split the night told me everything I needed to know.

Misha was gone.

A female's scream seemed to shatter my eardrums and a Grimm went sailing over my head, slamming into a rock fountain, shattering it, and landing on his face, skidding across a good fifty paces of snow-packed earth before striking a tree. The tree trunk cracked, and began to fall.

It was a big tree.

Which told me Tory had just discovered her lover's fate. And was no doubt destroying anything between her and Misha's body.

What was left of my heart blew away to ashes.

And the bastard before me laughed as he suddenly shifted to his human form.

I saw the terror in Ashley's face instantly replaced with disgusted horror, as Tory's scream dawned on her. Her eyes instantly welled up, but she didn't move. Gunnar let out a howl of mourning to match Raego's, and he crouched, ready to lunge at the werewolves before us. I laid out a hand on his back and he flinched, but remained by my side.

Geri stood before us, a dark grin on his face. "Surprise..."

Gunnar's muscles locked under my arm, preparing to pounce. I squeezed. Hard. He yelped instinctively, which caused me to release my grip. I must have unknowingly used magic to squeeze him hard enough to actually hurt him. But he got the point.

"What is the meaning of this, Geri?" The werewolf merely stared at me, and then Gunnar. He waved his hand, imploring Gunnar to shift back to his human form. Gunnar hesitated for only a second before complying. He stood from a crouch, *Bowflex* body tight and steaming from exertion.

And covered in yet more blood.

His face was as pitiless as a gravestone. "I will floss my teeth with your tendons. As you watch." Gunnar whispered in a tone that made me cringe.

I had never before heard him speak such words, or in such a tone.

Ashley let out a sob, and then a gasp as another werewolf snorted down the back of her neck in warning. Drool liberally dripped down her shoulder. Gunnar's icy gaze merely looked at them, but their shoulders sunk a bit.

"It's about time our Alpha had a true mate." Geri said absently. Everything happened at once. Geri snapped his fingers and Gunnar lunged, but he was too late. He struck an invisible wall and bounced back, shaking his head. The werewolves gripping Ashley hesitated. I knew this because I was staring at her, dumbfounded as to why I could suddenly not use my magic.

Then they bit down.

I heard bone crunch.

Ashley screamed.

Blood dribbled from the wolves' jaws.

Then they let her go, heads down as they backed off, tails between their legs. The two wolves' eyes were wet, as if they were crying. I frowned at that, still hammering against the invisible walls blocking me from my magic. I glanced to the side to find Ichabod staring at me and I scowled. God damn it.

Ashley kept right on screaming as the werewolf gene hit her. The next few days would tell if her body accepted it at all or if she was to die a slow, painful death. And even if she *survived* the change, whether or not she was strong enough to control her beast or if she was doomed to become a mindless thrall to the change, hungry only for blood, more beast than human. It was a fifty-fifty chance. Gunnar hammered into the wall again, knowing how futile it was. But doing it anyway. Again. And again.

And again.

I did the same.

The pack shifted uneasily behind Geri, looking torn. How was this even possible? Gunnar was their Alpha. This shouldn't have been possible. Not even counting Geri's word, which was worthless. I knew quite a bit about werewolves, thanks to my father studying them before helping Gunnar. What Geri had said rang true. This shouldn't have been possible.

Unless… the man Gunnar had killed hadn't been the Alpha.

But that was impossible. I had met him before. Met his pack. He was definitely the Alpha.

My mind raced, suddenly alarmed about Indie. She had been with Death, and I severely doubted anyone could have pulled one over on him. It was impossible.

But there was a lot of that going around.

"You are no wolf. You wouldn't be able to go against your alpha's command so easily." And I said the only thing that made sense. "Wilhelm." I growled.

"You got me." Then he shifted to a doppelganger of *me*. A perfect copy, and my blood froze. "Whoops, wrong one." He shifted to his true form, the man I had fought at Alistair's house. His eyes as black as midnight.

Everything fell into place. The man I had seen on video – me – quitting Temple Industries, and sending it into a freefall had been Wilhelm. Voice, looks, mannerisms, and dress all perfect. The only answer I could come up with was that at some point in his life he had encountered a skinwalker of some kind – one of those shifters that could change into *any* form. They were rare. And dangerous.

And Wilhelm had killed one.

Which meant that his amulet let him appear as the Geri. He had begun a chain of events leading Gunnar to kill the Alpha, but Geri had been no wolf, so his words had been a lie. But how were the wolves not forced to follow Gunnar? And whom else had he managed to copy lately? Had he been one of my friends the entire time? Maybe even listening in on my plans? No wonder we had never stood a chance.

"You and I are going to have a talk. A long one. At least, it will feel like a long talk to you. Pain and torture does that to one's perception of time."

"Oh, I know all about time perception… and manipulation. How do you think we got here so… *fast?*" His eyes glittered with humor. "I froze time as soon as you left. It took a bit of effort, canvassing that large of a place, and of course, the Academy stepping in helped. Gave me a few more minutes to get everyone here. We had to go by car. I am not familiar with your disappearing act. Yet."

My vision was steadily, solidly blue. Darker than I had ever seen. Almost black. But I couldn't touch my power.

It had been Wilhelm impersonating me, destroying my company. My father's company. This man had destroyed every facet of my life. No doubt behind the theft of my ring, destroying my company, turning supernatural groups against me. And he had been doing it for months, apparently. My stock options had been negotiated months ago. By me, speaking to my broker in person. Even then, Wilhelm had been setting this up.

This world of dominos.

And the first tile had been flicked.

It boggled the mind. Talk about your long con.

Wilhelm was grinning at us. "Now that that is settled." He turned to face me. "I wouldn't want you to feel left out, Nate. Your woman is with my brother, Jacob as we speak. And we have the... *gift* your dragons were guarding. Talk about silver lining!" He grinned excitedly. "Meet us at sundown to finish this. I'll give you the chance to at least watch your woman die. I'll make it convenient for everyone. *Chateau Falco.* We'll be needing to gain access to the Armory after our... chat."

Then he disappeared. As did all the other Grimms. The wolves remained. My power flooded back into me like a tsunami, sending me crashing to my knees. Then again, a gentle breeze could have done so at that point.

Indie was taken.

Ashley had been turned.

They had the books.

*Operation White Knight* had failed miserably.

And they wanted my Armory.

Gunnar was suddenly at Ashley's side, picking her body up as it convulsed. He yelled into the sky, and Tory's instant cry was a perfect complement, the sounds melding together in a damning harmony.

I fell face first into the snow, crying, my vision pulsing from red to blue. Then to black as I pounded my fist repeatedly into the snow.

# CHAPTER 37

*I* finally lifted my head. After another second, I managed to climb to my feet. Every single werewolf was on his knees, but only one spoke, softly, to Gunnar's retreating back as he carried Ashley in his bulging arms.

"If it means anything, they told us that since your woman was a Regular, they wouldn't kill her. Just turn her. If we hadn't complied they promised to force one of us to kill her instead. Not that it matters to you." Gunnar's shoulders stiffened, and Ashley let out a soft whimper of pain, very much alive, as if punctuating the werewolf's words. He carried on, voice heavy with both guilt and the burden of accepting full responsibility. "I have a daughter. Two years old. They... took her. They took all of our children." Several answering sobs and growls responded to this comment. The man continued on.

"They killed my son. I... they let me choose which child would live." A soft sob escaped his dry lips, and I saw his eyes wet with unshed tears, but he wasn't begging. He spoke clinically, not asking for forgiveness from Gunnar. Just stating the facts to his Alpha. "If you want to take my life, I submit myself to you, Alpha. Just... just look after my girl. She's innocent... Even though her father is a coward... The choice to act was mine and mine alone. Don't punish the pack for my actions. Punish *me... please.*" He never lifted his gaze, just turned so that his throat was available for a quick strike. Now he was begging.

But not for his own life. He was begging to sacrifice his life for the pack.

Gunnar's chest heaved and the pack was silent.

My friend finally shook his head and continued on his way.

The man let out a breath, whether in regret or relief, I couldn't tell. I don't think anyone else could tell either. The pack looked at each other thoughtfully, guiltily, and then they began to round up, murmuring softly as they helped the pleading werewolf to his feet. He called out to Gunnar one last time. "Call on us when you need warm bodies ready to die. We owe at least *that* to you."

"You owe me nothing, because to me, you *are* nothing," Gunnar growled over his shoulder, almost too softly to be heard. But we were talking about werewolves here. Supernatural hearing. They caught it and the emotion under the surface. And their shoulders sagged even further, a pitiful sight. Then they nodded once to Gunnar and began to lope off in pairs.

I snagged the pleading werewolf's arm. He looked down at my hand, and then very calmly at my face. I wisely let go.

"What happened?" I asked softly.

"Our Alpha was forced to obey the Grimms after they took our offspring and women. Then Gunnar killed one of us in the sewers and sent our Alpha into a rage. He wanted a duel. Anything to show the pack that he wasn't defenseless. We didn't know that Geri was a Grimm. We had no idea. Not sure what happened to the real Geri. Probably dead somewhere." His eyes grew distant.

"That doesn't explain you guys here."

He nodded sadly. "When Gunnar refused to accept us, he left us without an Alpha. He didn't say the words. *You are mine.* The new Alpha has to say the words to the Geri. No one really thought about it until after you left. That's when Geri told us if we ever wanted to see our kids again we had to go with him. That's when we realized we had been played. But we couldn't do anything about it. Pack first. *Always* Pack first. And without an Alpha, our pack was our *family*, and the Grimms had them. We had no choice." He spat, not venomous with accusation, but with the fury of a man helplessly condemned.

I nodded, patted his shoulder, and spoke. "I'll talk with him. We will need you, despite what he said. Can you do that? As a favor? Without him saying the words?"

The man stared at me, and then shook his head. "Sorry, Master Temple. Pack first. Which means our families." His shoulders sagged. A thought crossed his features. "How come your spirit wolves didn't fight today?" I somehow managed a smile, and decided to be honest in hopes that it might gain both his respect and possibly his help.

"They never existed. It was just magic. And some cool boots." I admitted, smiling wider at his incredulous expression.

"Magic. And cool boots," he repeated, staring at me, a small smile slowly creeping over his face. "I can't believe that all this time we feared your invisible pack of wolves." He shook his head with a weak laugh. "Well played." I nodded in acknowledgment.

"Change anything?" I asked, voice hopeful.

He shook his head sadly. "Pack first." He recited. And then he loped away to rejoin his brethren. I couldn't blame him, but it sucked.

A nearby dragon watched to make sure the wolves left the property. I patted my pocket and frowned. One of the amulets was missing. When had *that* happened? I muttered a curse of frustration under my breath as I pulled out my cell phone, and dialed the only number in the world that mattered.

Death.

He answered on the second ring. "Is it finished?"

"Where is Indie?"

The line was silent for a moment, and then I heard a voice from Heaven. "Nate? Are you guys okay?" It was *her*. My heart seemed to shutter to a stop and then pick up double time.

"They didn't take you!"

"Um, no. What are you talking about?"

"The Grimms. Wilhelm. He said he had taken you."

"No, I don't really know where I am, but I'm with Death. He's reading a book," she paused. "*Through the Looking Glass*. Is everyone alright?"

I nodded, throat tight, then realized she couldn't see me. "Yes." I thought of Ashley. "More or less." Then I thought of Misha and Tory. "No. I guess we're not." Indie knew me well. She waited for me to speak rather than hammering me with questions. "Misha is gone." Indie gasped. "And Ashley was infected with the werewolf gene. We don't know how her body will react." I trailed off, and heard Indie let out a soft sob.

"I'll be right there. Death can get me there fast."

"Absolutely not." I snapped. For one thing, now more than ever, I realized how important my proposal was. I had to do it. Tonight. We had until tomorrow to confront the Grimms. And after that… well, I wasn't giving up, but odds seemed pretty likely I wasn't going to see the sun set. Perhaps I wouldn't propose, but I desperately needed Indie to know my intentions. But to do that, I needed to bake a cake first. With Dean's help, of course. Which meant that Indie needed to stay put.

After this fight, I didn't think I would have any problem encouraging everyone to recover in private for a few hours, to grieve, and prepare for tomorrow morning.

"The Grimms want you dead. They already kidnapped Ashley. Geri wasn't whom we thought, but was in fact, Wilhelm. He was also the reason Temple Industries folded. He can shapeshift into other people entirely. It was Wilhelm in front of the cameras announcing my resignation. It was Wilhelm impersonating Ashley to get on that flight. I'm going to make him pay in blood." I promised.

The voice on the other end went silent, not arguing. "How?" She asked softly. I began to answer, and then remembered how our unhackable phones had been hacked. And that anyone could be listening to us right now. Even with new phones, I wasn't taking any chances. The Grimms had known my every move so far. Time to change tactics.

"Somehow." I answered cryptically.

Indie got it. "When do I get to see you? When do we confront the Grimms? Why didn't they end it today?"

"They want the Armory. We have until tomorrow at sunrise. We meet at *Chateau Falco.*"

"What about me?" She asked.

"You will prepare for a date. Tonight. I'm hungry."

"What! A dinner date? *Now?*"

"Pretty woman don't argue with man. Or man club pretty woman and drag her to cave," I grumbled in my best caveman voice.

"I'm open to that," she teased.

"Just get ready. Death can help if you need anything. He'll know where to take you. Hand the phone over to him?"

"I love you, Nate. See you at dinner, tiger." Her voice dripped promises that I wished I had time to explore.

"Yes?" Death answered. I told him where to take her and at what time. It would give me a few hours to bake the cake. Or cheat if I failed spectacularly, which wasn't out of the realm of possibility. He grunted acknowledgment. "And keep her safe. They already took Ashley from under our noses. She is my *everything*." I spoke harshly, remembering his wandering gaze earlier.

"I know. See you soon."

And he hung up. I glanced up to see I was entirely alone. Gunnar – carrying Ashley – and Tory – carrying Misha's now human corpse in her arms – entered the home, heads bowed. Raego approached me on silent feet, glancing here and there at the property to assess damage and verify that his dragons stood guard. He stepped up beside me, not speaking.

"I checked. They have your bargaining chip. Tory did her best to keep them away, but after Misha…" His eyes grew dangerous. "After that, well, she kind of lost it. That's when they took it." My shoulders sagged. *Operation White Knight*, my failsafe, had done failed. I couldn't blame Tory. This was on me. I shouldn't have left such a big responsibility to Raego and his crew. I shouldn't have let Raego out of my sight.

Dwelling on that wasn't going to solve the predicament though.

"We must rectify that. Or we're all dead." Raego merely arched a brow as if to say, *how is that any different than our current situation?* I grunted in response.

"Indie safe?" He asked. I nodded. "At least there's that." He muttered. "So… sunrise?"

"Yes."

"Good. I have a few things to say to these sons of bitches." His body rippled slightly, his dragon beast threatening to break free. I smiled sadly.

"Just make sure you speak loudly. I think they have hearing problems."

"Oh, I'll speak very loudly indeed." His eyes twinkled with malice.

"I need to run. Get everyone ready. I know this seems callous, but none of us stands a chance if we don't fight tomorrow. We must use our grief as armor. Or as a weapon." Raego nodded, eyes fiery. "*Chateau Falco* an hour before sunrise. I want to go over a few things before shit hits the fan."

He nodded. "We'll be there a few hours before sunrise then. Just to be sure they aren't setting up an ambush."

I grunted. "I really don't think they have any reason to do so. They already have almost everything they want. They just need my... *me* to show up." I changed my words. Raego studied me thoughtfully, but didn't press.

He extended his hand. I grasped it, squeezed hard, staring him in the eyes with a silent promise. "We'll make them pay for this, Raego. All of them."

He nodded, grinning expectantly. "Aye."

Then I made a gateway back to *Chateau Falco,* leaving my friends behind.

# CHAPTER 38

*O*nce back in the comfort of my own home, I had made some cell phone calls. To Othello. Achilles. Tomas, the dragon hunter. Jeffries, the FBI Agent *slash* walking lie-detector.

No one answered.

Then I made a magical *call*. The Minotaur.

Nothing.

Which was probably for the best. At least for them. Then again, these people had been one-time allies and could have already been under threat of annihilation. Perhaps that was why they hadn't answered. Or, more likely, they had heard that I was persona non-grata and that any interaction with me would be bad for their health.

I hoped it was the latter.

Either way, it left us on our own. But we all had a vested interest in the Grimm problem.

People had died…

That hit me hard. It was essentially my fault. Putting myself at risk was one thing. I was willing to pay the price. But now my friends had paid the price. And my secret operation may have just made me the biggest threat to the Academy in recorded – and unrecorded – history.

I had been debating on whether or not to propose to Indie, but after the recent fight, and the deaths, I decided that timing be damned. I wanted her to know how I felt. She didn't have to *answer* me. But she *did* have to know how I felt. Some may call that cruel. Selfish.

So be it.

My death would hit her hard no matter whether I proposed or not, so I had made an executive decision that I wanted her to know my feelings. That we weren't just boyfriend and girlfriend.

We were *more*.

If that was only known for a few hours, so be it. I could carry it to my grave with a smile. A weight off my shoulders. No regrets.

Which meant I needed a baked good of some kind since the bakery had fallen through.

I stared at the mess that was now my kitchen. Egg shells, loose flour, and various other spills marred the counter. I was no baker. But it sure smelled good. I clutched the towel around my waist, my only garment as I was fresh from the shower, and strapped on the *Avengers Infinity Gauntlet* oven mitt Indie had gotten me as a small gift, knowing damn well I didn't cook.

Heh. I would show her…

The *Infinity Gauntlet* had almost given Thanos, the mad Titan, the power to overcome the Avengers.

Surely its power could help me bake a cake. I leaned down to the oven door, gazing inside to check on my masterpiece. The timer was almost up. I smiled to myself, lifting my *Infinity Glove* oven mitt into the air in a fist. "The world is mine!"

Which meant that I looked rather ridiculous when Dean entered the room and blinked at me, eyes widening, mouth opening to speak but no words coming to mind for a second. He wore neat slacks and a pressed shirt, impeccably tailored. He even wore a tie under his matching vest. The chain from a pocket watch glittered conspicuously.

He cleared his throat and tried again. "Does the Mad Titan need assistance baking his cake?" He was the King of Deadpan.

"Pfft. I already did the hard part. Icing it will be a cinch." I pondered that. "You do know how to ice a cake, right?" I asked, turning back to the oven and opening the door.

"Yes. I will return shortly with the icing. Need anything else while I'm out at the store?" I shook my head, reaching into the oven to clutch the cake and pull it out. "Okay. I will deliver the cake to the restaurant once finished." I grunted acknowledgment and heard the door close as he left.

I studied the cake with a proud whistle after setting it down on the counter. It needed to cool for a while, so I would go get ready while I waited. I went to the counter to pour myself a small glass of wine, needing to fortify my courage for the upcoming proposal.

Listen, I wasn't scared.

Per se...

More, I truly wanted this to be a momentous... moment. I wanted the gravity of my feelings to be expressed properly. I did better with winging these kinds of things rather than having a prepared speech. More heartfelt. Organic. Genuine.

Like Indie.

I was pouring the wine when I heard the door open. Likely Dean had forgotten something and had returned to grab it. I set down the bottle and turned to tease him. The towel dropped as I picked up the glass, exposing my danger zone. Before darting to pick it up in embarrassment, my eyes caught on the two figures standing in the doorway. And I stopped. They were smiling.

And neither of them was Dean.

Grimms.

They wore black leathers, looking like a cross between special ops gear and stealthy hunting garb. Like thieves in the night. It all looked new too; I could smell the freshly oiled leather. And here I was, all naked.

God damn it. I snatched up my towel. "Cold, Maker?" One asked in a honeyed drawl. His face was a cinderblock, complete with scars and a stubble blonde beard.

"Looks like it." The other answered. He was leaner, face drawn, and he wore a perfectly curled mustache. But he still looked tough. Just fashionably tough.

"What are you doing here? We have an appointment for tomorrow morning."

"Yes, about that." One, the beefier blonde one, answered.

Mustachio finished his sentence. *Tweedle Dumb* and *Tweedle Dumber*. "We wanted to talk to you about two of our brothers. It seems you accidentally killed them." He said. "Outside the hotel."

"No accident, I'm afraid."

"You should be. Afraid," he clarified. His hand twirled his mustache out of habit.

I kid you not.

I scowled. "Let me get this straight. You two clowns are here to get a little revenge on me for defending myself against two ill-prepared assassins who tried to punch my ticket the other day? Do you realize how idiotic that sounds?" I thought about setting my glass down, but wasn't sure if that would signal a reaction on their part. I took a controlled sip instead, trying to hide my nervousness. Being outnumbered was dicey. Being outnumbered and naked was worse. Especially in your own home. "Anyway, I spoke to Jacob and Wilhelm. They need me in one piece tomorrow morning. And he will probably need you two in one piece to be used as cannon fodder when I put an end to you guys for good. You know, take a few bullets for them so they can last a few seconds longer."

The beefier blonde shrugged. "We can leave you in one piece. One bloody and bruised piece, more or less functional." And he began to advance with slow heavy steps.

Unbelievable. Here I was, stark naked, still wearing the *Infinity Gauntlet* mitt, and a glass of wine in my hand, and these two chuckleheads wanted to scrap.

Fine. I'd had enough. I'd oblige.

I didn't even wait for the telltale pulse of blue to tint my vision. My power was now familiar to me, and I knew I could call it at will. Even though I wasn't as diverse in my use of it as I had been with my wizard power.

I launched a blast of air at the approaching Grimm.

But felt a familiar shield fall into place before I could strike.

Mustachio smiled, raising a finger to shake at me. "Ah, ah, ah. No power. Just a good old-fashioned ass whooping, Temple."

Well.

Two on one was never good odds.

So, I threw my wine glass at Mustachio. The glass shattered in his face, right in the eyes and his stupid mustache, causing him to roar in pain. The beefier Grimm yelled and began stomping towards me. I grabbed my towel and high tailed it out of the kitchen. I needed a weapon. These guys were strapped.

I tore through the hallways of Chateau Falco, trying to determine the closest weapon from the layout of the house in my mind. I hadn't had time to nab anything from the kitchen. The rapidly approaching footsteps told me I wouldn't have a chance at reaching any of the swords, guns, or axes in time. Then I had a thought. I veered abruptly to the right, racing through the dining room. I knocked over any piece of furniture within easy reach, lamps, chairs, tables, anything to slow them down. Then I hit the foyer, smiling at the sound of curses from the larger Grimm. At least the scrawnier, faster one was still plucking glass out of his mustache. I shivered at the imagined sensation of what was to come next, my fingers wrapping around the door handle leading outside. I threw myself through the door before I could think about it too much.

Icy cold hit my still damp hair and genitals like a knife. I pressed on, racing across the snow in bare feet, ignoring the stabs of pain from the gravel, and bolted straight towards the stable. I remembered the old rusty knife I had been meaning to fix sitting on the workbench.

The knife had surprised me by still holding an edge. It had once been a real specimen, long, full-tang, and bound with a sinister bone handle. An antique of some kind.

I tore through the door, which was luckily open, and sprinted for the workbench.

Or I tried to.

Something hanging just inside the doorway clipped me in the temple and I went sprawling, seeing stars. I heard heavily booted feet just outside the door as the beefy Grimm tried to close the gap. Having boots helped while running through snow. My feet were numb and no doubt bleeding from the gravel, and my head still spun woozily in the darkness of the stable. I lurched to my feet and stumbled to the workbench.

My hand closed around the hilt and I dove to the side, rolling to my feet quickly on the icy concrete as I anticipated the attack. A club slammed into the workbench a hairsbreadth away from clobbering me. I stood from my crouch with a manic grin. It was McBeefy Grimm. He took one look at my knife, smiled, and dropped his club. He withdrew a truly impressive knife from his belt, blade glittering in the filtered light coming through the windows. Luckily it was a wide-open space. Knife fights tended to require a lot of room.

I wrapped the towel around my left forearm – the one with the Infinity Gauntlet still covering my fist, and palmed the blade in the other hand. I felt naked.

Look, not just *literally*. I *was* naked in that department, which also wasn't good for a knife fight.

But naked without my *power*. I had grown used to having it, and knowing these punks were blocking me lent me a bit of paranoia. No backup. Just brawn against brawn.

And these guys knew brawn.

McBeefy approached on the balls of his elephant feet, surprisingly nimble, grinning as he shook his head at the ridiculous situation of getting into a knife fight in a garage with a nude, powerless wizard who was wearing an oven mitt and a towel for armor.

It would just make my victory more impressive.

Or my beating more embarrassing.

I lunged, swiping at his thigh like a snake. Mallory had taught me the ins and outs of knife fighting. I wasn't sure where he had learned it, but judging by his scarred forearms, he had practiced quite a bit in his youth. I scored a hit, a deep cut lashing his thigh, but he hammered my kidneys with his empty fist on my way by, and I grunted as the pain struck my groin, like only a true kidney punch could do.

He grunted at the strike, wiping a hand on the bloody smear and holding it up to the light. Then his brother, Mustachio, tore through the doorway, face bleeding and furious. His mustache was now lopsided, one side perfectly curled, the other a ragged protrusion of loose hair.

"Wardrobe malfunction?" I asked, motioning towards my upper lip.

He merely set his lips in a tight line, and pulled out his own knife. Then closed off any chance of escape as he nudged the door closed with a boot, eliminating the additional light from outside. They circled me like wolves.

Lucky me, I *knew* wolf. Gunnar had been my sparring partner for *years*.

I feinted left, watching with a distant grin as the larger Grimm fell for it. Mustachio yelled in warning but was too late. I slashed McBeefy's wrist. The one holding the knife. The blade clattered to the ground but he had instinctively reached to catch it, so caught my knee on his jaw instead, which sent him into a dazed twirl before he crumpled to the floor. I immediately jumped to the side rather than stomping on the Grimm for good measure.

Lucky me. Mustachio had lunged to catch me in the back, but missed. He growled, kicking his partner lightly in the ribs. "Get up." No response.

"I read him a bedtime story. Just you and me now." I smiled back, chuckling.

He snarled and lunged. I caught the blade on my towel-clad forearm, but it cut through the fabric easily. I felt fire lash my wrist and I tried to slice back, but he was fast. Not superhuman fast, which he no doubt could have been. Just experienced fast. Lucky me, these guys were staying true to their word and relying solely on their skills as humans.

For now.

I felt another slice graze my ribs – deep enough to draw blood – and my counter swing missed again. He was chuckling now. He was good. I needed to end this fast. Before Dean showed up and became collateral damage.

Or leverage. Which seemed to be a common tactic for the Grimms.

I threw myself at him in a savage flurry, missing with my first two strikes. I hit him two times out of four, one of them on his cheek. And that's when he began to change the rules. He used magic.

A force slammed into me, spinning me around, and his knife sliced my back. Hard. I fell, the bloody towel unraveling from my impromptu knot. The hand holding the knife hit the ground and the blade shattered. The Grimm began to chuckle.

"Aw, that's too bad," Mustachio called from over my shoulder. I turned to face him, lifting my *Infinity Gauntlet* to defend myself, calling on my power one last time, but to no avail. Apparently, Mustachio was the one blocking me, not McBeefy, or the shield would have evaporated. The knife raced towards me in a blur.

A crossbow bolt abruptly punched through his throat, sending him into a spin. His blade managed to slice the outside of my thigh in a deep cut as he fell, which hurt. Mustachio twitched once, and then a pool of blood began slowly growing around his body. I glanced back, grunting at the knife wound in my thigh. Dean stood in the doorway, holding a crossbow and a grocery bag. He hit a button on his key fob and his car alarm chirped on.

"Really, Master Temple. I told you about the crossbow on the wall by the door. Why did you grab that rusty old knife you so cleverly hid from me?" I blinked at him. Surprised at him saving my life, but also that he had known about the knife I had tried hiding from him. He calmly surveyed the scene. "Is that all of them?" He asked. I nodded. He hung the crossbow back on the wall and left without another word.

I blinked.

Then I used the towel to tie a makeshift tourniquet around my thigh. I used zip ties to bind McBeefy. Several of them on each arm and leg for good measure. Then I padlocked him to a fender of one of the late model cars parked in the stable. The kind made of all steel, no fiberglass. He groaned lightly as I did so, but didn't wake. I punched him in the nose and his head rocked back, striking the fender with a satisfying *clang*. I disarmed both bodies, threw a tarp over Mustachio, and made my way back inside *Chateau Falco*.

Dean was calmly plucking glass out of the cake. He turned to look at me with a frown of disapproval before pointedly glancing back at the cake. "You should shower again and bandage those wounds. You need to leave in thirty minutes to make your reservation."

I stared in utter disbelief for a few seconds as he silently began icing the cake. Then I left to follow his advice, muttering under my breath.

*Goddamn Grimms.*

*Goddamn snarky Butlers.*

# CHAPTER 39

*I* sat in the middle of the restaurant, trying not to fidget. My wounds were aching and burning in a steady, reliable rhythm, matching the uncomfortable feeling in my stomach. Dean had bandaged me up, and I was using my powers to block the insistent throbbing pain threatening to overwhelm me from the brief but violent knife fight, among other injuries over the past few days. I masked my grimace. It might send the wrong impression to Indie.

I, Nate Temple, life-long bachelor, was about to propose.

And then likely be murdered in the morning.

I signaled the waiter again impatiently. He danced over to my side, having been watching me out of the corner of his eye. "Yes, Master Temple." I had already ordered dinner for Indie and I, knowing what she generally liked and disliked, but also because she enjoyed the surprise. We always took turns. Sometimes she ordered, sometimes I did.

"Make sure to keep an eye out for–"

"Miss Indiana Rippley. Yes. Of course, Sir."

I grumbled dark things under my breath at his interruption. In his defense, I *had* reminded him three times already. "And you have everything you need to proceed as I ask–"

"Yes, Sir. Everything is ready, only awaiting your signal." He showed me the signal.

"And the-"

"Yes, the... *token of love* is ready and waiting. I'm sure she will adore the sentiment." His tone may or may not have held an undercurrent of sarcasm. I scowled for good measure, and then nodded. He left. I took a sip of my wine, waiting impatiently.

As if on cue, Indie entered the restaurant, and time seemed to slow. Everyone turned to look at her. She was very... *noticeable*, to say the least. She wore an ermine gown, slit at the thigh to reveal a small, tasteful slice of pale leg, and the fabric clung to her well-curved frame like a second skin. I smiled as I stood. She returned the smile as she spotted me and then approached. Many people continued to watch, some looking confused, and others shaking their heads before turning back to their meals. Perhaps they were still upset at me for the failure of Temple Industries, and my seeming blatant disregard in the interviews. But that had been Wilhelm, not me. Still, they didn't know that, and I didn't care about any of that tonight.

Indie stepped up to the table and the waiter was suddenly there holding the chair back, looking composed but slightly startled. Perhaps she had snuck in before they could guide her. I hadn't seen a waiter leading her to my table. And waiters in places like this could take those kinds of slights personally. I reminded myself to tip well.

The waiter arched a questioning brow at me and I nodded. His lips compressed into a thin line, but he continued on without Indie noticing. What the hell was wrong with this guy? Was he really that upset about not escorting her to my table?

I sat down after her, and all the weariness of the fighting and near-death experiences over the last few days slowly dissipated. I was still in pain and nervous as hell, but some of the weight had lifted from my shoulders upon seeing her dressed to the nines. I began to think about Misha, and Ashley, and quickly had to shake away the thoughts. Indie noticed, dropping her gaze in understanding.

The waiter spoke. "Shall I-"

"I'll have what he's having." She interrupted, staring at my drink. Which was not her typical drink. Then again, it was not a typical night. We were on edge. The waiter, still looking ruffled, nodded once, and then departed. Indie smiled at his back in amusement before turning to me, eyebrows arched. "Should we really be celebrating right now?" She asked softly. "It looks like many in this room would skewer you alive if they could." She added as an afterthought, glancing around the room.

Indeed, we were garnering many looks. Some hostile, some interested; all package and parcel for me. I was a celebrity in town, and was used to it. Indie would eventually get used to it also. She would have to.

"Of course, we should be celebrating. We are *alive*." I spoke softly.

Indie nodded, looking down.

"After what I saw today, I needed to remember what we are fighting for. What is truly important." And just like that, I found myself ready to spill my guts to her, not even waiting for our food.

Or Indie's drink.

The waiter was exiting the kitchen, and saw my pointed double blink. Our prearranged signal. He halted, glanced at Indie with a frown, and then back at me. I nodded discreetly and he disappeared behind the curtain. Why did he look surprised? I had told him more than a dozen times what I needed him to do. Even if I was jumping the gun a bit. But I couldn't help myself. Thinking of spending another hour in front of this woman and not asking her to marry me sounded horrible, and impossible.

Indie was watching me thoughtfully.

"But that's not the only reason I wanted to have dinner with you tonight," I began, noticing the owner of the store now standing by the curtain leading to the kitchen, barely hiding his interest in the upcoming action about to go down at my table. The waiter approached, set Indie's drink before her, and took a step back, waiting patiently. Indie frowned at him momentarily, but my words suddenly caught her full attention.

"Indiana Rippley. You are the most stunning woman I have ever encountered. Despite our... *differences*, I have thrived in your loving arms. We come from different worlds," she sighed at my words, eyes glittering as she smiled so deeply I thought she would burst out laughing. "But you have never been far from my side. I am not worthy to hold one such as you so close for so long, but I would ask that you let me do so a little bit longer... *forever*." My eyes met hers, and she glanced again at the waiter, who suddenly knelt at her feet.

The restaurant grew silent as a tomb, chairs creaking and scraping as everyone turned their heads to watch with disbelief. Her eyes flickered from me to the waiter and back again. I stood, approached her, and knelt at her other side, clutching her hand delicately. "Would you do me the great honor of becoming my wife?" She stared incredulously at me, and then her eyes darted to the waiter as he produced the kind of engagement ring only a once-billionaire could afford.

The *Infinity Gauntlet* oven mitt.

I accepted the mitt, nodding for him to leave, and then carefully, with great reverence, covered her hand with it. "No one else would propose with an *Infinity Gauntlet*. They would keep the power for themselves." I said solemnly. "But I want to share everything with you. The good. The bad. The ugly." I smiled at her, waiting for her response, my heart racing wildly. I had done it. All she had to do was say one little word.

Several customers left. In fact, I realized that quite a few customers had left. And the ones still in the process of leaving now had disgusted looks on their faces. The owner stared slack-jawed at me, then began to quietly but insistently berate the waiter whom had just left my table. But I didn't care. They could hate me all they wanted. I didn't blame them after what they had seen. After Wilhelm had impersonated me so perfectly to the local news channel, sending Temple Industries into a nosedive.

Then they got to see me at a posh restaurant, apparently unashamed, proposing to the woman I loved. Typical billionaire arrogance.

I realized Indie hadn't spoken yet, so I turned back to her, ignoring the increasing exodus of customers. "Well?"

She stared back at me, eyes staring at me with disbelief, and then they slowly began to transform into a smile.

But something was... *off*.

The smile was sinister. Wolfish. Mocking. Full of glee, but not for my intended reasons.

"Oh, this is likely the crowning moment of my existence." An entirely different voice spoke through her lips. Time momentarily froze with the familiar pulse of power I had come to fear, and the restaurant was instantly silent. Completely. People frozen in midstep. Then Indie's form began to twist and transform into a different being entirely.

Wilhelm suddenly sat before me, still wearing my engagement *Infinity Gauntlet*.

And I was clutching his hand like my life depended on it. I flung it away but couldn't manage to work my legs. My blood turned to ice. I didn't know how it was possible. How he knew to be here at this moment. The most important moment of my life. But it didn't matter. Here we were.

*No... Not this, too.*

He nodded, seemingly able to read my thoughts. "Oh, I'm afraid so. Your little wench is currently under lock and key, but on her behalf, I feel I must give you at least some kind of response." He caressed the oven mitt with pantomimed seriousness. Then his cold, dead eyes met mine, flashing black. "The answer is *No*. Indie is mine. But you will see her in the morning. Perhaps." He winked.

Then he was gone, leaving me kneeling beside an empty chair as time warped back to normal. Several customers suddenly tripped, clutching onto a chair or table for support. They glanced over their shoulders to see me standing beside an empty chair and frowned in confusion. The waiter and owner looked equally startled.

My vision pulsed blue and I began to hyperventilate. The waiter, noticing the look on my face, rushed over, urged on by the owner. "Master Temple? I didn't want to say it while he was here, but did I mishear your instructions? I thought you had said Indiana Rippley would be joining you this evening..."

I was growling, an unending string of dark curses pouring from my lips, trying to prevent myself from unleashing my power and burning the building to the ground. "What did you see?" I hissed.

The waiter's eyes widened. "Um, a rather scruffy gentleman in leathers sitting at the table. And then... well, you *proposed* to him." He looked as if his tongue was about to dry up and crawl out of his mouth. Not sure if my anger was at his failure or the apparent negative response I had been given by my dinner date.

I was going to kill Wilhelm. And then I was going to kill Death. I had spoken to Indie only hours before on his phone. Was he implicit in her abduction? Had he been lying to me even then? On the phone? Was he the source of the leak I suspected in my crew?

I stood, heaving, pinpoint flickers of light clouding my vision. I needed to get out of here. Fresh air. Cool wind. No people. Before I did something stupid.

"It's time I left." I managed to whisper. The other customers still present looked horrified and confused. I would have too if I had just seen the city's billionaire celebrity heir propose to a leather-armored man in one of the more exclusive restaurants in town.

The waiter nodded, turning as if to go grab the check. I tossed three one-hundred-dollar bills on the table and, without giving a flying fuck, Shadow Walked out of the restaurant and back into the kitchen of *Chateau Falco*, where I found Dean and Alucard waiting for me.

They blinked in astonishment, eyes slowly sparkling with eager smiles as if anxious to hear how everything went. Their stares slowly faded as they got a good look at my face, which was hard enough to grind rocks.

"We need Mallory up and running. Whatever it takes."

They blinked at me. "He should be fine in a few hours. That old bastard is beyond tough." Alucard sounded uncharacteristically impressed.

I nodded. "In the morning, we are going to murder every single one of those bastards. Slowly. I hope there are survivors. I want to make their remaining existence... *memorable.*"

Alucard cleared his throat cautiously. "I take it the proposal didn't go as... planned?" He offered carefully.

I stared at him, eyes no doubt bloodshot, because they seemed as dry as dust to me. "They took her," I whispered, barely able to maintain my feet.

They leaned forward as if they hadn't heard me correctly. The granite countertop abruptly crumbled beneath Alucard's claws as he squeezed the stone at my words.

I also gripped the kitchen island with shaking fingertips, but didn't break it. "Indie's been..." I swallowed deeply, unable to finish as bile crept up into my throat. She was my responsibility. The love of my life. It was my fault she was taken. I had trusted Death, an immortal being with his own agendas, to look out for her, and I had been burned.

My world rocked, and Alucard lurched forward a step as if to catch me.

I held up a hand, took several deep breaths, and spoke in a snarl.

"Indie's been *taken*. Tomorrow their blood will feed my lawns. Their screams will be trapped inside *Chateau Falco* like a soothing lullaby. Their bones will lay buried deep under our maze. I will destroy everything they hold dear."

I paused, lifting my gaze to meet their eyes. "I have nothing else to give. So, I will just begin *taking* from them. They will not escape me. This I swear." I drew a bead of blood from my thumb, and uttered a spell, binding the promise to my soul. A Blood Debt. Alucard's eyes widened in disbelief, and Dean looked as if his heart had just been ripped from his chest. And then I left the kitchen, ready to arm myself for the biggest tussle of my career.

Wilhelm had warned me of his interest in her. And Jacob had all but admitted that she would be given to his brother. Why hadn't I seen this coming? I took another breath and strode through the house, stomping loudly without consciously deciding to do so.

I didn't even bother calling Death this time. I couldn't trust him anymore. If Indie were free, she would have been at the restaurant. So, she really was gone. This was not some ploy. Some trick. She had been taken. And Wilhelm had stepped into her place for the sole purpose of rubbing my face in it. The fact that I had been proposing was merely icing on the cake.

I began calling the crew, telling them to get here early. I was done playing games. My tactic for this battle was simple, but efficient.

Overkill.

Absolute, illogical overkill.

It was time for me to dig out the party favors I had secured over the last few months from Temple Industries. Several of my side projects that only some knew about.

The Grimms were history. They just didn't know it yet.

# CHAPTER 40

*W*e stood outside the front door of *Chateau Falco*, the centuries-old monolith towering behind us as if in encouragement of our decision to fight. A calming giant backing us up. If only it could do more than look imposing. Inside her halls, maybe, but that wouldn't help me today.

Sunrise was in a few moments.

Leather creaked.

Fabric rustled.

Metal scraped and clicked, whether from gun, blade, or armor.

We had tried to go over plans a dozen times, but there were simply too many variables. We had killed several Grimms, but how many had truly died, and how many were left? McBeefy, my captive Grimm, knelt on the ground before me, struggling as if sensing my thoughts.

I didn't even look down as I lifted my boot and kicked the Grimm squarely in the back of the neck hard enough to give him whiplash and possibly crack one of his vertebrae. He grunted in agony and head butted the icy gravel.

Tory watched the violent blow without emotion, face devoid of any empathy whatsoever. I hadn't had the proper chance to talk to her. But she hadn't wanted to talk about anything anyway. She just wanted vengeance. I got that. Still, I wanted to wrap her up in a giant hug, help her carry some of those burdens. Even if she didn't want me to.

It's what friends did.

She was grieving. And I doubted that the Grimms would enjoy being on the receiving end of her fury. "You okay?" I asked her softly, our first direct communication since Misha had been killed.

Her eyes met mine. They were bloodshot, pained, and full of dancing, malevolent carnage. She looked away, not answering me right away. "I don't think it's a good idea for me to get in touch with my feelings right now. But soon I'll feel *much* better."

I nodded, and several others murmured their agreement.

Everyone shifted from foot to foot, the non-shifters trying to get used to the Kevlar vests I had provided. It wasn't perfect, but it would help. I hoped. Gunnar seemed especially uncomfortable, sniffing the air hungrily as he subconsciously adjusted the Kevlar vest covering his torso. He was the only shifter wearing one. I was anxious to see how it would hold up, seeing as how it had been made to hypothetically adjust on the fly, reforming to his new wolf form so that if all went well, I had a bulletproof werewolf on my side. I wasn't sure if the Grimms were packing silver bullets, or even whether they would use guns, but I wasn't taking any chances. I had told him of my conversation with the werewolf. He had listened silently, grunted, and then changed the topic.

It didn't matter anymore. He had more important things on his mind.

Like Ashley.

She was currently in a safe location under the protection of Gunnar's long-time friend, Agent Jeffries. He would use his FBI credentials to try and run interference if any police activity arose, which I highly suspected as a result of my alleged insider trading crime. Ashley was being held within a silver circle, watched and monitored at all times. I knew that more than almost anything, Gunnar wanted to be there by her side.

But this was the one place he would rather be, to exact revenge, just like everyone else here. Alucard stood like a statue beside him, idly thumbing his umbrella. He was liberally coated with sunscreen, and wore clothing meant to block the rays of the upcoming sunrise. You know, the kind of fabric you see on those pasty kids at the pool that get sunburns at even mention of the word *sunlight*. It was an odd pair, to see a werewolf and a vampire standing side by side, neither snarling at each other, but instead compatriots in the fight to come. Silent comrades, blood brothers of war, almost as if they had fought beside each other for decades, no further words necessary.

Raego and his dragons stood off to the side, speaking quietly, ready to shift in a blink, and far enough away to not take any of us out when they suddenly transformed to creatures ten times the size – or larger – of their human skin. But I wished we had more. Most of them were off on assignments overseas or protecting the Dragon Lord's American interests thanks to the arrival of the Grimms. And Raego had adamantly refused allowing Misha's daughters to participate.

I agreed.

The injured, but not down for the count, Mallory had finally gotten a hold of Tomas, who had been lying low after attracting too much attention to himself. The two were up on the roof at discreet points, armed with sniper rifles, relying on mortal means to aid in the battle. With Mallory already injured, his best support was being on the roof.

But to me, the world felt empty despite all my friends willing to die by my side.

Indie was gone.

Taken.

Captured.

Either Death had betrayed me, or the Grimms had overwhelmed him somehow, but I doubted the latter. Despite how badass the Grimms were, Death was a legendary warrior. At the Armageddon level. Which likely meant he had switched sides at some point. Made a deal with the Grimms. I realized I was growling, only noticing so as Tory placed a calming hand on my wrist. Her fiery eyes met mine. "Not yet," I nodded back, regaining some semblance of control.

After my head had cooled a bit, I had tried reaching out to Death to confirm my fear. But he hadn't answered.

No matter now.

Glancing at the skyline, I realized it was almost sunrise. Time to get to work.

I knelt down on the ground. My friends formed a loose circle around me, and I murmured a word, not bothering with the ritual. I wasn't here to protect myself, or make a bargain. I was here to do a single, all-encompassing action.

Raise holy hell.

On the third repetition of the word, I felt my friends stiffen as one, and three heavy thumps struck the earth strong enough for me to feel it in my knees. I rose, sniffing the air, which suddenly felt like a spring or summer morning in the woods, and saw two figures standing beside a silver-clad goddess. Well, what looked like a goddess. She and her companions were petite, despite the loud sound of their arrival. Alucard murmured appreciatively and the sprite noticed.

I wasn't sure if it was possible for silver skin to blush, but the skin of Barbie's cheeks did shift color a bit. Enough for me to smile faintly. The sprite turned to me. "So, it is time," she said simply.

"Yes. I needed some thugs, and your name came up." I looked at her two compatriots. "Brought friends to the party?" She smiled, and nodded.

Two women stood beside the sprite, also human-sized at the moment, and equally naked. One carried a small ebony stick, oozing the gravitas of age and power. Her mocha skin, almost black, seemed to shine, and her inky black eyes seemed to glimmer with undisclosed power. She was wrinkled, and aged like her stick, but you could tell that she had once commanded great attention from the opposite sex. If not from her looks, then from her seemingly raw power. It was elemental to my senses. Her cool gaze promised pain and pleasure in equal measure, and she didn't mind which one you preferred.

The other sprite was green. Like the green of fresh buds on a tree. In fact, her skin seemed made of grass and leaves. Gnarled vines formed a makeshift outfit that only emphasized her lean body. She wasn't curvaceous, but more of an innocent adolescent, a nubile maiden found by a pond in the middle of the woods.

The kind of young slip of a girl only read about in stories that usually ended with a disappearance of an innocent young boy. Her smile was cool, detached, and predatory. I averted my gaze as her eyes drifted to me.

Neither spoke. Not a word. "They have their own... *reasons* for joining me today. Old business with your... *guests*." Barbie offered with a humorless smirk. I shrugged.

Dean popped his head out the front door behind us. "Jeffries just phoned. Police have been served with a warrant for your arrest and are mobilizing now."

I nodded. "Is everything in order?"

"Yes, Master Temple," he responded, voice tight with stoic calm.

"Seek shelter then, Dean." The door began to close. "And thank you for your service." I added. The door remained open as I heard a sharp intake of breath, then he popped his head back out. "Movement discovered in the old gardens." The door closed, latching shut with a metallic snap. Several bolts slammed home, barring access to the mansion.

"It's party time, folks." And so I led the group of bloodthirsty Freaks to meet the equally bloodthirsty assassins. I used currents of power to shove my captive ahead of us so that he could be a meat shield against his brothers. I didn't need him for leverage. Just to prove a point. I masked his presence, so that the Grimms wouldn't see him at all. I didn't need them attacking on sight. I wanted to see Indie. Make sure she was safe.

Or even alive.

As we began to move, fanning out in an arch, I suddenly felt the now familiar throb of power that signified a time warp. We were used to it now, although I heard Barbie growl to her companions.

We were going to battle in our own cocoon of time, unaffected by the outside world. Which would prevent the approaching police from becoming collateral damage. I wondered if that fact was a conscious decision by the Grimms, since they preferred not to harm Regulars. Well, Regulars that weren't friends of mine. Apparently, being in the Nate Temple fan club revoked that mortal protection.

We walked for a few minutes in silence, braving the icy path that led down to the gardens. Tall trees suddenly stood before us as we crested a gentle rise, looking down upon the ancestral Temple Gardens. Benches, fountains, and statues dotted the pathways meandering through the once thriving greenery of the gardens. A small hedge maze stood in the center, surrounded by a soothing collection of perennial and floral arrangements that had been created to inspire peace and tranquility.

But like my current mood, the area was now barren, devoid of all life but the stone sentinels rising up like cresting waves over the brown shrubbery. And the towering trees that formed a circle of protection around the garden – casting an eternal shade over the life inside – only seemed to foreshadow the bloodshed about to take place.

The statues were all depictions of my various ancestors, and my father had hinted that no secrets could be shared within eyesight of any of them.

Each statue had been erected using the cremated remains – if only a part – of the person in question to form either the statue itself or the base or the mortar. Regardless, each and every statue down there had a bit of the owner inside of it, and by extension, a form of immortal existence. I wasn't sure if it was possible to converse with them, but my dad never made idle warnings, and if he didn't want me spilling secrets near a statue, no matter how odd the advice, I damn well wasn't going to be uttering any secrets around them. A vast field of once perfectly manicured grass surrounded the gardens – now covered in a blanket of snow – gently rolling up to the foundation of the sprawling mansion itself, perched atop the hill like a living entity. From this angle, the house was foreboding, dark, threatening.

To everyone but my crew.

I noticed movement at the same time as Alucard and Gunnar. A dozen figures stood around a large statue at the edge of the gardens and trees. The *Gatekeeper* of the garden, my father had called him. No other description had been given to me, but I knew he was a distant ancestor of mine.

Indie was chained to the base of the statue with thick, heavy links of some kind of glittering metal. Thick enough to eliminate the chance of even most Freaks breaking free. I wondered if my magic would work against them. Perhaps that was the point. Indie stood no chance of escape on her own, and perhaps we didn't stand a chance of breaking her free either. At least not until the battle was concluded.

My blood began to boil at the sight. There she was. Helpless. Kidnapped. A Regular whose only crime was to love me.

And now she sat at the hands of monsters.

The Grimms turned to face us, eyes hard, glinting in the pre-dawn light.

We approached, and the Grimms waited, idly thumbing the weapons at their belts.

Well, all but Jacob and Wilhelm, who stood closest to the statue. Jacob's face was blank, but Wilhelm's was full of glee. I stopped before the two brothers, the other Grimms stepping a few paces out of my way to grant me unbroken sight of Indie and their Big Brothers.

My friends fanned out beside me, and the Grimms subtly squared off to match them, eliminating any holes in their formation, pairing off subconsciously. My eyes stayed on Indie for several long moments. She finally looked up and I practically felt the fear in her gaze. Her makeup ran down her cheeks, smearing her mascara, or whatever you called the stuff women smeared around their eyes. She was terrified, but seemed to have cried too much to have any more tears left. Seeing me seemed to rejuvenate her. She suddenly grew calm, confident, and resolved.

I didn't like that look. It gave me the Heebie-Jeebies for some reason.

Wilhelm tossed the *Infinity Gauntlet* oven mitt down on the ground between us with a smirk. "Looks like you won't be needing this any longer." Indie's eyes tracked the motion, locking onto the familiar glove, and her eyes grew sad as they rose to mine. She recognized it, and although not completely understanding the particular meaning of its presence, she seemed to at least understand its significance.

Perhaps she knew enough to realize it was a token of my love, and would only be in his hands if things had gone horribly wrong. She had no idea it was her engagement ring.

"Enough." Jacob murmured softly. Wilhelm grunted but complied, stepping back. Jacob nodded in thanks. "We have the book. We have your woman. We have shown you time and time again what happens to those who oppose us. It is time for you to end this pointless quest and accept your place in the new world. And that place would be six feet under the ground." He didn't sound menacing. He sounded clinical. Stating facts. Reading a report. I didn't respond. "The only thing left is to decide how painful you want your end to be. Give us the Armory, and we will make it swift. Painless. Or…" He held out a hand in invitation.

"They called you guys *Decapitares* during the Crusades, right?" I asked softly.

Jacob frowned thoughtfully, but nodded. In response, I shoved an unseen force ahead of me, and suddenly the beefy Grimm from my garage lay sprawled at my feet, shivering in pain and humiliation, abruptly visible where before he had been unseen. I withdrew the sword at my side – the confiscated weapon belonging to the Grimm – and decapitated him with one swift blow. His head thunked to the ground and I nudged it with a boot until it rested at Jacob's feet. Mustachio's head, which had been held by McBeefy on the way here, rolled towards Wilhelm's feet, touching his boot briefly before he angrily kicked it away. I dropped the sword. It clattered to the cold ground. Then I lifted my gaze to Jacob and shrugged, brushing off my hands. "His mustache offended me so I killed him, too."

I had their attention now.

Jacob's gaze smoldered with barely restrained rage. His brothers tensed, ready to destroy every last one of us. "Last chance, boy," I spotted Ichabod a few paces behind him. He looked sickened. I smiled back.

"But I gathered my crew and it would be such a waste to ruin a scrap when everyone's here to dance. No blocking my power. Let's see what you bitches can do without hiding behind that sad, old, pitiful wretch over there." I pointed at Ichabod.

Jacob nodded. Wilhelm looked anticipatory. Hungry.

"Good. Now, before we get started, I should probably warn you. You are trespassing." I said softly. "And we don't care for that 'round these parts." I did my best to sound like a Texan. I lifted a hand slowly, snapped my finger once, and one of the Grimms suddenly crumpled to the ground with an explosive exhale of breath and a bloody mist where his head had been. The crack of a distant gunshot echoed throughout the grounds a moment later. I snapped again. Jacob began to yell, but he was too late.

The same thing happened before anyone thought to seek cover, another Grimm collapsing in an explosion of blood. Two headshots. Most survivors threw up shields of power before them. Others rolled to safety behind a tree or bench or anything that would slow a bullet. Ichabod stared at the scene, unmoving. Jacob snarled at him to see to the men. Ichabod met my gaze... and winked.

I didn't have time to decipher what *that* meant, so launched a blast of power at him. It struck him true in the chest and he went cartwheeling into the statue, cracking it in half. I hurriedly sent another blast, knocking the collapsing statue to safety so that it didn't crush Indie. Ichabod landed in safety and didn't move. Indie shrieked as the stone titan crashed only inches away from her.

At least I thought that was why she screamed. My eyes met hers and I saw a spreading stain of blood surrounding an aged ivory knife handle buried in her stomach.

And there was Wilhelm, kneeling beside her, grinning at me.

I almost lost control right there, but managed to remember I was our only chance at survival. I tossed up my other hand in a prearranged signal as I used my other hand to cast an incomplete dome of power over my crew and a smaller complete one around Indie. A whistling scream shrieked past my shoulder and I instantly lifted the dome of protection the rest of the way. The ground where the Grimms had been standing exploded in a crater of fire and screams, sending rock, dirt, benches, and shrubbery in every direction.

Rockets were fun.

For some, more than others.

I wasn't sure how many Tomas had, or where he had gotten them, but I was thankful. I dropped the dome of power shielding my friends and let loose my restraints, leaving only enough power to keep Indie's dome up and running. My rage pulsed hungrily. She was dying. And the only way to save her was to end this quickly, and keep her safe from further harm with my shield. The rest of us were on our own for now.

On cue, my crew broke up in an explosion of shredded fabric as the shifters tore free of their mortal skins and raced after the regrouping Grimms, dragons and a werewolf already wreaking havoc. The Grimms answered in kind, barely hesitating as they met their foes with sickening thuds of flesh and claw and blood. I heard Raego's distinct bellow as he slammed into another black dragon. It reminded me of *How to Train Your Dragon*. Blue and purple fire slammed into each beast, but they didn't seem to notice the liquid fire splashing across their scales as they slammed into each other again.

Alucard was laughing as he danced between two Grimms, umbrella deftly swiping at their heavier swords. He moved like a wraith, cutting, slicing, stabbing, and biting. Their blood painted his face, and his ivory fangs glowed in the rising sun. Three familiar shapes suddenly swooped in from the darkness of the hedge maze, aiming straight for Alucard, fangs shining in the darkness.

Vampires. The ones who had stopped by my house to threaten Alucard.

Damn it. I had forgotten about them.

The two Grimms fled, leaving Alucard to fight his own subjects.

I tapped the bracelet on my wrist in a predetermined staccato. A distant wail instantly responded, the sound seeming to shred my eardrums, and then a freaking meteor shower of stone griffins slammed into the earth surrounding us, sending up geysers of rock and earth. *Chateau Falco's Guardians*. They immediately tore after anyone with an amulet, which was their only rule of engagement tonight, according to the command I had tapped out on my bracelet. It throbbed, letting me know all of them were active. Two exploded in a violent shower of gravel before they had a chance to enter the fray. I hoped they would even the odds a bit, but I didn't have time to worry about them now. They were effectively on autopilot until every amulet attached to a body was gone.

I looked up, but the vampires were gone. So was Alucard. I wished him well as my eyes quested the fight. A stone bench slammed squarely into Wilhelm, knocking him back a few paces before his boots planted themselves in the dirt. His face was a sheet of blood as he squared off against Tory.

She waved at him, flashing a teasing smile. Then she turned and ran.

Wilhelm pursued instantly.

Only to be met by my idea of the three Sisters of Fate, the sprites.

Trees and vines suddenly exploded out of the earth, wrapping around Wilhelm in a blink before morphing into obsidian, inky black tendrils of rock. Then a lance of pure silver light struck the trapped Grimm and the shockwave sent me flying backwards.

Roars of fury shattered the night as dragons slammed into each other in the skies, limned by the rising sun. I watched it all for a second from my vantage on the ground, trying to regain mobility. I finally scrambled to my feet to see Wilhelm standing in the same place, a steady ring of darkness surrounding him as he glared back at the sprites. Whatever he had done had protected him from the blast.

But not from a two-hundred-fifty-pound werewolf. Gunnar slammed into his side, actually managing to knock him out of one of his boots before the Grimm shifted into his own wolf form. Tory and the Sprites took off after a pair of Grimms racing to help a fallen brother who was struggling to his feet after being thrown from the skies by a dragon, judging by the claw marks on his chest. Crackling energy split the night as they did whatever mayhem they preferred. I didn't have time to watch.

Jacob stood before me. Waiting.

Gunshots cracked the air, which was already filled with the musky scent of beast and fire and dust. Neither Jacob nor I blinked. We just stared at each other, having a silent conversation. Howls, snarls, and the snapping of teeth surrounded us as Gunnar and Wilhelm fought to the death. I sensed that Gunnar was doing his best to at least keep Wilhelm from interfering with Jacob and I.

*Mortals are off limits, you bastard*, I snarled in my head.

He shrugged. *They are if they aren't aiding a wizard. Those that side with freaks are fair game. This all could have been avoided. All you needed to do was give me the book and die in silence.*

"Hey, Jakey?" I asked with a furrowed brow.

He frowned angrily. "My name is *Jacob*."

"Sure thing. Don't clench." I smiled.

Before he could react, I whipped out twin cords of purple fire and lightning-infused chains, sizzling and snapping hungrily as they latched onto his torso and legs, wrapping him up like a spider. I began to twirl in a circle, using my power to aid with his weight, and then launched him as hard as I could. He roared in fury, but just before he struck another set of trees, his body morphed into a dragon and he spread his wings, buffeting the air powerfully. He still struck the statues, pulverizing them, but his scaled skin was much tougher. He swooped down, racing straight towards me.

I dove and rolled as a blast of silver shards pelted the earth. I looked up to see that Gunnar wasn't watching, and was directly in the line of fire. I whipped out a blast of air and struck him in the back hard enough to give him whiplash. A second torrent of silver spikes slammed into the earth where he had been, and his body crashed into some bushes a dozen paces away. Wilhelm was already on top of him, swiping claws and fang at Gunnar's back as my friend tried to untangle himself from the brush with snarls of pain and rage.

Then he let out a terrifying bark of pain, instinctively jerking his head backwards. His jaws managed to clamp down on Wilhelm's foreleg, shattering the bone in powerful canine jaws. Wilhelm yelped and darted away, limping on three legs. Gunnar finally tore himself free from the shrubbery and slowly raised his gaze to glare unbridled rage at the Grimm.

His icy blue eye practically froze the Grimm in his place.

But the other eye socket was empty, a gaping, bloody, hole of mangled flesh.

My heart stopped in disbelief and shock. But Gunnar was having none of it. He took a single step, angling his head so that his one eye kept Wilhelm in his sight. Wilhelm crouched as if about to attack, then froze, whining as he stared over Gunnar's shoulders. I turned and saw a dozen wolves tucked low in the grass around the shrubbery behind Gunnar. Their growls filled the night, almost a cackling, bubbling snarl. Gunnar jumped ahead a step, so focused on Wilhelm he hadn't realized the pack behind him. I didn't see any amulets, but perhaps they were still enthralled by the Grimms.

Gunnar erupted in an explosion of furious warning growls and barks that I could feel deep in my chest. His ears perked towards Wilhelm since he had only the one eye now.

One of the wolves crouched low and lifted his throat, baring it in submission. Gunnar blinked with his one good eye. The other wolves mimicked the motion, in complete silence. Gunnar seemed to grumble an acceptance, and snapped his teeth once at them in warning. *"You... are... mine..."* a truly monstrous voice growled from Gunnar's canine jaws. My neck instantly pebbled. I had never heard Gunnar speak when in full wolf form. I hadn't known that he *could*. Then he slowly turned to face Wilhelm. His one good eye seemed to dance with laughter.

Then he fucking *howled*.

And I almost believed that I could see the sound wave of it. It was so primal and aggressive that the goosebumps simply jumped off my arms and ran away, replaced by pure adrenaline. It was a reminder of when mankind huddled in caves and beasts ruled the night. It was a hunting cry. No, a hunting *command*.

And Gunnar's wolves obeyed.

The wolves launched over Gunnar like a cresting wave as they tore after Wilhelm. I had never seen a wolf run away so fast. Which only pushed the pack to faster speeds. Gunnar chased after them, trying to become accustomed to his hampered vision. I smiled as Jacob landed beside me, now in human form, watching with a pensive frown.

"Looks like the wolves are mine again, Jakey." He didn't respond. "Just curious, but what do you think they're going to do to your brother? Disembowel him? Eat him? Or just kill–"

The blast of force should have been expected, but the *level* of power was not.

It slammed into my hastily prepared shield and I skidded back on my heels for ten feet or so. Sensing no other attack, I lowered my arms, brushed off my pant leg, and then smiled at Jacob. He was panting. The disgust flickering in his eyes almost hurt my feelings.

Now *this* was the man I had met several years ago. No more polite façade. This was the man who hated every single cell in my body. The polite, congenial, incredibly suave assassin had been so different from the beast of a man I had first met several years ago, that it was practically a Jekyll and Hyde persona. The man was mad. As mad as a hatter.

It was sort of a relief to see him back in his true form. Like Wilhelm. Now he was emotional.

And emotional people made mistakes.

The wolves were much faster than the injured Wilhelm, and they swarmed him, darting in for strike after strike, alternating and synchro-nizing with each other in a practiced, subconscious pattern. Tearing flesh here, snapping bone there, clawing a side here, and finally one wolf shat-tered the chain holding Wilhelm's amulet in an explosion of links. Wilhelm instantly transformed into his human form, broken, battered and bloody. The wolves stepped back, growling darkly as Gunnar approached on silent paws, head tilted to view the situation in his one eye.

Jacob instantly roared in defiance, morphing into his dragon form to defend his brother. I cast out a sizzling web of power that caught one of his wings, sending him crashing down to the earth, twitching and spitting in a furious snarl. Useless spikes of silver sailed off into the night as he tried to lock onto the wolves. Three of them broke off to harry the lamed dragon, but his skin was too tough for it to be too effective. Razor sharp silver talons practically ripped one wolf in half.

They seemed to realize all of a sudden that the dragon was *actually* silver, which was about as dangerous to a werewolf as one could get. They played defense, trying to instead wear him out and keep him distracted. I cast a few more spells at him, flashing lights and crackling explosions on either side of him, messing with his senses. Gunnar locked eyes with me, blinked, and then turned back to Wilhelm. He approached calmly, padding up to the wounded man, turned to glance at Jacob, snarled...

And then tore out Wilhelm's throat. He swallowed the meat, and then calmly strode off to find a new dance partner. The wolves slinked off to accompany their Alpha. Jacob writhed, roaring in pain, rage, and grief, eyes locked onto his fallen brother.

I had a moment or two to study my surroundings, the explosions, and fighting now more prevalent to my survival. My *Guardians* pelted the Grimms. Alucard slashed and bit at the other vampires – of which only two remained. Wolves harrowed. Tory physically *pummeled*. And the sprites, well, I'll let you imagine. I had a feeling that the stakes were about to rise a bit. We had just killed one of the infamous Grimms. Brother to the leader of them all.

And Gunnar had gobbled him up. No chaser.

I was sure repercussions would be severe.

# CHAPTER 41

*I*t was one of those moments when time stretched. Not literally, but perhaps my heightened adrenaline merely sped up my brain. So, I got a clear view of the battle.

The war.

I spotted Tory squaring off against a Grimm who seemed to be matching her strength, judging by the fatal blows they were swinging at each other, and the fact that they kept getting right back up. It was like watching two bulls go at it. Unbelievable power. Direct hits that would shatter vertebrae to dust. Then another one. Then another. Tory was moving oddly, and I began to grow concerned that she wasn't going to be able to stand up to him.

Then I noticed why.

Her arm was missing at the elbow. Her left arm. I blinked, unable to process. *How was she still moving?*

She moved slightly off balance, but the make-shift tourniquet – made from pulsing green vines, no doubt courtesy of the green sprite – seemed to staunch the flow of blood, and was in fact growing inside of her arm socket in one place, as if giving her a transfusion. On closer inspection, I noticed that parts of her skin seemed bark-like, shattering off in splinters with each blow from the Grimm. He tried to duplicate her new power when the silver sprite appeared out from behind him and whispered into his ears.

He froze like a startled rabbit. So did Tory. And another Grimm I hadn't even noticed also froze in the act of creeping up on Tory's unsuspecting back from behind a low bush, clutching a knife in his fist. He stood from his crouch, dropped his knife, and began to approach the sprite openly.

The first Grimm turned to face the sprite, face quivering as he tried to fight her power.

His erection was quite obvious.

Then Barbie enveloped his face in an open-mouthed kiss. He began to ravage her, and a very sinister, joyful laugh pierced the night, creepily contradicting the sounds of battle. She grabbed the back of his head and held it before her... well... *that* was new.

Her eyes rolled back in her head as she moaned in rapture.

Tory tried to take a step closer, a jealous, envious dark look on her face. The vine keeping her alive pulsed brightly and she stopped, eyes suddenly clearing. I followed the vines to find the green sprite on the ground, staring up at Tory with determined, pained eyes. Then I realized why. She sported several slashes across her nude form that let me see *inside* her. I saw bone and a few organs before averting my gaze harshly.

She was dying.

And her last act was to keep Tory alive long enough to destroy the Grimm.

The second Grimm had reached the first Grimm and Barbie. The silver sprite opened her eyes, stared at the approaching Grimm, smiled, and then beckoned him closer with a seductive wiggle of her finger.

The second Grimm decapitated his brother, and then kicked his body away, standing before her curvaceous form all ready to be sexed up by a creature that was anathema to him. His excitement was also... *noticeable*, judging by the prominent bulge in his pants.

Another figure approached from out of nowhere, strolled up beside the Grimm and the silver sprite in a seductive sway. Her ebony skin shone brightly in the rising sun. Her hand reached down and clutched his manhood. He grunted in anticipation, his gaze darting from one stunning creature to the other, as if not believing his luck.

A crackling sound emanated from her fist, then she released him and walked away. In the place of his manhood now rose a lump of stone in vaguely the same shape as his previous appendage. Barbie reached down, swept her fingers in the blood of the first Grimm, and then wiped it down her face like war point, swirling down around her breasts.

She gripped the surviving Grimm's head like a long-lost lover. He whimpered in agony. "Say *Please*." She cooed, gripping his hair tighter and tugging his body closer to her, enough for his chest to brush her nipples.

"Please..." He whispered in response. I didn't know whether it was in fear or expectation, but it was sickening how much he was in her thrall.

Without warning, she smiled, and squeezed her fist. His head simply ceased existing.

I stared, transfixed, forgetting Jacob was right behind me as I stared at the looping war paint covering her body. It was tribal, exotic, dark, seductive, and deadly.

I met her eyes, which instantly flew over my shoulder in alarm. I flinched, and my mind jolted back to my situation. Her warning saved my life. I felt the snick of a blade slide across my ribs, protected by my Kevlar vest, before a body slammed into me from behind. Even with my flinch and the Kevlar, it was a near thing, saved only by Barbie's warning.

I whirled, whipping up my hands while imagining a blade clutched in a defensive fist. Jacob's sword clanged into my metaphysical one in an explosion of sparks. I shoved him back with the aid of my Maker power, drinking in the quivering river of power beneath my feet.

And a vision of Indie filled my mind's eye.

These guys had stabbed Indie.

Gunnar had just eaten his brother's throat.

You could say that we were both more motivated than we had been at any point in our lives, and you would be underestimating our passion.

Our eyes met from a few paces away. Power erupted between us, sending up a cyclone of sparks that abruptly bloomed around us like a miniature big bang model.

I dove deep down into my mind, wading into the river of power that was so hungry to be utilized. I metaphorically dove in head first, allowing the power to roll and wash over me with violent, deadly, almost innocent glee. It crashed over me, rolled into me, fueled me, empowered me like an adrenaline shot to the groin. I reached out and introduced myself to the alien power. It recoiled, and then paused a few inches from my fist, as if smelling me. Like a dog with a new human.

It drifted closer, defying all laws of physics, and then slammed into my chest.

But there was no pain.

It was a high five.

Endorphins pummeled my mind and I somehow survived it. So much power coursed through me that the majority of it flowed right back out of me, having nowhere to take up residence. I studied my new roommate. It was pure emotion. Carnal. Beastlike. It wanted revenge for the Grimm's trespass and the harming of my woman. I sympathized, and allowed I knew not what inside of me, my mind beyond the realm of rationality.

It metaphorically beat me bloody, and I sighed in release. It felt right. No more thinking. Just emotion. Revenge. Make an example out of these killers. I almost let loose, but a small part of me was screaming defiance. I honed in on it and a flood of rational thought finally broke through, hammering me, slapping me in the face. Which woke me up just in the nick of time. I wasn't *just* emotion. I was *enlightened*. I had *thought*. *Rationality*. This presence did not. Sure, it was powerful beyond measure, but it needed a Captain.

I focused around that bubble of thought, forcing it back into the river like it had forced itself on me. I essentially slapped the shit out of it, and it calmed, startled.

Then waited, unmoving, the entire river of power completely still.

*Good…* I heard a voice whisper in my mind. *I can work with this one… But there will be a price.* I waited a beat, and then nodded my agreement. The voice laughed.

I felt a gentle, polite merging of the power with my soul this time, fortifying my resolve, strengthening my limbs, and whispering dark words of power that could be used to do *this*.

And to do *that*.

I opened my eyes to see only a second had passed, the sparks still falling around Jacob and I. He was glaring at me. I smiled back and unleashed some of those secret words.

The air exploded in a crackling wave that slammed into Jacob, forcing its way past his last second shield of power like a monsoon against a screen door.

He flew from his feet, body literally smoking. I noticed that the webs of sizzling energy I had first thrown at him had badly marred his body, leaving behind angry red welts, but they didn't seem to faze him.

He climbed to his feet, staring at me incredulously.

"What have you done?" He whispered, spitting out a tooth.

"I made a new friend." I whispered back, not fully understanding it myself.

And we fought.

He attempted to shift to dragon form, but I halted him midway, ripping the power out of him like gutting a deer. I don't know how I did it. It was instinctual. I merely told it *no*, and the power obeyed my wish, eager to be used by the world's last surviving Maker. Jacob coughed, instantly returning to human form, which had to hurt. Gunnar had once told me that abrupt shifts like that had broken the minds of many young shifters. One always had to be in control to shift like that, a master of their beast. Rapid shifts were often considered a sign of weakness.

Bullets rained down from the mansion, pelting the earth a few feet from Jacob. He snarled, rolling to cover, and began to flee.

Nope.

Again, without completely understanding what I was doing, I threw my hands up into the air. A purple vortex coalesced in the sky directly above me, growing larger as bolts of power emanated from its depths, forcing it to grow faster, wilder, and more erratic. I allowed emotion into the vortex then.

Fury.

Death.

Hope.

Absolution.

Then I threw my hands at Jacob. These monsters had a single purpose. An undying hope. To destroy the world of magic.

Fine. I would take away *their* hope. Not just that single hope for extermination.

But *all* hope. I would make their minds barren with any sense of motivation, replacing it with complacency and acceptance. I would neuter their souls by taking away their inner fuel. The necklaces would do no good being worn by broken warriors, terrified of their own shadows.

I remembered Death once teasing me about being the Rider of Hope.

So be it.

I embraced the moniker now, casting every particle of my being into the foreign spell.

The world seemed to groan, and then crack in two, and a blur of black flecks flew across my vision as Jacob was hammered by dozens of bolts of power within a second or two. Then all was still.

I realized I was lying on the ground. I sat up and my head swam. *Good...* the voice whispered approvingly in my head. Then it was gone. And so was the power. I was confident that I could still tap into it to do a basic spell, but the godlike power was gone.

I was myself again.

I decided to stay seated for a second, gather my wits. I looked around to find Tory running up to me, holding the green sprite over a shoulder in a fireman's carry. She set the body before the two surviving sprites. They didn't acknowledge their comrade, but instead stared at me with amazement... and horror.

Which should say something.

They were world-class sociopaths. What did that make me?

I shook off their looks as I noticed Gunnar pelting up to me with the pack close on his heels. They halted a dozen feet away and Gunnar continued on alone. He shifted back to human form, all naked manliness and scooped me up. Which was icky.

But I let him.

"Jacob." I pointed at the crater where I had last seen him. Gunnar grunted and carried me closer, the rest of the crew following. Alucard stepped out from behind a tree, clutching a vampire's head in one hand, eyes wild, and fangs out. He blinked a few times, composing himself, and then dropped the head before walking up to the crater. I noticed the two other vampires following him; head down as if in submission. That was good.

Gunnar reached the lip and we peered down. Jacob's battered body lay there unmoving. Then his body lurched suddenly and he gasped a labored breath. His eyes opened wildly, but he was too weak to do anything. I noticed the two surviving sprites suddenly dart off to equidistant points on either side of him. They pointed at Tory and then another spot, which would form a triangle. Tory blinked, frowned, but complied.

Once in their proper positions, Barbie spoke. "Just let us do the work, child. I only need you to be a conduit. You hold our sister's power for a short while. Let me use it. It will help you in healing. Consider it payment for the gift of life she gave you." Her voice was wrought with grief at the end. Tory nodded, looking guilty, and obeyed.

A ring of power suddenly rose from the ground, outlining the outside of the crater in a glowing azure light. Jacob's eyes darted to the sprites and he snarled, regaining some of his strength. His face began to morph into a scaly snout and Barbie belted out a foreign word. His amulet snapped free and flew to her hand, emitting sparks as it pierced the dome of power. Jacob collapsed with a groan and the dome fell, leaving only a broken, battered man behind.

I let him get his bearings, coming to his feet on shaky legs.

"I tried to warn you," I growled. Then I had Gunnar set me down and I began heading back towards the only thing that mattered to me.

Indie.

"Follow. Or die here, Grimm." I snarled. I heard the wolves spitting out warning growls as they shepherded my prisoner back to the entrance to the gardens.

"Oh, I've waited a long time to see this…" Barbie murmured darkly.

# CHAPTER 42

My eyes scanned the scene as I slowly began to trot, then run. Trees flew past me, broken, shattered, and uprooted. Benches, statues, the hedge maze, all were either broken, torn from the earth, or smoldering in flame, kept in check by the snow.

But I found no surviving Grimms. I saw several bodies. Grimms, dragons, and a few wolves, but none moved. It was a cemetery. Charon was about to have a busy day, but I hadn't seen him yet, which was odd.

I heard Gunnar lightly laughing off Tory's concern over his eye. "You're missing an arm." He said drily. She tried to laugh but only grunted in pain. I noticed that the green vines were growing weaker, but her wound looked better, not an immediate concern of bleeding out any longer. She murmured something to him that I didn't catch, but I did hear his response. "They were hiding on the grounds. When the Grimms left to fight us here, the pack was able to rescue their children. They apparently brought them to the mansion. Dean has them in a safe room inside *Chateau Falco*. The wolves wanted to make up for their disgrace. I accepted their offer as Alpha." His last words were dark, hungry, and a warning to the wolves trotting behind him. Tory wisely stayed silent. I idly wondered what he would ultimately decide to do with them.

But then I spotted Indie. She was lying on the earth, but no dome of power covered her any longer. A guardian fell from the sky and instantly dove to her side as if to protect her.

Then it opened its beak to rip her in half.

I began to panic.

*No...*

Then it hit me. When I had called upon the river of magic, I had directed all my power at Jacob. *But there will be a price...* the voice had said. And I had *agreed*.

*Anything but this*, I whispered to myself as I raced to her side. I didn't have a command to make the *Guardian* stop, not having planned on a need for it earlier. And I didn't have any power left.

But... the *Guardians* were *mine*.

Using my mind, I silently, frantically, commanded it to *stop*, hoping I wasn't too late.

It did, reverting back to a chipped stone statue, unmoving.

I let out a deep breath of relief. I didn't know what that had been all about, but I didn't care. Bloodlust, I guessed. She wasn't moving, and blood muddied the earth. She had fought, tried to escape. Maybe my power had prevented her from fleeing to get help from the house. Had I killed her by trying to protect her? My mind almost shut down with guilt, but I shoved it away. There might still be a chance to save her.

I gripped her shoulders, shaking her gently. "Indie, please. Wake up." My voice broke. Tears filled my eyes as I begged. "Please..." I shoved her chest several times, gripping her chin and forehead as I breathed air into her lungs. I lowered my head to her lips, listening for a breath.

Nothing.

I checked her throat for a pulse, my tears splattering her beautiful face.

Nothing.

I angrily slid an obstacle out of my way, not even looking to see what it was, as I checked her left wrist for a pulse, hoping for even a faint flicker of blood flow.

But found nothing.

My shoulders hunched as my watery gaze finally rested on the object that had impeded me. It covered the hand I had wanted to place my mother's ring on. To show her my undying love.

But that beautiful, delicate, hand was wearing the *Infinity Gauntlet* oven mitt, as if saying *yes* to the question she never got the chance to hear.

My heart shattered, then burst into flames, and I collapsed, body shaking. My mind flew, alternating between guilt, unbridled rage, sadness, and love at her wearing the ridiculous oven mitt.

"I love you, Indie..." I breathed as Gunnar rested a hand on my back, breathing heavily as he fought his own grief. A primal, beastlike scream shattered the night.

I didn't even realize that it was my own. Power raced out of me.

The earth cracked in a perfect circle around me, earth crumbling away to form a three-foot deep moat of living green fire that soared up a few feet above the ground. Screams and shouts of alarm filled the morning air. But I didn't have the energy to pay attention.

I was consumed with power. And it was beyond my control.

Energy poured out of me, deftly weaving to and fro at unseen commands by my subconscious mind, and the air abruptly formed a miniature tornado just inside the ring of fire, whipping our clothes and hair about with snapping cracks. My knees began to shake and my eyes instantly welled up. The ring of fire flared higher as a pillar of water waist-thick erupted into the sky, at least fifty yards high, originating near Indie's motionless body. A dozen bolts of lightning struck the top of the column of water in as many seconds, creating a dense fog to slowly fall to the ground like dry ice as the lightning effectively ate the excess water before it could rain down on us. The explosions abruptly stopped, causing my ears to ring, and gravity took hold, sending the water back down to the earth, the spigot abruptly ceasing. Jacob's eyes widened in disbelief, staring at me with shock.

Alucard suddenly darted out and latched onto a form hiding behind a bush. I heard fists striking flesh, and then a body landed on the ground at my feet. Without warning, I reached out and snapped open the collar around Ichabod's throat, not caring to discover what flavor of power he would use to retaliate. Then I stood and stomped on his back. I picked up a conveniently discarded nearby sword, ready to slice his throat.

Slowly.

Gunnar placed a restraining hand on my forearm, shaking his head defiantly. "Not like this. It will break you." His eye met mine in a blow of reality, bringing me back to myself. I was panting, muttering under my breath, feeling out of touch with reality, just a creature of emotion. Like a psychopath. Even the sprites were watching me cautiously.

I took a breath, closing my eyes for a moment. Then I opened them, and nudged the body, flipping him over so that I came face-to-face with their spell-slinger, Ichabod. His blue eyes were pained, momentarily stunned, but then they calmed, watching me in silence. I didn't spot one ounce of hatred at him losing the battle to a Freak. And his eyes weren't black.

Jacob sounded panicked, clutching his stomach in my peripheral vision. "He can heal..." He broke out into a fit of coughing, unable to finish. I had almost forgotten. I had seen Ichabod heal death.

I never broke eye contact with Ichabod. "You will heal my friends. Now. And owe me a favor later, no questions asked."

Jacob seemed to understand the implicit fact that to grant me a favor later they would have to be alive, which meant...

Jacob began to speak but I didn't look at him. "No questions asked." I growled.

He finally relented, realizing it was more than he deserved. "You took someone from the dragons." I told him, not breaking eye contact with Ichabod. "Where are they?"

Ichabod nodded at me, realizing Jacob no longer held any power over the situation.

A hazy silhouette became apparent off to the side, miraculously out of the danger zone and safe from the battle. They were wrapped in shadows, indiscernible other than as a vaguely human form. They turned to face us and I sighed in relief. The retaliation would have been profound if they had been harmed. I wasn't concerned for myself, but I was concerned for my friends. I was going to disappear after this. All I brought was harm to those near me.

My company was no more.

The threat was no more.

Indie was no more.

I had *nothing*.

Ichabod spoke in a dry voice. "They are unharmed." He mimicked my pronoun, not providing me an answer as to whether it was male or female. I wondered if he had done that subconsciously, or was it an effort to match my cloaked statement? Had he presumed that my choice not to name their sex was a subtle hint that those by my side shouldn't know? I pondered that, nodding finally at Ichabod.

Another thought hit me. He had used magic. But he was collarless...

He was a *Freak*.

On a leash. Well, he *had* been on a leash. Until I had broken it.

And I had seen him heal the dead. My heart began to beat faster at the potential. Perhaps Indie wasn't lost after all. I managed to keep my tone emotionless. "If you do this, I may let you two live." He met my gaze, unblinking, and then gave a single nod.

I pointed at Indie and he shook his head. "I need to... borrow some power from your friends to even have a hope at saving her. I'm spent." I didn't understand that, but waved him on to hurry. I didn't want to get my hopes up, but I also wanted to give him whatever chance he needed to bring her back.

He climbed to his feet, a hand slowly moving to his throat to reverently touch virgin skin, but eager to not make any sudden movements. He closed his eyes momentarily, and then approached Gunnar. My friend held up his hands, eyes on fire with distrust. "No. I'll go last." The Grimm hesitated, and looked at me. I nodded. He bowed his head deferentially, and then moved on to Tory. He gripped her shoulders, which made me flinch, and her arm socket began to glow.

I saw the form of a new arm growing instantly, and then she gasped, collapsing to the earth with a groan. Everyone simply stared. The sprites were watching him with thoughtful, incredulous gazes. They began murmuring softly to one another in a language I couldn't understand. Ichabod smiled idly as if understanding them, but said nothing.

He approached Alucard, who was covered in scratches, some deep enough to sport muscle, gristle, and bone to the naked eye. But the wounds hadn't slowed him down at all. He made short work of my friends, healing a few broken limbs and gouges from claws, burns from dragon fire, and any other injury.

He slowly approached me, wobbling lightly on his feet before coming to a stop, hands at his sides. I pointed at Gunnar. My friend again shook his head, pointing at Indie.

Ichabod looked from Gunnar to Indie, then his head sagged.

"I cannot..." he all but whispered in defeat.

"Pardon?" I growled. "You told me you would power up with my friends' magic. I've seen you heal mortal wounds before. Do it. Now." The sword may or may not have risen in my quivering fist, ready to draw blood.

He held up a weak hand. "I do not have the strength to do so. Not after the fight and healing your friends. They were all weak. Expended. At their limits. They put everything into this fight, and there isn't enough for me to borrow from in order to heal her. And..." he hesitated, "She is too far gone, and has no magic to aid me. Healing my... brothers was different. I could draw on their power to assist me. But everyone here is on their last legs." He lifted compassionate eyes to mine and shrugged in weariness, defeat, and resignation to his impending fate.

"Use mine, then." His head lifted.

"I cannot." He hesitated, as if debating to elaborate. "You should be dead right now." He looked at the still flickering green flames and the wet ground around Indie. "That shouldn't have been possible. You should be dead." He watched me thoughtfully. "Besides, I am barely standing. I have nothing left in me. Healing a dozen warriors without much remaining magic to aid me forced me to use my own reserves. I am depleted." He sighed, dropping his eyes, gaze locked onto the sword in my fist. "But even before healing your friends, I couldn't have helped her." He added, answering my fear.

I saw Gunnar shrug across from me, behind Ichabod now. He had circled him on silent feet. He wasn't going to be healed either. His pained expression let me know he shared my grief, relieving me of any responsibility or guilt I may have harbored on his behalf for sacrificing an eye.

Jacob began to wheeze in laughter. "You thought it would be that easy, Maker? Even *we* can't change fate."

I slowly turned to face him, confident that Gunnar could take out Ichabod if he tried to attack my defenseless back. "You look constipated, Jakey." I whispered.

"Wha–"

He abruptly cut off with a grunt as I slammed the sword into the earth all the way to the hilt. Bolts of green tracer fire instantly spider-webbed outside of the perimeter of the green fire, and I heard twin screams as they burned two unseen surviving Grimms to death. Jacob looked startled, sitting ramrod straight with wide eyes. Then he coughed, and blood bubbled out of his lips. Several took a weary step back, turning to me with confusion obvious on their faces.

I slowly withdrew the sword from the ground and it came out dripping crimson heart's blood. I wasn't sure how I had done it, but I had impaled him with the tip of the blade. From a dozen feet away. And it had killed two other Grimms I hadn't known survived. Hell of a way to go.

"There, now you should feel better." I muttered, turning away to face Ichabod again.

He was watching me. "You told him you would let us–"

"I lied." I answered bluntly.

He stared at me. Then he began to laugh. The motion actually seemed to wear him out because he fell to the ground and his eyes rolled back into his head. One of the sprites raced to his side and had him conscious again after a few moments. I didn't give him a chance to get his breath. My voice was cold, heartless. But I would at least do my duty. Keep my city safe.

"You are the last Grimm." The sprite made a choking sound, but Ichabod didn't flinch. "You will not bring your brothers back. You owe me a favor, and until then you are on a very, *very* tight leash. You so much as let out a fart without my permission and I will make your last days on this earth an eternity of pain." Alucard muffled a laugh, but Barbie looked agitated. I ignored her. Ichabod nodded once confident I was finished speaking. I flicked a hand dismissively and his body flew a dozen feet away, slamming into a tree trunk with a grunt of dispelled air. "Keep an eye on him." I muttered to no one in particular. I heard Gunnar begin coordinating some wolves to surround Ichabod, who very wisely hadn't moved.

I stared down at the love of my life, my cheeks dripping with unbidden tears. She was still sporting the *Infinity Gauntlet* oven mitt.

I smiled as I imagined a world where I had heard her shout, *Yes*, to my proposal.

A world where she had even heard the question in the first place.

# CHAPTER 43

*I* felt people beside me as I forestalled my next action.

Burying an innocent, beautiful, intelligent woman. A woman who had wanted to see my world.

My mouth tasted like ashes.

Well, she had gotten her wish. Gotten to see my world.

Gunnar stood on my left, unspeaking; his good eye closest to me. He held out a hand. I frowned, and finally found the muscles necessary to control my own hand to meet his. A cool metal object touched my skin, physically weighing practically nothing, but psychically weighing several tons. He murmured something about the wolves finding something, but I didn't catch it all as I opened my fingers and stared at my mother's engagement ring in my palm. Then I stared down at Indie, and the tears spilled faster.

Tory reached out from my other side and touched my arm briefly, and then she growled a curse and wrapped me in a bear hug. I stood motionless, accepting it the only way I could.

By surviving it.

I didn't have the energy to return the motion. It was all I could do not to run screaming for the nearest cliff.

She stepped back, face a mess, and gripped my chin.

She jerked it softly, attracting my attention to her own hands held out before her at waist level. She held my cherished feather, given to me by the Minotaur. It belonged, coincidentally to Grimm, Pegasus' brother, and grazing buddy to Death's own Horse, Gruff. The feather had been taken from me at some point, but I couldn't recall when. "One of them had it. He paid for his thievery." She whispered.

I murmured some form of thanks, which she apparently understood because she nodded, and then placed a large, bone white acorn in my palm. I frowned at it, lifting my eyes to hers. She shrugged. "It fell out of my wound after it was finished healing." I stared at it blankly. Then I shrugged, and bent down over Indie's body, resting on my heels as I shoved the feather into my pocket.

The ebony sprite was suddenly beside me, staring sadly at Indie's body. I almost growled at her to leave, but she calmly reached over and plucked the acorn from my palm before I could react. She placed it over Indie's chest, and then turned her sad eyes to mine. Their other worldliness seemed to pull at me momentarily, so I jerked my gaze away. After a moment, I nodded in thanks.

"Will you... I think she would have wanted you all to help me bury her." I rasped to no one and everyone. I heard several affirmative murmurs through emotional throats. The ebony sprite moved first, and a deep humming filled my ears. The ground began to respond, and suddenly began sinking down further into the earth, carrying Indie down into the ground at least a dozen feet before her motion slowed. She rested in a perfect curvature of smoothly rounded dirt.

I stared at her for a few moments, and then had a thought.

"Everyone... grab something important to you. Now."

I had meant to only talk to those immediately around me. But apparently, everyone involved in the fight was within earshot. I heard rustling all around. Then they began to step forward one by one.

Gunnar murmured a Norse funeral rite, and then bit his freaking wrist. Blood splashed into the earth. The sprites looked suddenly tense, and pleased.

Tory's face was blotchy, no doubt thinking of Misha. I promised myself that no matter what I did next I would at least go to her funeral. I could run away afterwards. Tory took a deep breath, and I watched her, not seeing anything in her hands. She took several breaths, closing her eyes for several eternal seconds.

Then she opened her eyes, and began to laugh. At first it was forced, tears wrecking her beautiful features. But the laughter soon infected her, and began to sound more genuine as memories flashed in her wet eyes.

And then they began to sparkle with pure joy. Soon the laughs were erupting from deep within her chest, and I noticed that it was affecting those around me. Everyone was smiling. Sadness was still predominant, but an undercurrent of joy now boosted their resolve. The laughter soon died away, and Tory knelt, kissing the earth, "I give you laughter, you dear thing. Carry it with you on your travels." Then she stood, head bowed in silence.

Barbie stepped forward and silently cast a tiny sphere of glowing light down into the grave. "May your path be ever lightened." The sphere touched her chest and erupted into a silvery dome, lighting the clearing. I noticed the vampires flinch protectively in my peripheral vision.

The ebony sprite stood and gave her a rippling black orb of power, the antithesis of Barbie's gift. "May this eat away any darkness your light cannot pierce." And the silvery dome of light evaporated, casting the scene back into the light of only the weak sunrise.

They then spoke in unison. "Our fallen sister gives you life, in the form of an acorn, a seed of hope for us to remember you both."

Everyone was silent until Raego stepped up. He calmly tossed a black dragon's scale into the pit. "To shield your soul from harm. You were a beautiful soul, Indiana Rippley. The world is now a darker place." He turned away, breathing heavily.

Alucard stepped up, looking uncomfortable. He looked torn. He met my eyes, kept my gaze for a few moments as he debated internally with himself. Then he tossed in his umbrella sword. "I didn't have the chance to know you, but anyone who commands such respect from such powerful people deserves my greatest possession. The blade has been in my family for centuries. Keep it safe and let it protect you from grief." He nodded at me and stepped back.

One of the wolves padded forward and silently dropped a mouthful of Grimm amulets into the hole. He whimpered at Gunnar, who nodded before interpreting. "He gives the trophies of the wolves. Those Grimms killed at their hands are pledged in honor to Indie." The wolf crept back out of the immediate vicinity.

Everyone turned to me. I debated. I too had nothing of value on me. Well, I did, but I didn't know what was more important.

The ring was the obvious choice, but I wasn't an obvious kind of guy. And I wanted to keep that for myself, as a reminder of the woman I loved more than life itself.

I withdrew Grimm's feather. The ability to call a fearsome beast for protection.

I let it fall from my fingertips. Everyone watched as it floated down to finally rest over her eyes. I knew that death wasn't always exactly an end, and I wanted to make sure she had a guardian. "To the woman who let me briefly see Heaven. She has gone home, and like Raego said, the world is a darker place for it. Let her passion be an example. She was the weakest of us, with no magic, but she was also the bravest of us. Whether she had been taken or not, she was going to be here to fight and help. Her courage was undisputable, and unparalleled. She was… my *everything*…"

*And now I have nothing.*

My breathing grew hoarse, deeper, faster, and pained. The blood of battle soaked the icy soil, as well as the dust of my long-dead ancestor's remains from the pulverized statue.

And the love of my life lay buried at the epicenter of the chaos. The restraint on my power crashed behind a torrent of raw power. I would create something beautiful out of this tragedy. It would be my last memorable act. Even if my world was now dead to me.

Even if it burned away all my power and killed me.

Indie deserved it.

I let out a yell, casting one fist into the sky and one down at her body – at the acorn – fusing *life* and *hope* into the seed. My broken dreams at a future life with Indie raged and screamed, producing the antithesis of my new reality.

Life.

Happiness.

Contentment.

My fists began to glow, one shining yellow as it pointed at the sky, and the other blue pointing down at Indie's body. Then they began to pulse, alternating, and I felt my soul washing away, power scouring away my existence. A bolt struck my fist from the heavens in a viridian explosion, and my eyes shot wide open. A heartbeat later, a purple blast slammed down into the earth in a web that halted a moment before striking Indie, coming to rest over her form like a blanket gently tucking a child in for bedtime.

The sprites were doing something, somehow complementing my power. Dirt began to fold in on itself and slowly cover up the purple blanket protecting the woman I loved. The ground quieted for a moment, now perfectly smooth and devoid of snow, and I realized that the sprites were singing in a haunting, angelic song of an unknown language. A language understood only through sensation, not words. Emotion given sound.

The entire earth began to rumble inside the ring I had made earlier, which was still guttering lightly with green fire. I stumbled, realizing that it was only growing stronger.

"Get back!" I roared, grabbing Tory's coat as I dove over the trench.

Moments later the ground rocked, and a sapling exploded out of the earth, growing in fast forward, widening, thickening, sprouting branches and leaves as it raced towards the heavens. I could feel and hear the roots screaming as they tore through icy soil and rock, but the tree didn't slow until it reached a height of at least a hundred feet at the entrance to the gardens.

And it was bone white, with pale silver leaves. Several fell from the force of the rapid growth, and lightly drifted to the ground. I reached out to catch one, sobbing openly at the beauty of the fallen sprite's gift of life from the acorn, and hissed as the leaf sliced through my fingertips like a razor.

I stared at my bleeding finger in disbelief and then began to laugh.

Just like Indie. *A mouth like a razor, that one...* I had once heard an employee describe Indie. I don't know how long we stared at the stunningly beautiful tree until a strange motion off to my right shattered the silent majestic safety of the sheltering branches.

I lurched to my feet, hungry to destroy something.

# CHAPTER 44

*I*t was the shadowy figure kidnapped by the Grimms. She was shaking, railing against an invisible force, and I assumed she was shouting.

I turned to Ichabod, who was staring at the tree with wide eyes, mouth opening and closing wordlessly. "Conceal her. But leave her senses accessible." He did so with a wave of his hand. "Now, it's time to call in my favor." He waited obediently. "Make a call."

"I have no... *phone.*" He said the word oddly, unfamiliar with such a device.

"You won't need one." I responded drily. His eyes squinted for a moment, and then he smiled in understanding.

He murmured several words and flung his hand out at the air between me and my friends, ripping a void in the fabric of reality.

A doorway.

Revealing Jafar.

He jumped to his feet from a chair, staring at me incredulously. Then at Ichabod. He began to shout over his shoulder. He was armed for battle. A dozen Academy Justices jumped through the opening ahead of their Captain, all strapped in battle leathers. That pretty much answered my question right there. They had been ready for this call. And had known it would happen around now. After my scheduled fight with the Grimms.

They had known it all.

Too bad they hadn't anticipated my success.

Or the fact that Ichabod had opened the gateway in the center of two aggressive fronts of Freaks who were a tad bit irrational at present. Several Justices let out a shout of surprise to see werewolves, vampires, sprites, and dragons surrounding them, and Ichabod the only Grimm in sight. And the last Maker in existence staring at them with cold, dead, heartless eyes. At least I was pretty sure I looked that way. It's how I felt, and I had no energy to put on a front.

I no longer cared.

"Well, I would love to hear you explain this one," I said drily, staring directly at Jafar.

He looked from me to Ichabod, no doubt wondering if I was under the man's control or if it was the other way around. As his eyes roved from face to face, he was bright enough to realize the Grimms were no more. He didn't look pleased, but he also didn't look disappointed. "Bravo." He muttered. "This was your little problem? This man?"

I didn't blink. "He had a friend or two. You can find bits and pieces of them around here somewhere. Well, *everywhere*, I guess." I pointed a finger at Jacob's body, which I suddenly noticed was very embarrassingly face down, exposing his rear end to the air. I decided to let imaginations run wild with the story of his demise. But I wasn't concerned with those stories, as entertaining as they may be. I was concerned with Jafar's reaction.

And he didn't disappoint.

There was a moment – a tiny, almost unnoticeable moment – where recognition flashed across his eyes. Then a flicker of disbelief. And then it was gone.

He turned to face me, poker face back in place. "This was approved through the proper channels? We don't condone murder," He growled authoritatively. Several Justices flexed fists at their sides, ready to throw down.

I began to laugh. No one moved. But Jafar's face darkened.

"Go right ahead," I chuckled. "Arrest us. There were no... *proper channels* involved. In fact, I killed this one with quite the *opposite* of the *proper channels*. I impaled him. A little out of fashion these days, but I found it quite satisfying." I straightened my face and enunciated each word, grinning openly. "I murdered this man in cold blood. He was defenseless at the time. I had hinted at letting him go. He was cooperating." Jafar's face looked victorious. "I killed him. Slowly. And I enjoyed every *second* of it." I shot him a wolfish smile, holding out my hands for imaginary handcuffs. "Do something about it, oh Noble Knight."

As if on cue, the dragons let out short puffs of fire and the wolves targeted individual Justices. Tory calmly picked up a stone pillar once belonging to a birdbath, calmly snapped off the bowl with her hand, and hefted the revised bludgeoning tool with a satisfied grunt. The sprites moved like wraiths, drifting closer to the action with predatory smiles.

The Justices, the most feared group of killers on the planet, *hesitated*.

Which seemed to infuriate old Jafar.

"I'm waiting, shit stain," I teased, using my grief to speak freely. I had no concern for my safety any longer. I was also *very* inclined to cut loose with my power again. I was slightly drunk off it from earlier.

Jafar quivered, but didn't make a motion to arrest me. I frowned, and lowered my hands. "So, how was this supposed to play out? You were obviously ready with a squad of thugs to go *somewhere*. And Ichabod here had a direct phone number to reach you. Almost as if you had worked together, or something."

He began to growl. "Very clever. It changes nothing. We hired assassins to take out a threat to our people. We were prepared to apprehend—"

I held up a finger, frowning thoughtfully as I blatantly interrupted him. "*We*? You're *sure* about that?" I asked softly. His eyes tightened. "As in, this was authorized via *proper channels*? You're telling me you had the backing of the Academy to take out a person who had signed a peace treaty with them in the presence of an Angel and a Horseman of the Apocalypse?" Even mentioning Death's name by proxy made my vision pulse blue. It was his fault Indie had been taken. I didn't know how or why, but he was going to pay. After that I would disappear.

Jafar threw up his hands. "Of course it was sanctioned. I'm the Captain of the Justices. Who do you think you are, questioning me? You are a *murderer*."

"Is it really murder when I defend myself from other murderers?" I smiled. "I don't see it that way. Neither do these guys. You're more than welcome to disagree." My eyes glittered hungrily, and I couldn't hide the interest in my voice. "*Please* disagree."

He did nothing. Just stared back at me, thinking furiously. Looking for a political loophole to weasel out of. But I didn't play politics. Neither had Indie.

"You hired the biggest threat in the world to take out little old me. A force so feared that they were locked away for hundreds of years to keep us all safe," I let the silence build, and then shrugged as I turned my back on him. "How did that work out for you?"

Several Justices moved, judging by the reactive snarls of my friends. I didn't turn around. It might have looked fearless and suave on my part, but to be honest, I welcomed someone to end me right here. The only thing I truly wanted to do was to kill the Horseman for letting Indie be kidnapped. After that I had nothing left to live for.

"How fucking stupid are you, Jafar? Did you honestly believe that they would act in good faith after they killed me? They are hungry to kill all of us. They don't even see us as human. We are pests in their eyes. We require extermination. *All of us*. Are you truly that arrogant?"

He snarled. "If you could beat them, so could I. You are nothing. You don't deserve to live after your blatant disrespect of the Academy. Your constant bending and shattering of the rules is a poison. You are a nuisance. An eyesore. A blemish that must be lanced. You are cancerous."

I turned to stare at him in surprise. "Do you truly believe all of that?" He nodded. "That's kind of… *mean*," I chuckled. "Anyway, you hired men who would kill us all to order a sanctioned…" I hesitated. "It *was* sanctioned, you said?" He nodded after a few seconds. "Right. To order a sanctioned hit on an ally of the Academy." I pretended to think for a minute, but I knew what it was really all about. The Armory.

"You really want the Armory that badly?" I shook my head in disbelief. "It's kind of amazing to me. To hunger after something so desperately. Not being given the toy must have really bothered you in grade school." I shook my head again.

"Well, this toy isn't up for grabs, like I told you last time. You're more than welcome to try and take it from me." I smiled, crossing my hands behind my back as I turned to face him. "Go ahead. Try."

Again, he didn't oblige. I sighed, shaking my head. "What do you think they would have done with the Armory after killing me?"

"It was to pass to our hands, of course." The, *you idiot*, was implied in his tone. "That's why we came prepared to fight. They wouldn't have stood a

chance against us after your battle, and with the Armory at our disposal."
He snapped, spittle flying.

I nodded, and then addressed one of the Justices. "You ever see an offi-cial order about this assassination contract?" He didn't answer. "Don't worry, you don't have to answer that. Answer this instead. Does this kind of subterfuge sound like it's official? And more importantly, do you agree with it... *Justice?*"

"Enough!" Jafar roared. "They answer to *me*, not *you*. Who cares if it was official? It was in the best interests of the Academy. When they hear how you slaughtered over a dozen humans, you will be finished. Friends helping you or not."

Which was actually a good point. Without the amulets, the Grimms were pure mortals. I would look kind of guilty.

Jafar's face looked victorious. I bowed my head in defeat for a few seconds, and listened as he commanded his Justices to arrest me. One took a single step, and I lifted my cold gaze to meet his. He rocked back a step, hands reflexively darting to the sword at his belt. I smiled, and held up a finger.

"Oh, I almost forgot..." I motioned to Ichabod. "Drop the veil on our guest. Entirely. Remove any hindrance on their senses. They were only placed there to protect everyone's safety until the proper moment." Ichabod smiled, and did as commanded.

To reveal the person Raego had kidnapped at the beginning of all this.

*Operation White Knight.*

I turned to Jafar, grinning like an idiot. I was going to enjoy this. His face paled, and a small part of my heart erupted in joy as he witnessed the person behind the veil. Then a surprising thing happened. Every single wizard dropped to his knees, and bowed their heads to the ground. Even Jafar. The Justices tore away their masks in a puff of fairy dust, which powered them. I frowned, turning in confusion. *What the...*

Then I froze, and might have made a small whimper.

A frail old woman stood only a few feet away; apparently having strode up to me in the few seconds I had been watching Jafar suffer. I held up my hands defensively.

"You've got to be kidding me! Raego! What the *hell* were you *thinking*? I didn't mean *her*! How am I supposed to regain their trust *now*?"

Her eyes were twin coals, and she seemed to be debating which one of us to skewer first. I couldn't attack *her*. I didn't think I stood a chance even if I tried. Even if all of us tried. Collectively.

Raego mumbled from the other side of Jafar. "You said an Academy Member. Someone of importance. She was the first one we saw. Easiest target." He turned to address her. "No offense. She must have mistaken me for one of her associates." He added sheepishly, hinting at his ability to shift into different people entirely. She didn't look amused, so he continued. "Why? Who is she?"

The old woman was tapping her foot angrily, glaring daggers at me, seeing as how I was the only person meeting her gaze. "Um, maybe because she's the *Grandmaster* of the Academy? You. Idiot." I swallowed, leaving my hands where she could see them. "This was a mistake. A very big mistake. I suspected Jafar's involvement and knew no other way to let the truth be known. With him as the detective, the Academy would only hear what he reported. Like last time." I lowered my hands slowly.

I wasn't concerned for my safety.

Okay, I *was* terrified to die, assuming that she could kill me in very creative, drawn out ways. But I was only terrified of the actual *experience* of dying slowly. I didn't care to live anymore, but that didn't mean I was going to go volunteer for the nearest torture house either.

But I *was* concerned for my friends. So, I assumed responsibility.

"This was all on me. These people did only as requested. They had nothing—"

She held up a gnarled hand. Despite her age, she moved with agility, authority, and the mantle of command. She had freaking *calluses* where the mantle of power rested on her shoulders. She was hundreds of years old, and the legends surrounding her life allegedly rivaled Merlin.

The first Merlin.

I didn't even know her real name. Just Grandmaster. Maybe *Madame* Grandmaster.

"You presumed he was acting outside his authority," I nodded. "But you had no proof when you kidnapped me. You weren't *sure*." I sagged my shoulders and nodded, not hiding my guilt.

"I only wanted one of the top dogs to see what their hound was doing behind their backs," I added honestly.

"Top dog?" She rasped in disbelief. "Yes, well, I believe you found your *top dog*." Her eyes could have frozen fire. "You will pay for your actions today. Even if you are outside my jurisdiction." She promised. And I shivered. When people like her made promises, they damn well kept them. I would have to run far, far away to escape her wrath. Then run *further*.

She turned to Jafar, and I relaxed a tiny bit. He seemed to sense her glare and lifted his face, looking guilty as guilty can be. She shook her head. "You have disappointed the Academy. You have disappointed *me*." She continued to watch him and each word struck him like a physical blow. "This man arranged for me to be kidnapped. But you betrayed morals for personal vengeance. Working with our greatest enemy, the Grimms. And you cloaked it with the Academy's stamp of approval. A nation that has spent hundreds of years to earn a reputation of trust – if not *peace* – from all supernatural persons. You abused that power and forced this *ally* to risk everything to prove his innocence."

Jafar crumpled in fear and submission.

She continued, addressing the Justices. *Her* Justices. "You are all on probation." They shivered in response, but didn't raise their heads. I was guessing probation meant something akin to a long trip to Siberia. In the nude. While being squirted with super soakers. "Jafar," her voice was pure frost, and then I realized it was literal frost as the fires around us died instantly. "You are hereby under arrest."

My anger jumped back to the forefront of my mind.

"Nope." Everyone froze. My friends suddenly tensed, sensing the imminent fight.

"Excuse me?" She whispered, slowly turning to address me as if surprised.

"It's not going to happen that way. He's mine."

She blinked. "That is not how this works, young man."

I held up a finger. "I think you forget who you are talking to," I answered respectfully. "Don't take this the wrong way, but this man's actions caused the deaths of many people. *My* people. He was under your control when initiating this."

She snarled. "If I hadn't been *kidnapped*, I would have caught on before it escalated this far." I sensed her gathering her power.

"Remember our truce, wizard." I warned.

"You broke our truce." Her power continued to build.

I shook my head. "I didn't kidnap you. True, I ordered it, but were you harmed? Even remotely?" Her face grew victorious, no doubt remembering the Grimms abducting her. "Harm caused directly by me and mine," I quickly corrected.

"Semantics," she stated flatly.

"Yet that is exactly what our agreement states, yes?"

She flinched as if struck, lips tightening impotently. "You do not want to press me on this. He is *my* responsibility. *I* will deal with him."

"Like I already told you. That's not going to happen. He abandoned his position the moment he broke the law. Under normal circumstances I would agree with you. But you see that tree?" her eyes darted to it, knowing full well what lay beneath it. She had witnessed everything, after all. She didn't respond. "That can't be given back to me. He dies. Here. Now. By my hand." Her eyes glittered with malice. "Whether you want it that way or not." I promised. "There are witnesses here to see what you do. Do you really want the world to know what truly happened here? That the *Grandmaster* of the *Academy* was kidnapped? That your own *Captain* betrayed you? What do you think that is going to do to your precious reputation? What were you planning on telling the Academy members when they asked why you were holding a decorated veteran in your prison?" Her eyes grew thoughtful, and I felt her power finally diminish. I hid my sigh of relief. I would have thrown down, but some of us would have died.

Perhaps *all* of us.

I waited for her to respond. Her eyes darted from person to person. My friends stared back, ready to go to war. And she realized that she couldn't win cleanly. Whether she won or lost, word would get out. And the respect for the Academy would evaporate overnight. Their Grandmaster kidnapped. Their veteran Captain a traitor. Collaborating with the Brothers Grimm, whose hatred for *all* freaks was well-documented.

She was essentially politi-fucked.

She finally turned to me, frustration apparent on her features. I nodded coolly. "He's mine." She nodded, and flung a casual finger at Jafar as he opened his mouth to speak. His mouth clamped shut and he lurched to his feet against his will where he stood motionless, face turning crimson as he struggled against her bonds.

She turned to me. "Remember my generosity. Also, remember that I would not have been as gentle as you are about to be." She watched me for a moment, assessing. "You will pay for this," She promised.

I waved a hand, pointing at the scene of the battle and the fact that I had just killed the legendary Brothers Grimm. "I'm really not that concerned about it. St. Louis is off limits. You want to fight, call me. My friends were only defending themselves. They were targeted by the Grimms, thanks to your poor management structure."

Her face darkened, but she kept her calm. "You are amassing quite the arsenal." The Armory was left unspoken, but it was obvious. She was also subtly referring to my crew.

"Not by choice. By necessity. Your people obviously went rogue. You need to clean house. Then we can talk. Maybe. I might be busy." Her face darkened, but she didn't respond.

Then a subsonic scream tore the night as a gateway appeared before her. The sound wasn't necessary. More like a parting slap directed at me. She shooed the Justices through the gateway and we were suddenly free from their meddling. Jafar looked panicked. I smiled at him.

"Let's see how gentle I can be." I grinned.

And I sent a blast of power into him before he could retaliate. He slammed into the base of Indie's tree, head cracking into the wood in a red splatter. Then I let loose. Twin bolts of lightning slammed into him as I cast him up into the air in a vortex of power. He evaporated into nothing, and my vision rippled, more black flecks racing across my eyes. A coil of darkness overcame me for a few moments. I felt like I had swallowed rancid oil. And then I found myself somewhere else entirely.

Somewhere familiar.

And terrifying.

# CHAPTER 45

*I* stood in a blinding white room. White couches, white walls, white tables... listen, you get it.

My *existence* was a stain on this place.

And I had been here before.

Last time I had been here was only a few months ago. Ironically, it was also after a fight with Jafar and his Justices. A rogue Justice. A sprinkling of Horsemen, Angels, and Demons had also made an appearance.

But even having been here before, I still wasn't sure what this place *was*.

Death had told me not to talk about it. And had seemed alarmed that I knew of it. Last time when I had been here I had stained anything I touched. Out of curiosity, I tried it again on a hidden corner of a lampshade. As I withdrew my fingers, I saw the stain. Although this time the stain seemed darker. I began to panic at that. What did it mean? Where was I?

And what was that *noise*?

I froze.

*Noise.*

Footsteps approached from somewhere in the house, and they were rapidly drawing closer. I began panting, willing myself back to the gardens outside my home. But nothing happened.

And those footsteps kept right on coming.

They sounded like boots on hollow wood – like everyone's upstairs neighbor in the morning when you were trying to sleep in. In fact, the pictures on the wall began to shake slightly with each step.

Whatever was coming was *big*.

I clenched my eyes, willing, begging, to teleport myself out of here. I began to hear heavy breathing as the footsteps entered the room just outside mine.

Please, please, *please*…

I *really* didn't want to meet the owner of this house. Especially not after staining his lampshade. He seemed like the kind of guy who might notice. And might take offense. Anyone who lived in a white house was undoubtedly OCD about things like that.

My eyes quested the room for any possibility of escape. They briefly settled on a book resting on the coffee table and I froze. The book was obviously white, but stained with grey fingerprints. The cover was a pressed image and the words of the title were legible from a few feet away. *Through the Looking Glass.* I had touched this book last time I was here, and the fingerprints were all mine. My skin began to prickle. This book had been on the bookshelf last time I was here. Which meant that whoever lived here knew of my previous intrusion, and had left the book out as a warning… or a conversation starter. But I really didn't want to have a conversation.

At all.

The handle began to turn, and my stomach roiled as the door began to open.

I managed to see a gnarly red beard and a giant booted foot enter the room before my body evaporated to a cloud of mist and I found myself suddenly back in the gardens, panting wildly. Sirens filled the air, and I heard bullhorns, slamming car doors, and angry shouting.

My eyes danced about wildly, trying to make sense of the room and my sudden change in surroundings. How had the cops gotten here so fast? It had been quiet only a few minutes ago. How long had I been unconscious?

As my mind struggled to overcome my fear at escaping the strange room and make sense of the sudden riot of sound, my phone began to ring. I answered it instinctively, glancing at my friends. All were in the same position, and Gunnar was just now racing towards me, as if I had only just fallen. *What the hell?*

"Nate!" The voice belted directly into my ear canal.

My breath froze. "Othello?" I asked incredulously, feeling a deep anger building as I remembered she hadn't answered any of my calls when I needed her most.

"Yes!" She was crying heavily. "You're alright. Oh, thank *God*. I was so worried about you. I saw all your calls once I broke free–"

"Wait, what?" My anger sputtered.

"I was kidnapped. Held in a cell. I couldn't escape. They didn't harm me, just kept me in a cell. Really weird. Then last night I found that the door was unlocked and no one was guarding me so I fled. It was an abandoned building in Cairo. In fact, the whole street seemed deserted. I couldn't find anyone. Not even a taxi. I had to walk a mile before anyone helped me. Then I couldn't get a hold of you. What happened? You're all over the news."

"Yeah, I'm going to need to call you back. My lawyer is here." I said, spotting Turner Locke running towards me.

"I called him, you idiot. An hour ago."

I blinked. "Oh." Turner reached my side, puffing heavily, the police racing up the grounds a hundred yards behind him. Talk about good timing. "Thanks. I'll... I'll call you back soon." I lied, hanging up.

"Nate!" Turner shouted urgently. "Do I have your permission to prevent them from entering the grounds?"

I smiled. "Oh, yeah."

He turned and ran back, waving his hands like a crazy person, a sheaf of papers in his fist. The cars stopped, men jumping out with weapons drawn. "Stop!" He commanded before they could whip out their bullhorns. Several cars sat idling by the entrance, calling for everyone to come out with their hands up, but they were just far enough back to not see any bodies. As were the cops now talking to Turner. "I have a letter from the mayor, signed by three judges that this man is innocent and your warrant invalid," he declared.

I smiled, and walked towards the tree, tuning everyone out.

My mind raced as Gunnar stepped up beside me, turning to face the police, guarding me in case Turner failed, saying nothing. Othello had been kidnapped. It must have been the Grimms. They knew of her and didn't want her blowing the whistle on their attack on Temple Industries.

What blew my mind was that they had had the foresight to do any of it. Something was missing. How could they have become so interconnected? There was another player somewhere helping them, and I didn't think it had been Jafar. He was a thug. Not a planner. Not a schemer. This reeked of a schemer.

And the more I thought about it, I could think of only one other person who might know.

Death.

I had to go kill Death for failing Indie.

But I would make sure to ask him some questions first. I stood, ready to go take care of business. I looked up to see that the cops were mostly gone, the last of them making their escape. As if unaware of the cops, I saw a man climbing off of a motorcycle only a few feet away from me. I was sure I heard it neigh like a horse. But I hadn't heard him approach. I found myself growling, and then the world suddenly halted, except for us.

Snowflakes floated in the air, unmoving, and the last of the policemen stood outside their car, one foot inside the vehicle, one still on the ground. My friends stood in various positions, some pointing, some mouths open as if speaking.

All were still.

Good. I didn't even need to leave my house to take care of killing Death.

# CHAPTER 46

*H*e began clapping, face serious, as he approached. "The Rider of Hope. I never thought you would be able to use it as a weapon so soon."

I didn't sense any magic other than the stillness of time. Which was odd. He normally reeked of magic, after you knew what to look for. "My hope is dead." I whispered, glancing over at the tree. "You saw to that." I finally lifted my eyes to meet his.

And he stopped.

Sure, I was kind of a badass and I had a reputation for being a hothead.

But this was Death.

And he had hesitated. Looking closer, I even noticed that he looked guilty, despite his next words. "I wouldn't be so sure..." he answered cryptically.

"You were supposed to keep her safe." My voice was a wreck, and my cheeks were wet with tears. "I thought that you of all people would understand that obligation. I trusted you." I let venom lace my words, alluding to the death of his family so many centuries ago. His face was tight, offended, but empathetic of my tone. "I have one question," he nodded. "Was it intentional?"

Death watched me in silence for a time, the world seeming to hold its breath. "You can speak freely. What you mean to ask is, *did I intentionally*

305

harm Indie in an attempt to hurt you? Or, *did I intentionally allow her to be taken in an attempt to hurt you?*" He clarified. His face grew harder. "No. Neither of those. Never."

I waited for him to continue. "That wasn't my question."

His face grew pained. "I'll answer your *true* question. Was I manipulating events from the outside? Yes. Was it to aid the Grimms and overthrow you?" He stared up at the tree, a lone tear forming before he wiped it away. "I did not collaborate with the Grimms to aid them in any way, shape, or form. I swear it on my power. What they did, they did. I might have been able to stop it, but larger pieces are at play. It was… *necessary.*"

"Necessary…" The word sounded foreign on my tongue. My fury bubbled over and I slammed my fist into the ground, causing a minor shockwave of power to roll outwards from me in a rippling ring. It struck an invisible force and the sound of a thousand bells crashed over us, and time lurched back to normal around us.

Death looked amazed, but not fearful as he turned from the previously unseen ward to me with thoughtful eyes. Gunnar caught a glance at me, and flinched, suddenly noticing I wasn't alone. He shouted and suddenly my crew was racing towards me. Most of them. Enough of them.

Although, I didn't need their help.

They skidded to a halt around Death, all too aware of my current opinion of the man. The place was silent as everyone watched me. I wanted to kill him. *Needed* to kill him. But… a nagging thought crept into my mind. I honestly wasn't sure what that would do to the world. Maybe we *needed* him. He was specifically tied to Armageddon. And I had met *actual* Angels and Demons.

They all walked cautiously around Death.

Not even considering his three brothers, War, Famine, and Pestilence.

I shook my head. Deciding that if at any point in my life I had needed a minute to clear my head, this was it. "Yeah. You should probably leave. I don't trust what I may do to you if I see you here for even one minute longer." He watched me, face looking torn with regret. He opened his mouth as if to speak, but shook his head.

He left.

On his motorcycle.

Again, I was confident I heard a neigh combined with the roar of the bike, but what caught me as odd was that he hadn't used any magic. He could have simply Shadow Walked – or whatever his version of it was – out of my garden.

But he hadn't.

A sign of respect? Not wanting to push the unstable Maker before him any further than necessary? Was I truly that dangerous in his eyes?

I didn't speak as I turned back to the tree, considering the conversation as I took deep meditative breaths. *Hope.* The Rider of Hope. A Fifth Horseman of the Apocalypse.

I chuckled, shaking my head.

Yeah, right.

They needed a new Human Resources department.

I couldn't even keep my girlfriend safe. Or my friends.

I had told Death that my hope was dead. And he had answered cryptically, as all ancient beings did, that maybe that wasn't the case. I watched the silver leaves swaying in the wind hundreds of feet above me. Thinking about it now, I had imbued the tree with my hope. My hope for Indie to have a pleasant passing onto whatever the next realm of existence was, if there was such a thing. Thoughts of the tree inevitably brought the memory of the White Room back into existence. I shivered, thinking about the giant ginger living there.

I would have to look into it.

Tomorrow.

After I decided what to do with Death.

After all, he had been in the room too. Or at least knew of it.

Regardless, the tree seemed to emanate a similar power as the gentle throbbing of the mysterious room. Also, it was a bleached bone-white shade. Pretty similar to the room.

Tory offered me her healed arm, face drawn in an attempt at a tired smile. I took it, and we slowly made our way back to the mansion. Gunnar was the first to speak.

"Ichabod is gone."

I halted, jarring Tory. His face was hard as we locked eyes. We had a silent conversation, where he promised to keep an eye out for him. I nodded, and continued on, strides more powerful now.

To be honest. I used my anger as a crutch. I wasn't angrily storming away to formulate plans to take out Ichabod and deliver the last dose of vengeance against the Grimms.

I was figuratively running. The towering tree seemed to chuckle at my cowardice as I fled. Laughing softly, silently, eerily familiar. I shivered, and blocked it away.

The conversation picked back up as we walked. I caught bits and pieces of the events after the battle, but to be honest, I didn't care. As long as they were safe, I was happy. They wouldn't have me around much longer to drag them into trouble anymore.

Small favors.

# CHAPTER 47

*I*t had been a week since the battle, and the mansion was thankfully quiet again. Having a pack of werewolves and their pups on the residence had been stressful, but I had never seen Dean so lively. Every spill and broken artifact had been met with ultimate happiness at being able to perform his function.

A Butler.

I had let everyone stay at my place for a while to verify that their homes were safe and that we hadn't missed any of the Grimms. Other than Ichabod, that is. We had yet to find a trace of the man, no matter how hard we tried. It seemed that his experience off the grid was coming in handy for him. Not the other way around. I had hoped that his ignorance would allow him to be caught on camera, or to accidentally challenge someone to a duel for stealing the milk he himself wanted at the grocery store.

No such luck.

I had made sure to hide the books well, under dozens of protection spells so that they could never, *ever* be found. The sprites had been satisfied, barely. They still believed that at least *Grimm's Fairy Tales* should be destroyed, but I couldn't force myself to burn a book, no matter how dangerous.

I was a bookstore owner. Books were like children to me.

I had finally regained entrance to the Armory, checked in on everyone, let Gunnar give Pandora and my parents the cursory details, and then fled before the conversation could branch out to more painful subjects. They deserved more, but I didn't have it in me yet to talk about it.

About *her*.

I fingered the ring I constantly carried in my pocket now. An idle habit. The wind buffeted my overcoat as I sat on one of the repaired benches outside the garden, staring at the bark of the alien tree towering over my home. Thinking. Reminiscing. Trying to move on. I hadn't had time to reach out to Death, what with taking care of the dozens of werewolf pups secreted away at *Chateau Falco* during the fight. Like Gunnar had mentioned, the wolves had taken the opportunity to rescue them when all the Grimms left to fight me at dawn. They, having been suckered by Wilhelm, had been aware of the final meeting place, and had brought everyone here during the battle, secreting them away with Dean in one of the safe rooms. Then the parents had come to join us in battle.

Well, to join Gunnar.

I hadn't seen much of my friend. He had been preoccupied with watching over his new pack of werewolves, and their fledgling member.

His fiancé. Ashley. She had pulled through. Successfully surviving her first change. That was the last I had heard from my friend. An almost guilty, proud phone call that she had taken to it like a natural. I smiled, thinking about it. Working for my parents, she had spent the majority of her life around Freaks, so I wasn't too surprised.

Tory had flown to Scandinavia with Raego and the dragons for a brief mourning period. They had taken Misha's daughters along, in hopes that the countryside would do them some good. A place where there was less chance for collateral damage. Tory had stepped in as a surrogate mother to the dragonlings, much to Raego's pleasure and approval.

Agent Jeffries – the supernatural lie detector and FBI Agent I had nick-named White Lie – and my lawyer, Turner Locke, had been in constant contact with me regarding Temple Industries. They – with Othello's help – had legally proven that my alibis held up, that I physically couldn't have been the one to cause all the mayhem and illegal short-selling of my own company, but it was too late. Trust in Temple Industries was at an all-time low, and for them to have any chance of surviving, Ashley and I had to stay out.

Temple Industries was no more. The best employees had already fled, joining the German firm. Part of me hated them for it, knowing that the Grimms had orchestrated it all, but part of me got it too. So, I was off scot-free, but not without consequences. I was, of course, being watched even closer now by the men in blue.

But I could live with that.

Money was my true concern. My mansion, *Chateau Falco* was actually owned in trust, with the funds held there sufficient to cover upkeep and maintenance in perpetuity, so I wouldn't have to worry about utilities or selling it any time soon. Still, I had no means of making income outside Plato's Cave, which was still undergoing renovations after a heavenly hit squad had disagreed with me a few months back.

I had lost billions of dollars, confiscated by my friends at the FBI, and it would take years and hundreds of millions of dollars, if not more, to get any of it back. So I had donated it equally to the families of those loyal employees. The ones who had stayed despite the news. St. Louis had an influx of *New Money* to contend with.

Which made me smile.

I thought of Greta, Ashley's assistant, the religious die-hard, and what she might do with all the money now at her disposal. Probably give it to a charity. Or make a charity specifically aimed at saving my everlasting soul. *That rapscallion, Nate Temple...* I grinned. Then my eyes fell back on the tree and it died slowly but completely as if it never were.

I heard a nicker nearby and glanced over to find Grimm grazing under the tree. He had become a permanent fixture on the grounds. I wasn't sure if it was a token of sorrow from Asterion, the Minotaur, or if Grimm sincerely wanted to be here, a shoulder for me to lean on. Or if he was drawn to his feather now resting over Indie's corpse deep underground. We had grown close over the last year; meeting up once a week or so, weather permitting, to go on a cross-country ride through Illinois or some other near locale. Of course, somewhere we wouldn't be seen. I had even taken Indie along once...

Grimm neighed as if in salute to my unspoken memory.

I wouldn't have been surprised to discover he really could read my thoughts.

Two ravens swooped down to stare at me, perching on one of the nearby trees. Their eyes were entirely too intelligent for my tastes as they studied me, but I just didn't have it in me to care too much. I ignored their presence.

It seemed the world had been holding its breath since the Grimms visit. The Academy was silent. In fact, I had been kind of expecting an invitation or threat from them every morning, but nothing had materialized. Perhaps I had finally made my point to them. I wasn't theirs. I wasn't to be bullied around. I was a free agent. The last Maker in existence. I had defeated the Brothers Grimm. With friends, true, but the stories never come out that way. They always seem to fixate upon one person, as if it was mere coincidence that anyone else helped at all.

I shook my head. To be honest, I had been a failure. Without my friends, and their sacrifices, we would all be dead right now. And I had lost the only thing that mattered.

Indie.

I stood, stomping my boots a bit for warmth, and approached the tree.

I had tried carving into it with a knife, but the tip of the knife had broken. I had even tried magic, but nothing seemed able to mar its bark. Which was puzzling. Grimm watched me as I placed a hand on the bark, closing my eyes in an effort to stop the lone tear forming.

What was I without Indie? A familiar flash of rage pulsed through me, thinking of Death, and yet again coming to no conclusion as to what to do with him. He had made a silent appearance several times over the last few days, staying in the shadows to watch me anytime I left the house. My very own Grim Reaper. We pretended each other didn't exist, and that it was a mere coincidence to run into each other here of all places. Like strangers on a sidewalk. Ships in the night.

I almost didn't care about him anymore. I didn't care that I had won. It didn't matter if he had betrayed me. Sure, I might try to avenge her, if such a thing were even possible. He was a freaking Horseman of the Apocalypse, after all. Pretty sure I didn't stand a chance, Maker or not.

The world tasted like ashes in my mouth.

My biggest fear had come true. I had warned her. She hadn't listened.

I crouched, murmuring to the universe. "I miss you so god damned much, Indie..." I rolled the ring in my fingers, the metal seeming to freeze my fingertips with accusations.

"*Nate...?*" a voice called from the depths of my mind, a taunting whisper, as if someone was messing with my mind. But it was most likely my own guilt. I ignored it, shaking my head sadly.

The bark grew warmer under my palm and I frowned.

"Nate..." The voice was louder now, closer, more corporeal, but weakened. Why was my subconscious so freaking twisted? Did it think I wasn't grieving enough already?

"Temple," a new voice commanded, sounding displeased. "It's rude to keep a lady waiting..." I jumped to my feet, whirling to find Death facing me.

He was smiling softly. His skeletal hand slowly rose to point over my shoulder. My body moved mechanically, heart hammering in my chest.

And then it stopped entirely.

Indie stood leaning against the tree, knees quivering, unable to fully support her weight. I froze, staring at her. She looked... different. A shade.

Death had brought Indie's shade to my home. Perhaps as a peace offering. I felt anger and desire building inside me in equal measure. Anger at Death, desire to gain even one more moment with Indie.

She began to fall, and before I could think about it, I was there, catching her.

And... a physical body hit my hands. I almost dropped her as my body went into shock, not understanding. I barely managed to prevent us from both collapsing, and groaned softly as my thighs flexed, my arms quivering as they clutched Indie's body to mine. My wounds screamed in protest, but I held her tightly.

"Nate..." her voice was barely a whisper, but gained strength with use. "I'm not that heavy... asshole." She finally managed. Then she smiled, and my soul exploded into a million fragments. I shook with laughter, squeezing her arms, her back, her face as my breathing quickened.

And then I was kissing her. Her forehead. Her cheeks. Her hair. Her eyelids.

And finally...

Her lips.

*Ohmygod.* My mouth exploded with tingles as flesh met flesh in a perfect fit. She was still weak, but gave the kiss her all, and I realized only afterwards that we were both crying.

Death cleared his throat behind us and we separated, smiling guiltily at each other. I turned to face him. He was smiling. My mind raced. "How..."

He smiled, opening his mouth to answer, but Indie beat him to it, struggling between exhausted breaths. The color was returning to her cheeks, and her eyes seemed brighter with each passing minute. I even sensed that her strength was returning as her muscles flexed now and again under my arms.

"It was a setup, Nate. Death *saw* me at *Achilles' Heel*. He *saw* my death in the near future. But even he can't stop Fate." I blinked at her, following, but not following. He hadn't said a word about any of it. Risking my hatred. My power. My fury.

My friendship.

All to save the woman I loved.

As if sensing my question, he spoke. "I am not at liberty to discuss Fate with those not directly affected by it," he answered softly. "The spell couldn't be broken until you chose to speak directly to her. Which you finally did today."

"Let me down, Nate. I'm fine now. Just a little shaky." I did, watching her like a hawk as I set her down on a bench one of the gardeners had repaired and moved closer to the tree. She sat down taking a deep breath, and rolling her neck. Then she withdrew a handful of amulets from her person, extending them towards Death. The metal was unfamiliar to me. The obsidian gem of each amulet hung suspended in the shape of a double crescent, surrounded by a ring of tiny rubies. I was reminded of the familiar power pulsing in time with my own Maker magic. But I ignored that for now, curious as to what was about to go down. Death stepped closer. "As agreed, Horseman." She said solemnly.

He held out a hand, took the amulets, but didn't do anything with them. They dangled by the chains from his fist. "Pick three." He murmured.

She blinked at him with a frown, but didn't argue, choosing three at random. He nodded, pocketed the rest, and then clapped his hands together. A green glow suddenly erupted from between his fingers, and the smell of burning metal filled my nostrils. His eyes were closed, and as the magic pulsed, I saw beneath his skin to see a fearsome skeleton in robes, with wings made of bone, and eyes made of fire staring down at his ten-inch long skeletal fingers. The power abruptly ceased and he stood before me as a human again, except now a single chain and amulet hung from his fist, thicker, wider, but still seemingly delicate.

Feminine.

He groaned with pleasure, muscles flexing underneath his coat. "Ah, I missed that." He murmured.

"Missed what?" I asked, frowning.

"My power. I lent it to Indie when I swiped your amulet at the bar." He winked. I stared back, shaking my head. How many freaking pickpockets was I friends with? I had assumed I lost it during the fight at Raego's house.

"Wait, when you offered to give her a ride, denying Ashley, it was all part of a... *plan?*" I asked incredulously.

He nodded. "I knew Ashley would go through trials and tribulations, but that she would ultimately survive, and *thrive* in the years to come. Indie, however... she was destined to die. All I could do was make it to happen at the right time. In the right way. Give you what you needed to bring her back. We worked together in secret after *Achilles Heel*. With her permission, I... *gave* her to the Grimms." He admitted softly.

My world rocked.

Indie had knowingly sacrificed herself to save me? To give me the chance to in turn save *her?*

Death used the silence to offer her the chain.

"Is this necessary? It's not really my style," she asked. He nodded once. She sighed and reached out for the chain. The moment her fingers touched the metal, a dozen bolts of black lightning slammed down in unison in a perfect circle around the tree. My skin instantly pebbled with gooseflesh, and my ears rang at the sudden lack of sound. That didn't make any sense. Something as large as the tree should have attracted every single one of those bolts. But instead, they had struck the ground in what I would guess was a perfect circle around Indie. She looked physically unfazed, but mentally startled.

Death was grinning as he spoke. "It is the bargain for your life. Indiana Rippley, the mortal, died. A Freak was born. Balance." He held his fingers out like a scale. His next words struck me like a hot knife to the heart. "You must not take this off. Ever. You are now the last Grimm. In this world, at least. I'm sure the others are still out there in their void, waiting for a chance to come back. As long as you hold this amulet you are powerful. Just like they were. Not invincible, but not helpless anymore. Use this power wisely, like you did with my gift." His eyes grew distant, and my mind raced.

Indie was a *Grimm*? Death finally continued, as if having debated the words. "You chose Jacob's own amulet, which makes you the de facto leader of the Grimms should they ever come back."

"*WHAT*?!" We both roared in unison.

Death smiled. But didn't elaborate. Grimm began to approach, plodding on delicate feet, ice and snow melting beneath the miniature craters of fire left by his hooves. He dropped his horn to Indie's chest and nickered, flashing his tail and flaring out his peacock-like mane. She placed a hand on the barbed horn, careful not to cut herself, and the beast calmed even further. She smiled.

I didn't.

"You risked your own power to keep Indie alive?" I asked, but he was already turning away.

He halted a dozen paces away, and turned to face me, eyes smiling as he answered softly. "It's what friends do. What Brothers do..."

Without warning, I Shadow Walked directly in front of him, satisfied at the sudden look of alarm on his face.

I tackled him to the ground.

And kissed him right on the mouth, crying and laughing uncontrollably. I punched him in the arm and jumped to my feet.

He climbed to his feet, brushing off the snow, and rubbing his mouth as if to wipe away germs, but he was chuckling in amusement. "Be wary, Brother. Whether you accept it or not, you used powers yesterday that could anoint you as a Horseman. What started out as a joke from us to you is now very much a... *possibility*. Not mandatory, but interesting nevertheless." He glanced over a shoulder as he walked away. "Be wary of the White Room."

His bark of laughter echoed across the grounds as a vertical ring of green fire exploded into existence, revealing a murky bar on the other side. He stepped through and the fire winked out like a snuffed candle, leaving Indie and I alone.

Charon suddenly appeared on his boat, hovering above the ground. "Freaking overtime." He growled through his sewn-up lips, the sound equivalent to a dozen rattlesnakes crawling through a pile of ancient bones. My skin instantly pebbled at the sensation of his voice and his presence. He took a heavy swig of a beer as he paddled his boat over the graves we had dug for the victims of the battle. Indie watched, wide-eyed.

"What took you so long, Charon?" I asked curiously.

He turned to me, polished off his beer, and then threw it in the back of his boat as several souls rose from beneath the earth and drifted up to sit beside him. The spirits looked at us with distant eyes, as if not seeing us. Perhaps the delay had pushed them too far beyond the land of the living to remember why they had died. Which was sad to me.

Charon finally answered. "Death lent her his power. Gave me a mini vacation. But you ruined that now." He grumbled, scowling at us for good measure. Then he began murmuring dirty limericks under his breath as he went about his work collecting souls. He waved one time and drifted off, having carted off all the souls he could carry.

Or just the ones he wanted to carry.

I wasn't exactly sure what his job requirements were.

I heard him crack open another beer and then he was gone.

I shoved my hands in my pockets for warmth, and for something to do as I turned to see Indie staring at me, face flush with the desire of life after her brief trip to the Land of the Dead. I had been fidgety since Indie's death, finding myself constantly needing to fiddle with something to calm my racing mind.

My fingertips clutched the cool metal of my mother's ring and my heart stopped.

Hope is a powerful, dangerous thing.

She had been gone. Now she wasn't. I had thought our *now* would last forever. Then I had experienced the realization that I would *never* have the chance to hold her again.

But everything had changed, thanks to Death. That sneaky, slimy, beautiful, incredible Horseman. I was grinning like an idiot.

Indie was shaking her head in disbelief, staring off at nothing, fingers caressing the necklace she now wore. "I'm not powerless anymore, Nate." She said softly, eyes thoughtful. "I can protect myself now. Well, after you teach me how to use it. Do you think you could do that?" I managed to disguise my smile as she lifted her gaze to mine.

"Only one way to find out." I answered, fingers sweating as they clutched the ring.

I stepped closer, only a few feet away now.

"Good, because I feel funny. We should probably make it a priority. Or find someone who can help. Pandora?"

"Maybe. But for now, I'll give it a try." I was only a step away now.

*A lot can happen between now and never...*

"Indie...?" I asked, practically quivering with nerves.

"Mmm?" She answered, smiling up at me. I spotted Alucard's umbrella sword leaning against the tree. With all the surprises, its presence didn't even make me bat an eye. I pointed it out to Indie, using it to distract my approach. "Oh," she exclaimed, picking it up thoughtfully. "For me?"

I nodded. "Alucard's parting gift. From your funeral..." Her eyes grew thoughtful, but I didn't elaborate. We would talk about all that later. I was close enough now.

I more or less fell to both knees, and extended the ring to her. Her eyes widened. "Will you—"

"Yes!" She shrieked, tackling me into the snow and burying her tear-stained face into my shoulder for a second and squeezing me as hard as she could. Her hair fanned out around me like angel wings as she leaned back to stare into my eyes. "Yes..." she repeated softly. I placed the ring on her finger, her eyes watching the motion in rapture.

"It's no *Infinity Gauntlet*, but I don't know what happened to that after..."

Instead of answering, she kissed me like it was her last night on earth.

But in fact, it was just the opposite. This was technically her first night on earth.

Indie. My fiancée. Dead. And reborn as a Grimm. *The* Grimm, if Death was right.

Like I said, a lot can happen between *now* and *never*...

I was kind of anxious to see what the world had for us next...

∾

DON'T FORGET! VIP's get early access to all sorts of Temple-Verse
goodies, including signed copies, private giveaways, and advance notice of
future projects. AND A FREE NOVELLA! Click the image or join here:
www.shaynesilvers.com/l/38599

ate Temple returns in **SILVER TONGUE**. Turn the page for a
sample... Or **get the book ONLINE!**

# TRY: SILVER TONGUE (TEMPLE #4)

*I* was going to kill him. "Do we really need to talk about this right now? This isn't as easy as I'm making it look," I hissed, crouching in the shadows of an old brick warehouse, focusing intently on the illusion spell I'd wrapped around the both of us. I clutched a book tightly, a slight tingle vibrating my arm as I caressed the embossed black leather cover. The sensation was no doubt caused by the residual traces of magic that were warding it for safekeeping, but I was masking that from detection now. *Success*, I thought to myself as I tucked it into my satchel.

Alucard's fangs glistened in the moonlight. I looked up between the buildings at the glowing sliver of moon, and spotted a dark tide of hungry clouds rolling in. A big storm. One of those old Missouri Summer storms that pounded the city clean with a vengeance of rain and ear-splitting thunder and lightning.

As if a premonition of the storm to come, guttural howls of outrage, and an inhuman hunting cry pierced the air, and then the pounding of many thunderous feet filled the streets. I shivered. They were onto us.

My accomplice didn't catch my tone. Or prioritize our current predicament.

"It's just that... well, the job is *hard*."

I rolled my eyes, tracking the heavy footfalls that were racing about in a frantic search just around the corner. "It's a fucking bookstore, Alucard." I wanted to grab him by his canines and throttle him. Worthless vampires.

"Yeah, but—"

I held up a hand, silencing him instantly.

A throaty basso voice rumbled, "Clear," from just around the corner. It was a harsh sound, as if unused to speaking in anything other than consonants and growls. The thud of his calloused feet continued off into the distance. I took a deep breath and rounded on Alucard, careful to put as much venom into my tone as possible without breaking our masking spell. I was good, but not good enough to cover a shouting match.

"Get your head in the game. Ogres don't appreciate being robbed."

"Why don't you just *buy* it from them, then? You know, like you *told* them you were—"

A barbed arrow struck the brick wall right behind Alucard's ear, hammering deep into the stone. A frustrated curse rang out at the near miss, and all of a sudden I sensed many bodies changing direction to come directly at us.

"Goddamn it!" I hissed at Alucard, careful to not use his name now that they had found us. He tensed, as if about to launch himself at the archer on the roof that had nearly pierced his ear. Twenty vertical feet wasn't difficult for a vampire. I immediately grasped his forearm, squeezing hard to stress the importance of my warning. "Remember to stay in character!" His lips tightened briefly, and then slowly morphed into a grin. He suddenly belted out a pious clarion call for all to hear.

"Usurpers, fiends, abominations, all!" And then he ran *up* the side of the building against our backs, and laterally launched his body across the alley to tackle the goblin archer on the adjacent roof. The goblin simply stared at his impending demise in utter disbelief, the second arrow in his calloused hand hanging loosely, forgotten.

Alucard slammed into him and the weapons went clattering down the fire escape loud enough to pinpoint our exact location. *Damn it, Alucard.* I didn't have time to go after him. I tapped a few buttons on my watch, the screen depicting an aerial view of the city block around us. A swarm of glowing red forms were converging on my position in the dark alley at the bottom of the screen. I tapped a few options on the screen to send the drone home and covered my watch. I still had a warehouse of technological goodies I had, um, appropriated from my company, Temple Industries, before it had been sold to a German firm. The FBI frowned on insider trading, even though it had all really just been a setup: The Brothers Grimm complicating my life a few months back.

Seeing no other option, I sighed and stepped out into the open. A dozen or so gargantuan ogres skidded to a halt upon seeing me. They were covered in tan hides over their grey, warty, scarred skin. Primordial weapons of bone and flint hung in their meaty fists as they seethed with hatred upon seeing me. Their heads were bald, but some sported beards. Even a few of the Ogresses had faint mustaches. Ick. Several looked amazed that a lone, weaponless human stood calmly against their gang.

But if my illusion spell was working as intended – and the look on the archer's face had kind of confirmed it was working flawlessly – they saw something else entirely standing before them. Something to be feared... or at least acknowledged with no small amount of respect. Then again, ogres weren't too bright. So, I was ready for anything.

The leader gripped a club as big as my torso in his meaty fist. He let the tip thump to the ground as he challenged me with an aggressive glint in his eyes.

"Pretty birdboy going to die," he growled.

I smirked back in what I hope looked like pious disdain – in line with my character. I was still getting the hang of my powers, and wasn't entirely sure how adaptable my disguise was. For all I knew, I was standing there with a mentally deficient look on my face. Or no emotion at all. I guessed either would work fine with this disguise. I didn't speak, not wanting to risk giving my true nature away. Instead, I tapped my cane on the ground and it rang out like a bell. The lead ogre stared at the cane with trepidation, but of course, he didn't see a cane at all.

The ogres were all seeing a monstrous Crusades-era sword, and it was glowing with crackling blue-white light. Because standing before them was a Nephilim, a child of an Angel of Heaven and a mortal. And most avoided Nephilim like the plague, because they were rather... *Old Testament*, you could say. No forgive and forget with them.

Illusions kind of rock.

I wasn't sure how much action the illusion could handle, so I was banking on the fact that simply seeing a Heavenly Warrior might be enough to keep them at bay. That had been my plan anyway, before Alucard had stumbled into an empty trashcan while we were creeping out of their vault, alerting every ogre on the block. I couldn't risk my illusion failing if I threw down with them here and now, revealing my true identity. Especially if I used any overt magic. Nephilim were dangerous, but wizards they ain't. Magic would give me away faster than a cockroach skittering across the linoleum when the lights flicked on.

I felt the strain of my spell tugging at me as Alucard drew further away. Tiny droplets of sweat began to pop up on my forehead. My vision began to grow blue with the strain, as sometimes happened. If the spell broke, these guys would know exactly who had robbed them blind. Which wouldn't go over well. Not at all.

So, I was bluffing. And I hoped they didn't call me on it.

No elemental whips. No fire, no Shadow Walking. Just my shiny new cane.

"No God here..." The leader snarled, and then raced towards me like a charging rhinoceros. I waited until the last second, feinted left, then darted to the right, lashing out with my 'sword' at his feet. The cane traced a line of white fire across his flesh, and boy, did he howl!

I sneered contemptuously. The remaining ogres watched him writhing in pain as he bled out, none offering so much as to help him stand. They exchanged glances with each other, and I watched as their features began to darken in outrage.

"Oh, shit," I whispered, under my breath. They slowly turned back to me, hungry grins on their cheeks, and then surged forward with a murderous roar that seemed to make the pavement quake.

I thought about that outcome for all of a millisecond, and then turned and fled. I took two running steps up the wall and catapulted myself to the lower rungs of the fire escape. I used a tiny boost of power to give me the extra juice to reach, and latched on, quickly pulling myself to safety. One of the ogres pounded the wall below me with his hammer fist, the brick crumbling. Then his pals began to join in. The old building groaned. I raced up the metal stairs, gaining the roof to find Alucard ripping the throat out of his attacker. He leaned in as if to give the goblin a kiss.

"Stop!" I hissed. "Nephilim, *remember?*" I enunciated the words in low tones as I ran towards him. He shuddered, eyes lidded closed for a moment before dropping the body to the roof. He turned to me, eyes swimming with the bloodlust of his inner vampire, irises flashing a crimson red. The illusion didn't work on us. We saw our true forms. I grabbed his shoulder and shook him until his eyes cleared. I waggled a hand for us to hurry as the building quivered again, the pounding of fairy fist against mortal brick like a steady drumbeat. He nodded, looking slightly embarrassed. "We're out of here. I'm sending an illusion of us flying away like good little Nephilim."

Alucard nodded as I squinted in strained focus, gathering my power and wrapping it around a single thought. The literal belief that what I was making was real. That two Nephilim were throwing themselves off a perfectly good roof before unfolding their wings and fleeing the ogres' compound. Once confident of every minor detail, I let out my breath in a rush and flicked my hand. Power drained out of me and my knees shook as the illusion took form.

Two rather scrawny Nephilim hurtled themselves off the roof, anxiously checking over their shoulders as they flew to safety. I nodded to myself, redoubled the illusion spell that was no longer disguising us, but hiding our presence entirely, and ripped a hole through reality. A verdant spherical Gateway of fire flared into existence, revealing a quiet street several blocks away on the other side. The flames limning the door reached toward the calm street with hungry, dancing claws, stating the direction of the intended travel. As far as I knew, no one would be able to walk from the other side to my current location – they would be eaten alive by the flames.

As long as those flames pointed the direction you wanted to go, you were safe.

Sparks sailed off the flames, darting through the opening and into the street beyond.

Alucard's dark eyes glittered in the moonlight as he turned from the portal to me. He looked impressed, but also thoughtful. I rolled my eyes at him. He was still getting used to how I handled things, but now wasn't the time. I shoved him through the opening, followed, and pulled it closed behind me as I heard the fire escape protesting under immense weight. A quick glance back revealed no pursuers, so I hoped no one had noticed our true getaway...

～

**_Get your copy of SILVER TONGUE online today!_**

～

*Turn the page to read a sample of* **UNCHAINED** *- Feathers and Fire Series Book 1, or* **buy ONLINE**. *Callie Penrose is a wizard in Kansas City, MO who hunts monsters for the Vatican. She meets Nate Temple, and things devolve from there...*

*(Note: Callie appears in the Temple-verse after Nate's book 6, TINY GODS... Full chronology of all books in the Temple Verse shown on the 'Books in the Temple Verse' page..)*

# TRY: UNCHAINED (FEATHERS AND FIRE #1)

The rain pelted my hair, plastering loose strands of it to my forehead as I panted, eyes darting from tree to tree, terrified of each shifting branch, splash of water, and whistle of wind slipping through the nightscape around us. But... I was somewhat *excited*, too.

Somewhat.

"Easy, girl. All will be well," the big man creeping just ahead of me, murmured.

"You said we were going to get ice cream!" I hissed at him, failing to compose myself, but careful to keep my voice low and my eyes alert. "I'm not ready for this!" I had been trained to fight, with my hands, with weapons, and with my magic. But I had never taken an active role in a hunt before. I'd always been the getaway driver for my mentor.

The man grunted, grey eyes scanning the trees as he slipped through the tall grass. "And did we not get ice cream before coming here? Because I think I see some in your hair."

"You know what I mean, Roland. You tricked me." I checked the tips of my loose hair, saw nothing, and scowled at his back.

"The Lord does not give us a greater burden than we can shoulder."

I muttered dark things under my breath, wiping the water from my eyes. Again. My new shirt was going to be ruined. Silk never fared well in the rain. My choice of shoes wasn't much better. Boots, yes, but distressed, *fashionable* boots. Not work boots designed for the rain and mud. Definitely not monster hunting boots for our evening excursion through one of Kansas City's wooded parks. I realized I was forcibly distracting myself, keeping my mind busy with mundane thoughts to avoid my very real anxiety. Because whenever I grew nervous, an imagined nightmare always—

*A church looming before me. Rain pouring down. Night sky and a glowing moon overhead. I was all alone. Crying on the cold, stone steps, and infant in a cardboard box—*

I forced the nightmare away, breathing heavily. "You know I hate it when you talk like that," I whispered to him, trying to regain my composure. I wasn't angry with him, but was growing increasingly uncomfortable with our situation after my brief flashback of fear.

"Doesn't mean it shouldn't be said," he said kindly. "I think we're close. Be alert. Remember your training. Banish your fears. I am here. And the Lord is here. He always is."

So, he had noticed my sudden anxiety. "Maybe I should just go back to the car. I know I've trained, but I really don't think—"

A shape of fur, fangs, and claws launched from the shadows towards me, cutting off my words as it snarled, thirsty for my blood.

And my nightmare slipped back into my thoughts like a veiled assassin, a wraith hoping to hold me still for the monster to eat. I froze, unable to move. Twin sticks of power abruptly erupted into being in my clenched fists, but my fear swamped me with that stupid nightmare, the sticks held at my side, useless to save me.

Right before the beast's claws reached me, it grunted as something batted it from the air, sending it flying sideways. It struck a tree with another grunt and an angry whine of pain.

I fell to my knees right into a puddle, arms shaking, breathing fast.

My sticks crackled in the rain like live cattle prods, except their entire length was the electrical section — at least to anyone other than me. I could hold them without pain.

Magic was a part of me, coursing through my veins whether I wanted it or not, and Roland had spent many years teaching me how to master it. But I had never been able to fully master the nightmare inside me, and in moments of fear, it always won, overriding my training.

The fact that I had resorted to weapons — like the ones he had trained me with — rather than a burst of flame, was startling. It was good in the fact that my body's reflexes knew enough to call up a defense even without my direct command, but bad in the fact that it was the worst form of defense for the situation presented. I could have very easily done as Roland did, and hurt it from a distance. But I hadn't. Because of my stupid block.

Roland placed a calloused palm on my shoulder, and I flinched. "Easy, see? I am here." But he did frown at my choice of weapons, the reprimand silent but loud in my mind. I let out a shaky breath, forcing my fear back down. It was all in my head, but still, it wasn't easy. Fear could be like that.

I focused on Roland's implied lesson. Close combat weapons — even magically-powered ones — were for last resorts. I averted my eyes in very real shame. I knew these things. He didn't even need to tell me them. But when that damned nightmare caught hold of me, all my training went out the window. It haunted me like a shadow, waiting for moments just like this, as if trying to kill me. A form of psychological suicide? But it was why I constantly refused to join Roland on his hunts. He knew about it. And although he was trying to help me overcome that fear, he never pressed too hard.

Rain continued to sizzle as it struck my batons. I didn't let them go, using them as a totem to build my confidence back up. I slowly lifted my eyes to nod at him as I climbed back to my feet.

That's when I saw the second set of eyes in the shadows, right before they flew out of the darkness towards Roland's back. I threw one of my batons and missed, but that pretty much let Roland know that an unfriendly was behind him. Either that or I had just failed to murder my mentor at point-blank range. He whirled to confront the monster, expecting another aerial assault as he unleashed a ball of fire that splashed over the tree at chest height, washing the trunk in blue flames. But this monster was tricky. It hadn't planned on tackling Roland, but had merely jumped out of the darkness to get closer, no doubt learning from its fallen comrade, who still lay unmoving against the tree behind me.

His coat shone like midnight clouds with hints of lightning flashing in the depths of thick, wiry fur. The coat of dew dotting his fur reflected the moonlight, giving him a faint sheen as if covered in fresh oil. He was tall, easily hip height at the shoulder, and barrel chested, his rump much leaner than the rest of his body. He — I assumed male from the long, thick mane around his neck — had a very long snout, much longer and wider than any werewolf I had ever seen. Amazingly, and beyond my control, I realized he was beautiful.

But most of the natural world's lethal hunters were beautiful.

He landed in a wet puddle a pace in front of Roland, juked to the right, and then to the left, racing past the big man, biting into his hamstrings on his way by.

A wash of anger rolled over me at seeing my mentor injured, dousing my fear, and I swung my baton down as hard as I could. It struck the beast in the rump as it tried to dart back to cover — a typical wolf tactic. My blow singed his hair and shattered bone. The creature collapsed into a puddle of mud with a yelp, instinctively snapping his jaws over his shoulder to bite whatever had hit him.

I let him. But mostly out of dumb luck as I heard Roland hiss in pain, falling to the ground.

The monster's jaws clamped around my baton, and there was an immediate explosion of teeth and blood that sent him flying several feet away into the tall brush, yipping, screaming, and staggering. Before he slipped out of sight, I noticed that his lower jaw was simply *gone*, from the contact of his saliva on my electrified magical batons. Then he managed to limp into the woods with more pitiful yowls, but I had no mind to chase him. Roland — that titan of a man, my mentor — was hurt. I could smell copper in the air, and knew we had to get out of here. Fast. Because we had anticipated only one of the monsters. But there had been two of them, and they hadn't been the run-of-the-mill werewolves we had been warned about. If there were two, perhaps there were more. And they were evidently the prehistoric cousin of any werewolf I had ever seen or read about.

Roland hissed again as he stared down at his leg, growling with both pain and anger. My eyes darted back to the first monster, wary of another attack. It *almost* looked like a werewolf, but bigger. Much bigger. He didn't move, but I saw he was breathing. He had a notch in his right ear and a jagged scar on his long snout. Part of me wanted to go over to him and torture him. Slowly. Use his pain to finally drown my nightmare, my fear. The fear that had caused Roland's injury. My lack of inner-strength had not only put me in danger, but had hurt my mentor, my friend.

I shivered, forcing the thought away. That was *cold*. Not me. Sure, I was no stranger to fighting, but that had always been in a ring. Practicing. Sparring. Never life or death.

But I suddenly realized something very dark about myself in the chill, rainy night. Although I was terrified, I felt a deep ocean of anger manifest inside me, wanting only to dispense justice as I saw fit. To use that rage to battle my own demons. As if feeding one would starve the other, reminding me of the Cherokee Indian Legend Roland had once told me.

*An old Cherokee man was teaching his grandson about life. "A fight is going on inside me," he told the boy. "It is a terrible fight between two wolves. One is evil — he is anger, envy, sorrow, regret, greed, arrogance, self-pity, guilt, resentment, inferiority, lies, false pride, superiority, and ego." After a few moments to make sure he had the boy's undivided attention, he continued.*

*"The other wolf is good — he is joy, peace, love, hope, serenity, humility, kindness, benevolence, empathy, generosity, truth, compassion, and faith. The same fight is going on inside of you, boy, and inside of every other person, too."*

*The grandson thought about this for a few minutes before replying. "Which wolf will win?"*

*The old Cherokee man simply said, "The one you feed, boy. The one you feed..."*
And I felt like feeding one of my wolves today, by killing this one...

∼

**Get the full book ONLINE!**

∼

*Turn the page to read a sample of **WHISKEY GINGER** - Phantom Queen Diaries Book 1, or **BUY ONLINE**. Quinn MacKenna is a black magic arms dealer from Boston, and her bark is almost as bad as her bite.*

*(Note: Full chronology of all books in the Temple Verse shown on the 'Books in the Temple Verse' page.)*

# TRY: WHISKEY GINGER (PHANTOM QUEEN DIARIES #1)

*T*he pasty guitarist hunched forward, thrust a rolled-up wad of paper deep into one nostril, and snorted a line of blood crystals—frozen hemoglobin that I'd smuggled over in a refrigerated canister—with the uncanny grace of a drug addict. He sat back, fangs gleaming, and pawed at his nose. "That's some bodacious shit. Hey, bros," he said, glancing at his fellow band members, "come hit this shit before it melts."

He fetched one of the backstage passes hanging nearby, pried the plastic badge from its lanyard, and used it to split up the crystals, murmuring something in an accent that reminded me of California. Not *the* California, but you know, Cali-foh-nia—the land of beaches, babes, and bros. I retrieved a toothpick from my pocket and punched it through its thin wrapper. "So," I asked no one in particular, "now that ye have the product, who's payin'?"

Another band member stepped out of the shadows to my left, and I don't mean that figuratively, either—the fucker literally stepped out of the shadows. I scowled at him, but hid my surprise, nonchalantly rolling the toothpick from one side of my mouth to the other.

The rest of the band gathered around the dressing room table, following the guitarist's lead by preparing their own snorting utensils—tattered magazine covers, mostly. Typically, you'd do this sort of thing with a dollar-bill, maybe even a Benjamin if you were flush. But fangers like this lot couldn't touch cash directly—in God We Trust and all that. Of course, I didn't really understand why sucking blood the old-fashioned way had suddenly gone out of style. More of a rush, maybe?

"It lasts longer," the vampire next to me explained, catching my mildly curious expression. "It's especially good for shows and stuff. Makes us look, like, less—"

"Creepy?" I offered, my Irish brogue lilting just enough to make it a question.

"Pale," he finished, frowning.

I shrugged. "Listen, I've got places to be," I said, holding out my hand.

"I'm sure you do," he replied, smiling. "Tell you what, why don't you, like, hang around for a bit? Once that wears off," he dipped his head toward the bloody powder smeared across the table's surface, "we may need a pick-me-up." He rested his hand on my arm and our gazes locked.

I blinked, realized what he was trying to pull, and rolled my eyes. His widened in surprise, then shock as I yanked out my toothpick and shoved it through his hand.

"Motherfuck—"

"I want what we agreed on," I declared. "Now. No tricks."

The rest of the band saw what happened and rose faster than I could blink. They circled me, their grins feral...they might have even seemed intimidating if it weren't for the fact that they each had a case of the sniffles

—I had to work extra hard not to think about what it felt like to have someone else's blood dripping down my nasal cavity.

I held up a hand.

"Can I ask ye gentlemen a question before we get started?" I asked. "Do ye even *have* what I asked for?"

Two of the band members exchanged looks and shrugged. The guitarist, however, glanced back towards the dressing room, where a brown paper bag sat next to a case full of makeup. He caught me looking and bared his teeth, his fangs stretching until it looked like it would be uncomfortable for him to close his mouth without piercing his own lip.

"Follow-up question," I said, eyeing the vampire I'd stabbed as he gingerly withdrew the toothpick from his hand and flung it across the room with a snarl. "Do ye do each other's make-up? Since, ye know, ye can't use mirrors?"

I was genuinely curious.

The guitarist grunted. "Mike, we have to go on soon."

"Wait a minute. Mike?" I turned to the snarling vampire with a frown. "What happened to *The Vampire Prospero*?" I glanced at the numerous fliers in the dressing room, most of which depicted the band members wading through blood, with Mike in the lead, each one titled *The Vampire Prospero* in *Rocky Horror Picture Show* font. Come to think of it…Mike did look a little like Tim Curry in all that leather and lace.

I was about to comment on the resemblance when Mike spoke up, "Alright, change of plans, bros. We're gonna drain this bitch before the show. We'll look totally—"

"Creepy?" I offered, again.

"Kill her."

≈

**_Get the full book ONLINE!_**

# MAKE A DIFFERENCE

Reviews are the most powerful tools in my arsenal when it comes to getting attention for my books. Much as I'd like to, I don't have the financial muscle of a New York publisher.

But I do have something much more powerful and effective than that, and it's something that those publishers would kill to get their hands on.

**A committed and loyal bunch of readers.**

Honest reviews of my books help bring them to the attention of other readers.

If you've enjoyed this book, I would be very grateful if you could spend just five minutes leaving a review (it can be as short as you like) on my book's Amazon page.

Thank you very much in advance.

# ACKNOWLEDGMENTS

First, I would like to thank my beta-readers, TEAM TEMPLE, those individuals who spent hours of their time to read, and re-re-read Nate's story. Your dark, twisted, cunning sense of humor makes me feel right at home…

I would also like to thank you, the reader. I hope you enjoyed reading *GRIMM* as much as I enjoyed writing it. Be sure to check out the two crossover series in the Temple Verse: The **Feathers and Fire Series** and the **Phantom Queen Diaries**.

And last, but definitely not least, I thank my wife, Lexy. Without your support, none of this would have been possible.

# ABOUT SHAYNE SILVERS

Shayne is a man of mystery and power, whose power is exceeded only by his mystery...

He currently writes the Amazon Bestselling **Nate Temple** Series, which features a foul-mouthed wizard from St. Louis. He rides a bloodthirsty unicorn, drinks with Achilles, and is pals with the Four Horsemen.

He also writes the Amazon Bestselling **Feathers and Fire** Series—a second series in the Temple Verse. The story follows a rookie spell-slinger named Callie Penrose who works for the Vatican in Kansas City. Her problem? Hell seems to know more about her past than she does.

He coauthors **The Phantom Queen Diaries**—a third series set in The Temple Verse—with Cameron O'Connell. The story follows Quinn MacKenna, a mouthy black magic arms dealer in Boston. All she wants? A round-trip ticket to the Fae realm...and maybe a drink on the house.

Shayne holds two high-ranking black belts, and can be found writing in a coffee shop, cackling madly into his computer screen while pounding shots of espresso. He's hard at work on the newest books in the Temple Verse—You can find updates on new releases or chronological reading order on the next page, his website or any of his social media accounts. **Follow him online for all sorts of groovy goodies, giveaways, and new release updates:**

*Get Down with Shayne Online*
www.shaynesilvers.com
info@shaynesilvers.com

facebook.com/shaynesilversfanpage

amazon.com/author/shaynesilvers

bookbub.com/profile/shayne-silvers

twitter.com/shaynesilvers

instagram.com/shaynesilversofficial

goodreads.com/ShayneSilvers

# BOOKS IN THE TEMPLE VERSE

*CHRONOLOGY: All stories in the Temple Verse are shown in chronological order on the following page*

## NATE TEMPLE SERIES

FAIRY TALE - FREE prequel novella #0 for my subscribers

OBSIDIAN SON

BLOOD DEBTS

GRIMM

SILVER TONGUE

BEAST MASTER

BEERLYMPIAN (Novella #5.5 in the 'LAST CALL' anthology)

TINY GODS

DADDY DUTY (Novella #6.5)

WILD SIDE

WAR HAMMER

NINE SOULS

HORSEMAN

LEGEND

## *FEATHERS AND FIRE SERIES*

*(Also set in the Temple Universe)*

UNCHAINED

RAGE

WHISPERS

ANGEL'S ROAR

MOTHERLUCKER (Novella #4.5 in the 'LAST CALL' anthology)

SINNER

## PHANTOM QUEEN DIARIES

*(Also set in the Temple Universe)*

COLLINS (Prequel novella #0 in the 'LAST CALL' anthology)

WHISKEY GINGER

COSMOPOLITAN

OLD FASHIONED

MOTHERLUCKER (Novella #3.5 in the 'LAST CALL' anthology)

DARK AND STORMY

MOSCOW MULE

WITCHES BREW

## CHRONOLOGICAL ORDER: TEMPLE VERSE

FAIRY TALE (TEMPLE PREQUEL)

OBSIDIAN SON (TEMPLE 1)

BLOOD DEBTS (TEMPLE 2)

GRIMM (TEMPLE 3)

SILVER TONGUE (TEMPLE 4)

BEAST MASTER (TEMPLE 5)

BEERLYMPIAN (TEMPLE 5.5)

TINY GODS (TEMPLE 6)

DADDY DUTY (TEMPLE NOVELLA 6.5)

UNCHAINED (FEATHERS... 1)

RAGE (FEATHERS... 2)

WILD SIDE (TEMPLE 7)

WAR HAMMER (TEMPLE 8)

WHISPERS (FEATHERS... 3)

COLLINS (PHANTOM 0)

WHISKEY GINGER (PHANTOM... 1)

NINE SOULS (TEMPLE 9)

COSMOPOLITAN (PHANTOM... 2)

ANGEL'S ROAR (FEATHERS... 4)

MOTHERLUCKER (FEATHERS 4.5, PHANTOM 3.5)

OLD FASHIONED (PHANTOM...3)

HORSEMAN (TEMPLE 10)

DARK AND STORMY (PHANTOM... 4)

MOSCOW MULE (PHANTOM...5)

SINNER (FEATHERS...5)

WITCHES BREW (PHANTOM...6)

LEGEND (TEMPLE...11)

Made in the USA
Coppell, TX
26 October 2019